SECOND CHANCES

To Kath.
Thank you for your friendship, and for always being kind to everyone.

SECOND CHANCES

Love,
Liz W.

Liz Wainwright

Book Two of the Lynda Collins Trilogy

Elizabeth Wainwright asserts the moral right to be identified as the author of this work.

Printed and distributed by Createspace Ltd

Loveday Manor Publishing
Copyright © 2013 Liz Wainwright

ISBN-13: 978-0957227927
ISBN-10: 0957227922

www.lizscript.co.uk

For Glyn
and
Our wonderful family.

CHAPTER ONE

As if the wind had gathered them up and then scattered them, the horses turned and raced away from her, heading towards the winter sunshine easing its way onto the frozen snow in the far corner of the field. Lynda, her blonde curls tucked away inside a soft woollen beret, snuggled deeper into her matching red scarf and sighed as she watched the horses. She envied them their exhilaration and freedom. Then she looked into the pram and smiled at the baby peeping up at her from the nest of fluffy white blankets. She leaned forward over the pram handle to talk to him.

'Hello, Michael. Have you woken up? Grandma had better get you home then, before you get hungry.' She pushed aside the imitation suede of her black glove and looked at her watch.

'Oh, hell, your Grandma's in trouble now. It's past your feed time. I shouldn't have brought you this far, we'll have to run to get home before twelve.'

Running and pushing a pram along pavements spread with large patches of lumpy grey ice wasn't easy, but Lynda was slimmer and fitter than many other women who, like her, had edged their way reluctantly into their forties. She managed to push the pram along at some speed until she came to the long steep hill that led up to the main road. She paused half way up to catch her breath and look across at the industry nurtured Lancashire town in the valley.

Milfield had looked better when the snow had covered its soot darkened stone. In the last couple of days some of the snow had melted, and the rows of stone terraced houses looked blacker against the mini-mountains and ridges of snow, which had been shovelled and stacked aside by people who had to get to work.

Michael was staring up at her, puzzled as to why the soothing motion of the pram wheels had stopped. Lynda smiled at him and started to push again. The wind had become much stronger by now and was throwing icy rain in her face, blinding her momentarily as, with her arms fully stretched she struggled to push the pram up the awkward sloping bend at the top of the hill.

'Lynda!' John's voice roared just as the wind threw another onslaught at her. Startled by his shout, she lost concentration for a fatal moment and slipped. She screamed as she felt the pram toppling over in slow motion towards the road. She was kneeling on the ground next to the pram when John, tall and strong, and angry, stepped in front of her and quickly lifted it upright. She scrambled to her feet as he pushed back the hood to see the baby.

'Is he all right?'

'Yes. No thanks to you! He could have been killed if there'd been a bloody car coming!'

Lynda was sobbing now. 'Oh, God! Let me look at him, he isn't hurt, is he?'

John shoved her aside. 'Get away, Lynda, and let me get him home.'

His harsh tone woke the sleeping child and, startled and feeling the hunger inside him, little Michael Sheldon began to cry. He was still crying, but louder, and with real anguish, when his Grandad carried him into the living room of the 1930s semi-detached house on Beechwood Avenue. This was his home, and also that of his parents, and his grandparents. John and Lynda Stanworth had felt they'd really moved up in the world when they'd become, courtesy of too big a mortgage, the owners of this semi in a suburb defined by sharply cut back rose bushes, and winter defying pink flowered viburnum. Today, however, the person very much in charge of that house was John's mother, Sheila Stanworth.

'Give him to me!' Sheila stepped forward and took the screaming child out of her son's arms. 'What's happened?'

She and her granddaughter, Carolyn, who had just woken up from a much needed sleep on the sofa, listened carefully to John's brief account of the pram tipping over.

Sheila's tone was full of reprimand. 'He's frozen, the poor little mite. What were you thinking of, John, letting her take him out on a morning like this?'

John responded, as he often did when his mother spoke to him about his wife, with a look of silent, shame-faced apology.

Carolyn held out her slender arms, 'Let me have him, Nana, he's hungry.'

Sheila passed the baby to her and pursed her lips as Carolyn took the baby upstairs.

'I wonder how long it will take this time? That child's always hungry. I keep telling her it's time she gave him a bottle, she's not satisfying him with what she's got.'

Lynda, a little afraid to face them all, had been slowly taking off her wet coat and shoes, and heard this as she came in from the hallway.

'She is, he's just growing, that's all. Breast is best, that's what they say.'

'Oh, do they?' Sheila sneered. 'And what do 'they' say about grandmothers who take a two-month old baby out on a freezing cold morning, when any sensible person would keep him indoors? You nearly got your grandson killed, from what I've heard.'

'It wasn't that bad.' Lynda's look accused her husband of failing to support her, but John was careful not to see it. He focused instead on the Sunday lunch cooking in the small kitchen which opened on to the living room. 'Mother, can dinner wait till our Carolyn comes back down? Steve's not here yet.'

'No, he's not, and he knows what time we eat.'

Lynda, as usual, defended her son-in-law. 'He doesn't like to leave a job unfinished.'

John asked again, 'Can't you slow it down for half an hour, Mum, please?'

The tightly-permed sixty-eight year old whose body was being pared down by age but showed few signs of frailty, demonstrated her annoyance by the way she removed, folded, and set aside her floral cotton apron.

'I can but it will spoil it.'

Lynda let out a sigh of impatience. 'It'll be all right.'

'And how would you know?' was Sheila's sharp response.

Lynda was silent, she knew the smirk on her mother-in-law's face was generated by the never-to-be-forgotten nightmare of the undercooked turkey a few weeks ago.

Sheila had always been the one who triumphed in the role of Christmas catering matriarch, and Lynda had made the mistake of insisting that, as Christmas 1984 would be her grandson's first Christmas, he should spend it in his own home, and that she would cook the dinner. The meal had struggled to be edible, and had been consumed in silence, with only Steve trying to be politely complimentary about it. The only parts of the Christmas mealtime offerings which had been perfect were the Christmas pudding, mince pies, sherry trifle and Christmas cake, all contributed with many a flourish by Sheila.

Steve Sheldon, when he walked in ten minutes later, grimaced at the atmosphere in the room and retreated quickly upstairs to change out of his working clothes, and to see his wife and baby. He paused for a moment at the bedroom door, just to enjoy seeing his child being nursed by the young woman he'd been lucky enough to marry.

Carolyn moved the baby to her other breast and brushed her short blonde hair away from her face before allowing her husband to kiss her cheek. He spoke quietly.

'Hello, love. How are you? It's daggers drawn again downstairs, what's happened this time?'

Carolyn's eyes filled with tears. 'My Mother took the baby out, and the pram tipped over.'

'Oh, hell! Is he all right?'

'Yes, but she shouldn't have taken him out. I told her not to, but she wouldn't listen. It was too cold for him to be out, and it's been raining.'

'There was a bit of sunshine earlier on, she probably thought the fresh air would do him good.'

'Oh, go on, make excuses for her, as usual – your drinking partner!'

Steve sighed. 'Are you still mad because we went out last night?'

'It should be you and me going out together, not you and my Mother.'

'You said you didn't want to come. I keep trying to get you to come out with me but you won't.'

'I'm too tired. And anyway we can't afford it.'

'I only had two pints,' he lied defensively.

'And the rest! I heard you and her giggling and falling about. And so did my Dad.'

'I'm sorry.' Steve drew a small fold of banknotes from his pocket. 'Anyway, I've got some good news. Mr. Clark paid me, and his wife was so pleased with the cupboards that she slipped me an extra tenner! You can get those winter boots you want now. Like those your friend had on.'

He immediately wished he'd not reminded her about that visit from her school friend, Tricia Holmes, who had called in after Christmas with a present for the baby. Tricia was a good friend, not one of the racy set Carolyn had become involved with at school. Tricia hadn't passed judgment on her when she'd got pregnant, just as Carolyn didn't judge Tricia when she found out Mr. & Mrs. Holmes spent an unwise amount of their income on gin.

Tricia had tried hard to say all the right things about Carolyn being lucky to have such a beautiful child, but she'd been unable to stop herself enthusing about the great time she was having at university, and about going out with Philip Lawson, a trainee solicitor who had once fancied Carolyn. After she'd gone, Carolyn had retreated with her hungry child to the small back bedroom, and Steve had found his wife still sitting there, an hour later, with tears streaming down her cheeks in mourning for the life she had dreamed of. She had the same look on her face now.

'Tricia hasn't got a baby to look after, she can afford to spend money on new boots. I can't. We need to give Mum and Dad extra money towards the gas bill. It's going to be massive after this winter.'

'I want you to have nice things.'

'I know you do, and I know you feel guilty about me not being able to go to university, but we've got to be realistic. We've got a baby and we'll have to get used to being short of money like everybody else.'

'Not everybody. That guy who bought the Dorchester isn't short of money.'

Sheila heard this as she opened the bedroom door. 'No, but he's the Sultan of Dubai not a carpenter.'

Steve would have liked to correct her, once again, about his qualifications as a skilled craftsman, but instead tried to laugh. 'Oh. Perhaps you should have married him instead of me, love.'

'She didn't get the chance, did she?' Sheila retorted accusingly before turning to Carolyn. 'We used to dream about going to London one day and staying at the Dorchester, or having afternoon tea at The Ritz, didn't we, love?'

Steve straightened and pushed his soft brown hair back off his forehead in a familiar gesture of defiance.

'Perhaps we will do that one day. I'll add it to our list, shall I, Caro?'

His wife gave her husband a gentle smile, but his mother-in-law ignored him. 'Anyway it's not afternoon tea we're having now, it's Sunday dinner and I came up to ask how long you'll be?'

Carolyn glanced down at her baby. 'About ten minutes, with any luck.'

'Right, I'll go and finish making the gravy.' Sheila turned to Steve. 'And you've got time for a wash.'

Steve watched Sheila leave the room, and knew he would never like her. He also wished she didn't have so much influence on the up-bringing of his child.

It had made sense, financially, that Carolyn, with her Nana helping her, would stay at home and look after the baby, while Lynda worked more or less full-time. When they'd all eventually had to accept her idea, Sheila had been very pleased, realising that she'd be able to spend as much time as she wished with her granddaughter and great-grandson.

Lynda hadn't liked the idea at all. She'd wanted to look after the baby, and get closer to her daughter, but they needed the money. And she was honest enough to admit to herself that she wouldn't really have wanted to give up her job.

CHAPTER TWO

Lynda loved running The Copper Kettle, the café opposite the Market Hall, it was her world and sometimes it felt more like home than Beechwood Avenue.

She was putting clean tablecloths on the pine tables when Dan arrived with the morning delivery of bread rolls and pasties. He could have asked one of his assistants at Heywood's bakery to bring them, but he knew that just seeing Lynda smile at him would help him through the day. Lynda turned to greet him as she heard him come in through the back door and put the trays on the work surface in the kitchen.

'Good morning, Dan. Thanks for those. Have you time for a cuppa?'

'Yes. I'll put the kettle on.'

Dan Heywood stood by the counter and looked round the café. Lynda had made a great success of the business which the previous owner had trained her to take over. Freda Wilson, who had been a friend of Lynda's Grandma, had been dead many years now, but would have been happy to see how her café had remained an important part of Milfield. Lynda had felt awkward about re-naming it, even though she'd

9

waited until a year after Freda's death. It couldn't remain 'Freda's café' for ever but Lynda had given a lot of thought to the new name. When she died Freda had left her an old copper kettle which had belonged to her mother, and it now stood in the centre of the window in the café, giving it its new name.

Lynda had always been surprised at the lack of interest Freda's son, Duncan, showed in the business. When she'd asked permission to spend money on re-naming and re-decorating the café he had given his assent with a shrug and a wave of his well-manicured hand, 'Do what you like.'

Lynda had talked to Dan about her puzzlement over his attitude, but Dan had just said that Duncan Wilson wasn't much of a business man. Dan, however, hadn't been at all puzzled at his lack of interest because he knew that Duncan didn't own the café – he did.

It had been bought by his father, Geoff Heywood and, as Geoff had kept his ownership a secret from Ellen Heywood, Dan also didn't see any reason to disclose this to his mother. He thought it was wonderful to see Lynda running the café so well, and he derived many simple pleasures from it, like now watching her spreading the clean red and white gingham tablecloths while he waited for the kettle to boil.

'They look nice and fresh.'

'Yes. They won't stay clean for long, but I like to put them on. It reminds me of Rose. She always had red and white tablecloths in her café.'

'Have you heard from her lately?'

She pointed up at a card on a shelf above the counter. 'Yes, I had that 'Happy New Year' card, and a letter. She wants me to promise I'll go and see her this year.'

'And will you?'

'I'd love to but, as you know, I can't even mention her name at home, let alone ask John if he'd like to go to Cornwall and visit her.'

'Yeah, I can imagine how his Mother would react to that!'

'Exactly. No chance of forgive and forget there — or from any of them really. That's why she has to write to me here. I'll have to give her a ring sometime and explain. It's a shame really, I'd love to have a little holiday in Cornwall, and Rose isn't getting any younger.'

'We none of us are.'

'Oh, now, what's up with you? Don't go feeling sorry for yourself just because you're forty-two next month.' She walked over to him and patted his cheek. 'You're still a good-looking fella.'

It was true. Dan Heywood wasn't one of those men who become more chiselled and handsome as they get older, but he was, as she said, still good-looking. And his sandy hair was still as thick and soft as it had been when, as a teenager, Lynda had caressingly run her fingers through it. She looked at him and knew that he, too, remembered those times.

A light but persistent tap tap tap at the window of the café took them away from that moment as Dan saw his three-year old niece, Katie, waving excitedly at him through the glass. Lynda unlocked the door and received a fleeting hug from the chubby little girl with auburn curls, who then flung herself into her uncle's open arms.

'Uncle Dan! Uncle Dan!' squealed Katie as her

mother, Jenny, shook her head apologetically.

'She spotted you through the window and insisted on coming to see you. Sorry, Lynda, I know you're not open yet.'

Lynda smiled at the young woman with dark brown shoulder length hair, and a figure which had not yet managed to lose all the weight left over from its second pregnancy.

'Don't apologise, Jenny, this café is always open for you and little Katie. We've just made a pot of tea, and there might be a treat somewhere for somebody, if that's all right?'

Katie was already gazing at the jar of lollipops Lynda kept on the counter as Jenny nodded her permission and settled herself down happily on one of the farmhouse style chairs.

Lynda grinned at her. 'These chairs are a lot more comfortable with those cushions you made for me, aren't they?'

'They certainly are!'

'A bit of a mistake these chairs,' Lynda explained to Dan. 'I didn't sit on one long enough before I bought them. Steve would have made me much better ones but I needed them quick.'

'Is he still wanting to go into business, making furniture?' asked Dan.

'Yes, he makes things now in the garage but he's no time for it at the moment. He's doing all the overtime he can at Bentham's, and does jobs for people, privately, at the weekends. They're still trying to save a deposit for their own house,' she explained to Jenny.

'They can have ours,' Jenny said, wishing that were true.

Lynda was surprised. 'Don't you like it, your new house?'

'It's far too big and flash for me, and we don't need five bedrooms. It's all for show. It's not what I call a home.'

Dan looked ruefully at Lynda. 'It was Richard's choice - and my Mother's.'

'Of course. Your Mother thinks she's got a talent for making decisions for people, as we know too well. The trouble is, they're not good decisions. And they can ruin people's lives.'

She stared at Dan with such misery in her eyes that Dan couldn't bear it. It was always there, that longing between them and Lynda had started reminding him of it, which scared him. The fear of his own feelings made him speak more sharply than he intended. 'That was a long time ago. We're all a lot older now, Lynda. And married.'

Jenny wondered what was behind this exchange, but was distracted by Katie offering her a lick of the red and white lollipop Lynda had let her choose from the jar. Lynda, feeling unreasonably hurt by Dan's sharp remark about being married, gave in to a need to punish him a little, and broached Dan's least favourite subject, his younger brother.

'And what about Richard, that husband of yours, Jenny? Is he behaving himself any better?'

Jenny bowed her head, and Dan, fearing the answer, said quickly, 'He's very busy at work, they're selling loads of cars, top end of the market, of course. They're buying the land next to the garage so they can display more stock.'

Jenny didn't want to talk about her husband. 'How's John? Still getting plenty of work at

Earnshaw's?' she asked.

'Yes, thank goodness. This council house sell-off is still bringing work in, plenty of rewiring going on, so he's not looking like adding to the three million unemployed just yet. You wouldn't think so, though, the way he worries. The only time you see him smile is when he's with little Michael. He's besotted with him, just like he was with Carolyn.'

'Tell him to give me a ring, and we'll go out for a pint,' Dan suggested.

Lynda ignored that, and went to play with Katie who was exploring the box of toys in the corner. Dan, disappointed with his visit, decided it was time to leave, and kissed Jenny on the cheek.

'Better get on with these deliveries. See you on Sunday.'

'Yes, I suppose so,' Jenny sighed.

'I'll do roast chicken, your favourite.'

'Thanks.'

Dan waved to his niece, 'Bye, Katie, see you soon!'

Katie dropped the truck she was holding and ran over to kiss him before reluctantly waving and watching him leave. Jenny stood up.

'Come on, Katie, we must be going, too.'

The little girl began to cry. 'Don't want to go home.'

'Five more minutes, eh?' Lynda asked. Jenny nodded and Katie ran back to play with the truck. Jenny sat down again and Lynda joined her.

'So how are you doing?'

Jenny glanced over to check that Katie was absorbed in getting more toys out of the box, and then slowly pushed up her sleeve. Lynda winced as she saw the bruises.

When Jenny had gone, Lynda set the tables and started preparing the meat and potato pies for lunchtime. It was such a dark, cold and miserable morning that she switched all the lights on in the café as soon as she opened. By eleven o'clock plenty of customers had been tempted in by the cheery prospect of a bit of banter in cosy surroundings and, for many of them, a plateful of home-cooking.

Jean Haworth came in just after one o'clock. She pulled off her rain hat and, catching sight of Lynda's bright blonde curls, ran her fingers through her damp and droopy brown hair, to try to fluff it up. It was half past before Lynda, signalling to her assistant, Debbie, had time to sit and have a chat to her.

'You've still got your Christmas lights up,' was the first thing Jean said, with a hint of disapproval.

'Yeah, they help keep the place looking cheerful. And you know me, I like a bit of sparkle. Treating yourself today, are you, Jean?' she asked, as Jean ate the last forkful of meat and pastry.'

'Yes. The heater's broken in the shop. I had to come here to get warm.'

'Not come for the food then?' Lynda joked, observing the empty plate.

Jean laughed. 'You can't beat your meat and potato pie.'

'Freda's recipe, not mine, God bless her.'

'Your pastry's even better than hers was though.'

'Thanks. It's better than Sheila's as well, but nobody will ever say so. Especially after the Christmas fiasco.'

Jean, who had been Lynda's friend since schooldays, had been the only non-family partaker of the awful Christmas dinner at Beechwood Avenue.

Ever since Jean's husband, Gordon, had died, Lynda had made sure, whenever possible, that Jean wasn't lonely. She had always been 'an honorary aunty' to Carolyn, and was hoping to have that same kinship with Lynda's grandson.

'You're a good cook.'

'Sometimes.'

'The food here is always lovely. I hope Duncan Wilson appreciates that it's you who's kept his mother's café going.'

'I've had a pay rise, but I'm not sure it came from Duncan.'

'Who else would it be from? He hasn't sold the café to anyone, has he?'

'I don't know, he's very evasive when I talk to him, as if he's not the one making decisions. Anyway, I'm not going to worry about it, as long as I can keep my job, I'm happy.'

'Like everybody else, including me.'

'How are you doing at 'Francesca's'? Oh, she does fancy herself, Frances Horton. 'Francesca'!

'I've only had one customer this morning, wanting a dress for a Valentine Dinner Dance.'

'Oh.' Lynda saw the sadness in Jean's eyes.

'Gordon always made it a lovely day. No Valentine for me this year.'

'No, not for me either!' She picked up Jean's empty plate, and grinned at her. 'Time for a slice of lemon meringue pie, eh?'

CHAPTER THREE

Jenny Heywood parked the car round the back of Kirkwood House, as far away as she could, so that the girls would have a chance to run around and enjoy some fresh air before they had to go inside for Sunday lunch. She hoped that their arrival would not have been noticed, she knew her mother-in-law would not be looking out of the window eagerly awaiting her grandchildren. Ellen Heywood, once she had returned from church, liked to spend the remainder of the morning reading 'The Sunday Times' and making a start on the crossword.

Jenny picked up the obligatory bouquet of flowers which had travelled beside her on the front seat. She watched as Katie ran and hid behind a laurel bush, while her five year old sister, Alex, covered her eyes and counted slowly.

'15, 16, 17, 18, 19, 20. Coming ready or not!'

Katie stepped out from behind the bush, and stood there beaming as she waited to be found.

'No!' cried Alex. You're supposed to be hiding! Mummy, tell her, she has to wait and let me come and find her.'

'You both hide and I'll come looking for you,'

Jenny suggested, and turned to look towards the house and count as they hurried away along the familiar 'fairy paths' through the garden.

Kirkwood House, a large Victorian villa, had been built with the intention of impressing anyone allowed the privilege of visiting its owners. The weightiness of its huge sandstone blocks and pillars was lightened in the autumn by the beautiful red leaves of the Virginia creeper which had ventured here and there up its walls, but now, in the early days of February there was nothing to take away the darkness of the building. Jenny had often wondered how different the house would look, and feel, if the soot ingrained by the industrial revolution which had paid for it were washed away. She and Geoff Heywood, Ellen's husband and Jenny's sympathetic father-in-law, had talked about that before he died, but Ellen, as always, had refused to change the house which had been bought by her father when she was a child.

Kirkwood House always made Jenny feel even smaller than she was, and had done ever since that day, about six years ago now, when Richard Heywood had brought her here and presented her for his Mother's disapproval. She heard Katie calling for her, and went to seek her precious children.

Everyone was hungry and so, at one fifteen, Ellen allowed them all to take their places round the candelabra on the dining table and begin their Sunday lunch, even though Richard had not arrived. Ellen, a tall, unfailingly elegant woman in her early sixties, fingered the three strands of pearls at her throat as her younger son removed the empty soup dishes from the table.

'This is very unlike Richard,' she declared, a little untruthfully. 'He must be discussing some business with James. You say he was taking a car to show him as well as playing golf?'

'Yes, I think so.' Jenny mumbled.

'You think so? Do you take so little interest in your husband's business? What time did he leave this morning?'

'I don't know.'

Dan saw his mother draw herself up like a bird of prey preparing for an attack, and swiftly moved to Jenny's side. 'Will you help me bring in the roast, Jenny?'

They hurried along the corridor to the kitchen, like two children escaping from the headmistress's study. They didn't start getting the food ready to serve, they needed to talk, and quickly while they had the chance.

'Where the hell is he?'

'I don't know,' replied Jenny. 'He didn't come home last night – again.'

'Didn't he phone to say he was staying over at James Hanford's?'

'I phoned James. Richard left their place after the dinner. James was a bit embarrassed. I don't think Richard had left alone.'

'Oh, up to those tricks again, is he? I'm sorry.'

'I'm not. To be honest, Dan, I don't care, as long as he's not sleeping with me.'

'As bad as that?'

'Yes.'

'I'm sorry that I couldn't make him stop hurting you. I don't understand why he behaves like he does.'

'I should never have married him.'

'No. But you don't have to stay with him. Get

divorced, like I did.'

'I want to. I don't love him any more and he doesn't love me – or the children.' She sat down at the kitchen table and put her head in her hands. 'He's even started tormenting them.'

Dan stared at her, clenched with fear. 'Then leave. You've got to leave.'

'I can't, not yet. I've been saving up, but . .'

'I'll let you have some money.'

'How can you? You said all the family money's been going into Richard's business.'

'I'll borrow some. You've got to leave him. I know my brother, Jenny. I know what he's like.'

'I used to tell myself Richard and I had to stay together for the sake of the children. But now . .'

'You have to leave him, for the sake of the children.'

'Yes.'

When they had finished lunch there was still no sign of Richard. They moved into what Ellen always insisted on calling the drawing-room. The children had learned long ago that in their grandmother's favourite room, with its antique chairs and displays of delicate ornaments, everything was a 'don't touch'. This included the grand piano which had belonged to Ellen's father, Alexander Buchanan, and which, like his ghost, dominated the room.

The two little girls, kneeling by the small table they were allowed to use, had grown tired of occupying themselves with colouring books and crayons. Katie was in need of a nap, and kept resting her head on her arms. Jenny, watching her, wondered when she would be allowed to take her children home.

She and Dan were next to each other on the sofa opposite Ellen who was sitting, as always, in her leather, winged-back chair by the fire. During the meal they had run out of any remarks or speculations about the reasons why Richard had not arrived, and they had been sitting in more or less continuous silence when the doorbell rang. Dan, glad of the chance to get out of the room, went to open the door.

The policeman, after formally introducing himself and the female officer who had accompanied him, scanned the room and as soon as he saw the children he nodded to his colleague. She bent down towards them.

'Would you take me out to play in the garden?'

Alex, wide-eyed, looked at her mother. 'If Mummy says we can.'

Jenny, swallowing hard, said, 'Yes, that will be nice for you,' and then, trying to keep her voice steady, addressed the police-woman. 'This is Alex and Katie. Their coats and hats are in the hall.'

Waiting until a few moments after the door had been carefully closed behind them, the policeman asked Ellen for permission to sit down. He positioned himself on the edge of the Chesterfield sofa which faced the fire. They all listened very attentively to what he had to say, and afterwards Ellen Heywood remembered every word of it, every chilling word. Jenny heard 'accident' and 'fatal'. Then she held her breath until she heard the word 'body', and knew for certain that Richard was dead.

The doctor arrived twenty minutes later to find Ellen Heywood still fighting for breath. Dan, whom she had impatiently brushed aside, was standing by his

Mother's chair, not daring to touch her. Later, when Ellen had been given a sedative and a neighbour had come to watch over her, Jenny took her children home, and Dan went to identify Richard's body. After that brief formality he was left alone with his brother. As he stared at the damaged face which had always been so handsome, so admired by women, especially his Mother, he felt, for a moment, nothing but anger. 'You bloody idiot,' he whispered, 'you bloody ungrateful sod.'

'The Oakwoods' - it was never referred to by estate agents or by its residents, as an estate - was a recent tasteful arrangement of a dozen large detached 'executive homes'. The houses were designed to endow their owners with the prestige of en-suite bathrooms, and large patio doors leading to gardens substantially larger than the ones usually allocated to new housing.

When Richard had shown her their new home, Jenny, to avoid an argument, had pretended to be impressed by its large, light, and coolly decorated rooms, and by the space the children would have to play in. The reality was that their toys were confined for most of the time to the fifth bedroom which Richard, on his mother's advice, had designated as their playroom. The only thing Jenny truly liked about the house was the oak tree which the planners had decreed must retain its place at the end of their garden. As she walked round the house that evening, with her children tucked safely under their duvets, not yet knowing that their father would never come home, Jenny felt cold and completely alone in the world.

Steve and John were watching television when Dan phoned on Monday evening. Lynda was upstairs with Carolyn enjoying her grandson's bath-time. John took the call and was surprised to hear Dan's voice, these days they only talked to each other when they happened to meet up in The Red Lion. John listened to the news, and could find no words to comfort his friend except, 'I'm sorry, mate. I really am. Terrible, for you and your Mother, and especially for Jenny and the kids. If there's anything we can do.' He listened again. 'Yes, well, let us know. And condolences and that.'

Steve, hearing John's sombre tone, had turned off the television, and sat respectfully silent while John told him the news. Steve had met Dan as one of John's friends in the pub, but had only met Ellen Heywood once, when Carolyn had tried to introduce him to her in the street. He remembered her as the disdainful woman who had ignored the outstretched hand of the young man who, in her opinion, had ruined the life of her protégée.

She had also, he knew, encouraged Sheila to campaign for Carolyn to have an abortion. He felt nothing but hatred for this woman who had threatened his child's life, but had had to keep that to himself, because Carolyn had forgiven the wealthy woman who, since childhood, had been her friend and mentor. And now Ellen Heywood had lost her son, and Steve could not deny her sympathy for that.

John sat quietly, trying to think it all through. 'I'll tell Carolyn and Lynda when they come down, and then I'll go round to my Mother's. Dan didn't want to phone her, but he wants her to go round and sit with his Mother tomorrow while he goes and sorts out some paperwork and stuff. It's complicated, with there having to be an inquest.'

Steve unwillingly recalled the experience of dealing with his mother's suicide. 'Yeah, that can take a while. So they won't have a date for the funeral yet.'

'Dan's hoping it will be a week tomorrow.'

Lynda entered the room. 'What's a week tomorrow?'

'Richard Heywood's funeral. He's been killed in a car crash.'

'Oh, hell. Are Jenny and the kids all right? They weren't with him, were they?'

'No.'

'Thank God for that.'

'Will you tell Carolyn? I'm going round to my Mother's to tell her now. Dan wants her to go to the house to look after Ellen tomorrow. She had a slight heart attack when she got the news.'

'Oh.'

Steve, noting that Lynda didn't ask, filled the gap. 'She's all right now, though?'

'Yes, but still in shock, of course.'

Lynda made her decision with no hesitation. 'I'll go and see Jenny tomorrow, I can leave Debbie in charge for the afternoon. And I'll stay with Jenny tomorrow night if she needs me to.'

'Oh. Well, like I said, they think the funeral might be next Tuesday. I don't think I'll be able to get time off work.'

'Do you want me to go instead?' Lynda almost laughed as soon as she'd asked the question. She answered it herself. 'No, of course not, she won't want me there. It'll be your Mother who goes.'

'And Carolyn,' John added.

'Oh, yes,' Lynda said, speaking to her husband, but looking at Steve. 'That's who she'll want, your Mother, and Carolyn.'

The sun came out as Lynda got off the bus on the main road which ran along the edge of The Oakwoods and she was glad of it. She hated February with its dark days which always made her feel lonely and depressed - especially since her beloved friend, Kathleen Kelly, Jenny's mother had died. Kath had always thought of something to cheer you up on a dark day, she'd wear a silly hat or anything to make people laugh, or she'd do something practical like cooking you one of her special apple pies. She thought of Kath as she walked past the large, expensive houses with their double garages and fancy gateways, and knew that Kath would have felt the same as she did about The Oakwoods.

Lynda had only been here once before, when Jenny had wanted to show her the house while Richard was away on business. She was just about to turn the corner into the cul-de sac where their house was when she saw Dan's car driving towards her. She waved and he pulled up by a dark row of trees a little way from the houses. She saw the look on his face, got in the car and instinctively gathered him in her arms. He leaned his head on her shoulder and sobbed.

After a while he spoke in a voice choked with pain. 'It should have been me, not him.'

'No.'

'That's what she feels.'

'No, she doesn't.'

'She does, she told me so. Oh, Lynda, I've never seen my Mother cry before. And she's so angry, so mad that it's Richard she's lost and not me.'

'She's a nasty woman, your Mother, to talk like that, and a fool. I'm not saying she's not got a right to grieve, she's lost a son. But it's the better son she's still got and she should be told that. We know the truth about Richard.'

Dan spoke more steadily now. 'But my Mother never will. At least, not yet, I hope.' He looked anxious now. 'It will be in 'The Milfield Express' tomorrow. But luckily the editor's a mate of mine from school so they won't publish any sordid details.'

'What do you mean?'

Dan took a deep breath. 'It will say in the paper that he hit a patch of ice. What it won't say is that he was still over the limit from the night before, and that he was on his way home from spending the night with another woman.'

'Oh, hell.'

'I've got to go now, Lynda, my Mother's expecting me back. Jenny will tell you the rest. Can you stay to keep her company for a bit after she's put the children to bed? She'll be glad of somebody to talk to, and apart from me you're the only person she can confide in.'

'Yes, of course I will. I'll stay as long as she wants.'

She watched him drive away, and then walked slowly to what would now be Jenny Heywood's house.

It was even harder than she had imagined, being with Jenny and her two little girls who were struggling to understand that they wouldn't see their Daddy again. Katie was easily distracted by whatever new little game Lynda was able to make up and play with them, but Alex kept losing concentration and staring out of the window as if what she had been told might not be true, and that her Daddy would drive a big shiny car up to the house as he had so many times before.

After Lynda had cooked their evening meal, and helped to give the children a bath before leaving their Mother to read them a story and kiss them goodnight, she opened a bottle of red wine and poured two glasses.

'I couldn't find any white.'

'No, Richard always preferred red.'

'He's got a good collection in that wine rack.'

'Yes.' Jenny sank down on to the cream leather sofa which faced the one Lynda was sitting on.

'I don't know what to tell them, Lynda. I've just said that Daddy's gone to Heaven, to live with Jesus.'

She gave a little laugh. 'Richard didn't believe in any of that.'

'No.'

'It's going to be in 'The Express' tomorrow.'

'Yes, I know. Dan told me.'

'I'll have to make sure the children don't see it. Did Dan tell you that he was . . .?'

'Drunk and on his way home from some woman's house, yes. Has anyone told her?'

'James has phoned her. Apparently, she's very upset.'

'It was lucky she wasn't with him.' A memory from another bereavement flashed through her mind. 'She won't be going to the funeral, will she?'

'No. They'd only just met that evening.'

Lynda snorted. 'He was a bastard.'

'You always said that.'

'Well, it's true.'

'That's going to be the hardest part – pretending he was a good man, a good husband, a good father.'

'A perfect son,' Lynda added in a sardonic tone.

The two women looked at each other with the trust of many years of knowledge and understanding. Then Jenny crumpled and held her head in her hands, and Lynda moved across to sit beside her and hold her until she had cried out some of her pain.

After a while Jenny looked at Lynda and asked, 'You'll come to the funeral, won't you?'

'No. His Mother won't want me there.'

'But I will.'

'Dan will make sure you're all right. I wouldn't want to cause any trouble by being at the church, and Sheila and Carolyn will be there to help look after Ellen. I'll have to stay at home and babysit our little Michael. But I'll come round to be with you when you're here on your own after the funeral. And any time you want me, Jenny, I'll be here.'

'Oh, thank you.'

'No need to thank me, it's only what your Mother did for me. Kath was always there to comfort me when I needed her.'

Jenny burst into tears again. 'Oh, I do miss my Mum. And my Dad. I miss them so much!'

Lynda held her even tighter.

'So do I, love. So do I.'

CHAPTER FOUR

Holy Trinity Church had a beautiful spire and a roof which had recently been repaired, thanks to the generosity of its congregation. The vicar, well aware of the inadequacies of the church's heating system had hoped that the sun would shine and give the congregation at least the partial illusion of warmth, but it was not to be; it rained steadily throughout the morning of Richard Heywood's funeral. Everyone who attended the service, mostly people who knew the family, and a few of Richard's friends, was glad to leave the church. There were even some among them who guiltily thought that they were glad there was to be a cremation rather than a cold, wet vigil by a graveside.

Ellen had been adamant that the funeral cortège would leave from Kirkwood House, and it was in that house that the few mourners who were invited gathered after the service. Ellen sat very still in her chair by the fire, and hardly spoke in response to those brave enough to venture close enough to say a few words to her. Edwin Lawson, her solicitor whose family had known her parents, had watched and waited until the other people he knew had presented

29

themselves to her, and observed that they had swiftly taken their leave. He bent his tall, still athletic frame towards her and gently took hold of her hand.

'I'm so sorry, Ellen. This is a great loss. Richard was very dear to you.'

Ellen's voice was hoarse with grief. 'He was my life, Edwin, my life.'

'Yes, but at least you still have Daniel.'

A flash of anger took him by surprise. 'He is not Richard. I have lost my darling boy. How shall I live without him?'

'It will take time. And faith.'

'Faith.' She looked at him with empty eyes, and there was a silence before she nodded curtly and said, 'Thank you, Edwin.'

He knew he was being dismissed, and bowed his head courteously before moving away and seeking out Dan. He found him standing near the door, shaking the hands of the rest of the mourners who had also decided that they could now decently leave.

'How are you, Daniel?'

'I'm all right, thank you, Mr Lawson. But my Mother . . .'

'Yes. It will be hard for her.' He glanced across to the window where Jenny was sitting with her arms round her children, 'And for Jennifer, of course.'

'Yes. I don't know what she's going to do, how she's going to manage.'

Edwin Lawson spoke quietly. 'It's too soon for me to say this to Jennifer, but if one day she should wish to seek employment again, she will always be welcome back at Lawson and Broadbent.'

'Thank you. I'll tell her that, when . . .'

'Quite.' Edwin Lawson fastened the second button

of his charcoal grey suit, and stepped towards the door. Then, remembering that what he had just said had not been his idea but that of his partner, Reggie Broadbent, he added, 'Mr Broadbent, Reginald, wished me also to present his condolences.'

Bob Horton, a property developer in his early fifties, whose tailor never quite succeeded in disguising the muscular arms which had developed while Bob had learned his trade initially as a bricklayer, kept looking at his watch. His wife, Frances, was a petite, fashion conscious woman who had managed to infiltrate the refined ladies' circle which Ellen Heywood had carefully selected. Frances went with them to concerts and art exhibitions, but preferred musicals. She often despaired at her husband's lack of decorum and, seeing him look at his watch again, discreetly applied a sharp elbow to his rib-cage.

'Stop it, Bob,' she whispered.

'I've got a meeting with the site-manager at half past one. You go and offer our sympathy to Richard's wife and I'll speak to Dan, and then we'll go.'

'What about Ellen?'

'You have a word if you want, but she doesn't look to me like she wants to talk to anybody.'

He was right. When Frances dutifully walked towards Ellen she found Sheila and Carolyn were sitting with her, shielding her from the rest of the guests. Sheila gave Frances a little flick of her hand to indicate that Ellen was too distressed to speak to anyone, and so Frances, and the rest of the people who remained, decided they would leave without trying to approach her again.

Bob Horton had only really spoken to Richard Heywood once, when Richard had considered buying one of his houses but had decided it wasn't grand enough for him and his family. Bob had been glad he hadn't bought it, he hadn't like Richard Heywood, or anything he'd heard about him. In business Bob Horton was prepared to be polite to everybody, but didn't believe in being hypocritical, so when he spoke to Dan he focused the conversation on him and his widowed sister-in-law.

'It's not going to be easy for that young woman, with two children to bring up.'

Dan, who had found himself feeling much older in the last few days, stated firmly, 'I'll look after her. And her daughters.'

'And your Mother? And the bakery? You'll have your hands full, lad. And you'll still be missing Geoff.'

Dan liked this big straight-talking man who had been a friend of his father's. 'Yes, I miss my Dad a lot.'

Bob held out his broad, rough hand and held Dan's in its strong grip. 'I'm no substitute, but if you ever want a bit of free advice, or just a chat, I'm always willing to meet up for a pint.'

Dan smiled for the first time that day. 'Thanks, Bob, I'll take you up on that.'

Bob Horton turned to beckon to his wife who was sitting next to Jenny, helping to entertain Alex and Katie by helping them dress their dolls. Before they had left for Kirkwood House that morning Jenny had hastily stuffed some toys and books into the appliquéd bag she had made for them. Frances gave Bob a brief wave which told him she would see him later, and turned back to Jenny.

Alice Smith, who worked in the cake section at Heywood's bakery, but liked to present herself as almost part of the family, approached with another tray of food. Alice and her late father had, many years ago, established a tradition of always being at weddings and funerals in the guise of 'helpers'. Alice received only small cash payments for these services, but was usually well rewarded in another commodity which was a staple of living for her, gossip.

She placed the tray of sandwiches and cakes on a small table and perched on a chair, which she moved forward so that she was sitting close enough to listen to, and possibly guide, the conversation between Jenny Heywood and Frances Horton, who were talking about the children.

'They're so lovely at this age,' Frances cooed, 'I had such fun playing with my daughter's dolls when she was little. It goes so quickly, they're grown up before you know it. You have to make the most of these years, don't you?'

'Yes,' Jenny said softly.

Alice knew that she shouldn't be asking Jenny this question, but asked it anyway. 'Will you be able to cope, financially, without going back to work?'

Frances was shocked, but also couldn't stop herself admiring Alice's brazenness, and was keen to hear the reply.

'I'm hoping so,' Jenny said quietly, relieved that the girls were engrossed in their play and not listening to the adults.

Emboldened by Alice's trampling over the barriers of discretion, Frances remarked, 'I saw Edwin Lawson having a chat to Dan, there'll be a lot of things to sort out.'

'Yes, but Edwin will take care of everything. You couldn't wish for anyone better.'

'Oh, of course!' Alice enthused. 'You used to work for him before you were married, didn't you?'

'Yes.'

Alice, who had been helping herself to the cooking sherry in the kitchen, as well as the glasses on offer to fellow mourners, went into full flow now. 'Isn't that how you managed to meet Richard?'

'Yes.'

'Perhaps they'll want you back. Reggie Broadbent keeps spending more and more time on the golf course, so they'll need people in the office to cover for him.'

'Is Mr Broadbent the other partner?' asked Frances.

Jenny smiled at the thought of Reggie. 'Yes. He's a lovely man, very jolly.'

An image came into Frances Horton's head, 'I think I may have met him at a Chamber of Commerce 'do'. Isn't he the one with, slightly exotic taste in ties?'

'Garish, you mean,' Alice corrected her, standing up briefly to help herself to a cream cake, and then settling back down for a more confiding conversation.

'I've heard that Mr Lawson's son is joining the firm as soon as he's qualified,' she continued. 'Not much fun for a young man like him but, from what I've heard, Reggie Broadbent has persuaded him. He used to be a bit of a tearaway at school did Philip Lawson, I hope he's settled down a bit since then.'

Frances saw that Jenny wasn't comfortable with Alice's opinions, and decided to assert her authority as the wife of a local businessman.

34

'I'm sure he has. It's a very good firm, Lawson and Broadbent, very well respected.'

Alice, aware of this now slightly reproving tone, wanted to remind Frances that she and her husband had not been part of the Milfield community as long as she had, and so carried on with her theme.

'I remember that Philip used to go around with Carolyn Stanworth's husband when they were at school. Steve took him to a couple of those parties at your parents' house, didn't he Jenny? Mr Lawson didn't approve of him going to them at all, thought they were a bit too wild.'

'They were wonderful parties,' Jenny protested, her eyes brimming with tears. Alice sought to make up for the offence she suspected she had caused but, as so often happened, made things worse.

Turning to Frances, she said, 'Yes, they were famous, those parties. I've only heard about them, I was never invited.' She changed to a more intimate tone with Jenny. 'The last one was your Father's farewell party, wasn't it, before he went back to live in Ireland?'

'Yes.'

Alice saw that Jenny was about to cry again, and didn't want to be seen as the cause of more upset, so looked for a brighter note. 'I heard it was a fantastic night, and your Dad made it Steve Sheldon's twenty-first birthday party as well, didn't he?' She beamed at Frances, 'It was quite an event, that party, I heard people talking about it for weeks afterwards.'

Frances followed her lead. 'You obviously come from a wonderful family, Jenny, it must be good to have the comfort of such lovely memories.'

Jenny, taking strength now from those thoughts of

her Mum and Dad, smiled at her. 'Yes, ours was a happy home.'

Frances touched her arm reassuringly. 'And I'm sure you'll make a happy home for you and your daughters once all this sadness is past.'

'I hope so.' Jenny began to pack away the children's toys. 'I think it's time we went home.'

Alice had expected that Ellen would require her daughter-in-law to remain at the house to support her.

'Oh, I thought you'd be staying here.'

'No.' Jenny looked across at Dan who immediately came over.

'Are you ready to go, love?'

'Yes. The girls have had enough.'

Alice saw that she had misjudged what was happening within the Heywood family, and quickly readjusted her view.

'Yes, not the place for children, is it, a funeral?'

Alice saw the look which passed between Dan and Jenny, and realised for once that she should have kept that particular opinion to herself. Dan spoke in the firm, measured tone his father had used when Alice had gone too far.

'Jenny and I felt it was best that they should be there, to say goodbye properly.' He did not say that his Mother had been strongly against allowing her grandchildren to be at the funeral.

Frances, watching the pale young woman gathering her daughters closely to her, imagined her walking into an empty house. 'Are you going with her?' she asked Dan.

'No, I'll be needed here,' he said, looking across at his Mother and then at Jenny. 'You'll be all right,

Lynda will be with you, won't she?'

'Yes, I'm picking her up from the café on my way back. I'll give her a ring now to let her know I'm coming.'

Frances Horton heard Alice catch her breath, and then whisper, 'Lynda Collins, so that's the way it's going to be,' as they watched Jenny walk into the hall, followed by Dan and her children.

All snobbish thought of superiority were swiftly set aside now as Frances was too intrigued by Alice's comment, and had to ask, 'What do you mean? Who is Lynda Collins?'

Alice Smith, needing to share the excitement she felt at the dramas she could imagine unfolding, pulled Frances Horton towards her. 'She's Lynda Stanworth now, but I always think of her as Lynda Collins. She's Carolyn Sheldon's mother, though they've never been close. And Ellen Heywood won't want Lynda spending time with Jenny, I can tell you that.'

'Why not?'

'They're old enemies, but Jenny and Lynda are old friends, through Jenny's Mum and Dad.'

'Oh.' Frances Horton was finding that the Milfield community was becoming more fascinating by the minute, and Alice, recognising an enthusiastic audience, was happy to entertain her.

'You remember that party I talked about, Frances?'

'Yes.'

Alice pointed discreetly to Sheila Stanworth and Carolyn who were still protectively close to Ellen. 'That party was where Sheila Stanworth's granddaughter met Steve Sheldon – and the result of that, of course, was a shotgun wedding.'

'Oh.' Frances was struggling to keep up.

Alice enjoyed the spellbound expression on Frances Horton's face, and knew that she had achieved respect from a kindred gossip. She gave her a knowing smile, and then went off to the kitchen to put together a bag of cakes and sandwiches to take home for her tea.

Dan had put the children's coats on, and now brought the two little girls back into the sitting room to say goodbye to their grandmother. Ellen, however, hardly acknowledged them, she just raised her right hand which seemed to have no strength.

'Carolyn and I will stay here while you take Jenny home, if you like,' Sheila offered.

'No, it's all right, Jenny's driving herself home. But thank you.'

Dan took the children out to the car where Jenny had switched on the engine to warm it up. He fastened their seat belts carefully, and gave them a kiss before moving to the front of the car to take hold of Jenny's hand.

'Don't worry, love. I'll look after you.'

'I know you will,' she said gratefully. 'And I'll look after you.'

He tried to smile and ran behind the car, waving to the girls as he usually did, trying hard to show his beloved nieces that everything could go back to normal now that this terrible day was over. Then he walked back up to the front door. As a teenager, Dan Heywood had sometimes felt that Kirkwood House was like a prison. That feeling came back to him now.

CHAPTER FIVE

Milfield football team were never going to be famous, but they were a good excuse for a bit of freedom and fresh air, and both John and Steve were glad of that on a Saturday afternoon. They'd enjoyed the match, and there was the added bonus that Milfield had won for once. After the match they'd managed to get out of the ground quickly and so were able to stroll the half mile to the car park at a conversational pace.

John looked at his watch, 'We've got time to call in at the Nelson Arms for a pint.'

Steve, aware of the limited amount of cash in his wallet, shook his head. 'No, I'm not bothered.'

'Don't want to go home smelling of beer, eh?'

'No.'

John didn't like seeing Steve so downcast. 'She'll lighten up in a bit, you know, our Carolyn. I think it's just that she's so tired with the baby.'

'Yeah.'

'Her Mother's not helping at the moment, either,' continued John, 'She's spending too much time looking after Jenny Heywood and her kids.'

Steve understood better than John, why Lynda was doing this. 'She feels sorry for Jenny, with her having no mother to turn to. Lynda thought the world of Kath, and she promised her she'd look after Jenny.'

'I know. But she has her own daughter and grandchild to think about as well. Our Carolyn was quite upset the other day when Lynda went there straight after work instead of coming home.'

'Yeah, and I was late home as well, which didn't help. I got a right telling off. But I can't turn down overtime.'

'No. Are things still all right at Bentham's?'

'They've announced they're 'looking to make some changes' – whatever that means. But it doesn't look like there'll be any pay rises, so I think you'll be stuck with us for a while yet, John.'

'Don't you worry about that, Steve, we like having you.'

They'd reached the car park and the battered Ford Estate that they shared.

'Thanks. But I am desperate for us to have our own place, and our own car. You look tired, John, do you want me to drive?'

John handed him the keys, 'If you don't mind. I hope Lynda's ready to be picked up, we don't want to get stuck in the football traffic.'

'She won't be late, because she's going out tonight, round to Jenny's to keep her company again.'

John paused before closing the car door.

'Yes. And that'll mean another row with Carolyn.'

'I know.'

While she waited for Lynda to usher out the last few customers and finish the clearing up, Jean Haworth re-read the Houses for Sale section in the coffee stained copy of 'The Milfield Express'. She

40

loved to imagine what it would be like to live in one of the 'new executive homes, houses of a style to suit the 1980s'. Her small stone terraced house, however much you tried to modernise it, would always belong to the nineteenth century when it had been built to house a family who had all worked in the cotton mills.

She was finding it difficult to concentrate on the details of the houses as Lynda was singing loudly to help out Elaine Paige and Barbara Dickson with their hit version of 'I know him so well'.

Jean shouted above the music. 'You've played that twice while I've been in, have you been playing it all day?'

'On and off. I love it.'

Lynda stopped wiping the tables for a minute as she wanted to put her heart into her favourite bit of the lyric.

'Isn't he good, isn't he fine? Isn't it madness, he won't be mine?' she sang at the top of her voice, and carried on singing till the end of the track.

Jean closed the newspaper. 'Can I take this home with me?'

'Of course you can.'

'There's a house advertised that's like Jenny Heywood's. They're asking big money.'

Lynda finished the tables, as she said, 'And they'll probably get it, the way house prices are going.'

'Do you think Jenny will sell hers?,' asked Jean. 'It's a big house for her to run on her own. Has she got a big mortgage?'

'Not now. Richard's life insurance sorted that out.'

Jean was embarrassed. 'Oh, yes, it will have done, I forgot.'

Lynda looked at the clock. 'John won't be long.'

Jean didn't want her thoughts interrupted. 'It must be awful for Jenny on her own at night. I remember when I lost Gordon, it took a lot of getting used to, you hear noises all the time.'

'She puts the tele on.'

'Do you think she will move?'

'She'd like to.'

'I suppose she and the children could move in with Ellen Heywood, there's plenty of bedrooms in Kirkwood House.'

'That, I think, would be Jenny's idea of hell – I know it would for me.'

'Well, you and Mrs Heywood have never got on.'

'Got on? I hate the woman.'

'It was all a long time ago. You need to forget about that, you know.'

'Her stopping me marrying Dan, you mean?'

Jean put on her 'prim face' and looked searchingly at Lynda.

'That's why you like that song, isn't it? I don't understand you, Lynda. You got to marry John, you ought to realise how lucky you are! Some people would give anything for a husband like him.'

'He's not that good.'

Jean pursed her lips and concentrated on folding the newspaper into a neat parcel small enough to fit in her handbag.

'Speak of the devil,' Lynda announced as John entered the café.

'Are you ready?' he asked brusquely.

Lynda nodded across to Jean. 'We both are.'

John quickly changed his tone of voice. 'Oh, hello, Jean. Are you all right, love?'

'Yes, thank you, John,' she replied with her brown

eyes widening a little, as they always did when she saw John Stanworth.

Lynda put on her coat, locked the door to the kitchen and started to turn off the lights as she told John, 'I said you'd give Jean a lift home.'

'Yes, of course I will.'

'You can drop me off at the bus stop and then run her home,' Lynda instructed him.

John paused in the doorway. 'Where are you going?'

Lynda, not wanting to see John's expression, concentrated on locking the door of the café as she said, 'I'm going round to Jenny's. I told you.'

'I thought that was later tonight.'

'It was, but I phoned her and the kids want to see me before they go to bed.'

'What about your tea?'

'I'll have something with Jenny.'

'Our Carolyn's cooked a big casserole for us all.'

Lynda looked at Jean, who was standing in the street, waiting silently for them to finish their conversation.

'I know. Tell you what, Jean can have my share of the casserole. She can go back to our house with you and you can take her home later, before you go and pick your Mother up from Ellen Heywood's. You'd like to go round to ours, wouldn't you, Jean?'

'I'd love to.'

Lynda fixed a smile on her face as she presented another idea to her husband. 'Perhaps Jean can help you babysit, then Steve and Carolyn can go out for a drink. Would that be all right with you, Jean?'

The thought of an evening on her own with John was a remembered dream, and Jean replied eagerly,

'Of course it would.'

'That's settled then. Where have you parked, John?'

'Round the corner,' was the rather surly reply.

'What are you scowling about?' Lynda asked as she and Jean hurried along beside him.

'You. Upsetting our Carolyn.'

'She won't be upset.'

'She will. You need to make more effort. You said you wanted things to be different.'

'I do, and I thought they would be after Michael was born.'

'But you're making a mess of it again.'

'There's other people at fault here beside me!'

She became aware of Jean's embarrassment at witnessing yet another row between her and John.

'Sorry, Jean, you don't want to hear all this. Give it a rest, John.'

They'd reached the car now.

'You sit in the front, Jean,' Lynda said, 'I'll be getting out first.'

John held the door open for Jean and watched his wife get in the back seat.

'I'm just saying, Lynda, that you need to choose who's important to you, Jenny Heywood or our Carolyn.'

'Don't talk rubbish!' she shouted as she slammed the door closed.

'I'm not!'

Dan Heywood had long ago given up hope of being able to go out regularly on Saturday nights. He could only manage it if his Mother was going with friends to the theatre or a concert; otherwise his presence was required in her drawing room, or at least somewhere in the house. It was even worse since Richard had died. Dan had now to sit, night after night, and watch this grey shadow of a woman resting her head against the wing of her chair, and gazing at Richard's graduation photograph on the piano. This Saturday night, however, thanks to Sheila Stanworth's offer of a visit, he was able to escape and join his friends in the Red Lion. It would even be possible to drink a few pints with them because Sheila, who sometimes felt sorry for Dan, had demanded the services of her son as her chauffeur on this occasion.

Over the past few weeks Sheila had learned how best to comfort to Ellen Heywood. She'd learned when to listen, and when to contribute a few gentle words. And she was glad to offer this help, for she would never forget how Ellen Heywood had guided, and protected her through the shame and gossip of her husband's desertion.

When Ted Stanworth had left his wife it had been the talk of the town, at least, that was how Sheila had perceived it. In fact, it was just a small group of women at the church who had forgotten their Christianity for a while, and had given in to the temptation of rejoicing that, unlike her, they had managed to keep their husbands from straying into sin. Sheila sought to protect Ellen now, as she had protected her then.

Ellen clutched her glass of sherry and shook her head. 'I do not understand why he was driving along that road.'

Ellen had posed that question many times, it was part of her going over and over the terrible event which had torn her life apart. Sheila had heard the rumours about Richard, but would keep them from his Mother for ever if she could.

Sheila was not perceptive enough to realise that Ellen Heywood had a strong suspicion that her son had not returned home the night before the accident. Also, although Sheila was aware that Ellen could be a very determined woman, she did not comprehend that that strong determination encompassed the capability of deciding, not only what the facts about certain matters would be, but also who would be condemned to carry the burden of any culpability.

Sheila only saw that Ellen was vulnerable in her grief, and that she needed, at this moment, to confide in someone who would understand.

'May I speak to you in confidence, Sheila?'

Sheila, feeling flattered, straightened her spine a little and clasped her hands neatly in front of her.

'Of course, Ellen.'

'I know for a fact, that Richard would not have been out on that road, he would have been at home, had he been happier there. Do you take my meaning?'

Sheila nodded sagely.

Ellen continued with a sigh. 'Neither of us have been fortunate in our son's choice of wife.'

Sheila echoed the sigh, and sought to offer some comfort by adding, 'At least Daniel managed to avoid the disaster of marrying Lynda Collins, thanks to your guidance. I only wish I had been able to make John listen to me and change his mind about marrying that girl. She will never make him happy.'

'No. Just as Jennifer Kelly was incapable of making my son happy. There can be no consolation for me, ever. But if there were, it would be that my son is free of her now.'

Sheila was shocked, but quickly moved on in her endeavour to help Ellen. 'At least you have his children. They are a part of him which you can hold on to.'

'Indeed. As you have your granddaughter.'

'Yes, it's been marvellous watching her grow up, and she's been such good company for me.'

'Carolyn has been a great comfort to me these last few weeks. I appreciate her spending time with me, especially when she has a young baby to care for.'

'Carolyn thinks the world of you.'

Ellen sighed. 'Life should have been so different for her.'

'Yes, I think you are as disappointed as I am that our Carolyn had a brilliant future taken away from her.'

Ellen continued to speak with bitterness. 'And we know who we have to thank for that. Lynda Collins. Or rather, Stanworth.'

Sheila's mouth became a thin line. 'No, Lynda Collins. I always think of her by that name, you know, she will never be a Stanworth.'

Ellen leaned forward and poured more of Harvey's Amontillado sherry into Sheila's glass. As she put down the decanter she gave her friend a steady look.

'There is such a thing as divorce. Normally one would not seek to break the vows of holy matrimony, but in some cases one has little choice.'

Sheila, who had, for a while, been wondering about this possibility, eagerly reminded Ellen, 'She and John were married in a registry office, not a church.'

'Quite so.'

Sheila took a long drink of sherry, and didn't notice that her voice became a little shrill. 'He doesn't need her. None of us need her. I've told John and Carolyn, and I've told her, she does nothing but cause trouble.'

CHAPTER SIX

Lynda had always loved Sunday mornings; she wasn't bothered about reading the Sunday paper, listening to the music on the radio was what she liked. They were playing the Wham hit 'Wake me up before you go go' so she turned it up full blast, and was singing and dancing around with the baby in her arms when Steve and Carolyn came downstairs.

'Turn it down! You'll damage his ears!' her daughter shouted.

Lynda did as she was told, a habit she'd been trying to get into since Michael was born. She didn't find it easy, but she was happy to accept that everything had to be right for the baby.

'Sorry. He was enjoying it, though, weren't you, Michael, dancing with your Grandma?'

Steve headed for the kitchen with the coffee mugs he was carrying. 'Thanks for the lie-in Lynda. Great to be able to have a cup of coffee in bed, isn't it, Caro?'

'Yeah. Where's my Dad?'

'Gone round to your Nana's of course.'

Steve, who had been looking forward to a Sunday without Sheila's critical presence, said, 'I thought she was going out to lunch with the women from church.'

'She is, but she wanted your Dad to get her some compost. Any excuse to get him round there.'

Carolyn immediately justified her Nana's needy demands. 'Sundays are lonely for women on their own. And she wants to get the garden ready for her spring planting.' She turned to explain to Steve, 'When I was little we always had to do a lot of work at this time of year. I used to love being in the garden with her.'

Lynda, thinking fondly of the man who had been her friend, also reminisced, 'It was your Grandad's pride and joy that garden.'

'Till he abandoned it and his wife,' Carolyn said pointedly, copying the tone of resentment used by Sheila whenever Ted Stanworth's name was mentioned – which wasn't often.

Lynda wished, yet again, that it was easier to move away from the past and build the closeness she craved with her daughter. She didn't want to rake up an old conflict, and so changed the subject.

'Did you enjoy going out last night, a bit of time on your own?'

Steve watched and waited for his wife's reply, and was disappointed.

'It was all right,' Carolyn said without enthusiasm. 'I wanted to go to The Peacock but we ended up at the Red Lion.'

'We'd have had to have had a meal if we'd gone to The Peacock, they're doing dinner dances on Saturday nights now,' Steve explained.

'Oh, gone up-market have they? They fancy themselves too much at The Peacock, always did. They need to knock their prices down.'

Carolyn swiftly contradicted her. 'It's a lovely

hotel, with beautiful decor and comfortable armchairs. You have to pay for that, and it's worth it.'

'If you can afford it,' Lynda argued back.

Steve, calling on his reserves of natural optimism, said, 'Wait till I've got my own business, we'll be able to dine at The Peacock then.'

Carolyn, who had struggled to find anything decent to wear to go out in last night, wasn't in the mood for fanciful day dreaming.

'Oh, stop it, Steve. We've no chance of that at the moment, where are you going to get the money to set up on your own?'

Lynda changed the subject again.

'Did you see anyone you knew at The Red Lion?'

'Dan Heywood was there.'

'My goodness,' quipped Lynda, 'you mean his Mother had let him out?'

Carolyn glared at her.

Steve didn't know Dan Heywood well but recognised long-term unhappiness when he saw it.

'He seems to me,' he observed, 'to be having a tough time at the moment, bound to, I suppose, with his brother dying. Were they very close, Lynda?'

'No. Richard was always trouble.'

Carolyn looked disapprovingly at her Mother. 'You shouldn't speak ill of the dead. I don't think Ellen will ever get over losing Richard. I must go and see her again this week.'

Lynda had always resented Ellen Heywood's influence over her daughter, but didn't dare try to discourage her visit.

'Well if you do, see if you can time it so you can give Dan a break. He told me he's having to be with her nearly all the time. She lets him go to work, but that's about it.'

Carolyn didn't like the criticism in Lynda's comment. 'She's lost her son, it's only to be expected that she needs Dan.'

'She's always been too demanding with him. He deserves to have a life and be happy.'

'I'm sure Ellen wouldn't want him to be unhappy.'

'Dan's happiness has never been a priority for Ellen Heywood. Believe me, I know.'

John walked in on the silence. 'What's up?'

'We were talking about Ellen Heywood,' Lynda informed him.

'So was my Mother.' He turned to his daughter, 'She said Ellen was hoping you'd go and see her again.'

Carolyn gave her Mother a steely-eyed look. 'I am doing.'

Steve didn't like Lynda and Carolyn disagreeing, and it was happening too much lately. He was glad to find a reason to separate them for a while. 'Shall we take Michael for a walk now?' he suggested. 'It will do him good to have a bit of fresh air before dinner.'

After they'd gone John settled down in his armchair with 'The News of the World' while Lynda went into the kitchen to cook the midday meal. She was trying a new recipe with chicken fillets in a mushroom and pepper sauce, which she was hoping would impress everybody. When it was cooking in the oven, she went back into the living room, took a holiday brochure out of a drawer and sat down opposite her husband.

'John, can we have a chat for a minute?'

'What about?'

'A holiday.'

'Oh, not again! I told you, we can't afford it, Carolyn's going to need loads of stuff for the baby.'

'How many times have I heard that?' Lynda snapped resentfully. 'All our married life it's been 'Carolyn needs'. What about what I need for once? I can't remember the last time we had a holiday. I'm working all the hours God sends, here and at the café, and for what? What do I get out of it?'

'You're not the only one who's working.'

'We need a break, John. I've been saving up, and if we all put some money towards it we could rent a flat or a caravan by the sea for a week. Carolyn and Steve would love that.'

'Our Carolyn's not keen on caravans. And neither is my Mother.'

'What's your Mother got to do with it?'

'Well, she'd want to come with us.'

'No way.'

'We couldn't leave her here on her own, while we went swanning off to the seaside.'

'I don't want a holiday with your Mother in tow!'

'Just as well we're not going on holiday then, isn't it?' John said, satisfied, as if he'd won the argument.

He opened the newspaper again.

Steve was glad to be alone with his wife and child, walking through the park, and seeing that spring was finally persuading winter to make an exit. He thought it was wonderful being a Dad. He loved pushing the pram and gazing at his son, whom he regarded as a little miracle. It was a pity Carolyn seemed to still be in a bad mood.

'Good to get out for a bit.'

'Yes,' she replied, staring ahead and not noticing the snowdrops and crocuses at either side of the path.

'What's the matter, Caro?'

'My Mother. I thought it was going to be different after we had the baby. I thought she'd change. Be a proper grandma.'

'She is. She's thrilled to bits with her grandson.'

'She doesn't seem sure how to look after him.'

Steve hesitated, wondering if his wife would be able to cope if he told her that she was the problem, showing that she didn't trust her Mother with the baby.'

'She's learning, just like we are. She says she's forgotten a lot, because it's a long time since she looked after you when you were a baby.'

'She didn't look after me then. It was always my Nan.'

'Your Mum and Dad were short of money. Lynda had to go out to work.'

'She wanted to. She enjoyed it, like she does now. She loves going to the café. Sometimes I think she'd rather be there than at home. I'm not sure she was cut out to be a mother or if she wanted children really. We've never been close, you know. And you should be close to your Mother, she should always be there for you.'

'She is.'

'No, she's not! She's spending more time looking after Jenny Heywood than she is looking after me!'

Steve didn't contradict his wife, because he thought what she'd just said might be true.

'I know you like her, Steve, but it's not easy that we're having to live together in the same house.'

'You and Lynda do seem to argue a lot.'

'We always have done. My Dad's great, but me and my Mother have never really got on. And she won't change. My Nan's got no time for her.'

Steve couldn't stop himself muttering, 'Oh, well. Your Nan.'

'Don't be like that.'

Steve looked around for a distraction from the conversation he wasn't enjoying, and was pleased to spot Jean walking through the park. He and Carolyn waved, and Jean, who hated being alone on Sundays, hurried towards them excitedly.

'I didn't expect to see you again so soon,' she trilled. 'You'll have had enough of me for one week! How's little Michael? Did he sleep all right?'

Steve grinned. 'Yes, what did you put in his bottle?'

'Nothing, you cheeky so-and-so.'

Steve was ready for a bit of teasing. 'Hey, I've something to tell you, Jean.'

'What?'

'Dan Heywood was asking about you last night.'

'Was he?'

'Yeah. You and Dan ought to get together you know, go for a night out on the tiles.'

'Oh, no, not me and Dan,' she protested. 'It was always Lynda he wanted, not me.'

Carolyn was wide-eyed. 'Dan Heywood and my Mother? Did they go out together?'

'Oh, yes. It was the big romance for your Mother after she left school. But Dan was forced to finish with her and she started going out with your Dad.' Jean drew her coat tighter around her as she remembered how much that had hurt her.

Carolyn was open-mouthed, 'But it was Dan

Heywood she wanted really.'

'Yes. But, it was all a long time ago.' Jean felt she had said too much, but Carolyn was very keen to learn the truth.

'My Nana told me my Mother chased after my Dad, and blackmailed her and my Grandad into letting him marry her.'

Jean, who had had reason to follow the progress of that particular romance very closely, selected her information carefully. 'I don't know about that. I only know Lynda's Grandma was desperate for her to get married.'

'So she married my Dad on the re-bound,' Carolyn concluded. 'That explains a helluva lot.'

Steve looked warily at his wife, and wished he'd never made the joke about Jean and Dan. He could see Carolyn was again heading towards thoughts which were far from positive. He looked to his son to lighten the mood, and leaned over and tickled him.

'Do you hear all this, Michael? Take my advice and keep clear of women, they make life too complicated.'

Little Michael Sheldon smiled, and loudly broke wind. And as Steve had hoped, even Carolyn laughed.

The Ford Estate had to go into the garage for its M.O.T test, and John was hoping it would get through without costing much. The rain was pouring down that morning, and he was really pleased when Dan's bakery van drew up beside him as he stood at the bus stop near the garage. He was always glad to see Dan, and he'd been worried about him the last few weeks.

'You'll have been having to look after your Mother quite a bit lately.'

'Yeah.'

'Even more than usual, eh?'

'Yeah.'

John wasn't used to Dan being so quiet with him. He'd known Dan long enough to realise that his friend was suffering.

'Not easy, is it, having your Mother so dependent on you?'

'No.'

'Mine gives me the run-around when she feels like it, as you well know. It's always been the same for us, hasn't it?' He smiled at Dan but he was staring at the road ahead and gripping the steering wheel tightly.

'Not quite,' he replied. 'The difference is that your Mother loves you, in her way, but mine doesn't love me.'

John found it hard to talk about such feelings, but knew he had to try to reassure his friend. 'She does, Dan, in her way.'

Dan's throat was so tight he could hardly say the words, but John was his best friend, someone who might truly understand.

'Not as much as she loved Richard.'

John bowed his head for a moment, as he sought some words which would ease Dan's pain. 'Now he's gone, she'll be able to appreciate you more.'

Dan looked at his friend with gratitude but little conviction.

'Maybe. I hope so, anyway.'

They drove along in silence for a while, then Dan, needing a happier thought, joked, 'I hope your car gets through its M.O.T. or you'll be asking me for your motorbike back.'

'Have you still got it?'

'Oh, yes. Me and my Dad kept it hidden in a shed at the bakery. I used to take him out on it sometimes, you know. He loved it.'

'And your Mother's never found out about it?'

'No. I sneak off for a ride whenever I can. It's still a good bike.'

'I know it is. It was hard to have to sell it, even to you. It meant a lot to me, that Norton. Lynda bought it for me.'

'I know. For your twenty-first birthday.'

'Yeah.'

John smiled at the memory, and spoke out with rare emotion.

'I really loved her that day.'

Dan hesitated for a moment, but he had to know.

'And you still love her, don't you?'

John was surprised at the question, and found it awkward to answer. He eventually decided to say what would be expected, even though he wasn't sure it was true.

'Oh, yes. We have our ups and downs, but she's still the girl I married. Worrying about money and that gets in the way now and again, that's all. And she's hard work sometimes is Lynda. And women are never happy anyway, are they?'

CHAPTER SEVEN

Lynda was upset that she was missing Michael's tea-time and bath time. On Tuesdays, as most of the market stall holders and shopkeepers of Milfield closed at lunch time, Lynda closed the café at three o'clock. Usually she hurried home to have that precious extra time with her baby grandson. For the last few weeks, however, she'd had to give Jenny and her children priority. It wouldn't, she hoped, be for much longer.

She'd tried to explain to Carolyn that she'd promised Jenny's mother, Kathleen, who'd been a best friend to both Lynda and to her mother before her, that she would look after her daughter.

Carolyn had just given her that cold stare that she'd inflicted on her Mother from her teenage years onwards. She had also, Lynda had noticed, seemed to reduce the times she allowed Lynda to cuddle or care for the baby, a sort of revenge, Lynda supposed it was.

She was glad to see that Alex and Katie were playing and arguing and making a lot of noise when she arrived. Jenny apologised for the din and the mess.

'Don't be daft It's good to see them back to normal.'

Jenny gave her a questioning look, and then realised what she meant.

They talked about it later when the children were happily asleep after insisting on having 'Aunty Lynda' read them an extra story.

'It's been hard for them. I think even Ellen has begun to realise that now,' Jenny told Lynda. 'In fact she's much better with them now than she's ever been.'

'That's good, I suppose.'

'I'm not so sure,' Jenny said. 'I don't want to take a negative view, but I think Ellen looks on them mainly as her strongest link to Richard. I only hope she doesn't try to take them over. Does that sound mean?'

'No. It sounds sensible. We both know what she's like, your mother-in-law.' Lynda paused before asking quietly. 'How is she with Dan?'

'Terrible. It's as if she resents him being there instead of Richard.'

'I hate that woman. She doesn't deserve to have a lovely son like Dan. He needs to get away from her. And so do you, before she takes over your life.'

'I know the dangers, Lynda, but she needs her grandchildren and I want them to have a family round them. I need to get out of this house, though, it has too many bad memories. And it was never a house I would have chosen.'

'I know. At least Beechwood Avenue was my choice. But it's never been my house, not with his Mother having her say about everything. And now it's Steve and Carolyn's more than mine. I don't mind that really. I love having the baby there, even if I don't seem to get much of a look-in sometimes. Sorry, I shouldn't be moaning – especially to you.'

Jenny poured her another glass of wine and claimed, with a little laugh, 'We're entitled to moan, both of us, like we're entitled to have a drink. Mind you, I'll have to be careful, I found myself pouring a glass in the morning, one day last week.'

'You little devil! Why shouldn't you, though? You're bound to get depressed.'

'I was feeling a bit sorry for myself, and thinking about what lovely grandparents my Mum and Dad would have been for the girls.'

'Yeah. I wish they were still here, especially your Mum.'

'So do I, she was wonderful.'

'They both were, and full of fun. That's what we're short of now, a good laugh. I used to escape to their house as often as I could, you know. That's what I feel now, that I need to escape for a bit.'

'Can you and John not go away for a few days?'

'He won't even consider it.'

'Go on your own, then.'

Lynda opened her bag and took out a letter. 'I'm thinking about it. You remember I told you about Rose Milner – the woman Sheila's husband went off with?'

'Yes. She went to live in Cornwall after he died, you said.'

'That's right. She's been asking me for ages to go down there to stay with her. And at Easter she and her friend are having a big joint birthday party – like me and your Mum did. I'd love to go. She's getting on a bit is Rose, and I'd like to see her again.'

'Go then.'

'I can't, because I'd have to tell John, and he'd go mad. His Mother always blamed me for Ted going off to live with Rose.'

'Did she?'

'Oh, yes, so it would cause ructions even having her name mentioned. But I'd love to go and visit her, and I'd love to go to Cornwall. Sometimes I get this feeling that I need to be by the sea, walk along a beach on my own. It's been something I've always needed.'

'Oh, it would be lovely, Cornwall in the spring.'

'Yeah. But I can't do it.' She folded the letter carefully and put it back in her bag. 'The story of my life, not being able to do what I want.'

Jenny re-filled Lynda's glass, and proposed a toast.

'To us, two women who want to get away, but can't. But we will, one day, Lynda, I'll get out of this horrible house, and you'll get to go and walk on that beach!'

It was a long time before Lynda could get to sleep that night. She kept thinking about how cruel Ellen Heywood was being to the son who, Lynda knew, loved her more than Richard had ever done. When she did finally sleep, she dreamed of Cornwall and of walking barefoot on the sand in the early morning sunshine.

When Dan came to deliver the bread the next morning he looked so pale and tired that as soon as she saw him she put her arms round him and held him close.

'Jenny told me your Mother is being nasty to you.'

He pulled away briefly, but saw the love and

compassion in her eyes and allowed himself to cling to her, needing to be held in her arms. 'Yeah,' he said, his voice hoarse with pain. 'She keeps saying she has no reason to live now he's gone. What about me? I said. You still have me. But she looked at me, and . . .' He shuddered. 'You don't know what it's like, Lynda, how it feels, not to be loved.'

She took a deep breath. 'Yes, I do,' she whispered. 'John doesn't love me.' She paused and looked steadily into Dan's eyes. 'And I don't love him. I love you, Dan. I still love you.'

He instinctively held on to her, and then those old feelings he'd kept trying to drive away took hold of him again, and they clung to each other just like they used to as teenagers.

They kissed and found a happiness they had not felt for years. Then she whispered, 'We need to be together, Dan. Let's get away from all this misery, let's go away and have the life we want.'

He pulled away from her. 'Get away? How can we?'

'We'll just do it, get in a car, get on a train – just go.'

'No. Stop it, Lynda. Stop this! We can't do it. John does love you, Lynda. He told me only the other day. I can't do this to him. You're not being fair, to him or to me. You've got to stop trying to have what isn't possible.'

'We love each other.'

'No!' He held her away from him and looked at her searchingly. 'Lynda, you've got to stop yearning for a life you can't have. I know you're not happy, neither of us are, but that's what happens, life's not perfect. And to be quite honest, I think you don't know what you want.'

'I do, I want you.'

'Why? Because you can't have me?'

'What a horrible thing to say!'

'You don't really love me, Lynda. What you love is just the romance, the way we felt about each other as teenagers. What's hurting you is that you've had to give up your dreams, like we all have. But the trouble is, you're not willing to be content with what you've got.'

She was angry with him now. 'No, I'm not. And why should I be?'

'Because we have to take what we're given in life. I love you, Lynda, but I can't have you, and I've learned to accept that. But you talking about what can't happen is a torment to me, especially now. You've got to leave me alone. Sometimes I wish that you'd go away so I could forget about you.'

'No, Dan, don't say that.'

'Our big romance was over when we were teenagers. You married John, and he's the one you have to love. You have to stay with him. You belong to John.'

She stood there, staring at him and not wanting to believe what he was saying; but she saw that he meant every word.

'The trouble is,' she cried, 'I don't feel as if I belong to anybody.'

He was gentle now, 'Lynda, love, it's no good either of us looking for a different life. We have to be satisfied with the life we've got.'

'I can't.'

'We have to be, we've no choice.'

He looked at her with eyes full of misery and longing. Then he shook his head, and turned to leave. And she knew he was walking out of her life.

CHAPTER EIGHT

On Friday Steve came home from work with what he thought was good news. He'd been worried that the small workshop that was the Milfield part of Ralph Bentham's business was about to be closed down, but that afternoon it had been announced that, although that workshop would be closed, Bentham's were moving to bigger premises in Milfield.

There would be some re-organising and a few early retirements would be necessary, but once that was dealt with, the rest of the jobs would be safe – at least for the time being.

Steve announced the good news as they were sitting round the table together that evening.

'Victoria Mill, we're moving to. Do you know it, John?' he asked.

Lynda smiled. 'I do, it's where my Grandma used to work. It's a big place.'

'They're not taking over all of it,' Steve explained, 'but it sounds as if there'll be room to do a lot more work. Randerson was talking about doing bedroom fittings as well as kitchens.'

John reacted like someone who'd been thumped in the chest.

'Randerson? Do you mean Tony Randerson?'

Steve, who hadn't noticed the look which passed between John and Lynda, nodded with enthusiasm.

'Yes. He's going to be in charge. He's Ralph Bentham's son-in-law and next in line to the throne apparently. I've heard he's a bit of a tough bastard, but I'll cope, as long as he brings work in.'

'Bastard's right,' muttered Lynda, and headed for the kitchen. 'I'll make a cup of tea.'

'Do you know this Randerson?' Carolyn asked her Dad.

'No.' John winced as he heard the name again, and he went and sat in the armchair by the fire.

'Victoria Mill is further out, will it be all right if I take the car and drop you off on the way, John?' asked Steve, embarrassed again by such practicalities. 'I'll be able to get my own car soon, if we start to get more overtime.'

'Yeah.'

Carolyn saw her father had slumped down in his chair, staring at the fire. 'Are you all right, Dad?'

'Yeah. Yes, of course I am.'

Steve eyes were still sparking with excitement.

'Tell you what, John. I'll take you out for a pint. Is that all right, Caro?'

Carolyn kissed him on the cheek, happy to see him so full of hope. 'Go on, celebrate.'

Steve called out to Lynda. 'Don't make tea for us, love. I'm taking your Dad to the pub. Come on, Johnny boy, get your coat!'

Lynda stayed for as long as she could in the kitchen, slowly washing and rinsing the plates they'd used for their evening meal, watching the water flow over their surface and trying to slow down the pounding of her heart. The memory of that night with Tony Randerson still made her feel physically sick. When she could find nothing else to do in the kitchen, she made two beakers of strong tea and took them into the living room.

She was standing by the sideboard, adding a drop of whisky to hers when Carolyn came down from checking that Michael was asleep. She was surprised to see the whisky bottle, which usually never emerged from the back of the sideboard cupboard, except at Christmas or when someone was poorly. 'What are you doing with that? Oh, celebrating, are we?'

'Do you want some?'

Carolyn sighed in that patronising way which made Lynda feel more like a stupid child than a mother. 'I'm breastfeeding – remember?'

She watched her Mother sink down into the armchair, and bow her head to stare into the cup of hot liquid she was clutching in both hands.

'Is something the matter?'

'I don't want Steve working for that man.'

'Tony Randerson? Why not?'

Lynda didn't reply, but concentrated on raising the cup to her lips.

Carolyn never had been perceptive where her mother was concerned, and merely gave a sardonic laugh.

'Is he an ex-boyfriend of yours?'

'I don't want to talk about him.'

'For goodness sake! Steve and I get a bit of good news for once, and all you can do is look miserable.'

'It's not good news.'

'Oh, shut up. Don't go spoiling this, just because you had a fling with this Randerson guy and he dumped you, or whatever.'

'No!' Lynda yelled.

The cry made Carolyn stop and wonder what this was about. Then a memory came.

'Oh, I get it. He was the one you and Dad had that big row about when I was a teenager. Randerson was the one my Dad found out about, was he? It was bad, that. I remember. Nana and I thought you were going to get divorced.'

'Perhaps we should have done. I'd have been happier, if we had.'

'How can you say that? My Dad forgives you, and all you do is moan about him! You're never satisfied, that's your trouble.'

'You can talk!'

'You got my Dad to marry you — blackmailed him into it, my Nan says — and you've never been satisfied, never appreciated how lucky you are. She's right. I've watched you all these years. You've never been happy with him and you've never made him happy.'

'You don't know what you're talking about Carolyn. You've never understood me, never bothered to get to know me. It was always your Dad for you, or your flaming Nana. Never me, your Mother. I never counted for anything with you.'

'You were never there! You were always off out when I was a kid, going to the pub with your mates. On the lookout for another fella. Always wanting some other man instead of my Dad. Who is it this time? Dan Heywood?'

'What do you mean, Dan?'

'Aunty Jean told me you used to go out with him, that you and he are still keen on each other.'

'Is that what she said?'

Carolyn hesitated now, wondering if she'd gone too far, and not wanting to get her Aunty Jean into trouble. 'It was just a remark, she didn't mean to say it, I don't think. But judging from your reaction, it was true. What's going on?'

'Nothing!'

Lynda felt herself begin to shake, with fear and with anger. In the last hour, in that room, it was as if the past had roared up to attack her.

'It doesn't sound like nothing,' Carolyn persisted.

'Jean Haworth is a mean minded trouble-maker. What did she tell you exactly?'

'That it was Dan you wanted really, not my Dad. He wasn't the one for you, you knew that, but you still married him. It wasn't right, it's never been right. You should have split up years ago. He should have divorced you when . . .'

Lynda stood up now, glaring at the daughter who, for many years now, had never loved her as she'd hoped to be loved.

'When what?'

'Like I said, when you and Randerson . . .'

'What? 'Miss 'Know-it-All'! What?' Lynda shouted.

'God knows! Nana says she warned Dad that you were a flighty piece who'd make his life a misery. No wonder she said that. How many men have you been out with? Nana says you'll never change.'

'No, and neither will she! And neither will you. I let you spend too much time with her, and she's made you like she is.'

Lynda looked away, blinking back tears now.

'I thought when Michael was born, we'd get closer, be friends like a mother and daughter should be. All these years you've made it clear that you think I'm rubbish, that I'm wrong about everything. I thought with Michael to bring us closer, we could make a fresh start, but now I see that nothing's ever going to change.'

She opened the door to the hallway.

'I'm going out. I need a walk. I need . . .'

'Another drink?' mocked Carolyn.

'Another life!' cried Lynda as she slammed the door, and took her tears and her pain out into the cold night air.

The following morning, after dropping Steve off on the way, John drove Lynda to work as usual. They had hardly spoken a word since the night before. Lynda had pretended to be asleep when John had come to bed. She often did. She didn't like him to touch her any more, but he didn't seem to notice that. If he wanted sex she didn't refuse him, but she felt demeaned by it.

She'd cried for hours last night, walking the streets and then lying between the cold sheets of their double bed. She'd almost laughed to herself as she got into bed and shivered, the sheets seemed to symbolise what was wrong with being married to John Stanworth. He refused to have what he called 'one of those continental eiderdowns', John was a man stuck in the 1950s, and always would be.

She felt cold again now and folded her arms around her body as she sat in the passenger seat watching the windscreen wipers struggling to push aside the rain. John was aware of the silence between them but was almost afraid to speak because of the pressure of the anger within him. Randerson was back in their life and there was no way to get rid of him, or the memory of what he had done.

John had always felt his manhood had been diminished by his inability to take revenge against that man and his crime. And it was something he still could not talk about. But he had to talk to Lynda, she was his wife, they could not live together without talking, so he decided he must find something to say.

'When they move to Victoria Mill it'll cost more in petrol for Steve to go to work.'

He cursed himself as soon as he'd said it.

Lynda gave him a scornful look.

'Don't worry, he'll pay you the extra.'

'I know he will. I wasn't worrying about that. You always take things the wrong way.'

'Oh, me in the wrong again, is it? I'm not surprised. I've been in the wrong for a long time, haven't I, John?'

'What do you mean?'

'Ever since that night. No, let's be honest, ever since we got married.'

'That's not true, we used to be happy.'

'Used to be. So you admit we're not happy now.'

Furrows appeared on his brow, and he shook his head slowly, as if trying to solve a puzzle.

'No, Lynda. We are happy.'

'I'm not.'

'Why not? We have a family, a nice house, a lovely little grandson – why can't you be content?'

'Why can't you love me enough to make me happy? You don't love me, John. Admit it.'

'Don't talk stupid!'

They'd reached Hudson Street but John didn't turn on to it, he drove down a quiet side-street before stopping the car. He didn't want to have this row parked in front of the café where passers-by might recognise them and wonder what they were arguing about.

'What's going on, Lynda?'

Lynda, her face tight with pain and certainty, paused before she answered.

'I saw it in your face last night, John. You'll never forgive me, and you'll never forget. Things will never be right between us, John. I've not made you happy, and you've not made me happy. We should have ended it then, all those years ago.'

'But we didn't.'

'No. But I've been doing a lot of thinking lately, asking myself questions. Big questions.'

He folded his arms and sighed impatiently. 'Like what?'

'Like, where's our marriage going? Where's my life going?'

He switched on the engine again.

'Oh, I'm not listening to this. We'll talk about it tonight.'

Lynda got out of the car and walked away, without looking back at him. She knew that they wouldn't talk about it tonight, or ever.

CHAPTER NINE

Jenny Heywood had been dreading Mothering Sunday because she knew it would become a day of mourning when they went to Kirkwood House. Alex and Katie had leaped into bed with her that Sunday morning and given her the cards they had made at school and nursery. They also gave her a box of chocolates with a picture of a cosy country cottage on the lid. She thanked her lovely girls, and kissed them and shed a few tears.

'We made the cards,' Alex told her, 'but Aunty Lynda bought the chocolates for us to give to you. She said you'd like the picture.'

'I do. I love it. Thank you so much.'

Alex looked puzzled. 'If you like it, why are you crying?'

Jenny hugged her close, 'Because the picture is like the ones at my Mummy and Daddy's house. They used to cut out chocolate box lids like this and hang them on the wall.'

'And that makes you sad?'

'Yes, but it makes me happy as well.' She hugged both her little girls. 'Now come on, let's go downstairs and have a lovely breakfast.'

Kirkwood House was as gloomy as expected, but at least after lunch they managed to persuade Ellen to move into the sunny Victorian conservatory, and watch the children play with their dolls and some of Dan's old toys he had brought down from the loft.

Jenny and Dan were glad, as usual, to take refuge in the kitchen, washing the delicate crystal and the Royal Doulton dinner service.

'Thank goodness that's over,' Jenny said, feeling she could breathe at last.

'Yeah. Big mistake with the flowers though. I've always bought her flowers on Mother's Day, it's tradition, but I never thought of them as a reminder of the funeral, there's no lilies among them.'

'She just chose to see them that way. Shall I take them home with me?'

'Oh, please, get them out of the way, unless they'll be funereal to you, too.'

'No, they'll give me double pleasure, knowing you bought them.'

'Thanks. I don't know how long it's going to go on like this, Jenny. She hardly talks to me, but when she does, they're strange conversations, as if she's full of dark secrets.'

'Perhaps she is. I've heard she's been asking questions in the coroner's office. I think she knows the truth about what happened. But of course she'll never admit it.'

'No, she won't,' Dan agreed. 'She wouldn't hear a word against Richard when he was alive, so she certainly won't now he's dead. And we have to listen to her going on about him, and keep quiet, even though we know that most of it isn't true. It must be even harder for you than it is for me.'

'I don't mind. It's enough that she's lost her son, without losing the good memory she has of him.'

'You're too generous. She doesn't deserve a daughter-in-law like you, especially the way she treats you.'

Jenny finished drying the crystal glass in her hand, and stared at it thoughtfully as she set it down next to the others.

'I look upon it as part of my punishment for marrying her son. And I know Ellen is domineering and sometimes cruel, but she's still my children's grandmother. I never knew any of my grandparents, they were in Ireland and died before I was old enough to be taken to see them. Or rather, before Mum and Dad could find the money to take me there.'

'I still think you might be better off getting away from my Mother.'

'I can see why you're worried, but Milfield is my home, and I haven't got the courage to move away and start again somewhere I don't know anyone. And unless I can sell the house I haven't got any money apart from what my Mum and Dad left me, which isn't a lot.'

'It's a wonder Richard didn't take that off you.'

'Yes, he liked to have control of all the money. But he seemed to understand how I felt about my Mum and Dad. That was the last time I remember him being kind to me, when my Dad died.'

'I'm glad you've got at least one good memory of him. It's more than I have.'

Jenny laughed ruefully and gave Dan a hug.

'You'll just have to share your Mother's then, won't you?'

He looked at her and shook his head slowly.

'Stuck, aren't we, you and me?'

'Yeah. But I can't think of a better person to be stuck with.'

They could tell the children were relieved when they walked back into the conservatory. They ran up to their Mother and clung to her skirt.

'When are we going to the party, Mummy?' Alex wanted to know.

'When you've tidied away Uncle Dan's toys.'

Ellen, who had been staring out of the window and remembering Richard and his friends playing among the trees, turned towards them sharply.

'What party?'

'It's their little friend's birthday party. I promised they could go'

'You should not have done so. It's not right that they should go to a party so soon after . . .'

Dan saw Alex's lip was already trembling with disappointment. 'They're children, Mother. No one's asking them to forget about Richard, but they have to live, and have their childhood. Richard wouldn't have wanted . . .'

'Don't you presume to tell me what my son would have wanted. You didn't know him.'

'He was my brother.'

Ellen paused, taking a deep breath. 'You were not close.'

'No, I admit that. We weren't close.'

'You didn't understand him.'

'No. I didn't.'

'I did. I understood him. But what I will never understand is why he was out on that icy road.'

She looked pointedly at Jenny before continuing, 'Why was he not at home with his wife?'

Dan forced himself to speak out. 'It's no use keep asking these questions, Mother. It's hard for you, I know, it's hard for all of us. But we have to move on.'

'Move on! Stop thinking about it, do you mean?'

'Yes, Ellen. At least some of the time.' Jenny looked at her mother-in-law with pleading as well as compassion in her eyes.

Ellen's voice was harsh with anger and pain. 'I see. You wish to forget. I tell you now, you will not forget him. You will not forget his goodness, his generosity, his wonderful love of life. He will live on in this house, just as my Father does.'

She paused and looked at them both, daring them to speak against her. Then, knowing she was in control, she decided to display another aspect of her power, that of finance.

'Thinking about my Father reminds me that I must discuss some business with you, Jennifer. You need to come without the children one day next week. I suggest Wednesday.'

'Yes. I can come on Wednesday morning, when Katie is at nursery.'

'Good. We must discuss your finances. I want to check that I am making adequate provision for my grandchildren's upkeep.'

'You are, you're being very generous, Ellen. But I think it would be sensible for us to move to a smaller house.'

'Out of the question. My son provided that house for you and I will honour that commitment. Now, Daniel, would you make us some coffee please?'

'I'll skip coffee, if you don't mind.' Jenny stood up and gathered her children close to her. 'We have a party we must go to.'

Dan beamed at them and waved 'Bye bye'. Ellen, however, was furious that she was being disobeyed.

'What an ungrateful girl she is,' she remarked almost before Jenny had closed the door behind her.

'Jenny's not ungrateful, she's just trying to sort out her life after losing her husband.'

'A husband she was not worthy of. Richard should never have married her. She didn't love him, she just wanted his money, the life he could offer – and now she's wanting to sell his house!'

Dan knew better than to contradict his Mother when she was in this mood. It had never been easy, living with this autocratic woman who rarely changed her opinion of anything or anyone. Since Richard had been killed she seemed to be living within herself, her mind weaving its way around a reality she could not shape into what she wanted.

Ellen decided it was time to declare what she believed. 'I blame her for Richard's death.'

'Mother, you can't.'

'I'm not a fool, Daniel. I know Richard was not happy with her. He would have been home that day if Jennifer Kelly had been a loving wife.'

Dan shook his head. 'You can't blame Jenny for the accident, Mother.'

'But I do blame her. And if she continues to show disrespect for my son's memory, I shall tell her what I believe.'

'No! You can't do that.'

'I can. And I shall.'

Dan didn't want to have to do this, and he was

afraid, but he had to protect Jenny.

'Mother, Richard didn't die because he wasn't happy at home, he was killed because he was driving too fast and he'd been drinking.'

Ellen took a step towards him, her eyes darkened with malice.

'Shame on you! He was your brother, but you did not love him. You were jealous because he was such a fine, handsome young man, such a contrast to you. Are you so jealous of him still, that you would slander the son so cruelly taken from me?'

She turned away from him in disgust and opened the door.

'I shall go to my room. I cannot bear to be here with you, when I wish to be with him.'

Dan listened until he had heard her safely ascend the stairs and close her bedroom door. He sat down slowly in an armchair, and then saw a toy the children had left under the settee. It was the little wooden baker's van his Dad had made for him. He knelt down on his hands and knees and reached out to retrieve it. Still kneeling, he held on to the toy, and wept.

They hadn't opened their Mother's Day presents until Sheila had arrived at Beechwood Avenue. Carolyn was delighted with the dress which Steve, with Lynda's help, had bought for her as her first Mother's Day gift from her little boy. When John presented his Mother with a large pink azalea, she exclaimed with pleasure. 'Oh, I'm glad it's a plant because I've already had a beautiful bouquet of flowers from Sylvia and Graham. It would have been nice if they'd brought it themselves of course.'

'It's lovely that Graham has taken Sylvia away for a weekend-break, though,' commented Carolyn enviously.

'I know. Enid has gone to stay and look after the children,' Sheila said, not sure whether she would have wanted to do that, but still jealous that Graham's Mother had been chosen. 'I don't know why they have to live so far away.'

'Graham has no choice, he has to go where the Bank sends him,' John explained for the umpteenth time.

'I know.' Sheila sighed looking round for sympathy. Carolyn, seeing that her Nana was about to search for her handkerchief, placed another present in her hands. Carolyn had bought this one with the money her Dad had secretly given her. Sheila was delighted with the Italian woollen wrap she had admired so much, and so persuasively, when she and Carolyn had been looking round the shops together a few weeks earlier.

'You're spoiling me. How did you know I wanted one of these?'

She beamed at them - a picture of innocence.

Lynda tried not to show her disappointment as she unwrapped the cheap, brown imitation leather shopping bag which was her present from her daughter. She knew Carolyn and Steve were short of money, so she hadn't expected a lot, but a bag like the ones she saw all the old ladies in Milfield carrying to the market was about the worst thing they could have bought her.

'Do you like it, Mum? You said you needed a new bag for work.'

'Yeah. Yes, it's very good for that. Thank you.'

Steve realised that Lynda was upset, but knew he could do nothing about it. He put his arm round her as he asked, 'Are we off to the pub, then?'

'It's a hotel,' Sheila corrected him.

Sheila Stanworth liked The Peacock Hotel, it had been the scene of her greatest triumph, the wedding of her daughter, Sylvia, to Graham Laycock. That had been in the 1960s and the hotel now had new owners who were superstitious and had got rid of the peacock feather patterned curtains, replacing them with a more fashionable design in a peachy pink and green. The chairs in the dining room had been re-upholstered to match and there was new table linen, pale pink with a burgundy trim.

The Stanworth family shuffled into their places along a table in the corner. Steve parked the baby's buggy in a space at the end of the table and sat beside it, ready to take Michael out if he woke up and started to cry.

John had been commanded to sit at the head of the table next to his Mother and his daughter, and Lynda, wanting to avoid sitting next to her mother-in-law, chose a chair at the end, next to Steve. They ordered beers and lager shandies, and then settled down to enjoy reading the menu.

Carolyn smiled happily as she took in all the details of her surroundings. 'They're lovely, aren't they, these new curtains, Nan?' she enthused.

'Yes, I like them, and this new table linen,' Sheila agreed, fingering the edge of the napkin to test its quality. 'Quite an upgrade.'

'They've upgraded the prices as well,' grumbled John.

'You're not paying for it,' his Mother pointed out a little tartly.

He glowered.

Sheila had demanded that John should book a table at The Peacock Hotel as a special treat for her and her granddaughter. John and Steve couldn't afford it, she knew that, and had, not very discreetly, given John some money when the waiter came to take their order.

Sheila had requested that Carolyn should accompany her to church for the Mothering Sunday service that morning, and this was one of their topics of conversation during the meal.

'Ellen Heywood wasn't there,' Sheila informed John.

'Oh.' John wasn't interested in their visit to church.

Steve wasn't interested either, but he was aware that Lynda was grim-faced as she listened to the two women dissecting the situation in the Heywood family. He noticed, though, that she didn't comment. In fact she hardly said anything all through the meal.

Steve had been aware of a lot of tension in Lynda the past few days, and that she'd been very quiet. He had seen that she was very much aware of either being ignored or having her opinions disregarded. And today he'd been carefully observing everyone's behaviour, and he wondered how many times in the past he hadn't noticed what had been going on.

He watched and realised that, apart from himself when he wasn't busy with Michael, no-one engaged Lynda in conversation. They didn't even speak to her to offer her the salt, or the jug of cream which came with the dark chocolate gateau they'd all ordered for dessert. Twice he heard her ask Carolyn to pass it to her, but her daughter didn't hear her, she was too busy talking to her Nana. In the end Lynda stood up angrily and reached across the table for it – prompting a disapproving comment from Sheila.

'Manners!'

Steve was annoyed when, at the end of their Mother's Day lunch, they failed to include Lynda in the order for coffee and tea, and asked pointedly in a loud voice, 'What about you, Lynda? Would you like a coffee?'

'Yes, please, love,' she said quietly, and her grateful little smile broke his heart.

CHAPTER TEN

Lynda had never pictured it like this. She'd always imagined there would be shouting and yelling, and doors slamming, and clothes stuffed hastily into a suitcase. But her leaving had been quiet, secret and calm.

On the Wednesday after Mothering Sunday she'd gone to work as usual in the morning, but had returned home at half-past ten, when she knew that Carolyn would have taken the baby to Stanhope Road to be shown off to a friend Sheila had invited for coffee.

She'd carefully folded her favourite clothes, all washed and ironed and had packed them in the one decent suitcase they possessed. She'd also put in a couple of skirts and pairs of trousers she wore for work; she was only going for a few days, but she wouldn't want to wear her best clothes all the time. She'd put on her best coat, a three-quarter length camel jacket she'd bought in a sale, and then, as an afterthought, had stuffed her raincoat into the bottom of the suitcase, which was by now very heavy.

The last thing she did before the taxi came was place the letter in the centre of the dining table. It was only short, written the night before, after everyone had gone to bed. There was so much she had wanted to say in that letter, so many things that had happened or been said, all the things which had made her so miserable. But when she'd tried to write them down, they had sounded petty and trivial, and selfish, so, in the end, she didn't write about any of them. All her letter told her family was that she was going away for a few days, that she needed a holiday, and some time to think.

So there she was, sitting on the Penzance train, staring out of the window at the towns and villages, and the wonderful English countryside between them. She had expected to feel excited at the idea of being on holiday, going somewhere entirely new to her, but as soon as she'd started to travel away from Milfield she'd felt afraid, and lonely. What she felt most of all, however, was an overwhelming sense of relief.

Her loneliness came to an end when she got off the train at Truro and Rose Milner wrapped her arms round her in a motherly embrace. It had been over ten years since the two women had seen each other, but Lynda had no problem recognising Rose with her comfortable figure and bright smile. Her hair still framed her face with soft brown curls, a shade or two lighter than they used to be when Ted Stanworth had stroked them gently. Her eyes still danced with laughter and her light, teasing tone was just the same.'

'You've lost weight, Lynda. Wish I had!'

'You look marvellous, the climate in Cornwall must be good for roses.'

'It'll soon put some colour in your cheeks,' Rose said cheerily – hiding the concern she felt at the sight of the lines and shadows on Lynda's face which, she remembered, had once been smooth and glowing.

'There's Patrick.' She waved at a tall, dark-skinned, well-groomed young man in his early twenties, who strolled towards them.

'Patrick, this is my friend Lynda.'

'Hi, Lynda. I've heard a lot about you,' he remarked with a slight drawl. His smile was wide and appreciative as he touched the brim of the black cowboy hat tilted on the back of his head. He shook her hand firmly and took hold of her suitcase as if it weighed nothing.

'Patrick works at the hotel. He's, . .' Rose hesitated, 'how would you describe yourself, Patrick?'

'Multi-racial and multi-talented! I do just about everything in that damned hotel. I cook, I clean, I keep an eye on the finances – and of course, I keep the ladies entertained,' he added mischievously.

He put down the suitcase next to an old white Rover 3500, and with a flourish held open the rear passenger door.

'Your carriage, ladies. You're honoured, Lynda, Robbie has sent his main status symbol, with me playing the role of chauffeur, to transport you to the hotel. He's obviously keen to make a good impression.

Lynda turned to Rose who had settled herself comfortably beside her on the soft grey leather seat.

'Is Robbie the owner of the hotel you told me about?'

'Yes, Robin Skelton, we all call him Robbie. He owns The Springfield Hotel where you'll be staying.'

Lynda felt a flutter of panic, she hadn't expected to be paying for a hotel room. Rose saw it, and was still good at reading her mind. She patted her hand.

'Don't worry, Lynda, you're my guest. Robbie and I have an arrangement when anyone comes to stay with me. My cottage only has one bedroom, but when I bought it off Robbie we agreed that I'd have free use of one of the hotel bedrooms if I had a guest.'

Patrick turned briefly to comment, 'A crazy deal by most people's standards, but that's Robbie, crazy where women are concerned.'

'You can talk!' laughed Rose.

Lynda was grateful that Rose kept their conversation light and discreet on the journey to the Roseland Peninsula. And for much of the time she wanted just to stare out of the car window at the countryside, and the beautiful coastline. It was just as she'd always imagined it, with its golden sand, and the sunshine which lit up the rocks and created all the shades of blue in the sea. She felt her limbs relax into a softness she hadn't felt for a long time. She hadn't been aware how tense her body had become over the past months, or was it years?

The Springfield Hotel was set back a little on a grassy headland which looked out over the sea and the gentle curves and tight little inlets along the coast. It was a large old two-storey villa, painted white with a powder blue veranda along the side facing the sea. At one end was a small round tower, a Victorian fantasy of an extension, only slightly taller than the rest of the building, and with a conical roof which looked as if half its tiles were about to slide off. The sun was setting as they arrived, and Robbie Skelton, in the dark blue jacket he wore when serving the evening meal, hurried out to greet them. Patrick took Lynda's case to her room while Robbie led them straight on to the veranda.

'I have to go and finish supervising dinner, I'm afraid. I'd like the two of you to sit here and have a drink, and watch the sunset, and I'll see you later.'

Rose sat on an old cane settee filled with plump, flowery cushions and patted the space next to her. She watched Lynda slowly sit down, as if in a dream, and held her hand as they watched the pink, gold and turquoise streamers of the sunset gradually lead the day away.

Rose then took her on a tour of the hotel, through the main lounge with its chandelier and squashy chintz-covered sofas, and coffee tables with fresh flowers in their centre, and into the library. After a brief look into the dining room where the hotel guests were enjoying their evening meal, Rose led Lynda up the narrow staircase at one end of the reception area. At the top of these stairs was the room in the tower which was to be hers for the next few days.

'Patrick's brought your suitcase up. There's the chest of drawers and plenty of room in here.' She opened a wardrobe painted white and stencilled with wild flowers, rabbits and butterflies. 'It's a bit of a fantasy room, this. Robbie's really into Walt Disney, 'Snow White and the Seven Dwarves' and 'Fantasia', that sort of thing. Whacky, but nice though, isn't it?'

'I love it.'

Lynda walked over to peer out of the window. 'There'll be a lovely view of the sea from here in the morning. It's a dream, having a room like this. Are you sure it's all right for me to stay here?'

'Absolutely sure. Robbie's already given me his approval signal.'

'What's that?'

'He taps his fingertips together and raises his eyebrows.'

'What does he do if he doesn't like somebody?'

Rose laughed and gave a demonstration. 'He strokes one hand across the other, as if brushing something away.'

'Oh, I'll have to watch out for that one.'

'No, you've no need to worry. He's very quick to make up his mind about people, is Robbie. Do you want to unpack and then come down for dinner? We usually eat when all the guests have finished, about nine o'clock. It's a bit late, but it means we can relax and enjoy ourselves.'

'That's fine by me. Do you work here full-time?'

'Oh, no. I used to, but now I just help out washing up or setting tables when they're busy, and serving teas in the afternoon. It reminds me of when I ran the café, I love it.'

'You're really happy here.'

'Yes. I knew straight away when Janet invited me after Ted died, that it was the right place to run to. It's where I needed to be. And I think it's where you need to be now, isn't it?'

Her look was as perceptive as ever, and Lynda blinked back tears and couldn't trust herself to speak. She just nodded, and Rose gave her a kiss on the cheek before swiftly going back down the stairs, leaving Lynda to enjoy the feeling of being safe and welcome.

Lynda unpacked slowly, and was amazed to find that she had brought with her not only most of her decent clothes, but also all her most precious possessions, and her favourite photographs. She couldn't remember packing them, she just remembered the silence and coldness in the bedroom, and the fear of someone coming to the house and finding out what she was doing. She struggled to decide what to wear to go down for dinner that first evening; she didn't want to dress up as if she was an important guest, so she chose a soft white shirt and a denim skirt.

Rose came back up to tap on the door at about ten to nine.

'Are you ready, love? I thought I'd take you to meet Janet before we go in for dinner.'

Lynda knew that Janet Meredith was Rose's closest friend, and that they'd met during the war when Rose had been sent to the area as a land girl. She had stayed as a worker and lodger at the old farm Janet and her husband, William, had inherited. Rose had been there in 1944 when the news came that William had been killed in Normandy.

Janet, Rose had told her, shared the cooking with Robbie, and so it was in the hotel's large, well-equipped kitchen that they met. Janet was standing in front of the Aga, spooning butter-glazed carrots and creamy leeks into serving dishes. Lynda knew that Janet was approaching her sixty-fifth birthday, and so was a few years younger than Rose, and was surprised to see that, in fact, Janet Meredith seemed older than her friend.

She was a tall, thin woman with calm, observing

eyes and long grey hair, which was streaked with pale gold and piled up somewhat haphazardly on the top of her head. She shook hands with a strength which took Lynda by surprise.

'Pleased to meet you, Lynda. I'm nearly ready. Just got to get the meat back out of the oven.'

She put on some oven gloves and bent down to retrieve a tray of pork already carved, and garnished with slices of honey-glazed apple.

'Can I help carry anything?' Lynda offered instinctively.

Janet looked at her appraisingly. 'Yes. Always glad of a pair of strong, young arms, aren't we, Rose?'

'Yes, better if they're on a good-looking fella, of course,' quipped her friend.

Janet gave a sideways smile. 'She always was a flirt.'

She took off her full length apron which had frills all round its edges, and observed Lynda looking at it.

'Not all that practical, is it?' Her face softened, and for a moment Lynda caught a glimpse of the young and beautiful Janet Meredith.

'My husband always said that if I had to wear an apron nearly all day, it should at least be a pretty one.'

Patrick was opening bottles of wine at the table where the hotel staff always sat together for their evening meal. He introduced Lynda to two teenage girls who were already sitting at the far end of the table, and then held out a chair for her in the centre, 'We'll make this your seat, shall we, so we can all gather round you and ask awkward questions.'

Lynda smiled. Rose had told her that she needn't worry about questions, because she'd told them what they needed to know about her family, and that she was just having a short break. She found she was able to sit back and relax, and enjoy the banter which flew back and forth across the table. There was a roar of laughter when Robbie came to join them, wearing a brightly coloured Hawaiian style shirt.

'Summer's here already, is it, Robbie? Why did nobody tell me?' Patrick complained.

Robbie proudly smoothed his hands across the exotic flowers on his chest, 'I just thought I'd give it a little encouragement. We want the sun to shine while Lynda's here.' He smiled at her. 'May I sit next to you, darling?'

Robbie Skelton was a big man in his late fifties, with smooth fair skin and cheeks which were always pink, either from sunbathing or cooking. His hair was thinning, but from the front all you could see were the reddish blonde curls which he preserved carefully. His still recognisable Liverpool accent, and the way he leaned on the table, with his head on one side and clasping his chubby hands in front of him, made Lynda think of those old Northern comedians who dressed as women, and had made her Grandma laugh so much .

'Do you like your room, Lynda?' he asked.

'I love it. I feel like a princess up in that little tower.'

'That's what Milady – my Mother, Elizabeth – used to say. It was her favourite room, she had a larger bedroom with an en-suite but she like to go and sit in that room, used it as a private sitting room.'

'She never missed a thing, on the lookout up there with her binoculars,' Patrick remembered. 'Heaven help me if I dug up a couple of flowers by mistake when I was weeding,'

Robbie laughed, 'Well, she knew you didn't know a dandelion from a dahlia, being the city boy you are. Patrick comes from London,' he explained to Lynda. 'We all keep hoping he'll go back there, but he doesn't take the hint.'

'I fancied a bit of sea air, and a bit of swimming – not that I get a lot of time for that these days,' he complained, wagging a finger at Robbie.

Lynda, trying to get used to being in a world which seemed at the moment a bit unreal, tried to act normally. She smiled at her host. 'How did you come to live here, Robbie?'

'Me and my Mother came from Liverpool originally,' he began.

Another shout of laughter from Patrick, 'Never have guessed, would you?'

'Like you can't guess I come from Lancashire,' sympathised Lynda.

'I don't worry about it, and neither should you,' said Robbie. 'My accent is part of who I am, and I'm proud of it.' He squeezed her hand, 'You just be yourself here, Lynda, and make yourself at home. And to answer your question, my Mother had always fancied Cornwall and I'd always fancied running a hotel, and this place was going cheap, so we upped sticks and came here.'

Janet smile and added, 'And he needed somebody to show him how to cook and clean, so the children and I moved in the following year. And it's been our home ever since.'

'And now it's yours, Lynda!' Robbie beamed at her and raised his glass. 'Welcome!' Everyone else joined in the toast, and Lynda had to fight back tears as she said quietly, 'Thank you. Thank you so much.'

CHAPTER ELEVEN

Lynda thought about Robbie's phrase 'just be yourself' as she was walking across the sand the next morning. The sunshine Robbie had ordered had been delivered first thing, and she had quickly dressed, and had almost run across the garden and down the steep, sandy path which led onto the beach. The sea was calm and she felt its gentle movement begin to soothe her mind.

She knew she needed to think, but she didn't want to. She took off her sandals and wandered barefoot through the sifting pale gold sand, and then along the edge of the sea, letting nothing come into her mind but the softness of the sand and the coolness of the water.

When she returned to the hotel, several of the guests were already in the dining-room, and one of the girls serving breakfast indicated a small table by the window, but Lynda hesitated. She retreated back into the corridor and went instead into the kitchen, where she found Janet busy frying eggs.

'Can I help?'

'Oh, good morning, Lynda. Yes, if you could just finish these off for me while I plate up the bacon and stuff I've got ready in the oven. That'll be the last of the early risers taken care of, then we can sit down and have ours. If you want to have yours in here with me?'

'Yes, please. They'd set a place for me in the dining room, but . . .'

'I understand. However, friendly people are, it always feels awkward walking in somewhere and eating on your own. I've never got used to it, never go out on my own even now, if I can help it. It's been great having Rose here again, keeping me company when I need it. She's told you how we got to know each other, has she?'

'Yes, that you looked after her when she came here as a land girl.'

'She looked after me, more like! I had a two year old, Chrissie, and was just about to have Tom when Rose turned up like a blessing from Heaven. I'd never have got through that time without her, nor when I lost my husband.'

'He was a lovely man, Rose told me.'

'The best.'

'And you've never married again. Sorry, that's none of my business. I'm always doing that, being a bit too personal.'

'I don't mind. No, there's no point in looking for somebody else when you've known how good a marriage can be, that's my view, anyway.'

When the breakfasts had been served to the hotel guests, Janet dished out theirs. Lynda was ravenous and ate the 'full English breakfast' so quickly that she had finished well before Janet. Embarrassed, she apologised again.

'I'm sorry. Another of my faults, eating too fast. I

think it comes from when we used to rush to get seconds at school dinners.'

'And from being hungry. There's an egg left in the pan if you want to make yourself some toast to go with it.'

Lynda hesitated, but Janet smiled kindly at her. 'Go on, we don't want it wasted.'

'Thank you. Would you like some toast?'

'Yes, I will, thanks. It's a treat, having something made for you, isn't it, after cooking for other people all day long.'

'Yes,' Lynda laughed. 'Even if it is only toast!'

'Rose told me you run a café,' Janet said.

'Yeah.'

'Have you closed it while you're away?'

'No, I've got a girl called Debbie who helps me. She's managing the café while I'm away. I'd got everything in stock or on order before I left, so she'll be all right.'

'Good. So you can be away for a while then, if you want to.'

'Yes.'

Rose came to the hotel in time to help out with the washing up and bed-making, and then she and Lynda walked down into the village of St. Benedict. Facing the sea was the main street, just a row of cottages and small shops. Tucked away behind them was another street with a mini supermarket and a post office. There was also a stone cross, with stone tablets arranged beside it, bearing the names of men who had lost their lives at sea, or during the war. At the far end of the street stood the tiny church of the patron saint.

Rose showed Lynda around the harbour with its upturned boats and its popular pub, The Angel &

Compass, and then took her along the main street to a primrose yellow cottage with window boxes full of primulas and daffodils.

'Welcome to my little haven,' she said, opening the door and watching Lynda's face light up as she recognised the rose-patterned sofa and armchair which had been in Rose's little house behind the café in Blackpool.

'It's just the same as I had it in Blackpool. I've had the sofa and chairs recovered in the same fabric. I suppose I should have had a change, but . . .'

'No, it's nice to have things stay the same. Ted teased you about your roses, but he loved them.'

'All the things in here are reminders of some very happy times.' She handed Lynda a photograph album. 'Would you like to look at this while I make us some lunch? It's photos and mementoes of Ted and me.'

Later they sat on the sofa and looked through the album together.

'You made him so happy Rose. Ted told me it was the best thing that ever happened to him, meeting you.'

'Sheila didn't think so. I feel very guilty sometimes, that I took her husband away from her.'

'It wasn't just because of you that he left her. It wasn't because of me encouraging him, either, though they all still think I was to blame.'

Rose saw how bitter Lynda felt about that. 'Have they still not forgiven you for taking Ted's side?'

She looked at Rose, this little woman full of compassion, and all the strength of spirit which had held her together over the years, suddenly seemed to melt away.

'They don't do forgiveness, John and his Mother — not where I'm concerned anyway.' She shuddered. 'Sheila hates me, always has done. And John, half the time he looks at me as if he's wondering why the hell he married me. There's no love there for me, Rose, not in that house.'

'There's Carolyn and Steve, and your grandson. I thought you said Carolyn was much closer to you since she had the baby.'

'She was at first, but now it's like it always was before. It's her and her Dad lined up against me, or her and Sheila. Steve tries his best to stand up for me, but when he does it only causes trouble between him and Carolyn. That seems to be what I'm good at, Rose, causing trouble. Even Dan says that.'

'Dan Heywood?'

'Yes. We had a row before I came here. You know I've always thought it was Dan that I really loved, but I'm not even sure of that any more. Dan told me I just needed something to dream about, and 'our big romance' was one of my escapist fantasies. And I suppose he was right.' She looked through the window at the view of the sea. 'This is one of the things I used to dream about as well, coming here. Oh, I'm so glad I could come here, Rose.'

'So am I. I'd always wanted you to see you again and share this with you.'

Looking at this younger woman, who had once been so full of energy and hope, Rose was worried. Lynda was clasping her hands tightly in front of her, trying to hold on to her self-control. She took a deep breath.

'No-one wants me, Rose. There's no-one there who loves me, or ever will. I looked round last

Sunday and realised that. And I couldn't take it. I felt so lonely, so cold and lonely. I had to get away.'

The tears begin to stream down her cheeks, and Rose was shocked to see this resilient young woman crumple as if all the strength had been taken from her. Held in Rose's loving arms, Lynda cried like a child.

She cried almost all of the next two days, and Rose and Janet quietly took care of her. They reassured her that it was all right to stay in her room, or go for walks alone. These two strong, older women had both known what it was like to reach breaking point – they understood Lynda's needs, and prayed she would come through this crisis in her life.

By the following Tuesday Lynda was feeling stronger and calmer, and on the Wednesday, while they were having lunch at her cottage, Rose suggested that perhaps, as Lynda had been away from home for a week now, she should phone her family to let them know she was all right.

Lynda panicked at first, thinking she was being asked to return to Milfield, but then realised that Rose was right, and that she should phone. She decided she didn't want to make the call from Rose's cottage, or from the hotel. She went instead to the phone box at the end of a quiet road leading to the beach. After the phone had rung several times Carolyn answered.

'Hello? Who is it?' she demanded, sounding breathless and irritated.

Lynda took a deep breath. 'It's me. Your Mother.'

'What a time to ring! You know it's when Michael goes for his nap. I'd just got him to sleep and now he's crying again up there.'

'I'm sorry.'

'So you should be! What do you think you're playing at? Just going off like that, without telling anybody.'

'I left a note.'

'Oh, yeah. 'I need a holiday.' We all need a holiday! It's just typical of you, that. Selfish! No thought for anybody else – not even for our Michael.'

'That's not true.'

Carolyn wasn't listening, her anger shut out everything. 'It's all about you, isn't it? Always has been, always will be. Well, if that's how much you care about us, we'd be better off without you!'

Lynda hadn't known what to expect, but it wasn't this. Shocked and angry, she fought back. 'Bloody hell! Better off without me, eh? OK if that's how you feel, I'll clear off for good, shall I?'

There was not a moment's hesitation. 'Yes. You do that! Take a permanent holiday. And don't bother ringing us again. And don't bother ever coming back!'

She slammed the phone down and ran upstairs to comfort her child.

CHAPTER TWELVE

Carolyn was still upset when, shortly after Lynda's phone call, Sheila arrived, bringing a cake and some ironing she'd done for them.

'You've been crying again. What's the matter?'

'I've had a phone call from my Mother.'

'Oh? Where is she?'

'I don't know,' replied Carolyn, realising that she hadn't asked.

'When is she coming back?'

'I'm not sure.'

Sheila knew when her granddaughter was being evasive, and feeling guilty. She felt a little flutter of hope and said, 'Well, it's not as if she's needed here, is it?'

Carolyn didn't reply.

Sheila opened the bag of clothes. 'I'll take this ironing upstairs and put it away, and then I'll make us a cup of coffee to go with the cake I've brought.'

'Michael's only just gone to sleep.'

'I won't wake him up.'

The baby whimpered as he heard his great-grandmother opening a drawer to put away Carolyn's clean nightdress, and then hanging her husband's shirts in the wardrobe. Sheila didn't like ironing for Steve but it would have looked churlish to iron John's and not his. She took her son's shirts into the back bedroom he occupied with his wife, and opened the wardrobe door. Carolyn had told her that Lynda had taken most of her clothes with her, and there was a small sigh of pleasure as Sheila paused for a moment to take in how few of Lynda's clothes remained there.

She quickly went to the chest of drawers and found there weren't many clothes in there either. She opened the shallow drawer in the centre of the cheap, cream plastic, spindly-legged dressing table where Lynda kept her more personal possessions, and found an open envelope positioned carefully on the top of a jumble of cards, lipsticks and broken necklaces.

In the envelope was a letter and a picture postcard of a sunny beach and blue sea. There was an address in Cornwall at the top of the first sheet of scented, rose garlanded notepaper. Sheila looked at the bottom of the second page of the letter and saw the name 'Rose', followed by a row of kisses. A hatred which would never fade took Ted Stanworth's widow in a hard, cruel grip which clenched itself around the letter and crushed it. Hearing the bedroom door open, Sheila thrust the letter and the card into the large square pocket of her cardigan as Carolyn stepped into the room.

'What's that?'

'Nothing.' Sheila kept her hand closed over the letter.

Carolyn looked at her Nana, but had learned from childhood when not to ask further questions.

'I've made the coffee.'

Sheila followed Carolyn down the stairs and when she went into the kitchen to get the coffee, Sheila quickly stuffed the letter deep into the bottom of her handbag.

'I didn't realise how few clothes your Mother had left here.' she said, sipping her coffee and watching her granddaughter carefully. 'It doesn't look to me as if she's any intention of coming back. I don't believe she has just 'gone for a few days holiday', like she said in that note, do you?'

'No.'

'And when she phoned, she didn't say she was coming home?'

'No.'

Sheila saw how Carolyn looked away. 'Did she say she wasn't?'

Carolyn thought of the way her Mother had shouted at her. 'Yes.'

Satisfied, Sheila sat back in her chair. 'I thought so. I knew it would happen. Your Dad should never have married her. She doesn't love him, you know. I knew she'd run off and leave him one day. He'll be upset for a bit, but he'll be a lot better off without her in the end.'

'Do you really think so?'

'Oh, yes. You said yourself they were always having arguments.'

Sheila got up and walked across to the table where the Victoria sponge now seemed, to her, to be transformed into part of a celebration. She cut two large pieces, beaming as she handed one to Carolyn.

'Don't worry, love. Everything will be fine.'

Carolyn didn't tell her Dad about the phone call,

his Mother did.

He was almost too stunned to speak. 'What do you mean, she's not coming back?'

'That's what she said, isn't it, Carolyn?'

'Yes.'

'She bloody well is coming back. She's my wife. I'll go and find her and bring her back.'

Sheila's voice was gentle and patient. 'We don't know where she is, John. We've no idea where she's gone.'

Steve thought his wife looked confused, like a small child. 'She must have said something, Caro.'

'She was calling from a phone box but she didn't say where.'

Steve put his arm round his wife. 'Don't worry, love, we'll find her. Perhaps we can get the police to trace the call.'

Sheila had developed a habit of looking at Steve Sheldon as if he were not only ignorant, but also a little stupid.

'From a phone box? And anyway, why would they try to find her, Steven? Lynda left a note, remember? She is not a missing person, she's a wife and mother who has decided to run off and leave her family.'

John rarely contradicted his Mother but spoke angrily now. 'She has not run off, and she has not left anybody!'

Sheila folded her arms and sat back to wait for him to see sense. 'Well, that's what it looks like to me!'

Steve Sheldon had never been told the full story of Carolyn's Grandad and the lady friend he ran off with. He had, however, seen the postcards on the shelf in The Copper Kettle and Lynda had told him they were from a friend.

Not realising what a minefield he was about to step into, he said, 'What about that friend in Cornwall? If Lynda wanted a holiday she might have gone to see her.'

There was a long silence. Steve saw the horrified looks on John and Carolyn's faces.

'What's wrong?'

Sheila's tone was cold and strong. 'We have no friend in Cornwall, have we, John?'

'No.'

Jenny Heywood didn't know where in Cornwall Lynda's friend lived, but she knew that would be where she'd taken refuge. However, like her Mother, Jenny had an instinct about when you needed to keep knowledge to yourself.

She learned that Lynda had actually gone when Dan told her that Debbie had been left in charge of the café for a few days. Dan didn't seem to want to talk about Lynda, so Jenny kept her thoughts to herself.

She was beginning to keep many things to herself, including the fact that she was already looking for a new home. She had been driving around looking at houses during the week, while Alex was at school; she knew that her eldest child would quickly guess that something exciting was happening, and she didn't want it to be mentioned in front of Ellen until everything was settled.

It was the week before the start of the school holiday that she found the place she'd been looking for. It was in the small village of Hadden Lea, which clung on to the edge of the moors a few miles from Milfield. The village was little more than two rows of terraced houses and a couple of shops, which faced each other across a quiet road which was part of a country bus route to Milfield. There was also a small Methodist Chapel, and a Sunday School hall, relics of earlier days when the village had been a small farming community of people content with a pie and peas supper on Bonfire Night, and other modest celebrations in the hall as the highlights of their social calendar.

The house formed the end of one of the rows of six large terraced houses, set on the hillside so that they offered a view across the dry-stone walled fields and the moorland beyond them. The houses had slate roofs with neat attic windows like miniature houses perched half way up, and they were built of ancient stones, many of them reclaimed from earlier settlements which had not survived the centuries. They had elegant bay windows and solid wooden front doors reached by well-worn stone steps. There was a garden at the side of the property, with a stretch of grass big enough to play on, a once lovingly tended herbaceous border and a vegetable patch at the far end.

As soon as Jenny, with Katie in her arms, followed the estate agent into the house, she felt welcome, as if she had come home. And the house did remind her of her childhood home on Bennett Street which, like this, had been a stone, terraced house with a bay window in the front room. The house needed to be stripped of layers of aged wallpaper, which she looked forward to replacing with her own decoration, but it also needed a new bathroom and kitchen. The money left her by her parents would just about cover the deposit and a modest new bathroom, but everything else would have to wait.

Jenny made her decision, she would buy the house straight away, before her mother-in-law could stop her. She knew the only way she could overcome Ellen's opposition to her moving from the house Richard had bought was to present her with a fait accompli.

A few days later she went to call on Ellen one morning, having arranged that Dan would also be at Kirkwood House, to give her his support. They sat on the sofa opposite the woman who wore the dark garments of mourning with defiant, proud elegance.

When Jenny announced her news, Ellen Heywood rose to her feet, trembling with grief as well as anger at being disobeyed.

'You have no right to sell my son's house! Why are you doing this? Is it that you cannot wait to cast aside his memory?'

'Of course not.'

Jenny's denial was uttered quietly, and was a lie. She admitted to herself that that was exactly what she was hoping to do. She was desperate to forget her cruel husband and the miserable, and fearful time she had spent with him in that house. She felt the need to defend herself now, but could not add to the pain in his Mother's heart by telling her any of those truths about her violent son.

Ellen's sharp eyes saw her discomfort.

'Not even two months have passed since my beloved Richard was taken from us, and you wish to move away from your marital home. What did that marriage mean to you, I have to ask myself. What did my son mean to you? He meant everything to me.

Can you say the same?'

Jenny bowed her head, her long brown hair forming a curtain across her face. 'Ellen, please.'

Ellen Heywood's mouth twisted into a bitter smile.

'I see you cannot. Some people said, you know, that the reason you married my son was not love, but money. And it is money that is behind this wicked scheme of yours now.'

She took hold of the photograph of Richard which, since his death, she had kept on the shelf next to her chair. 'What a wife he chose, my poor Richard.'

Dan placed his hand on Jenny's, and managed to keep his voice steady.

'Mother, you have no right to speak to Jenny like this. She was a good wife to Richard, and she is a wonderful mother to his children. And yes, it is a matter of money, but not in the way you seem to suggest. Jenny is just being sensible. She cannot afford to live in that house, and has found something cheaper which, hopefully, with the money from the sale of the one at The Oakwoods, she will be able to manage.'

Ellen observed his hand holding that of his brother's widow, and scrutinised him.

'She is my son's wife, and I will honour my duties to her, as will you,' she paused, staring at his hand still holding Jenny's, 'as far as is decent. I forbade you to sell that house, Jennifer, and you disregarded my wishes, and my feelings. I shall not forget that.'

'I didn't mean to hurt you, Ellen.'

Ellen raised her eyebrows. 'Really?'

She turned to Dan. 'You should have informed your brother's wife that it was not necessary to sell that house. I have money which . . .'

Jenny looked at her steadily. 'Which I could not accept.'

'I did not mean it for you, but for my grandchildren. Would you deny them my help and comfort? Richard would wish me to look after them. You have to accept that.'

Jenny knew the power of money, and the need for independence. 'They are my children, and it is up to me to keep and clothe them as well as to care for them.'

'And I am their grandmother. Do you wish to deny me that role in their lives?'

'No, of course not.'

Dan wanted to end this.

'Mother. Jenny will always be grateful for your help. And you will always have your grandchildren. But Jenny has found a house which is more suitable for her circumstances, and her needs. And it's all settled.'

Ellen Heywood's eyes narrowed as she surveyed her two opponents. 'So it seems. You will leave now. Both of you.' She clasped Richard's photograph to her heart and glared her hatred at them.

CHAPTER THIRTEEN

At one end of the Springfield Hotel was an extension which had been built to house the kitchen and laundry, with rooms for the staff on the floor above. A small conservatory had been added a few years ago, with a door leading to the garden and the path down to a small inlet they called Springwater cove, where the staff could swim and sunbathe away from the hotel guests.

Lynda had started having a cup of coffee in the conservatory with Janet before she went for her morning walk on the beach, and before Janet began the preparations for breakfast. This morning, however, Janet was sitting there wearing her best coat instead of her frilly apron; she was waiting for Robbie who was taking her to the station to collect her daughter.

Janet stared doubtfully at the grey sea and the slow moving clouds. 'I hope the sun will have come out by the time we get back. I don't want it raining when Chrissie gets here.'

'It rains in New Zealand as well, doesn't it?' Lynda said with a grin.

'Yes. But she won't be here that long and I want it

to be nice for her.'

'It will be. Is it a while since she's been over for a visit?'

'Yes, five years. It's a long way and a lot of money, but she came for my sixtieth.'

'And drove me round the bend!' Robbie declared as he and Rose came to join them. 'She bosses me about worse than my Mother did. Always has done, hasn't she, Janet?'

Janet laughed, 'Only because you let her. He spoiled her when she was a little girl, so he can't expect her to behave for him now!'

'At least she'll have her brother to boss about as well on Saturday, so perhaps she'll leave me alone then. Honestly, Lynda, I don't know how I'm going to cope with the whole of the Meredith family giving me the run-around. And they want a party as well!'

Rose patted him on the shoulder, 'Don't worry, Robbie, I'll be here to help.'

'No, you won't, you'll be one of the party girls, ripping it up on the dance floor and getting tipsy. Lynda, I've been meaning to ask, will you be able to stay and help with the party so that these girls can just concentrate on enjoying themselves?'

'Yes, I'd love to. I can stay as long as you want me.'

'For ever then! Brilliant! Now, come on, Mother Meredith, we have a troublesome child to collect.'

Lynda and Rose waved as Robbie and Janet drove off in the Rover, which had been specially polished for the occasion, and went into the kitchen to begin preparing breakfast. Rose, sitting at the table patiently making butter curls, tried to sound casual as she asked, 'So you're not planning to go back home yet?'

Lynda, concentrating harder than was necessary on wiping and chopping mushrooms, said quietly. 'No.'

She felt she had to explain. 'When I came here I wasn't sure if I'd be able to stay on for your party. But now, I've no plans to go home. I didn't tell you the truth, Rose, about that phone call. I'm sorry.'

'Oh.' Rose stood up, put the butter curls in the fridge, and then sat down next to Lynda.

'What did Carolyn really say?'

'Don't bother ever coming back!'

Rose couldn't bear to see her friend's misery. 'She didn't mean it.'

'She did.' Lynda spoke slowly. 'I've done a lot of thinking, Rose. I'm not sure I can love John any more. I'm not sure I ever did love him as he deserved to be loved. He'll be better off without me.'

'No.'

'And as for me and Carolyn – I don't know what to do about that. To be honest, at the moment, I don't feel I have a family, or anyone.'

Rose put her arm round Lynda's shoulders. 'You've got me, love. And I'll help you get through this.'

Lynda looked at Rose with bewilderment in her eyes.

'Dan told me it's no good wishing things could be different, he thinks we've got to learn to be satisfied with the life we've got. But it can't be right to be so unhappy, can it?'

'No, of course it isn't. But I'm sure John loves you and wants you back. Did you tell him where you've gone?'

'No. I haven't told anybody. But I've left one of your postcards, and your last letter, where John's bound to find it. So he'll know where I am. And if he does love me, he'll write, or come to take me home.'

They all stayed up late at The Springfield Hotel that night, opening bottles of wine, and laughing as they remembered the early days when Janet first came to work at the hotel and live there with her children.

'We have to celebrate all our family being together again,' Robbie explained as he beamed at everyone and filled Lynda's glass again.

'Hey, who are you calling family?' Patrick protested, 'I've my reputation to think about.'

Christine Meredith, a well-rounded, confident woman in her early forties, leaned her weather-tanned arms on the table and tilted her head on one side

'With women, do you mean?' You won't know this, Lynda, but his big sister keeps hoping she can find a nice girl and turn Patrick into a respectable married man. That's why he ran away and came to work here.'

'I did not run away. I came here to try to sort this place out!' was his laughing retort. 'But it gets crazier every week, Lynda, as you'll see. Take my advice and leave now, before you get too involved with this lot.'

Janet smiled at Lynda and said firmly, 'She can't leave, she's promised to make the sandwiches for me. And I refuse to make sandwiches on my birthday. You all know how I hate that fiddly job.'

'Yes,' boasted Rose, 'don't forget we're going to be two ladies of leisure on Saturday.'

'That'll make three, then,' commented Christine dryly. Lynda looked round, wondering who the third could be, so Christine, ignoring her Mother's disapproving look, provided the answer.

114

'Suzanne, Tom's wife. Never been known to lift a painted talon, sorry finger.'

'Chrissie, don't start,' Janet admonished her daughter. 'At least she's coming this time.'

'Don't bet on it. Mind you, we'd all have more fun if she didn't.'

'Christine, that's enough.'

'O.K.. I'll keep my mouth shut, if only to keep the peace for Tomkin.'

'Oh, don't do that, it'll get boring,' said Robbie, who liked to watch a bit of sparring. He turned to Lynda, 'Suzanne's just been spoilt by her Mummy and Daddy and Tom was the one brave enough to take on the consequences, that's all. What time are Meredith and Son arriving?'

'They'll set off as early as they can on Saturday and be here by lunchtime, Tom reckons.'

Christine clapped her hands together with excitement. 'I can't wait to see Mark, I love nine year olds. My boys are teenagers,' she told Lynda, 'hell on wheels, literally, at the moment.'

'They take after their Mother,' quipped Janet.

The next few days were hectic with preparations for the party to which, it seemed, all the village was invited. There was to be a hog roast and barbeque as well as a buffet serving savouries and desserts non-stop, and a generous selection of beers, wines and ciders. Lynda spent a lot of time in the kitchen, and found it was fun to work in the team led by Robbie and Janet. Christine and Patrick were in charge of room preparation and making the place as festive as possible, with the hotel and garden to be full of balloons and fairy lights.

On Friday morning Lynda went down to the beach. As usual, she went there before anyone else was up, so that she could be alone and enjoy the tranquillity of a walk along the sand. This morning, however, Christine was already there, swimming in the sea, but as soon as she saw Lynda she came out of the water and, wrapped in a towel sat beside her, sharing a flask of coffee she'd brought with her.

'I put a drop of rum in it. Family tradition, apparently. Mum told me my Dad used to do it - when they had the money, of course. Did your Dad like a drink?'

'Too much. And we lived in a pub!' Lynda smiled ruefully as she remembered Ray pulling pints out of hours for himself and his mates.

'I hardly remember my Dad, I was only four when he was killed. Did Rose tell you he died in Normandy, saving Suzanne's father?'

'Yes, she said that's why there's a close connection with the Heston family.'

'Yeah, Vic Heston was a good guy, he came to find us after the war, and all his life he did everything he could to help us. He felt so guilty that we'd lost our Dad because of him.'

'It must have been terrible for your Mum, though.'

'Yeah. She doesn't talk much about all that. She's still very angry that she had to lose Dad, and she was mad with Vic Heston even when he was trying to help. You should have heard the row when he got Tom a job in London.'

'That all worked out well though, he met Vic's daughter and married her.'

Christine laughed out loud. 'My Mother didn't thank him for that either – saw it as the Meredith

116

family rescuing the Heston family again!'

Lynda knew she was being nosey but couldn't help herself. 'What do you mean?'

'She was out of control was Suzanne, been having an affair with a married man – she seems to have a taste for them. Vic thought the world of Tom, and decided he'd be a good, steady husband for his wild child. And Tom fancied her something rotten, so there you go. Sex is the very devil, isn't it? Makes life entertaining, though.'

Lynda laughed, 'I suppose that's one way of looking at it.' She got to her feet, 'Talking of entertaining, we've got a party to set up.'

CHAPTER FOURTEEN

Everyone ran around the morning of the party, except for Janet and Rose who were ordered to sit in the conservatory and enjoy the novelty of watching everyone else work. Lynda had never been to a party like this; she stood and gazed at the garden full of trestle tables with bunches of green, white and silver balloons bobbing in the air above them, and more balloons tied with large bows all along the fence at the end of the garden. There were boxes of spring flowers attached to the fences as well as flower arrangements on each table.

And beyond this festive garden the sea glittered and danced in the sunshine, and the air was filled with the scent of herbs burning on the charcoal of the large barbeque which had been fired up. The hog which was roasting had, with callous familiarity, been named Hooray Henry by Robbie, and its aroma was already being appreciated by a group of men clustered round it with pints of beer and cider in their hands.

The party was scheduled to start at two o'clock but just after midday many local friends started arriving with plates of home-made cakes and scones accompanied by bowls of strawberry jam and cream. A small marquee had been set up at one end of the garden with Janet and Rose, who had been banned from the kitchen today, waiting to thank their guests and set the food out on the tables arranged around the sides of the marquee.

Robbie had hired a local band, and they quickly tuned their instruments and struck up a lively dance tune just as Lynda came across the garden with a tray of sandwiches she'd made. She put down the tray and held out her hands to Janet and Rose.

'Come on, girls. We're dancing.'

'Not me,' said Janet, but Rose took Lynda's hand and they were jiving on the lawn when a red MG drove up and parked by the edge of the garden. The driver tooted the horn loudly and Lynda saw Janet's face light up with a smile she'd never seen before. Tom Meredith, tall and muscular with tousled brown hair, crossed the garden in easy strides, lifted his Mother off her feet, gave her a big kiss and swung her round.

'Tom Meredith, you put me down this instant!'

'No, we're dancing,' her son insisted.

He turned to call to the nine year-old boy who was following him slowly, and who looked so like his father it made you smile at the wonder of nature.

'Come on, Mark, your Gran will show you how to jive.'

The boy stood shyly at the edge of the grass and then was swept up in a bear hug by his Aunty Chrissie, while his grandmother, following her son's firm lead, laughed and jived like a teenager to 'Blue Suede Shoes' until she was out of breath.

'Lynda, take this madman off me, please,' Janet

commanded.

She thrust her son towards Lynda who had, like Rose, stopped dancing to watch mother and son celebrating being together. Tom Meredith laughed and, caught a little off balance by his Mother's determined push, held on to Lynda to steady himself.

He was about to put his arm round her waist, ready to dance, when he looked into a pair of blue eyes which were so like a reflection of his own that it made him catch his breath. It was as if the air stilled around the two of them, and Lynda heard nothing but silence and her heart pounding with what felt like fear.

Christine's voice cut across this stillness.

'Hey, little brother, have you not got a hug for your big sister, who's come half way round the world to see you?'

'Hello, Chrissie.' Tom Meredith turned and held his sister close for much longer than she expected. She gently held him by the arms and looked into her brother's troubled face.

'Hey, Tomkin. Are you O.K.?'

'Yeah. Of course I am.' He blinked, and looked round for his son. 'You see how my boy's grown?' He put his arm round Mark's shoulders and smiled at Christine. 'And how are your two, and Jim?'

'They're all fine. They'll be running wild while I'm away, no doubt.'

'But you're missing them like hell.'

'No! Well, I might be. But it's great to be here for Mum's birthday.'

'And mine,' chipped in Rose, who'd been standing a little way off, enjoying the reunion of these people who had become her adoptive family.

120

'It's my 70th birthday party, too, remember, only a couple of years late.'

Christine, wagging a cheerful finger at her, said, 'Yes, don't you give us a scare like that again. Fancy being ill for your own birthday!'

'Blame my age, not me! I'm not getting any younger, you know. I keep trying but no success yet. I'll have to try some different tablets.'

Tom glanced over his shoulder to check his Mother wasn't close by, 'How's Mum doing? She sounds bright as a button every time I phone, but we all know how good an actress she is when she wants to be.'

Rose shook her head resignedly. 'She sneaked off to the doctor's a few weeks ago, but don't dare ask her what he said. But today we're going to be young women in our twenties again, and teach you lot the lindy hop. I saw you can still dance,' she teased Tom.

'Yes, but I lost my partner. Who was she, the young lady I was about to dance with when I was so rudely interrupted by my spoilsport of a sister?'

Rose, who had witnessed that moment between them, watched Tom carefully as she answered, 'That was my friend from Milfield, Lynda Stanworth.'

'Oh. Is she here on holiday?'

'Sort of. I think she may be here for a while. She fits in well, and Robbie's keen to get your Mother some help. He keeps telling her that sixty-five is past her retirement age. He's planning to retire before too long, you know, and keeps saying he wants Janet to go with him to the South of France. That's his retirement dream, a villa near Saint Tropez, with a pool.'

'That seems to be a popular idea. It's certainly

where Suzanne wants to be. Her Mother heads off to Cannes in the spring and spends her time, floating around the Mediterranean with her gin-palace friends.'

'When is Suzanne arriving?' Rose enquired.

'I don't know. She said she'd get a cab from the station. You know Suzanne, she sets her own schedule. Now, where did Mark disappear to?'

'His Gran is showing him off to her friends,' Christine told him. 'Now, let's have a beer and something to eat, and you can tell me everything I need to know.'

Lynda was exhausted by five o'clock but was still helping Patrick to serve drinks at the bar set up next to the marquee. Robbie, taking off the hat and apron he'd been wearing while cooking at the barbeque, came over to them.

'You're off duty now, you two. Everyone has had enough to eat and plenty to drink, so it's time for us to take it easy. They can help themselves from now on.' He saw the expression on Lynda's face. 'Don't worry, Lynda, it's the way we do things here, they're all friends. They'll just get what they need, and they'll stay on and help us clear up afterwards. Now, come on, Janet and Rose are about to blow their candles out.'

He led them across to the marquee where the two women were already standing together behind the cake which had been placed on a table in the centre. Robbie went to stand with his arms round both of them, and led an enthusiastic rendition of 'Happy Birthday to You.' Then he nodded to Tom Meredith who came to take his place. There was immediately a respectful silence as he started to speak.

'Ladies, gentlemen and children, we're here today to celebrate two remarkable women. You'll notice I call them women rather than ladies.'

He paused to allow a ripple of surprise and laughter.

'No, that's not meant to cause offence. I say it because they're not, and never have been, ladies of leisure, either of them. They've both been working women all their lives, and they should be proud to be called that because it's women like them who make the world run right, and who look after everyone,' he turned to raise and admonishing finger at his Mother 'Except themselves.'

He took a deep breath to help hold back his emotions, before continuing.

'My Mother has looked after me and my sister, and it's not been easy, but she's been the best Mum in the world. She brought us up without our Dad by her side, and that's been the hardest thing. But fortunately she had Rose with her. Rose shared my Mum's most difficult days, and it's a strong friendship when it comes from a time like that.' He raised his glass, 'So the toast I give you today, is working women, and friendship!'

Like many of those listening to that speech, Lynda wiped tears from her eyes as she watched Christine bring young Mark to join her Mother and Rose, and all of them hug each other very tightly. That was how family was supposed to be, Lynda thought, and she knew it was something she had never experienced.

CHAPTER FIFTEEN

The party was slowing down as the sun began to set. Most of the guests with young children had said their thank-you and wished everyone goodnight, and were making their way home when the taxi stopped outside the main entrance of the hotel. Suzanne Meredith, wearing a short-skirted white suit and stiletto heels, stepped out of it like a fashion model and waited for the driver to retrieve her white leather suitcases from the boot.

All the guests who saw the taxi arrive paused and stared for a moment at this beautiful creature. Suzanne stood there in the last of the evening sunshine, poised, very aware of her impact on the crowd. She brushed a few glossy, dark brown curls away from her face and smiled sweetly at the departing guests. She knew none of them, but several recognised her as Janet Meredith's rarely seen, or talked about, daughter-in-law.

Her husband and son had been looking out for her, and hurried forward now to take her suitcases.

'You've missed the party, Mummy.'

Suzanne bent to kiss her son on the forehead, 'Have I? Surely not all of it. Not everyone has left yet, have they?'

'No, but you missed Granny and Rose cutting their cake. And you missed Dad giving a speech.'

She took his hand. 'I'm sorry, darling, those trains take ages,' she said, looking across at her husband who, she could see, wasn't accepting the excuse.

Mark reassured her. 'It's all right. I've saved you a piece of cake.'

'Thank you, that was very kind. I'll have it later. I must go and have a shower, even first class compartments are filthy these days.'

Tom Meredith spoke firmly, 'Not till you've said hello to everyone.'

His wife's response was tinged with petulance. 'OK. But at least take my cases to my room and give me a couple of minutes to freshen up a little.'

Tom turned to his son, 'Mark would you tell Granny that your Mother is here. We won't be long.'

Mark looked doubtful but went off back to the party and passed on the message to Janet. He then headed towards the barbeque where Robbie had started to cook sausages again.

'I thought you said there was no more food, Uncle Robbie.'

'I said I wasn't going to cook any more food, but then I found out this new friend of ours has a passion for hot dogs and hasn't had one. Have you met Lynda? Lynda this is Mark Meredith, the best crab catcher in Cornwall.'

The boy looked shyly at the beautiful woman with the big smile, and politely held out his hand which she took solemnly in hers. 'Pleased to meet you, Mark. Are you staying here for the Easter holiday?'

'Yes, Dad has to go back to work tomorrow, but

Mummy and I are staying.'

Robbie grinned, 'That's good. Lynda hasn't been to Cornwall before, Mark, perhaps you can show her round. He's an expert on rock pools,' he told Lynda.

'Oh, I'd like that,' she responded enthusiastically. 'If you wouldn't mind?'

'No, I don't mind. Please may I have a hot-dog too, Uncle Robbie?'

'Of course you can. These sausages are nearly ready and Lynda's just finished frying the onions.'

'Yeah, got to have loads of onions on my hot-dog,' Lynda declared.

Mark smiled at her, 'And me! Oh, there's Mummy. Do you want a hot-dog, Mummy?'

Suzanne, holding on to Tom's arm as she stepped hesitantly on to the grass in her high heels, grimaced, 'No thank you, darling. I'm just going to wish your Granny a happy birthday.'

Lynda watched her and saw the guests move aside to let her take centre stage with Janet. Suzanne Meredith had class, Lynda thought, you could tell that as soon as you saw her. She envied the way Suzanne stood there, graciously accepting attention, with the self-assurance that money and stunning looks had given her throughout her life. Robbie saw her interest and nodded.

'Quite a girl, Suzanne. She's French aristocracy, you know. Mark's other grandmother is from a French family who have their own chateau in Normandy.'

'Wow,' Lynda said, partly for Mark's benefit, 'I am impressed.'

He was pleased at this, and added. 'Yes, and Nicki,

my Nana, goes to Paris to buy her clothes. She's there now, I think, en route to Cannes.'

'Sounds like a movie-star,' Lynda said.

'She looks like one, too,' Mark said proudly. 'And Mummy does as well, doesn't she?'

'She certainly does. I must make sure I don't stand next to her,' Lynda commented wryly.

'Especially not with this hot-dog stuffed in your mouth,' Robbie chuckled as he handed it to her.

Lynda bit into it. 'Mmm, yummy yummy!'

Mark forgot his manners for once, and spoke with his mouth full, 'Yes, yummy, yummy,' he echoed, sounding like a little boy at last.

By the time the sun had finally disappeared most of the guests had gone, but several stayed to help Robbie and the hotel staff to finish off the clearing up. They left the balloons tied to the fences and trees but later a strong wind brought heavy rain, so Robbie and Lynda set off to tour the garden and gather up the boxes of flowers to stop them being spoilt. They left the Meredith family to sit round a table in the dining room and make the most of their precious time together.

As Robbie and Lynda walked round the side of the hotel, after rescuing the flowers, they were surprised to hear someone talking on the telephone in Robbie's office.

'That's wonderful, darling. How clever of you. Of course I'll come.'

There was a secretive, very intimate tone in Suzanne's voice which made them instinctively creep past without making a sound. Then Robbie, never one to overcome his curiosity, took hold of Lynda's arm and signalled for her to stand with him against the wall by the open window. He put his finger to his lips, and they listened.

'I'll leave in the morning and get the first flight to Nice. Simon, are you sure she doesn't suspect?'

Suzanne listened for a moment and then laughed softly. 'You're a naughty man – I'm glad to say. See you soon.'

As soon as they heard her put down the receiver, the two listeners sped away.

The next morning Lynda worked in the bedrooms and avoided the kitchen as she knew the family had gathered there. She and Robbie had said nothing about the conversation they had overheard.

It was Patrick, not Tom, who drove Suzanne to the station. He'd taken Mark with him to give him a little more time with his Mother, and had tried to cheer up the young boy by promising him a visit to his favourite model boat shop in Truro.

Tom Meredith, with his hand resting on the little cleft in his chin, was sitting at the kitchen table with his Mother and his sister.

'I have to go back today. I've a group of business men arriving, they come every year, and they expect me to spend time with them. Mum, can I leave Mark here with you till Chrissie goes back?'

'You can leave him here for the rest of the holiday. Is that O.K. with you, Robbie?' Janet asked as Robbie joined them.

'No problem. But why has Suzanne left?' he asked, already knowing the true answer to his question.

'Apparently her Mother needs her to go and visit

her aunt in Cannes, who's very ill and asking to see her.'

Christine was glad that Suzanne had gone, but was always suspicious about her actions.

'I thought Nicki didn't get on with her sister.'

Tom, grim faced, was finding it difficult to talk about his wife and her Mother who, it seemed, were yet again putting their needs before those of his son.

'She doesn't, but it's family.'

'It's family money, you mean, Suzanne's her only other relative, so Nicki will be setting her up to inherit when her sister dies.'

'Christine, don't talk like that,' Janet reprimanded her.

'I just tell it like it is, Mum. How often does Suzanne do this, Tom, skip off to play in the South of France instead of helping you look after your son and the hotel?'

'Too often, but what can I do?'

Christine had her reply ready. 'Divorce her?'

He looked at his Mother and sister and knew that nothing but honesty would do for them.

'I've been thinking about it. I've even been to see a solicitor, to find out how I should handle it.' He paused, and then said quietly. 'Suzanne's been having an affair.'

Janet, who had never been happy about her son's marriage, gave a heavy sigh, 'Who with?'

'A married man called Simon Lennox. She's told me all about him. He has a wealthy wife and no children, and all the things that I don't have, like a yacht and a luxury apartment in Monaco.'

Christine was furious. 'For goodness sake, Tom, divorce the bitch!'

Her brother shook his head.

'She's Mark's Mother, I can't risk her getting custody of him. I have to give her a second chance. She's ended their relationship and has promised she'll never see him again.'

Robbie hesitated, but couldn't bear to have anyone make a fool of this fine man whom he loved like the son he could never have.

'I'm sorry to have to tell you. Tom, that she's breaking that promise now. I heard her talking on the phone last night, to this Simon. She's flying to Nice to spend some time with him. There was no mention of her aunt, and Nicki is in Paris, buying clothes.'

There was defeat in Tom Meredith's eyes now, and his Mother reached out and put her hand on his clenched fist.

He shook his head as he looked at her. 'I want to divorce her, but I don't see how I can. I wouldn't want to make her homeless, and anyway I can hardly force her to leave the hotel her father bought for us both.'

Janet, who usually didn't give advice unless it was requested, made a suggestion.

'Let her have The Gatehouse at Loveday. Tell her she can come and visit Mark there whenever she wants.'

'Yes,' Christine added her support. 'From what I've seen of Suzanne as a mother, she'll be happy just to visit him when it suits her.'

'She does love him,' Tom defended his unfaithful wife.

'I'm not saying she doesn't. But, be honest, she's never been a devoted, full-time Mum, has she?'

'No.'

'Then do it, Tom,' Christine banged out the command with her fist on the table. 'Divorce her, and stop putting yourself through the humiliation and frustration she keeps dishing out to you.'

Tom looked at his Mother. Janet Meredith took her son's hand in both of hers, and nodded her assent.

CHAPTER SIXTEEN

Lynda had sent Janet Meredith to have an afternoon siesta in the little conservatory at the side of the hotel, but Janet had observed Mark wandering disconsolately down to the beach. She had gone to stand at the edge of the garden, and was watching her grandson angrily throwing stones into the sea.

Lynda came out of the kitchen, and walked across to stand beside her.

'You're supposed to be having a sleep. You promised Robbie that you would.'

'I know. But I saw Mark on the beach. I wish I was twenty years younger and could run down there to join him. That boy needs company, but it's been in short supply all his life. That's the problem with bringing children up in a hotel, you always have to see to the guests' demands first.'

'Yeah, I know what that's like,' Lynda sympathised. 'The customers always came first when we lived in the pub. I used to enjoy the social side, though, a good sing-song on Saturday nights.'

Janet laughed, 'I don't think he gets that sort of thing at Loveday Manor.'

'Oh, too posh, is it?'

'Yes, thanks to Suzanne and her Mother, but it was what Tom wanted. He's always been ambitious, aiming to be rich and successful. Vic Heston opened up a whole new world to Tom, even sent him to Paris to learn about hotels and restaurants.'

'Wow! I wish somebody would send me to Paris.'

'You're like my son was, aren't you, wanting a different life to the one you've got?'

Lynda looked into the eyes of this woman who seemed to have a special insight into the lives of those around her.

'I don't know what I want, to be honest, Janet. That's always been my problem, according to my husband.'

'You don't talk about him much.'

'No, and I'm grateful that I don't have to.'

'I've always thought that if people want to talk to you about something, they will do eventually.'

'I'm very mixed up about it all at the moment.'

'But missing your family.'

'Yes. But I won't go back until I'm asked,' she found herself saying defiantly.

Janet saw the pain in her eyes and wondered how she had been hurt, but then Lynda tilted her head back and Janet saw that she had learned to defend herself.

'Anyway, I'm happy here, and I can't tell you how grateful I am that you've made me so welcome. And if ever I can do something to help you, let me know. I'll be glad to do anything for you.'

Janet hesitated only briefly before saying, 'That's a very timely offer, Lynda. May I take you up on it?'

'Of course. What do you want me to do?'

'Since his Aunty Chrissie left Mark has seemed a

bit bored. Would you mind spending some time with my lonely young man?'

'You think he's lonely.'

'Yes, I do. I think he's often lonely. Mark's Mother has never encouraged him to bring many friends home, only ones of her choosing. And, as I said, living in a hotel has its limitations for a child. I'm afraid my grandson has learned to keep himself out of the way, to let the adults get on with their work.'

'He enjoys helping you in the kitchen, though, and having a laugh with Robbie and Patrick.'

'Yes, he loves it here, but have you seen the way he's throwing those stones in the water? Those aren't the actions of a happy child. He needs to talk, and I have a feeling that he might talk to you.'

'I wouldn't be too sure about that. I must look like an old woman to him.'

'Not as old as me and Rose,' Janet laughed. 'And you have a young spirit, and a bit of the daredevil in you that I think he would respond to.'

Lynda looked at her in amazement. 'My goodness, you have the world worked out, don't you, Janet Meredith?'

Janet surprised her with an impudent grin.

'Not as much as I'd like to!'

Lynda gave her an impulsive kiss on the cheek, and headed down to the beach. Janet sat on the bench at the edge of the garden and smiled as she watched Lynda approach her grandson.

She didn't walk up to him but picked up a few flat pebbles and bent down to skim them across the water. Mark watched for a while and then slowly walked over to Lynda. Janet heard him laugh as they competed with each other to achieve the highest score of bounces. Reassured that her instinct had been right she went contentedly to have the sleep she knew she needed.

That afternoon on the beach with Mark was the first of many Lynda spent with him. She was as glad of his company as he was of hers; she found he had a good sense of humour, and was well-mannered enough not to ask her awkward questions about herself and her 'other life'. They played games on the beach and built sandcastles and all kinds of fantasy structures in the sand. Mark had refused to join in such activities at first.

'They're for little kids,' he protested.

'And big kids like me. Why should you give up enjoying something just because you're a bit older?'

'People will think you're silly.'

'They think that anyway. Some people think I'm stupid at times, as well.'

'But you're not. You're quite clever in some ways.'

Lynda burst out laughing.

'Very good of you to say so, young sir!'

Mark was horrified, he didn't usually give his opinion so freely. 'I'm sorry, Lynda. I didn't mean to offend you.'

'You haven't offended me, you silly sausage,' she said and grabbed hold of him to give him a hug. He stepped back, startled at this show of affection, but then smiled.

'Silly sausage yourself,' he said cheekily, and Lynda was thrilled to realise that this reserved little boy was now confident enough to tease her.

Janet observed the friendship between him and Lynda, and it solved a problem for her. She had a chat with Rose first, to make sure she wouldn't mind, and then put her proposition to Lynda, as they worked together in the kitchen.

'Tom can't leave the hotel to come and fetch Mark home, so he's asked me to take him on the train, but he says someone young and strong has to come with me to carry the bags. I told him I could manage perfectly well, but he's decided that my sixty-fifth birthday put me firmly in 'the old lady' category, and therefore in need of a companion. Will you come with us?'

'If you want me to. But what about Rose?'

'Don't worry I've explained to Rose, and she says she'll be happier helping out here. So, do you fancy a trip to Surrey? We'll stay there a few days, have day out in London as well, if you like.'

'Oh, I'd love that. I've never been to London.'

Janet tried not to sound too surprised. 'Haven't you?'

'No, it's a long way from Milfield, and a lot of money to stay in a hotel there.'

'Well, this hotel will cost you nothing. Tom insists you will be his guest. Don't argue! Just enjoy it. I think you'll like Loveday Manor.'

'What's it like? It sounds very grand.'

'It's bigger than this place, and I suppose it is quite grand. Nicki and her Mother have filled it with antiques from the Marcellin's chateau, which I don't think suit the place, but it's their choice. It was originally an old manor house, and then became a Georgian mansion with a few Victorian additions. It was quite dilapidated when they bought it, and still is, in parts, but Tom thinks it's wonderful.

Tom Meredith came to pick them up from Guildford station in the silver Mercedes which he used to collect valued clients who chose not to bring their own cars. Mark sat in the front seat next to him and Janet sat in the back, asking about the hotel bookings, and carefully avoiding any mention of Suzanne.

Lynda, sitting next to her, didn't want to talk, she just wanted to enjoy riding in this luxurious car, and gazing at the gentle loveliness of the countryside, the spires of the ancient churches, and the delightful cottages in the picturesque villages they drove through. She didn't make any attempt to participate in the conversation until Tom spoke to her.

'I gather you've been entertaining my son during his holiday, Lynda.'

'He's been entertaining me!' she responded.

'Keeping you out of trouble, you mean,' chipped in Mark, turning round to grin at her. Tom glanced at his son in surprise at the easy relationship he had with this woman. He looked in the rear view mirror and saw his Mother give an approving smile.

'I hope you can persuade my Mother to stay at Loveday for more than the couple of days.'

'You're not the only one with a hotel to run,' Janet reminded him, 'but we will stay for a while. I'm under orders to take it easy.'

'Whose orders?' was his quick and concerned response.

Janet was annoyed at having let slip that she'd been advised to rest, but covered her mistake quickly, 'Robbie, of course. He bosses me about all the time these days. I'm thinking of giving in my notice,' she joked.

'You can always come and work for me,' laughed her son.

'No chance!'

They turned through what had once been the grand gateway of an extensive country estate. They drove past a large gatehouse, and through an avenue of beech trees until they reached a huge garden of gently sloping grass, box-edged flower beds and colourful herbaceous borders lovingly tended for centuries. They drove slowly up to the house, and Lynda fell in love.

Loveday Manor was a house pieced together by history and a little eccentricity. Only a small part of the original fourteenth century manor house remained, tucked in at the side of a modest Georgian mansion. A Victorian owner had added an extension with large elegant bay windows facing the garden, and a conservatory. Loveday Manor could hardly be described as elegant, but it had character and, above all, charm.

Lynda knew it was fanciful, but the house seemed to be waiting to welcome her.

'What a wonderful home,' she breathed.

'Have you got time to give Lynda 'the tour' while I unpack and have a little snooze?' Janet requested as they entered the hotel.

Tom nodded and then smiled at Lynda. 'My pleasure.'

Lynda felt the small flutter of panic she always seemed to experience when Tom Meredith looked at her. 'Thank you, but I'm happy for Mark to show me round. You must have plenty of better things to do.'

'I don't think so.'

'Dad loves showing people around.'

'And you've a television that needs watching,' Lynda teased.

Tom laughed as Mark made his escape.

'I see you know my son well.'

'He's a lovely lad.'

She paused as Tom showed her into a huge lounge filled with elegant sofas and armchairs, and huge oil paintings of peevish-looking gentlemen and fox hunting scenes. Tom waited for her to be impressed, and was a little disconcerted by her silence.

'What do you think?'

Lynda didn't want to be ungracious, but hadn't been quick enough to hide her reaction to this intimidating room.

'It's very impressive.'

'But you don't like it.'

'It's, very grand. I expected something a bit cosier, it looked a lot more cosy from the outside. I'm sorry,' she apologised, seeing her host's displeasure. 'It's me, this is too classy for me.'

'I'll show you the dining room, and the conservatory, and then I'll take you upstairs.'

To Lynda's horror, she felt herself blushing, and Tom Meredith noticed. He laughed, and Lynda felt ridiculous. She told herself to stop being stupid, and concentrated on finding favourable comments to make as she was shown round some of the unoccupied bedrooms. But Tom saw her grimace as he showed her a room with a four-poster bed.

'Do you not like this?'

'I'm sorry, it's just four-poster beds. I read that they had curtains over the bed to keep the rats off them at night. I've never fancied a four-poster since. I told you, I've no style, me.'

'You certainly have a very different style to my wife's.'

She was about to ask if he meant that as a compliment, but managed to stop herself just in time. This tour was turning into an ordeal and she was relieved when Tom took her outside to show her the garden and the old stables.

'What lovely old buildings. You could make really good use of them, convert them into really nice apartments or something.'

'I'd like to, but it would cost too much at the moment. We've had to spend a lot on the place over the last few years, and there's still much more to do.'

'How long have you lived here?'

'Since 1972, it was a wedding present from my in-laws, well, my father-in-law, really. He thought it would make a good home, and a good business for me and my wife.'

'Quite a wedding present.'

'Yes. Would you like to unpack now? I've put you in the room next to the one my Mother uses, it's in that small annexe at the back. She'll be looking out for you. I'll take you round there.'

'No, it's all right, I'll find it.'

He seemed relieved to be free of her company. 'Dinner is any time after six. If you'll excuse me, I need to go and start cooking.'

'Yes, of course. Thank you.'

She watched him stride off towards the back of the hotel, and knew that she had not made a good impression.

She tried to make amends by being very complimentary about the food that evening, but Tom just thanked her politely, and his smile did not reach his eyes.

His eyes were the first thing you noticed about Tom Meredith – the constant amused twinkle in them, as if he was laughing at the truth you couldn't hide from him. There was usually also kindness in those eyes, but there was no kindness in them tonight, at least, not when he looked at Lynda.

'What's wrong, do you not like her?' his Mother asked when they were having a cup of tea together after Lynda had gone to bed early.

'She's not exactly tactful, is she?'

'She's a bit outspoken, I suppose, but I like that. At least you know where you stand with somebody as straightforward as Lynda.'

Tom looked at his Mother, and knew that she was thinking about how different that was from his wife.

'I'm sorry if I was rude.'

'You weren't rude, just not as charming as you can be.'

'No, I'm sorry. I'm a bit on edge, I've had a phone call from Suzanne. She and her Mother are coming back on Monday.'

'Oh, I'll go home then, shall I?'

'No, stay till Wednesday as planned. I'll need your support, I've told Suzanne I know she's been with Simon, and that I want a divorce.'

'What did she say?'

'She was too shocked to say anything, except that we'd talk about it on Monday.'

'Not in front of Mark.'

'No,' Tom said quietly, 'not in front of Mark. How am I going to tell him, Mum?'

'I don't know. Find some time with him on your own. That's what he needs, you know, more time with his Dad.'

CHAPTER SEVENTEEN

Nicki Heston had been annoyed to have to return from Cannes almost as soon as she'd arrived there, but she had been waiting for this day. She was sixty-one, but took such good care of herself that very few people would have guessed. She had crisply styled, short blonde hair and the golden look characteristic of wealthy women who live on the French Riviera.

She had been a widow for almost four years now, and although she had a marvellous life with her friends in London and in France, there were times when she was in need of her daughter to keep her company. She could definitely see advantages in Suzanne being divorced – especially from someone as unsuitable as Tom Meredith. She had tried to brief Suzanne on how to handle this divorce, but the child didn't seem able to take in her instructions, so she had made her promise that she would not have any meetings without her being present.

Alert and in control, Nicki perched on one of the chairs in her son-in-law's office, and played carelessly with the diamond and pearl necklace which rested against the bronzed skin displayed between the folds of her cream silk shirt.

'You do realise that you will have to sell the hotel? My husband and I paid for it, and the money must come back to the family.'

Tom was ready for this. 'You know very well, Nicki, that Vic made sure that I own half of Loveday Manor in my own right.'

'My husband was a fool. But what you don't know is that he used some of my money as well as his own. I gave him a loan, and I shall want it repaid. So you will have to repay me, as well as giving Suzanne half of the value of the hotel. Do you have the money to do that?'

Tom Meredith was not a man who told lies, but he was desperate enough to stretch the truth at this moment. 'I will have. I have a business associate who will put up what money I need.'

He turned to his wife. 'I don't want to sell Loveday, Suzanne, you know that. And you know that Loveday is not just the business that provides income for the family, it's also Mark's home.'

'And mine,' she said, with a pleading look at her Mother.

Nicki sighed with exasperation, as she repeated what she had already told her daughter. 'Yes, Suzanne, but you don't want to live here, do you?'

'No. I want to live with Simon.' Suzanne adopted the pleading, petulant tone of the child her father had despaired of. 'You understand that, don't you, Tom? With Simon I get to live, to have a good time. I'm not having the life I want with you.'

Tom struggled to keep the emotion out of his voice. He was about to negotiate to keep his child.

'And what about Mark?'

'Simon doesn't want him . . .'

144

Suzanne heard her Mother's hiss of anger, and turned to her. 'I'm sorry, Mummy, I know I shouldn't have said that, but it's true.'

They became aware that the door to the office was now open, and that Mark, who had rushed home early from school to see his Mother, was standing there, trying to fight back his tears.

'Who doesn't want me?'

Janet Meredith hadn't wanted to be present at the confrontation between her son and his wife, and so had planned to take Lynda to London that day. They sat together upstairs on the front seat of a double-decker bus and Janet pointed out the sights to an awe-struck Lynda. Later they walked round Trafalgar Square, then up to Piccadilly, and Covent Garden.

'It's such a wonderful city. I'd never realised it would be like this. You can feel the history. I used to love history at school, and here it's all around you, you're actually on the streets where all those famous people walked.'

They strolled along Shaftesbury Avenue to see the theatres and Leicester Square before turning off into Soho for a late lunch, as Lynda had said she wanted to have a Chinese meal. Janet watched, amused, as she tried to eat with chopsticks, but soon abandoned them in favour of a knife and fork.

'I like my food hot,' she said, and then apologised as she realised she was talking with her mouth full. 'Sorry, I'm always doing that when I'm excited. Carolyn gets really mad with me.' She paused, eating slowly and trying to sort out the thoughts which were scurrying around in her head. 'She'd love this, being in London and eating in a restaurant. John can't stand

Chinese food. He only had a takeaway once, but that was enough for him.'

'Are you missing miss them a lot?'

'I am today. Wishing Carolyn was here having a good time with me. We haven't had many good times together. And I feel guilty, enjoying myself so much, while she's stuck at home, trying to cope with a crying baby.'

'I expect it's your grandson you miss the most.'

'Yeah. You're a Grandma, so you'll understand that it's a special love I have for him.'

'Yes, as much as you love your children, but different.'

'Yes. My friend Jean doesn't know how I could do it, walk off and leave little Michael. She hasn't got any children, so she thinks I'm stupid and the most selfish person on earth.'

'You've spoken to her?'

'Yes, I phoned her before I came away with you. I was thinking I should be going home instead of coming to Loveday with you and Mark.'

'What did she say?'

'She couldn't cope with talking to me. We've been best friends for years, and she couldn't talk to me. She just kept going on about how selfish I was, and we ended up shouting at each other. She said I didn't deserve to have a family, and a husband like John Stanworth. Mind you, she's always thought that. She's always wanted him for herself, you see.'

'And will she get him now?'

'What do you mean?'

'Will you get divorced?'

That was something Lynda had been avoiding thinking about.

'I don't know,' she whispered. 'John was very upset at first but now, according to Jean, they're all managing very well without me.'

'But that's according to Jean,' Janet said, thinking Lynda deserved a better friend. 'I'm sorry, I shouldn't have asked you that question, but divorce is on my mind at the moment. You may as well know, my son is going to divorce Suzanne.'

'I thought he might,' Lynda said, and confessed to Janet that she, too, had overheard the phone call Suzanne had made to her lover. 'It should be straightforward if she's confessed to adultery.'

'Yes. The money won't be, though. But that doesn't matter, as long as Tom gets custody of Mark. That's all he cares about, having his son with him.'

'It's usually the Mother who gets custody isn't it?'

'Yes, I just hope Suzanne decides she can have a better life without a little boy to take care of.'

'I gather she likes to have plenty of holidays with her Mother.'

'Yes. Suzanne does love Mark, but she's always been too willing to hand him over to an au pair or someone if she wanted to go away. And Nicki has encouraged the view that he doesn't need to be with either her or his Mother if it's not convenient.'

'I'm not the only one who's selfish, then.'

'From what I've seen of you, I think it's more of a case of being unhappy than being selfish. And it's not wrong to want to be happy. The question is, where do you need to be to find happiness?'

Lynda shook her head in wonder at this woman's perception. 'You always seem to know what questions I'm asking myself.'

Janet smiled. 'It's a gift. But I don't know the

answers to your questions. Only you can decide.'

'You mean, where do I go from here? That's the question. Do I go back to Milfield, or back to Cornwall with you?'

'Yes. Like I said. Where will you be happy?'

CHAPTER EIGHTEEN

Cherry blossom was adding a touch of fairyland to Alexandra Park, and many of the inhabitants of Milfield had come out to enjoy it with their children, dogs and, in some cases, their husbands. Carolyn and Steve had been lucky enough to find a bench where they could sit together and, as their son was still asleep in his pram, enjoy a few minutes of being just a young couple in the sunshine.

Steve had his arm stretched along the back of the bench, and pulled his wife closer as he said, 'This feels like when we were courting.'

'That seems a long time ago. Another world. Another Carolyn Stanworth.'

'Carolyn Sheldon, you mean.'

'Yeah. And Mother of Michael Sheldon.'

'That's all right, though, isn't it?' Steve checked anxiously.

'Yes, but like Dr Brennan said, I will be better if I have a break from being just a wife and mother sometimes.'

'I know we need the money, now there isn't Lynda's wage coming in, but are you sure you'll cope with working as well as looking after Michael?'

149

'My Nan will come round full time if I need her to. And it will be good for me to do something, Steve. It's been really getting me down being at home all the time.'

'I know.'

'And this job that Mrs Heywood's found for me sounds ideal.'

'You haven't done accountancy type work before.'

'I haven't been out to work before.'

'And you don't have to now.'

'I do. I need to use my brain, to be me again. You know what the doctor said about the depression.'

'Yeah.'

'And we do need the money. Especially now that my Mother's not coming home.'

'She'll be back.'

'You're kidding yourself, Steve, just like my Dad is. She didn't even send him a birthday card! Face it, she doesn't give a damn about us, about any of us.'

She looked into the pram where the baby had started to stir.

'He'll be waking up soon, let's get back, so I can have my tea in peace before he does.'

'O.K.' Steve sighed and stood up to push the pram home. 'Been nice to be on our own for once, though, hasn't it?'

When they got back to Beechwood Avenue they found Sheila and John in the front room, and they had company.

'Jean called in with some news about your Mother,' John said to Carolyn. 'She's had a phone call.'

'Oh?' Carolyn, still haunted by the vivid memory

of her telephone conversation with her Mother, was apprehensive.

'Yes.' Jean Haworth folded her hands primly on her lap. 'Not a very pleasant phone call, I'm afraid.'

Steve phrased the question that was most important to him. 'When is she coming back?'

'She's not. In fact, she was on her way to London.'

John's eyes were full of misery. 'She's always wanted to go to London. Ever since she heard our Sylvia talking about it.'

'My daughter and her husband went there for their honeymoon,' Sheila explained to Jean. 'Graham has a good job at The County Bank, so they were able to afford it.'

'Yes,' Jean remembered, 'Lynda told me about it. She was quite jealous.'

'Where's she staying?' Steve looked at John, who shook his head.

'Jean doesn't know. Lynda didn't tell her anything, and she was calling from a phone box again.'

Sheila had had enough of seeing her son getting upset about his wife. 'Anyway, she seems to be continuing to enjoy her freedom, so I suggest we forget about her and have our tea.'

Carolyn found she wanted to talk about her Mother, and Jean was her link to her. 'Would you like to stay to tea, Aunty Jean?'

This was what Jean had been hoping for.

'Well, if that would be all right?'

John looked at his Mother, who wasn't keen on anyone who was a friend of Lynda's, but Sheila nodded.

'I suppose so.'

Later that evening, when Sheila had gone to attend the spring concert given by the church choir, and Carolyn was enjoying a chat with her 'Aunty Jean', John and Steve took the opportunity to go out for a pint together.

John had stopped going to The Red Lion, he was sick of the customers there asking him about Lynda, so they went to The Britannia instead. John hadn't been there for years, but it hadn't changed, apart from having a new barmaid. He nearly walked out when he saw who it was, but Steve had already ordered two pints of their best bitter. John turned to walk away but she'd already spotted him.

'Hiya, John! Long time no see.'

Lorraine Garvey hadn't changed much, she was well into her fifties but still had long dark hair, thanks to regular sessions at her kitchen sink with a bottle of 'Chestnut Bronze'. She'd put on a bit of weight, John noticed, but still wore figure hugging clothes and jewellery that drew your eye down to her cleavage.

'Hello, Lorraine. Working here now, are you?'

'Needs must, I like my holidays in the sun. Have you been to Spain?'

'No.'

'Oh, I'd have thought Lynda would have had you over there on one of these cheap packages. You are still married to her, aren't you?'

'Of course, I am,' he said with a scowl. 'We'll sit over in that corner, Steve.' He strode away to claim a table well away from the bar.

'How do you know her?' Steve asked as he placed the two beers on the table and sat down next to John.

'She used to work at The Black Bull, where Lynda

lived till it burned down. She was the barmaid there, and Lynda's Dad's bit on the side.'

'I think she fancies you,' Steve joked, and then wished he hadn't. His father-in-law wasn't coping well with being without a wife.

'I can't get away from it, can I?' John said angrily, 'People asking about Lynda. Wanting to know where she's gone, when she's coming back. Why can't they mind their own bloody business?'

'She'll come back when she's ready. She hasn't forgotten about us. She phoned Jean.'

'Yes, but not us.' He looked at Steve with anguish in his eyes.

'I'd go looking for her, if I knew where to start. I was thinking of going to Cornwall in the summer.'

'You've no address and it sounds like she's in London now. Where would you start looking there?'

John shook his head and stared into his glass.

'Our Carolyn doesn't want me to look for her. I wish she wasn't so angry with her Mother.'

'She's more than angry. I hope the doctor's right and this part-time job will make her feel better about herself, give her something else to focus on beside the baby. I don't really want her going out to work, though. What do you think?'

'The money would come in handy. We're missing Lynda's wage.'

'I know. But, do you think Caro will cope?'

'Yes, if the job's right. And Mrs Heywood seems to think it is. Our Carolyn's always been good at figures, it might suit her. And my Mother will look after Michael.'

'I know.'

Steve wasn't keen on the idea of Sheila being even

more involved in bringing up his son, but it looked as if there was no choice. He wasn't spending as much time as he would like with Michael, but while there was paid overtime on offer he had to take it. When he went into work the next day, he found that that extra income was under threat. There was a notice on the door of the workshop, stating that there was to be a cut in the amount paid for overtime.

The move to the nineteenth century outbuildings of Victoria Mill had proved to be less advantageous than the employees at Bentham's had been led to believe. There was more room in the workshop, certainly, but it was a cold, echoing space with a high ceiling. Today, because it was raining, it felt cold and clammy. To comply with regulations which required him to provide some semblance of an adequately heated working environment, Randerson had reluctantly had electric storage heaters installed, but they warmed only the air beneath the ceiling and today, of course, because it was officially summer time, they were not switched on.

The stone walls were not clad in insulation but merely whitewashed to reflect the light from the huge stone pillared windows. The dull day made the room even more gloomy than usual. The rain was forming slender rivulets in the dense dust on the outside of the glass, and the strip lighting flickered as it struggled to maintain a believable imitation of daylight.

As soon as Steve walked in that morning Gary pulled him to one side.

'Have you seen that bloody notice?' They can't do that, cut our flaming wages!'

Hoskins, the supervisor, heard Gary and stepped quickly towards the two workers to head off any trouble. 'Technically, they're not cutting our wages. They're reducing the amount they're offering us for over-time.'

Steve had considered Gary Pearson a mate ever since he'd allowed Steve to join his gang, and they'd kicked a football around on the scrubby patch of grass at the end of the street where they'd both lived, unwillingly, with their parents. Gary had always been more than ready to look for a fight, and he moved towards Hoskins now, pushing his face close to his.

'It's a pay cut. Dress it up as much as you like, you smarmy bugger, it's still a pay cut.'

Hoskins, who was only interested in a quiet life until he reached his pension in a few months time, said smoothly, 'You don't have to accept it, nobody's forcing you to do overtime, if you don't want it.'

'They can stuff their overtime,' exclaimed Gary, turning his back on Hoskins and lighting a cigarette. Steve took off his jacket and walked resignedly towards his workbench and the stack of timber waiting to be made into kitchen cupboards.

The rain had cleared by the afternoon, so when Reggie Broadbent called at the house in Hadden Lea he found Jenny and her daughters out in the garden. When the big, red-faced man in a loud check jacket walked through the gate, the girls looked up warily from the rockery where they were constructing a hideaway for their fairy dolls.

'Afternoon, Jenny,' Reggie greeted her loudly. 'Thought I'd drop by and see how you were settling in. Hope you don't mind.'

Jenny put down her trowel and took off her gardening gloves as she hurried over to meet him.

'How lovely to see you, Reggie. Alex, Katie, this is Mr Broadbent, who Mummy used to work for.'

'And will do again, before too long, I hope.' Reggie reached into his jacket pocket and pulled out a large bag of sweets. 'Would it be all right if your young ladies shared these between them while you and I talk a little business?'

'Thank you. I was just about to make a pot of tea, so you're timing is excellent.'

They sat together on the ancient wooden bench which faced the moors. 'Good little spot you found here, Jenny.'

'You were the one who tipped me off about it coming on the market.'

Reggie tried unsuccessfully to feign innocence. 'Did I? Well, it was the right thing for you to do, have a fresh start. Which is sort of why I've called to see you today. I've had a chat with Edwin, and as soon as Katie's settled in at nursery, we can offer you some part-time work.'

'Oh, Reggie, that would be wonderful!'

'Well, as you can see,' he indicated his casual dress, 'I think at my age I should be spending more time on the golf course. And you've always been interested in the property side of the business.'

'Yes, I'd love to help you. I'll need to learn about conveyance, though.'

'You'll soon pick it up.'

'Are you sure it's all right with Mr Lawson?' Jenny knew that, although Reggie's gregarious energy attracted many clients, it was Edwin Lawson who kept the firm on financially solid ground.

'Edwin has given his approval, as long as your mother-in-law is told it was all my idea. He doesn't want to lose a valuable client.'

Jenny grinned at him. 'Don't worry, I'll make sure you get all the blame, Reggie.'

'I have broad shoulders,' he sighed. 'Now tell me, have you had the grand inspection yet, or is Mrs Heywood refusing to grace your new abode with her presence?'

'Dan's managed to persuade her to come for tea on Sunday.'

'Well, you must be so looking forward to that,' he said, with a much practised wink. 'Now, I must be off. Just give me a ring as soon as you've fixed up some available hours. Edwin will be very relieved to have someone sensible to keep an eye on me!'

CHAPTER NINETEEN

On Wednesday afternoon Sheila Stanworth and Carolyn were guests at a little celebratory tea-party in the conservatory at Kirkwood House, but there was a delay in the proceedings as the cakes had not yet arrived.

'I do apologise,' Ellen said, 'Daniel promised that he would call in with them. I don't know where he can be.'

'It doesn't matter, Mrs Heywood,' Carolyn said, 'we're just happy to be here. Shall I pour the tea?'

'If you would, my dear. And I think you may call me Ellen, now you are a wife and mother, and a career women, of course!'

Carolyn beamed at her. 'Thank you.'

Sheila was delighted that Ellen thought so much of her daughter. 'Carolyn is so grateful to you for arranging for her to have this opportunity.'

'Andrew Howell's father was a friend of my father, so he was happy to take my recommendation. I hope it will be a first step towards the career you deserve, Carolyn.'

'She's very excited about it,' Sheila enthused.

'And nervous,' Carolyn added. 'But it's just what I

need, a chance to learn a profession. I'd love to study accountancy.'

'There is no reason why you shouldn't, in the evenings at least. And a bright young woman like you should have a profession. We had such plans for her, didn't we, Sheila?'

'Yes,' Sheila said quietly, still feeling the shame of her daughter having to end her education and get married in haste.

With a glance at the pram outside the conservatory, Carolyn quickly defended the decision she had made against their wishes. 'I wouldn't be without Michael, though.'

'Of course not,' Ellen conceded. 'But these days the future holds so many more possibilities for young women. You could have your own business one day.'

'That's what Steve wants, his own business,' Carolyn said. 'He's very talented, you know.'

Ellen Heywood looked at Sheila, who knew that she shared the same view of Carolyn's unsuitable husband.

'I'm sure he is, but don't ignore your own ambitions. One never knows what will happen in the future.'

Their conversation was interrupted by a tapping on the door of the conservatory and they looked up to see Alice Smith flourishing the cardboard boxes she was carrying. Sheila, not at all pleased to see Alice, who, it seemed to her, was a frequent intruder upon her afternoon visits to Kirkwood House, opened the door.

'Good afternoon, Alice.'

Alice marched into the room, chattering away like a budgerigar.

'Good afternoon, ladies! An urgent order came in, so Dan asked me if I'd deliver these on my way home. It's not really on my way home, of course, but he said I'd be rewarded for coming out of my way on my free afternoon.'

Ellen sighed. 'Did he?'

'Yes,' Alice squeaked happily, 'he said he'd put an extra chocolate éclair in the boxes. He knows they're my favourite. Shall I go and ask Mrs Thompson for some more tea, and four plates?'

Without waiting for permission, she scampered off towards the kitchen.

'Oh, dear, I'm afraid this won't quite be the afternoon I had planned. I do apologise, but one can hardly refuse.'

Sheila was irritated by Alice's gate-crashing, but politely reassured their hostess. 'Don't worry, Ellen. We're quite used to Alice Smith.'

As expected, Alice's presence limited the conversation a little, all three women being well aware that Alice wasn't capable of grasping the concept of confidentiality. Once she had claimed more than her share of the cakes, Alice put all her energy into making the most of the sources of information within this small select gathering.

'I saw Jean Haworth the other day,' she volunteered, while manoeuvring an errant portion of cream from the éclair into her mouth with her finger. 'She's my cousin, you know, though my Mother and her Father never got on. She said she'd had a phone call from your Mother, Carolyn, but didn't say anything about her coming home.'

Ellen, well practised in handling Alice's probing

questions, tried a side-step.

'Isn't Mrs Haworth a widow?'

'Yes,' Carolyn replied. 'He was a lovely man, Gordon. I feel so sorry for Aunty Jean, being on her own. She's offered to babysit, Nana, if ever you can't do it.'

Sheila didn't like that idea. 'Has she?'

'Perhaps she should re-marry,' Ellen suggested, and Alice darted back into the conversation.

'She used to be very keen on your Dad, you know, Carolyn. If there's a divorce, she might end up being your step-mother.'

Ellen's reprimand was firm. 'Alice, you really must suppress such fanciful thoughts.'

Alice had her retaliation ready, in fact, even rehearsed.

'You never know how these things work out, Ellen. It's the same with your daughter-in-law, Jenny, she could easily marry again.'

Ellen sat bolt upright. 'Over my dead body!'

Dan Heywood was happily looking after the café on Saturday while Debbie attended her sister's wedding, when Alice Smith's candidate for divorce walked in. Dan was clearing away at the end of the afternoon, and saw John stand by the door for a moment, checking that there were no customers inside before he entered.

'Hiya, John. Not often we see you in here.'

'No.'

John knew too well, and Dan had learned from Debbie, that the last time John Stanworth had visited his wife's place of work was when he'd been desperate enough to ask the young girl if she had any idea where Lynda had gone. Debbie had told him about the postcards which she'd seen tucked away on the shelf behind the storage jars in the kitchen. They were no longer there, and she didn't know where they were from.

'Do you want a tea or a coffee? I was just about to have one,' Dan lied.

'No, thanks.'

'Are you all right?'

John spoke in the brusque manner Dan recognised as a warning. 'Yes, of course I am.'

'Been to the match today?'

'No, Steve's working, and anyway I couldn't be bothered. I've come to ask a favour.'

'Anything you like, mate.'

'Can I borrow the bike this weekend?'

'Of course you can. Fancy a ride in the country, do you?'

'Yeah.'

Dan put his hand in his pocket. 'You know where it is. The helmet and leathers are there as well. Here's the key, just help yourself whenever you like.'

'Thanks.'

'Carolyn and Steve all right, are they?'

'Yes. They could do with their own place, though.' He hesitated before adding, 'That's partly why I'm going out tomorrow, to give them a chance to have some time for themselves.'

'Oh, yes, your Mother will be on that church Sunday lunch outing with mine.'

There was a pause where the question about Lynda should have been, but Dan could judge his friend's mood well enough to know not to ask it. Dan didn't like the darkness in John's eyes, and sought a way to reach him.

'If you happen to be riding out towards Hadden Lea, why don't you call in at Jenny's new house? Here.'

He scribbled the address on a sheet from an order pad.

'I've managed to persuade my Mother to go there at long last, this Sunday, after the church 'do'. It'll only be a short visit. Just long enough for her to find out she disapproves,' he attempted a laugh but it wasn't taken up by John.

'Thanks, but I'll be riding further out, over the moors.'

'Oh, where you can get a bit of speed up, eh?'

'That's the idea.'

'Well, if you change your mind, I'm sure Jenny would be pleased. You used to have some good times at her Mum and Dad's, didn't you?'

'Yeah.'

John hesitated, he knew that this enquiry had been made, via his Mother and Ellen Heywood, but didn't trust their answer. 'Does Jenny know where Lynda's gone?'

'No, I'm sorry, John. I've already asked her. She thinks it's Cornwall, but she's no idea where.'

'Right. See you then, and thanks for the bike.'

It had not taken Jenny Heywood long to make the house at Hadden Lea more of a home than the Oakwoods house had ever been. Trying not to think about what her mother-in-law's reaction would be, she had sold the leather sofas and a lot of the other furniture which Richard had bought. She'd purchased a new sofa in a plain olive green fabric, and had made cushions of colourful contrasting material which she'd bought in the market. There was another smaller sofa which she'd spotted in the small ads of The Milfield Express and which she intended to re-cover.

At a second-hand shop she'd found a round table covered in paint and varnish which she had stripped away to reveal the warmth and beauty of the natural mahogany. It stood in the bay window and was used not only for dining, but also for the children's painting and model making, as well as Jenny's sewing.

She and the girls sat at this table for lunch on the Sunday, with Dan as guest of honour, but as soon as the children had finished their dessert of apple pie and custard they were allowed to leave the table and go out to play in the garden.

'Shall we treat ourselves to another slice of apple pie?' Dan suggested as he reached over for the blue and white striped jug in the centre of the table. 'There's plenty more custard left, unless you want the pie for the children tomorrow?'

'No,' Jenny smiled. 'Help yourself, there's another one in the kitchen, I'm getting into the habit of cooking for more than one day and making good use of the freezer. It will be useful when I start work.'

'When do you think that will be?'

'As soon as I'm sure that Katie has settled in the nursery. I didn't want to send her to nursery yet, but I have to start earning some money. Your Mother is being very generous, but I need to be independent. You understand, don't you, Dan?'

'Yes, but I'm not sure my Mother will.'

'I know, and I'm dreading what she'll say when she sees I've sold the furniture from the other house.'

'You've a right to have the things you want. Richard's taste was all for show.'

'Yes. I feel so sad that I couldn't keep any of my Mum and Dad's old furniture, but Richard wouldn't have it. At least I managed to hang on to things like this jug, and other bits and pieces. It's surprising how you need to have a tangible connection with the past.'

'Yes, but not when you take it to extremes like my Mother. And it has to be good memories you connect with. There are only a few things I treasure at Kirkwood, like my grandmother's chair and the cushion she made for me to sit on as a child. Kirkwood House isn't a home like this is.'

'I know your Mother needs you at the moment, Dan, but you ought to marry again, have a home of your own.'

'You have to have the right person to make a home with. It would have been wonderful I'd been allowed to marry Lynda. My whole life would have been so different.' He laughed ruefully. 'I wouldn't have married Sandra Burnett for a start, and what a disaster that turned out to be!'

'Do you think Lynda will ever come back?'

Dan was silent for a moment, thinking of what he'd said to Lynda. 'I don't know.' Dan turned away to look round the room, he couldn't bear to talk about Lynda any more. 'This place is lovely, so cosy and relaxing.'

'Yes, it's strange, but we've all felt the house welcome us, the girls are happy here, they sense the different atmosphere. It's been worth going through Ellen's disapproval.'

'You might have more of that to come when I go and fetch her here for tea. She's going to walk in here and compare it to a chicken coop, and a junk shop. It's the way she is and she's not going to change.'

'I know.'

'But why should you take all her criticism, and the way she talks about Richard? I can't bear to listen to her saying what a wonderful husband he was, when he was such a vicious sod. You'll have to tell her the truth one day.'

'And break her heart again? I couldn't do that to her, Dan.'

She stood up and began to clear away the dishes. Dan stared out of the window, and felt angry at his helplessness. Jenny put down the dishes, and leaned over to kiss the top of his head.

Don't worry. I'll manage to cope with Ellen as my mother-in-law. Now, let's have a cup of coffee in the garden and enjoy ourselves while we can, eh?'

The countryside was unfurling in bright ribbons of fresh green and gold as John Stanworth rode the motorbike out of Milfield and along the narrow country roads which passed through fields and hedgerows. He drove at a reasonable speed on his way to the wooded hillside and the river bank where he and Lynda had spent many hours lying on the grass, making love and talking about the exciting future they were going to have.

He parked the bike under a hawthorn bush and sat and watched the river tumble and race to throw itself against boulders and stones, and then slide away into still, calm shade under the trees. He let memories slip into his head and bring emotions and thoughts to be carefully sifted through and examined. He tried to form them into some kind of contentment, some kind of hope, but failed, and his mind and soul seemed to sink with them into the depths of the river.

His limbs were aching when he finally pushed himself up off the ground and walked slowly back to the motorbike, the symbol of the time he was happy. He stroked his hand along the leather seat and remembered the warmth of Lynda's arms clasped tightly round his waist, her head resting against the strength of his back. He looked at the helmet lying on the grass, left it there, and got on the bike. He began to move away towards the gate which opened on to the narrow track he'd ridden down. When he got off the bike to open the gate, he turned to look at the helmet. He walked back, snatched it off the ground and fastened it on his head.

Driving very fast he went past the fields black-lined with walls fashioned by work-hardened hands, and sped up on to the moors, away from everyone and everything. The engine roared as he pushed for more speed until the countryside disappeared from his vision, leaving only a blur of anger and tears.

He was heading towards grey clouds and a dark horizon now, and accelerating beyond control of the bike. It felt like the road had seized hold of the machine and him with it. He thrust his head towards oblivion, and stopped all thought. He felt the bike swerve beneath him. Instinctively he applied the brakes and steered towards a bank of grasses and shrubs which caught him, safe. He stayed there for a while, astride the bike, letting the tears run down his face.

At Stanhope Road Sheila Stanworth stood by the window of her living room, and watched the clouds drift towards the end of her garden. She had not turned on the radio as she usually did when she walked back into her empty house. She was waiting in silence for her son whom she had insisted should come for tea.

He was late. She looked at her watch, and then at the table set with china plates and cups, just for her and John. In the centre of the table she had placed a chocolate cake as a treat for him. It had always been her husband's favourite.

CHAPTER TWENTY

The Springfield Hotel was fully booked when Janet and Lynda returned from Loveday Manor, and Lynda was worried that her room would be needed. One afternoon she was walking through the reception area after serving coffee to some guests, when she heard Robbie again turning down a booking.

'Robbie, could I have a word with you?'

'You can have as many as you like, as long as they're polite and complimentary,' he joked.

'It's about my room. I know you said I could stay a bit longer, but I can see you might need it for a booking.'

'No, I told you, it's not a room I let out.'

'Oh, if you're sure. But I must start paying for it.'

Robbie had been talking to Janet and finding out as much as he could about Lynda's circumstances, so he knew he could pursue this conversation. 'You're definitely not planning to go home yet, then?'

'No.'

'In that case I have a proposition to put to you. I'm going to need more help, and I'd like to offer you a job, if you want it.'

Lynda felt as if she'd been given a medal. 'Yes,

please! What do you want me to do?'

'Everything, sweetheart. A bit of cooking, a bit of cleaning, a bit of book-keeping – I've seen you can handle all that, and I think you'd like to learn more about the hotel business? Am I right?'

'Yes. I love this place, and I'm willing to learn whatever you want me to do.'

'Your official job title will be 'General Dogsbody' – will that suit you?'

'Perfect!' she laughed. 'Do you mind if I go off and tell Rose when I've done the veg for tonight?'

'The afternoon is yours. Take Rose a slice of that lemon tart we had at lunch time, it's one of her favourites.'

Lynda prepared the veg and cleared the kitchen at top speed. Her head was spinning with thoughts of what her life would be like at Springfield. She was almost dancing as she made her way along the road towards St. Benedict. She could stay here, she could look at the sea every day, and be with people who were fun to be with.

She couldn't believe it when Rose didn't share her delight.

'It's a big decision, Lynda. And I'm sure Ted wouldn't have wanted you to leave John.'

'I haven't left him.'

'Haven't you? You left home for a few days holiday, and now you're talking about staying away all summer, and autumn too.'

'John hasn't come looking for me,' she said defensively. 'I left that postcard and the letter with your address.'

Rose shook her head. 'He might not have found

those. You haven't written to him to tell him where you are. Why not?'

'I sent him a birthday card with the address of the hotel, but he still hasn't contacted me. And Jean says they're doing all right without me.'

'Do you really believe that? Or is it that you won't admit to yourself that it's you who doesn't want to go back to your family, to your grandson?'

Lynda bowed her head. She knew that all the reasons she had given for not returning didn't seem strong enough to Rose. They sat and had a cup of tea, but almost in silence. Lynda was glad when there was a knock at the door and Janet came to join them.

'You forgot the lemon tart, Lynda, and Robbie thought I could do with a bit of fresh air and exercise. As if I didn't get enough exercise working for that slave-driver!'

Rose made some more tea and Janet shared out the lemon tart.

'One of the perks of working for Robbie,' she said as she handed Lynda her slice. 'He told me you've agreed to join the staff. I'm very glad.'

'Rose isn't.'

It was not Janet's way to take sides, she'd found over the years that, very often, listening seemed to be a good way of letting people find their own way through something. She looked at Rose, noting that she was unusually agitated.

'Should I leave you two alone to finish your conversation?'

Lynda, hoping that Janet might make Rose think differently, spoke quickly. 'No, it's all right, Janet. You know enough about my situation already. And you may as well know what Rose thinks.'

'All I've said, and I've told Lynda this before, is that it's a big decision, not going back to her family. And the longer she's away the harder it will be to go back.'

'I know. But they don't want me back.' She turned to Janet. 'I told you, didn't I, that Jean says they're not missing me. They don't want me, any of them.'

Rose spoke up strongly again.

'Not your little baby grandson, you can't say that he won't want you.'

'No,' Lynda admitted, her voice softer now, 'I can't say that. Little Michael is what makes me cry the most. I'd love to be with him, watching him grow up. But it was starting to be just like it was when I had Carolyn. I was out at work and Sheila was taking over, just like she did then. And she'll turn little Michael against me as he gets older, just like she turned Carolyn against me.'

Rose shook her head and looked first at Lynda, then at Janet.

'It's not right.'

Lynda's voice was full of anguish. 'I know it's not right – any of it. But I don't know what I can do about it. Don't look at me like that Rose, I know what I've done, left my family. But they don't need me, and they don't love me.'

Rose turned to her friend. 'What do you think, Janet?'

'Lynda has to make her own decision. And it looks like she's made it. Just like you made your decision to divorce Harry. You asked me then if you were doing the right thing. And do you remember what I said?'

'I remember. You said I had to decide what I wanted the rest of my life to be like. But that was different, Harry was making my life unbearable, refusing to look for work, and drinking away the money I earned. He was destroying me.'

Janet said nothing for a moment, and then asked her friend, 'And do you remember what you told me when Lynda first came here? How she'd changed from the girl you knew.'

Rose looked at the woman who was younger than she, but had always seemed older and wiser.

'Yes.'

'She needed to come here, didn't she?'

'Yes.'

'And maybe she needs to stay. But like I said, it has to be your decision, Lynda.'

Lynda, white-faced, nodded.

Janet stood up. 'Now it's time for me to be off. I was thinking of calling in to see my friend, Benedict, on my way back. Have you been to have a look at the church yet, Lynda?'

'No.'

'Perhaps you'd like to come with me?'

Lynda was surprised at how welcome the invitation was.

'Yes, I'd like that, Janet. Thank you.'

St. Benedict's was a simple church, built slowly and steadily, a few centuries ago, by local men who knew the limitations of the stone they harvested from the fields and the seashore. There was no elegant spire to reach up to the heavens, but a square tower which was tall enough to signal to the farms and cottages, some quite a distance away, that here was a place of prayer to come to, if they needed it.

There were no richly coloured, stained glass windows, just narrow shafts of light through plain glass in the side walls. At the far end of the nave, behind a small, simply carved wooden altar, there was an arched window through which there was a view of the cliffs and the sea beyond them. The walls were painted white, and there were small stone alcoves with small vases which local women kept filled with fresh flowers.

The church's only signs of glory were a modest statue of the Saint, given a kindly face and welcoming arms by its sculptor, and the curved ceiling above the altar, painted bright blue and patterned with gold stars.

Janet pointed up at those stars and smiled before taking a seat near the back of the empty church.

'I'll just sit here for a while and have a little conversation,' she said quietly. 'Robbie laughs at me, says I only come here to tell God where he's going wrong. You have a look round and then choose somewhere to sit for a while, and listen.'

Lynda didn't feel confident enough to walk towards the altar, so she moved slowly round the sides of the church, peering through the small windows and reading the wooden panels with the golden names of those lost at sea or in the wasteland of war. There was a peacefulness here which she'd never found in a church before, and Lynda felt it wrap itself around her until she felt calmer, and safe.

She eventually went to sit at the end of a hard, straight-backed pew not far from the altar. She looked up at the sunlight streaming through the windows and brightening the starry sky above the altar. She sat

174

silently until the thoughts jostling through her mind drifted away. Then she listened. After a while she heard two words. Lynda Collins.

That evening there was a party atmosphere as the staff gathered together for supper round their table in the dining room. Robbie had brought up two bottles of champagne, and tapped on a glass to call them all to order.

'I have some good news for you all. Patrick is leaving us. The bad news is, it's only for a few weeks. His services, such as they are, are required at another establishment.'

'Robbie, stop waffling, I'm going to help Tom at Loveday Manor, his assistant manager has been taken ill, and Tom needs help as he's got guests who expect him to accompany them to the races.'

'Oh, yes, it's the start of the season at Epsom,' Lynda remembered.

Janet was surprised. 'I didn't know you followed horse-racing.'

'My Grandma loved to have a bet on the gee-gees. And she could pick a winner.'

'Perhaps you've inherited her luck, I'll have to get Tom to take you to Epsom one day.'

For a moment Lynda enjoyed the image of being at Epsom racecourse with Tom Meredith, but quickly brushed the idea aside, 'Oh, he wouldn't want to take me.'

Robbie, feigning impatience, tapped his glass again, 'When you've all quite finished! I have another announcement to make. Lynda has agreed to join the staff. He picked up his glass. 'So here's to Lynda Collins, the new member of the family!'

Janet looked questioningly at Lynda. 'Lynda Collins?'

'Yes,' she whispered in reply, 'it was what I heard when I listened.'

Janet looked at her thoughtfully for a moment, then nodded.

They all drank the toast and Patrick, raising his eyebrows at Lynda, commented, 'Champagne, eh? Can't believe his luck, persuading you to stay in this hell hole.'

Lynda smiled. 'Feels more like heaven to me.'

'You just wait. He'll show his true colours now he's got you to sign a contract. It'll be 'do this, do that. Spit Spot – he fancies himself as Mary Poppins, don't you, Robbie?'

'Oh, yes, it was my Mother's favourite film.'

Janet laughed. 'She did look a bit like Julie Andrews, she had beautiful skin.'

'All that rain you get in Liverpool, marvellous for the complexion. Mind you, she was desperate to get away from the place, and live somewhere with sunshine. She loved to sunbathe.'

'Oh, yes,' Patrick chipped in. 'And she liked to have her handsome black servant bring her cocktails, too. Do you know, Lynda, she even bought one of those long-handled fans for me to waft over her!'

Janet laughed out loud, 'You got your own back, though, when you turned up one day in that loin cloth thingy.'

Robbie grinned at Lynda, 'Yes, a precarious looking garment if ever there was one – nearly gave Eliza a heart attack!'

'That's what he used to call her, you know,' Patrick complained with mock outrage, 'Eliza Doolittle. And she worked so hard!'

'Yeah.' Robbie wagged a finger at Janet. 'Too hard, like you, Janet, but at least she did as she was told later on and took it easy.'

Janet smiled at him. 'She was a lucky lady, having you for a son. It was her dream, to live here by the sea, and you made it happen for her.'

Lynda sighed with happiness. 'And now he's doing the same for me. It's a dream come true for me, too, living here.'

Patrick laughed as he watched Robbie fill Lynda's glass with champagne again.

'You won't think that tomorrow morning, when you've got a hangover and a mountain of fried eggs and bacon to cook!'

CHAPTER TWENTY ONE

Patrick was away until the end of June and when he returned Robbie announced, with some sadness, that he would soon be going to work permanently at Loveday Manor. Lynda understood now why Robbie had been training her to do some of the work which was usually Patrick's responsibility. She realised that this job wouldn't come to an end, she really was needed. She worked even harder and loved it. She rejoiced in doing work she knew she did well, learning to cook meat and fish in new ways, and receiving compliments from the guests. And she was in Cornwall; swimming in the sea and walking along the cliffs was a constant thrill for her. This life made her feel so good.

She found the old confidence she used to have and was able to reassure Robbie, 'I won't let you down. I'll do everything you need. I know it will be tough for you, coping without Patrick at such short notice, and in the middle of the summer season.'

'I've been expecting it for a while, and it was Tom who sent Patrick to me in the first place, when he was looking to get out of London. They're good friends, and Tom needs Patrick now, especially with this horrible divorce to cope with.'

'Oh, is it bad?'

'Bound to be, love, when there's money involved.'

A week after Patrick left, Tom Meredith arrived early one morning, and brought his son with him. Lynda was in the kitchen with Janet, who had told everyone that her grandson would be staying with her for the rest of the summer. She, like Janet, was shocked to see how much weight Tom had lost, and that there were dark shadows under his eyes.

'I have to get straight back,' he stated tersely.

'You'll stay and eat first,' Janet insisted.

'I can't. Someone has arranged an important meeting for this afternoon.'

A look passed between him and his Mother, who guessed who had arranged that meeting.

'With the solicitor, Dad?'

'Yeah. Nothing for you to worry about.' Tom ran his hand through his son's hair. 'You'll be OK, won't you?'

The boy nodded but his eyes were full of misery as he watched his father stride out of the room, slamming the door behind him.

'Mummy and Nicki are going back to the South of France.' Mark explained to them. 'Mummy was going to take me, but, it didn't work out.'

'And your Dad's busy,' Lynda added, knowing it wasn't her place to say anything, and that she'd no right to feel as angry as she did. She found a bright smile for Mark, and put her arm round him.

'Well, never mind, there's a fish pie for lunch, with extra prawns in it. Your Nana made it specially. And after we've had that, we'll go down to the beach and see if your batting's improved. Is that all right with you, Janet?'

Janet smiled her gratitude to Lynda, 'Fine.'

Everyone devoted as much time as they could to entertaining Mark. Robbie took him fishing, and to the cinema, his grandmother and Rose found him jobs to do, and taught him to cook and bake. Lynda went swimming with him, played cricket and boules, and together they went for long walks, exploring the bays along the coast.

'You don't have to come with me, you know,' he declared one afternoon as they met up outside the hotel, ready to set off on one of these walks.'

'What?'

'I can go on my own,' he insisted in a surly tone. 'You don't need to look after me.'

'What's brought this on?'

'Nothing!'

'Have you gone off me or something?'

'No.'

'Well, let's go for this walk then.'

They walked for at least a mile with only the calls of the seagulls piercing the silence between them. Lynda, wondering how to reach the young boy she'd grown fond of, couldn't find a subtle way to express her concern.

'I'm not doing this out of pity, you know, I like going for walks with you.'

'That's a lie.'

Taken aback at the vehemence in his voice, she sparked back at him. 'What's a lie? The bit about pity or liking the walks?'

'Both.'

'I see. Well, I do like going for walks with you – truly. But, yeah, you're right about the pity. If I'm honest I do feel a bit sorry for you.'

'I don't need you to feel sorry for me.'

'No. It's not helpful, is it? I don't like people feeling sorry for me. But talking, that's helpful, I've always found.'

'They don't talk to me.'

'Who? Your Mum and Dad?'

He nodded.

'My Mum just sends me postcards, like the one I got this morning telling me she has to stay in France a bit longer.'

'Oh. Is that why you were upset?'

'Yeah. If they don't realise I know what's going on, they must think I'm stupid or deaf. You should hear them shouting at each other. I don't understand why they ever got married.'

'They loved each other, I expect.'

'Not according to Nicki. She says he only married my Mother for her money.'

'Oh.'

'They only had me because the marriage was falling apart and my Mum didn't want to lose my Dad. And when Grandpapa died she was afraid of being without Dad to look after her. So they stayed together, but now Mummy has found Simon she wants a divorce, and they need to get on with it.'

'And your grandmother Nicki told you all this?'

'Some of it,' he flushed a little guiltily, 'after I told her what I'd heard.'

' Oh. I see,' she said, and then muttered almost to herself, 'It's a lot to be told at your age.'

'What do you mean?'

'Nothing.'

'You won't tell anyone I've told you all this, will you? Nicki said it should be a secret.'

'I bet she did. Have you not even told your Grandma Janet?'

'She knows already, I think, but she doesn't want to talk about it.'

'No. And I don't blame her, it's not easy, talking about stuff like that.' She looked at the boy trudging along beside her with his head bowed, and couldn't bear to see his anxiety. 'Tell you what will be easy, though?'

'What?'

'Persuading me to buy you an ice cream at Toni's. Have you ever had a Knickerbocker Glory?'

She could have cried when she saw him manage to smile.

'What's that?'

'I'll get Toni to make you one, and one for me, of course!'

When Lynda shared these unwanted secrets with Rose, she advised her to keep them to herself but confirmed some of what Mark had said.

'Tom was influenced by Suzanne's money. He always was ambitious, ever since he was a teenager. He didn't work hard at school, though, he just wanted to get away from all the silly rules and work in the hotel. He wanted to earn money, and he always was convinced that he would have his own hotel one day, and go to London and make his fortune.'

'And he's done it. By marrying Suzanne. Did he love her?'

'He found her attractive. Who wouldn't? But Janet thinks it was mainly wanting to be in 'the smart set' with money and flash cars, and all the rest of it. But don't let her know I told you that.'

'I won't. But Tom Meredith needs to get it sorted out, and he needs to spend more time with his son.'

'You're right. All he can think about at the moment is how to hang on to Loveday Manor. But from what Janet's told me, he's about to lose it.'

'He'll lose his son if he's not careful.'

'Lynda, you're getting too involved. It's nothing to do with you.'

'I know. But when I see how upset that little boy is, I find it hard to keep my mouth shut.'

'So I've noticed. You need to learn to keep quiet.'

'That's what Carolyn used to say. I need to learn a lot of things, and I need to change, big style, according to Carolyn. But I'm not sure I can. And anyway, I quite like me as I am.'

Rose looked at the defiant woman sitting before her, and was glad to see Lynda sounding confident again. But she was also worried about how much she still had to learn about the world.

'Like I said, Lynda, don't get too involved.'

Towards the end of the school holidays Tom Meredith came to take his son home, and to try to reassure his Mother that he was coping with Suzanne's demands. When Mark had gone to bed Tom sat with Janet and Robbie at the kitchen table, and talked about his divorce. He seemed to have forgotten that Lynda was still in the room, quietly preparing some of the food for the next day.

'She, or rather her Mother, who's dictating all this,

183

says she wants to have The Gatehouse made over to her legally, not just by a reasonable mutual agreement. I'm sorry to be losing the place, but if Suzanne having The Gatehouse means I can keep Mark at Loveday with me, then that's how it will be.'

'And what about the money?' his Mother asked, looking at the son who, she knew too well, took risks.

'I've been to the bank, and they'll let me have some of the money I need. But,' he took a deep breath, 'I'm depending on Nathan Tyler to lend me the rest.'

Robbie frowned. 'The American guy who comes across for the racing?'

Tom hesitated but then claimed, 'Yes. We've become quite good friends. I think he might eventually invest enough in Loveday to allow me to make some improvements. But all I want at the moment is enough money to hold on to the place. '

Janet didn't want her son to lose hope, but felt she had to warn him.

'Be careful, Tom. I know I only met him once, but he struck me as a man to whom only one thing matters, and that's money.'

'It's what matters to most people,' Lynda chipped in as she approached the table. 'Would anyone like a tea or a coffee – or a Horlicks?' she added, teasing Janet as usual about her choice of bedtime drink.

Tom Meredith got to his feet. 'Not for me, thanks. I'm off to bed, it's that damned long drive home tomorrow.'

Lynda was shocked, and didn't stop herself from saying what she thought.

'You're not going home? I thought you were staying to have some time here with Mark. He's been looking forward to it.'

'I know, and so was I, but I've a hotel to run.'

'And you've a son who needs some time with his Dad.'

She became aware of the silence among the people sitting round the table, but all she could think about was the delight on Mark's face when he'd told her that his Dad was staying for a few days.

She went for it.

'That boy thinks he's going to go swimming and walking with you tomorrow. Are you telling me you've changed your mind and you're going to let him down?'

His voice was cold. 'I'm not telling you anything, because it's nothing to do with you. Do you make a habit of this? Interfering in something that you know nothing about?'

'I know what I see.'

'And you don't like it.'

'No.'

'Well, fortunately, it doesn't matter to me what you think.'

He turned and walked out, but when he got to his room, he stared out of the window, and realised, with some astonishment, that it did matter what that infuriating woman thought. And he was honest enough to realise there was some truth in what she'd said.

He admitted to himself that night that he was avoiding being alone with Mark, spending time talking to him. He knew that he was dreading facing his feeling of guilt that he had failed in holding his marriage together, and had thus failed his son.

The next morning he went back into the kitchen where they were all gathered, preparing breakfast, and told everyone he had changed his mind, and that he and Mark were staying a few more days. He avoided looking at Lynda while making this announcement but noticed that his Mother, after she had smiled and nodded to him, also gave a smile to her outspoken friend.

It was true that he couldn't afford to spend many days away from his business, but those days on the beach with his son formed, he realised, a precious memory which he hoped would help him keep his nerve in the months to come.

He wasn't looking forward to returning to Loveday Manor and the letters he knew would be waiting for him. The solicitors who were representing Nicki and her daughter were very skilled at what they did and, on the occasions when he'd had to meet them in their office, they'd gave him the impression that they regarded him as someone who had done too well for himself, and married far out of his league as a non-gentleman.

On the morning he was due to drive himself and his son back into this battlefield, he woke up feeling as if he hadn't slept. He managed not to wake Mark as he crept out of the room and headed for Springwater cove for a swim. He needed to be alone, to rid himself of the memories and imaginings which had so disturbed his sleep, and he was annoyed to find there was someone already there. He hesitated, but wasn't going to be denied the pleasure of an early morning swim, and started to unfasten the belt of his thick cotton beach robe.

He stopped as he realised who the swimmer was, and stood in the shelter of the rocks as Lynda walked out of the water, and towards him across the sand. He couldn't prevent himself from appreciating the loveliness of her body, but immediately remembered they hadn't spoken since her criticism of him as a father. She stood before him and waited for him to move.

'Can I have my towel, it's behind you.'

He spoke to her as if correcting an ill-mannered child. 'Please. And Good Morning to you, too!'

He handed her the towel. Embarrassed she lowered her eyes as she wrapped it around her, and tried to think of a way to make amends for her brusqueness, but all that came was, 'You're going home today, then.'

'Yes. And you are staying here, I gather. Lucky you!'

She hit back. 'And you're going back to Loveday Manor – so lucky you, as well!'

'I don't feel exactly lucky at the moment. In case you don't realise, I'm in the middle of what they call 'an acrimonious divorce.'

'Well, that's what happens if you marry the wrong person.'

'Yes. Did you do that, too?'

She looked at him, wondering how much he had been told about her. He read her mind.

'Robbie told me you were married, but don't seem to have any plans to go home. So I assume you married the wrong person, too.'

'At least I married for the right reasons,' she snapped back.

'And you think I didn't?' he challenged her, feeling

anger pushing at his mind.

She knew she shouldn't have made such a comment.

'I'd better be going.'

He stepped in front of her. 'No, just a minute. What did you mean?'

'Nothing.' She sensed his aggression, but felt she didn't deserve it. 'Forget it, it was just something somebody said.'

'What did they say?'

'Nothing!'

'Oh, no, I'm not going to let you get away with that,' he snarled, taking hold of her arm. 'What reason?'

She pushed his hand away. 'Money. She has money, hasn't she, your wife, and her family?'

'And you, you who know me so well,' he said with a smile full of sarcasm, 'you think that that was why I married her.'

'Well, you wouldn't be the first one to do that.'

She was desperately trying to think of a way out of the confrontation, out of the offence she knew she had caused.

'I know somebody who married for money,' she found herself gabbling on, 'and her marriage ended in a mess, as well.'

'And who was that?'

'My friend, Jenny. Her Mother never wanted her to marry him. And I expect your wife's Mother never wanted her to marry you either.'

'Too right she didn't,' he said bitterly. 'I wasn't good enough for her wonderful daughter who, like her bitch of a Mother, is never satisfied with just one man to take to bed!'

She saw his face darken with pain and anger, and she shuddered, pulling the damp towel closer around her body. He saw that she was shivering, and instinctively took off his beach robe. Before she realised what was happening, he put it round her and pulled her to him to warm her as a parent would a child.

They stood very still, transfixed by their intense closeness. Lynda wanted to move, but found she couldn't. He moved away for a moment, and then kissed her, a rough, hard embrace that expressed emotions that were frightening. She broke free and slapped his face.

'What the hell was that for?' she cried out, 'Revenge?'

With tears in her eyes, she threw the robe to the ground and ran back to the safety of her bedroom, where she wrapped her quilt round her as she had so many times as a child, waiting for the shivering to stop.

CHAPTER TWENTY TWO

After the October half-term holiday the Springfield Hotel was very quiet, but Robbie managed to keep the hotel open by advertising special offers of weekend breaks. He needed less staff so, apart from Lynda, there were now only a couple of local girls who came in when needed. Lynda was worried, and confided in Rose as they went for one of their regular walks along the coast. They were wrapped up warmly against the cold November wind which gusted in from the sea.

'There are only four guests booked in next week. Robbie won't need me, and I can't let him keep me on if there's no work.'

'He wouldn't do that. Don't underestimate Robbie, he's a business man. He used to run his own company in Liverpool and knows all about balancing the books. He won't keep you if the hotel can't afford you.'

'That's what I'm afraid of. I can't see him needing me much longer. And where will I go?'

'Home?'

'Oh, don't look at me like that, Rose. I can't face the thought of going back to Milfield, I really can't. I'm so happy here. I'm a different person here.'

'Are you?'

'Yes, I'm Lynda Collins again. And I'm a lot happier being Lynda Collins than I was being Mrs John Stanworth! Please don't tell me to go back. Ted didn't go back to Sheila, did he?'

'No. He stayed with me, and it was the right thing for him, and for me.' Rose patted her arm reassuringly, 'I'm sorry, love, I don't mean to push you into doing something you don't want. It's just that I thought you might want to go home for a visit at Christmas.'

Lynda, too, had been wondering about that.

'I don't know. Part of me wants to, but the idea scares me a bit. But I do know that I want to keep working here.'

'I think you may be able to. Janet's told me she's going to visit Loveday Manor in the New Year. Tom has asked her to go and spend some time with him and Mark. She hasn't seen them since the summer. They usually comes down at Mark's half-term holiday, but Tom couldn't manage it this year.'

Lynda had noticed that Tom Meredith hadn't come back to Springfield since that day on the beach, and that moment which she'd found herself thinking about every day.

Rose, unaware of the thoughts disturbing Lynda, continued, 'So I think you'll find that Robbie will be asking you if you could take over some of Janet's work for a while.'

'Oh, that would be great.'

'And he'll probably ask if you'll be able to work over Christmas. The hotel is fully booked all through December, so you'll need to let him know in advance if you're going to need any time off.'

She paused and watched Lynda carefully, 'Time to spend with your family, for example. What are you going to do about Christmas, Lynda?'

'I don't know.'

The little furry jacket that she sent for Michael had a hood with cute little ears on top, so he would look like a little bear. A few of her tears had hidden themselves in the soft fabric as she'd pictured her one year old grandson wearing it. She'd wrapped it carefully in paper with bright Father Christmas figures doing a dance across it, and had enclosed a Christmas card for the family. She'd written the 'sender' address very clearly on the back of the brown paper parcel, and had posted it at the beginning of December, allowing plenty of time for a response.

It came back a few days later. Robbie had examined the parcel carefully, and had guessed what it was. He was upset to see Lynda's face turn white as he handed it to her.

'It says 'return to sender'. The post office must have delivered it to the wrong address, love.'

'Yeah. Thanks.' She clutched the package to her breast and fled up the stairs to her room. She sat there for a while, just looking at the battered parcel, turning it over and over to see if there was any sign that it had been opened, or acknowledged. There was none. Carolyn had obviously just taken it straight to the post box and shoved it inside.

Robbie didn't mention the parcel again, but watched anxiously as Lynda came back down the stairs and walked out of the hotel into the driving rain. She walked along the cliff for a couple of miles, before going to Rose's cottage, where she burst into tears as she told her she wouldn't be going home at Christmas.

'They don't want me. I can cope with that, Rose. I can understand that. But I wanted Michael to have something from his Grandma.'

'Of course you did, and it's only right that he should. I don't know how they could do that to you. Perhaps you should ask your friend, Jean, to go and talk to them, and tell them you want to come home for Christmas. It's a special family time.'

'It should be, but it's no good with Sheila around.'

'No, I remember Ted saying how difficult she used to make it.'

'She still does. Last year was a nightmare for me, one failure after another! To be honest, when I think about it, Rose, I'm not sure I do want to go home for Christmas.'

'Well, at least find out how they all are. Give Jean a ring. And do it from here this time. Give her this number, and ask her to tell them they can arrange to phone you if they want to.'

Lynda remembered her last phone call to Jean, and hesitated, but didn't she how she could refuse.

Rose was already moving towards the kitchen. 'I'll go and make us a cup of tea, so you can have a chat with your friend in private.'

As it turned out, it wasn't a good time to call.

'I've just got back from putting flowers on Gordon and his Mother's grave. It's freezing here. What's it like where you are?'

'Not too bad. I'm phoning about Christmas, Jean.'

'Oh, are you coming home?'

'I'm not sure.'

'Well, either you are or you aren't.'

'I sent a present for Michael, but it's come back.'

'Oh.'

'I wondered if the post had messed up. Can you ask John or Carolyn if it got there?'

'No, I can't! I can't talk about you to them, because Carolyn won't have your name mentioned, and John just gets upset. And if you're not coming home there's no point, is there?'

Jean's voice became shrill.

'I can't cope with this at the moment, Lynda. I'm here on my own, and it's lonely. You've got a family, I haven't. It's them you should be phoning, not me. Don't call me again. I'm not going to act as a flaming go-between. I don't want to go round to their house causing upset. So either come home, or forget about us! I don't want any more damned phone calls from you – ever!'

And she slammed the receiver down so hard it made Lynda jump.

Rose, who had been standing in the doorway with a tray of tea and biscuits, looked at Lynda and then put the tray down in front of her.

'Not a good call.'

'No.'

Mark Meredith's grandmother didn't come home for Christmas, either. She had told him that she would, but, in the end, Nicki Heston had sent her grandson a present and a card saying she would see him some other time. For a while Mark had wondered if his Mother was also not going to come, but she arrived on Christmas Eve and they joined in the Christmas Festivities with the guests.

Tom, knowing he couldn't afford to close the

hotel at Christmas, usually allowed a few selected guests to come and spend the holiday at their favourite hotel. They were pleased to see that all the Meredith family were there, and the way Suzanne played hostess to the guests reminded him of the charm and sophistication which he had once found so attractive.

Tom also remembered how they had argued last year about the Christmas decorations, with Suzanne unwilling to accept that the hotel could not afford new ones every year. It was she who, two years ago, had chosen the festive decorations for the hotel, and she conceded now that none of the guests seemed to mind that they had seen them before.

The dining room of the hotel, with light sparkling from its two crystal chandeliers, was decorated in green and silver, with holly and ivy woven together round silver candles on the window sills and shelves. There were silver candles and bows in the centre pieces on the tables, and pale green linen set with crystal glasses.

Suzanne, graceful as a willow in her full length silver and white dress, was like a snow princess as she moved among the guests, smiling benevolently and making each of them feel special. As they enjoyed their brandy and coffee at the end of a superb Christmas dinner, she walked over to stand beside Tom and enjoy the satisfaction of having created a festive delight for the guests.

'As my Dad would say, I think that could be described as a success, don't you, Tom?'

Tom briefly imagined he saw Vic Heston, wise, courteous, and generous, standing as he had so often in that room, surveying the guests and smiling.

'Definitely.'

'Unlike our marriage,' she sighed. 'A pity, that.'

He blinked as he focused on a candle that was flickering in the centre of one of the tables. 'Yes.'

'It's a shame that this all has to go.'

'It doesn't have to, Suzi.'

'But you have to agree, that with property prices as high as they are round here, it makes sense to sell.'

'If, like your Mother, all you're interested in is money.'

'That's not fair. Mummy is just trying to do the best deal for me.'

'And what about the best deal for our son? This place is his home, does he have to lose that as well as losing his parents?'

'He's not losing us. He'll just not have us together, that's all.'

'He's upset that you're not staying for the holiday as you promised.'

'I did not promise. And he'll be fine here with you and Patrick. And as Mummy said, he could go to boarding school, if you don't have the time to look after him here.'

'I'll always find the time to look after him, unlike his Mother.'

'Oh, for god's sake, don't start that again. Why are all men such little boys, wanting a woman to stay at home all the time and make beef stews and sponge puddings for them? I was never going to be the kind of wife and Mother Janet was, you should have known that when you married me!'

'Yes, I should. And I should have known a lot of other things about you, too.'

'Like what?'

'Like your reputation with men. It was ages before I realised that your father was desperate for us to get married, because he thought I'd look after you and keep you out of trouble.' He looked at her in disgust. 'He was wrong there, wasn't he?'

She glared at him and walked away.

At Springfield Christmas was a much more colourful, family affair. The hotel was festooned in red and green, there was a huge Christmas tree in the dining room, and a collection of red-nosed reindeer and Father Christmases who surprised you round every corner. There were stockings of all colours and sizes hanging along the walls, and the whole hotel felt like a big family home.

It was packed with regular visitors who were more friends than guests, and on Christmas Day there were also some local friends who booked every year for Christmas dinner. Boxing Day was more relaxed, with just the hotel guests, who knew to expect to serve themselves from a buffet for their meals, and were also willing to help whenever needed.

Janet had a sore throat and a high temperature and Robbie sent her to bed after lunch, asking Rose to keep her supplied with warm drinks and aspirin. He was grateful that Lynda was there, and she'd never worked so hard in her life as she did that Christmas, but was glad to have little time to think about her family in Milfield.

CHAPTER TWENTY THREE

On the afternoon of New Year's Eve a large group of friends came for Robbie's annual children's party. Lynda helped to organise a game of 'pass the parcel', and after that she and Robbie joined in the game of musical chairs. It was a free-for-all, with Robbie pushing Lynda aside, and both of them laughing and shrieking louder than the children. When, at the end, she made a dash for the last empty chair she collided with a large body and, thinking it was Robbie, she pushed her bottom hard against him to force him off the chair on to the floor. She turned round giggling to find it wasn't Robbie sitting on the floor at her feet, but Tom Meredith laughing up at her.

She laughed, too. 'I was pregnant the last time I did that to a fella.'

'And who was that lucky man?' he grinned as he got to his feet.

'Nobody you'd know, and it was a long time ago. Have you seen your Mother? She's not very well.'

'Yes, I've just been up to see her and left Mark having a good old chat with her. I tried to insist she stays where she is but she's determined to come down to see the New Year in.'

'I don't blame her, it's a special moment that.'

He looked at her with approval. 'Yes, full of hope.'

Lynda's voice was wistful. 'That's what me and my friend, Kath, used to say.'

Tom Meredith saw the sadness in her eyes. 'A special friend, is she?'

'Was. Yes, a very special friend. And she'd have wanted us all to be having a good time. She'd have loved that.' She pointed to the disco which had now started up for both parents and children to dance together. 'And she wouldn't want to see anyone without a drink in their hand, so can I get you one?'

'You certainly can, I've something extra to celebrate.'

'What's that?' She checked herself. 'Oh, I'm sorry, I'd no right to ask. I've always been too nosey.'

'There are worse faults, and I don't mind your asking. I've just had a phone call from my American friend, telling me he's pretty sure he'll be able to lend me the money I need. If he does, it means I can keep Loveday Manor.'

She smiled, 'Oh, I am glad.'

'Are you?'

'Yes. For you and Mark. It means a lot to you both.'

'Yes, it does.' He looked down at her with those blue eyes which she found hard to look away from. 'You're a kind soul, aren't you, Lynda Collins?' he said softly, and she became aware of how close to her he was.

She blushed, and stepped away, saying brightly, 'I'd better get you that drink, and one for Robbie by the look of it!'

She pointed at their host who was staggering away

theatrically from the exertions of the disco he'd set up. He came towards them like a man on the verge of collapse.

'Thank God for a sit-down,' he exclaimed as he sprawled on a chair in mock exhaustion.

'We're not taking any notice,' Rose said as she followed him, 'we all know you love it.'

'No, I'm getting too old for this. Your Mother and I are retiring next year, Tom. I'll be selling this place and, if she'll let me, whisking her off to a villa in Saint Tropez.'

'Oh, don't say that,' Lynda protested, 'I've only just got here.'

'No, don't worry, I've got it all planned, you and Rose will stay on here, I'm selling you along with the hotel as fixtures and fittings.'

Rose laughed. 'You won't get much for me.'

'I will,' he replied. 'With your skills as a belly dancer – I think you'll be worth a fortune. Trust me, girls, I'll make sure you're all O.K.'

Tom had been watching him carefully.

'You're serious, aren't you, Robbie?'

With an apologetic smile, he said, 'Yes. I wasn't going to say anything till later, but your Mother's already guessed. You know what she's like, you can't keep anything from her. The thing is, I've met somebody. An old flame, actually, from way back. Connor and I were at school together. His parents took him off to Australia but he came back a few months ago, and we met up.'

'And?' Tom asked.

Robbie gave a gentle smile.

'You never get over your first love, do you?'

Rose was anxious. 'And now he's back, and you're

leaving Springfield?'

'Yes. I'm sorry, Rose, I'd have told you sooner, but I didn't want to spoil your Christmas. And I meant what I said, I'll make sure you can stay on if you want to.'

'Don't worry about me, Robbie, love, I've got my cottage and plenty to do. But are you serious about Janet going with you?'

'I am, but at the moment she's saying she won't leave St Benedict – I always said she fancied him! She'll be able to stay in Springfield cottage, if she decides that's what she wants. I'll make that part of the deal when I sell.'

Tom had other ideas. 'Perhaps I'll be able to persuade her to move into Loveday at last. When do you think you'll sell?'

'Around Easter time, there's already someone interested in buying it. But let's not think about it now. This is New Year's Eve, and probably our last one here, so let's make the most of it. Tom, are you up for a bit of cooking tonight?'

He turned to explain to Lynda, 'Tom always cooked us his special roast beef on New Year's Eve when he lived here.'

Tom smiled at Robbie.

'Of course, I am. I'll get straight in the kitchen now. But I'll need some help.' He looked at Lynda. 'How about it? Do you think you can cope with working with me?'

'If I can work with a fruit and nutcase like Robbie, I can cope with you,' she joked, trying to look confident, but wondering what it would be like to be in a kitchen with Tom Meredith.

'Just do as you're told, and you'll be fine,' Robbie

laughed.

'Oh, I've never been any good at that.'

'Neither has Tom, so you should make an interesting combination,' commented Robbie with a mischievous smile. 'You'll have to put up with the women in his life, Ella Fitzgerald, Peggy Lee, and my beloved Dusty Springfield of course.'

Tom gave a sideways smile, 'As you can tell, I got all my musical education from Robbie.'

'And your Mother,' Robbie added. 'It will be all Sinatra and Nat King Cole for her.'

Lynda blinked back a tear, 'My Mum loved those as well, and Doris Day. I always used to have to sing 'Que Sera' for her in the pub.'

Tom looked at her with interest, 'Oh, you can sing, can you?'

'She's brilliant!' Robbie enthused. 'Leave the kitchen door open so we can hear you both belting out the numbers while you cook.'

'You might hear a bit of swearing as well, when the Yorkshire puddings won't rise,' Lynda warned him.

'Who says we're having Yorkshire Pudding?' Tom protested.

'You can't have roast beef without Yorkshires, can you Robbie?'

'Oh, leave me out of this. You two will have to sort things out between you. Off you go, and good luck!'

Lynda tried not to look embarrassed at being alone in the kitchen with Tom Meredith. She'd felt her heart starting to beat faster as he'd walked in, and she told herself she was being silly, letting herself get nervous.

'What do you want me to do?' she asked. 'You cook and I'll skivvy, if you like.'

'Oh, no, we'll share the dirty work, and we'll share the cooking. Then, if it all goes wrong . . .'

She finished the sentence for him, 'I'll share the blame.'

'That's about the size of it.' He walked towards the CD player in the corner of the kitchen. 'Now, shall we start with Ella?'

'O.K. by me.'

She'd never enjoyed herself so much in a kitchen, singing Cole Porter songs softly at first, and then louder as Tom's velvety baritone gave her a confident accompaniment. She even found herself dancing round the kitchen to 'Anything Goes.'

They worked hard preparing vegetables and Tom showed her how he set the beef on a bed of onions, celery and carrot with fresh sage leaves and garlic. When it was in the oven he came to stand beside her and watch as she made the batter for the Yorkshire puddings.

'Is that the way your Mother made it?'

'No. My Mother wasn't the best cook, I learned most of what I know from Freda who owned the café I worked in.'

'Are they holding the job open for you till you get back?'

'I don't know.'

'What? If they're keeping the job for you, or if you're going back?'

She stirred the pudding batter slowly, avoiding looking at him.

'Both.'

'What does your husband say about it?'

'Nothing. But then John never had much to say about anything, except when I didn't do what he wanted.'

'Does he love you?' He saw how startled she was by this very intimate question, and placed his hand gently on her arm. 'Sorry, I've no right to ask personal questions like that, but I don't like to see anyone hurting.'

Lynda took a deep breath. 'No. No, I don't think he does love me.' Her eyes filled with shame and sorrow, and she turned her head away. He gently brushed aside a lock of her hair.

'It's just one of those things, choosing the wrong partner. We're a couple of life's 'Unfortunates' aren't we? Your husband doesn't love you, and my wife doesn't love me. What should we do about it, eh?'

She gave a little laugh. 'You're getting a divorce, or had you forgotten?'

He gave her one of those sideways tilting smiles of his which she'd found caused her a flutter of unwanted excitement.

'Oh, yes, I knew there was something that was making my bank manager scowl at me. They should warn you when you get married, to start saving for the divorce. Have you saved up for yours?'

'No. I got married for good, so I didn't think I needed to.'

He was watching her carefully, just like his Mother, with those eyes that read secrets. She felt a compulsion to tell the truth to this man.

'I did save up, though. What my Grandma called my 'mad money'. She thought every woman should have a bit stashed away on the quiet, in case she needed to get away.'

'And that's the money you used to get here?'

'Yes.'

'And, if it comes to it, will you have enough to pay for a divorce?'

'I won't need to. He'll divorce me, his Mother will make sure of that. She's probably found him a solicitor already!'

He laughed, 'Like Suzanne's Mother. She couldn't wait for the marriage to end, she never thought I was good enough for her daughter. And she was probably right.'

'Oh, no! I don't believe that for a minute,' Lynda blurted out.

He stared at her intently. 'Thank you, Lynda. But you don't know me well enough to judge. I hope one day you will, though, and that you'll still want to defend me.'

She looked up at this man who seemed to her to have all kinds of strength, and smiled at the idea of his needing her to defend him. Then she saw the self-doubt in his eyes, and into her mind flickered the image of her arms round him and his head on her shoulder.

They both heard the music end, and paused to listen as Ella Fitzgerald began the next song. It was 'Just One Of Those Things.' They laughed and began to sing and move to the music as they carried on with the cooking.

They were banned from the kitchen after the meal, and were ordered to sit on a sofa by the window to look out at the moonlight on the sea, and the stars in the clear night sky. Two large glasses of brandy were placed in front of them, and they raised them in a silent salutation to each other before leaning back against the cushions to sip their drink and enjoy its aromatic warmth.

After a while Tom said softly, 'Like you said, a very special time, New Year's Eve.'

'Yeah. Kath and I always used to step outside together and make a wish under the stars.'

'Was your wish granted this year?'

'No. A big disappointment. I was full of hope that my baby grandson would make everything right between me and my daughter. But it all went wrong. And I ended up walking out.'

'And coming here.'

'Yeah.'

'Do you want to step out under the stars and make a wish tonight?'

'No, I don't think so. I'm a bit fed up with being disappointed.' She sipped her brandy and then sat up straight, tilting her chin. 'I'm sorry, I don't usually indulge in self-pity. Being negative doesn't do anybody any good, does it?'

'No. But sometimes it just takes over, especially when things don't turn out the way you expect.'

'What about you, did you get what you wished for this year?'

He laughed ruefully. 'I don't think so. I certainly didn't wish for an acrimonious divorce.'

'No. Look at the New Year as a fresh start, that's what Kath used to tell me. It's a time to start again and ask forgiveness for your mistakes.'

'Sounds good. Do you think I could ask your forgiveness for my mistake?'

Lynda wondered what he meant.

'That kiss,' he explained. 'I'd no right. Can you

forgive me?'

'Yes,' she whispered, and hoped that he would assume it was the brandy that was making her cheeks glow. She also hoped he wouldn't guess how many times she had thought about that kiss, and all the crazy emotions it had fired within her.

She felt him watching her and was relieved when everyone came into the room to get ready for the midnight toast. Janet had insisted on being escorted downstairs and her son moved swiftly to her side. He made sure she was comfortable in an armchair in the centre of the group which gathered together to have Robbie fill their glasses with champagne.

When the clock struck midnight they toasted the New Year and then linked arms to sing 'Auld Lang Syne'. Lynda found she had linked arms with Rose on one side and Tom Meredith on the other, but he moved away when everyone began to exchange kisses and wish each other 'Happy New Year'. Rose saw her watching him go and stepped forward to give her a kiss.

'Happy New Year, Lynda. And a happy new life. Wherever you choose to live it.'

'Thank you.' Her eyes filled with tears, 'I wish I knew where that will be.'

'You will, one day.'

Rose gave her another hug and then went to wish Janet 'Happy New Year' and to sit beside her to watch the dancing. They both saw what happened a little while later, when Lynda was standing alone in the shadow of the Christmas Tree.

Tom Meredith walked slowly towards her and gently kissed her on the cheek. She looked up at him and he took her hand and kissed it. Then his eyes sought hers, and asked permission before he took her in his arms.

They kissed just once more but with a warmth which drew them closer and closer. After a while he moved away, but they looked at each other, and there was an understanding that this was a moment in their lives that they would never forget.

CHAPTER TWENTY FOUR

In February 1986 Janet Meredith let her God know that she was ready to stop work and be reunited with her beloved husband. She had a similar conversation with Rose and Lynda who had nursed her through the flu which had eventually developed into pneumonia. Her son and grandson were allowed to come and visit, and Christine to book her flight, only when Janet judged it was the right time for them to know she was about to leave them.

The service at the church of St Benedict was simple and short, and overcrowded, and the sun came out as this beautiful soul was laid to rest in the churchyard which, over the years, had spread itself up the hillside, and so offered a view of the beautiful coastline she had loved since childhood. As she had instructed, there was a party at the Springfield Hotel afterwards, where everyone had the chance to celebrate and give thanks for this quiet, hard-working woman who had been such a treasured part of so many lives.

Tom Meredith made sure he had a chat with everyone, and many a laugh. He was surrounded by people who knew and loved him and his Mother, and he had never felt so lonely in his life. Robbie, Lynda and Rose made sure everyone had plenty to eat and drink, and listened to the memories, but they also anxiously watched Tom Meredith and his son.

It was Lynda who saw Mark walk quietly out of the room and down the path to the beach. She went and got his coat and her own, and told Rose she was going to be with him. She found him huddled in the shelter of the rocks which surrounded his favourite rock pool, and wrapped his coat round him as she sat down beside him.

She didn't say anything, just hugged him close and they both stared at the rock pool and the sea shore. He didn't move; he sat taut and straight for quite a while, until, like melting snow, he slid down and, putting his arms round her, set free his tears of grief and pain, and loneliness.

The next day Tom Meredith had a long conversation with Robbie, and then surprised Lynda by asking her to have a coffee with him in the little conservatory. She'd spent so much time talking to Janet about her son during the weeks of her illness, and Tom had been so appreciative of the care she and Rose had given his Mother, that Lynda found she felt comfortable in his company. She thought how exhausted he looked now, sitting in his Mother's favourite chair, and looking out at the sea as if searching for some answers to the dilemmas in his life.

He watched Lynda sipping her coffee, and thought how lovely she looked in the pale February sunshine which had stayed with them since his Mother's funeral. The last few days had drained him of the energy required for small-talk, so he found himself asking straight away the question he'd meant to approach gently.

'Have you made any decisions about what you'll do when Robbie sells Springfield?'

It was not the conversation she had expected, but it was a question which she'd been considering for quite a while. She tried to make it sound just 'a matter of fact' as she answered him.

'Robbie says he'll ask the new owners to keep me on, but there's no guarantee that they'll want me. And I'm not sure I'll want to be here without Robbie and your Mum. Rose feels the same.'

His voice became hesitant. 'Will you go home?'

The vehemence of her reply shocked her as well as Tom. 'No. I won't go where I'm not wanted, so I won't be going back to Milfield, ever.'

She found her hand had begun to shake, and she quickly put down her cup. 'Bloody hell, it's a shock when you say it out loud like that.'

He saw panic in her eyes, and reached across to take hold of her hand before asking gently, 'Will you come home with me and Mark?'

'What?'

'I'm sorry, Lynda, to have to present you with this so soon, but I'm worried about Mark. He's taken it very hard, losing his Gran. She was a big source of security for him, and when he came here she gave him that mothering and feeling of home that he craved. He's going to feel the loss of that so much, especially as his Mother won't be there waiting for him when we go back to Loveday.'

Lynda couldn't stop herself. 'She knows he's lost his Gran, and she's not coming home to comfort him! What kind of a Mother is she?'

There was anger in his eyes as he thought of Suzanne, but he spoke calmly.

'I've often asked myself the same question. But she won't be there, and I've no idea when she'll return from France, which is why I'm asking you to come back to Loveday with us. Mark seems so fond of you. He talks to you, and he'll need someone to talk to while he comes to terms with all he has lost. You see, it's not just his Gran.'

She was quick to understand. 'No, it's Springfield, too, a big part of his childhood. It's going to be a shock to realise that this place won't be here for him any longer. It's a big loss for you, too.'

'Yes. Chrissie and I went for a walk this morning, up to the farm and then all round the village and back here, to say goodbye, and to remember.'

'That's the important bit, the remembering. It'll always be a part of you.'

'Yes, and we'll always be grateful for the life we had here.'

Lynda turned away so he couldn't see the tears that threatened as she whispered, 'So will I.'

He watched her for a moment, and then asked again, 'Will you come to Loveday with us?'

She knew it was what she wanted, but tried to think practically.

'I'd love to look after Mark, but he's at school. What would I do the rest of the time?'

He laughed, 'There's plenty of work at Loveday, believe me! I'm offering you a full-time job, I can't pay much more than Robbie, but . .'

She was embarrassed to talk about this in terms of money, and said quickly, 'That's all right. When would you want me to come?'

'Tomorrow. I'd like you to come back with us, so Mark won't notice his Mother's absence too much.'

'I can't leave tomorrow, I can't let Robbie down.'

He became Tom Meredith the business man again now, organised, in control.

'I've talked to Robbie. It turns out his buyer is wanting to complete the deal faster than he expected, so it's a good solution for Robbie, if you have a job to go to.'

'What about Rose?'

'You can invite her to come to Loveday with us, if that will make you feel better.' The tilting smile she hadn't seen for so long accompanied his next remark. 'If you'd feel happier with a chaperone.'

Lynda was annoyed to find herself blushing, and she quickly stood up and collected their cups.

'I need to ask her what she wants to do. I don't want to leave her here alone so soon after losing her best friend.'

'No. Go and see her now, and talk it over. And tell her she'd be very welcome to come to Loveday.'

Lynda was glad of the walk to Rose's cottage, she needed time to think. She saw the tower of Saint Benedict's church in the distance and knew she had to visit Janet's church for one last time. It was hard to walk into that cold empty space and remember saying goodbye to a remarkable woman she had not known for long, but whom she had learned to trust. She sat quietly on the same pew she had chosen on her first visit, and said a little prayer, asking God to look after

Janet Meredith. Then she stayed for a few more minutes, and listened.

She found that Rose was expecting her and already had the kettle on.

'Robbie phoned me and told me what he and Tom had agreed. You know what he's like, he can't keep anything to himself, but he wanted me to have time to think before I spoke to you.'

'And what do you think? Will you come to Loveday Manor with us?'

Rose slowly put down the teapot, and shook her head.

'No love. When we knew we were losing Janet, I started to give a lot of thought to how I would feel, living here without her close by. I love Cornwall, and I love my little cottage. And, more important, I feel I belong here. I've made good friends in the village, and I could be useful here, Betty is always glad of a bit of help in the café in the tourist season.

She picked up her cup of tea and smiled at Lynda.

'What I'm saying is, I'm too old to move again now, and this is home. But I will come and visit you at Loveday when you're settled.'

'You think I should go, then?'

'That's for you to decide, but Janet said you loved the place.'

'I do. It felt really special to me. And I think Tom is right, it will be good for Mark to have me there.'

'You've grown fond of him, haven't you?'

'Yes, he's a lovely lad.'

'Janet was really glad that you and he got on so well. She'd suggested to Tom that he should ask you to go to Loveday.'

Lynda tried to keep the disappointment out of her voice. 'Oh. It wasn't his idea, then?'

'No. He's been too distracted by this divorce to think about anything. Janet was worried about him having to borrow so much money, but she was more worried about the effect the divorce was having on Mark. He needs mothering, and Janet thought you were the right person to give him that.'

'Crikey. She had it all thought through, didn't she, Janet.'

A tear came with Rose's smile. 'Always.'

Lynda put her arm round this tender-hearted little woman who seemed to have grown older in the last few weeks. 'You're going to miss her so much.'

'Yes.'

'I feel awful going off and leaving you so soon after the funeral.'

Rose looked at her steadily.

'You can't always choose the time to do something. It's right for you to go to Loveday. But before you do, I have to tell you something else Janet said. It was about you and Tom.'

Lynda sat back apprehensively. 'What do you mean, me and Tom?'

'She saw him kiss you on New Year's Eve. We both did.'

Lynda's cheeks matched the colour of the most exuberant of the roses on the chintz covers of the sofa.

'Janet said that she was going to warn Tom that he must not get involved with you until this divorce is through. If Nicki Heston can find any grounds for accusing Tom of infidelity, she'll have the weapon she needs to force him to sell Loveday Manor. So do you see that there must be nothing going on between you and Tom Meredith?'

'There is nothing going on between us. And I'm married, Rose. I'm still married to John. Look, I'm still wearing his ring.'

'You don't feel married to him, though, do you?'

Lynda had always been honest with Rose and wasn't going to change that now. 'No. No, I don't. Not since I came here. I've gradually come to feel free, free of everything and everyone. Being here has given me back my life, who I am.'

'You're Lynda Collins again.'

'Yes. The young Lynda who laughed out loud, and sang at the top of her voice, and had fun. They were stopping all that, and taking away all my confidence, and I can't forget that.'

She was almost in tears as she remembered how she had felt, and she looked down at her hands and found she was twisting her wedding ring round and round.

She took a deep breath and slowly slid the ring off her finger. For a moment she shivered, feeling naked without it. She looked at Rose who was watching her, wide-eyed, and then carefully put the ring in her bag. There was a pause as they stared at each other, both overwhelmed for a moment by the significance of what she had done.

Rose's eyes met hers steadily as she confirmed Lynda's future. 'And now you're going to Loveday Manor.'

'Yes. I don't know how it will work out, but I know I want to live there, at least for a while.'

'And Tom Meredith?'

Lynda held up her left hand. 'Like I said, in spite

of this, I'm still married. And that marriage has damaged me, a lot. I feel I don't want to get involved with anyone ever again. So don't worry, I won't be giving Suzanne and her Mother any help with this divorce.'

It was still the half-term holiday when they arrived back at Loveday Manor, so Mark was able to spend time with his Dad, and when Tom had to work Lynda made sure she was, by chance, in need of some help or companionship.

Mark insisted that, as she was going to live there now, he should show her all around Loveday Manor. He took her into every part of the hotel, even up into the attics where they delved into musty old trunks full of discarded ornaments and curiosities.

Lynda peered under the dust sheets and discovered pieces of Edwardian furniture which Suzanne and her mother had banished to make way for the French antiques Nicki had brought over from her parents' Normandy chateau.

They explored the grounds and the long neglected old kitchen garden and orchard, and went for walks by the river which wound its way along the wilder more wooded part of the garden and the meadows beyond.

They spent a whole afternoon in the coach-house and stables which still seemed to have the sweet scent of horses and hay, even though it was a few years since horses had been kept there. Mark pointed to one of the stables which had a new door. 'My Grandad used to keep his horse in that stable, and my pony used to be in the one next to it.'

'You had your own pony? You lucky boy.'

'Grandad bought it for me, but when he died, Nicki decided we couldn't keep his horse, and it was best if my pony went as well.'

'Oh. Well, at least you had some good times, riding with your Grandad. I was desperate to have a pony when I was your age. I kept entering all these competitions in my comic and the Sunday newspaper, to try to win one.'

'But you didn't?'

'No. And I stopped trying after my Dad pointed out that there was nowhere to keep a pony in our pub.'

'Did you not have a field close by?'

'We didn't even have a garden, never mind a field.'

'Is that why you like it so much here?'

'I suppose it's part of the reason. I also like the potential the place has?'

'What do you mean?'

'There's such a lot you could do with all this garden, and this courtyard with the coach-house and stables.'

'That's what Dad used to say. He used to get so excited about it, and so did Grandad, but it was all going to cost a lot of money. And then Grandad died. And now, everything's going to change I think, with the divorce.'

'I suppose it is. What a shame.'

'I don't mind, but Dad does. He won't give up, though, he says you've got to hang on to your dreams.'

'He's quite right. And the dream I'm hanging on to at the moment is of a nice cup of tea, and a big slice of that walnut cake I made this morning.'

Mark's eyes twinkled. 'Oh, I think that dream is achievable.'

'Do you indeed? Well, let's go back and see if you're right.'

'Race you!' he shouted.

CHAPTER TWENTY FIVE

Lynda talked enthusiastically about the stables that evening as she had her supper in the kitchen with Tom and Patrick.

'The coach-house is huge, big enough for at least three coaches. This must have been a very grand estate at one time.'

Tom enjoyed the chance to talk about his beloved Loveday.

'It was. This house used to be a huge mansion, but parts of it were pulled down when the owners found they couldn't afford to maintain it, and it kept being altered according to the fashion of the time. That's why it's such a crazy combination of styles. Suzanne's Mother thought it was rubbish compared to the Marcellin Chateau in Normandy.'

'I love its quirkiness, and all the different bits of history. You could make that a feature, that all the rooms are different.'

Tom grimaced, 'I'm certainly going to have to do something with at least one of the rooms before the Tylers get here.'

Lynda heard the anxiety in his voice. 'Who are the Tylers?'

'Tom's American friends,' explained Patrick.

'And my only source of private finance. I need to persuade Nathan that he can be sure Loveday is worth investing in, and to sign the cheque for the rest of the money he said he might lend me.'

'Of course it's worth investing in, it's wonderful. Anyone would love to come and stay here.'

Tom, looking perplexed, said, 'Helen Tyler wasn't too impressed when she came with her husband last year.'

'What didn't she like?' Lynda wanted to know.

'Their bedroom mainly.'

'Which one did you put them in?'

'The one with the four-poster.'

'Oh, well, no wonder she wasn't happy.' Lynda turned to Patrick for support. 'What do you think of that room? Don't you think it's creepy?'

'Depends who's in bed with you,' joked Patrick.

Tom was on the defensive now.

'Most Americans love that sort of thing. If you look in the brochures for high-class hotels in America, you pay a premium for anything with old oak furniture and a four-poster bed. I once stayed in one in Savannah that had all the rooms like that, and they were charging a fortune.'

Lynda had her question ready. 'Did you enjoy being in the room?'

'I wasn't in it much, I was working for the owners of a hotel chain and had a lot of meetings to go to.'

'But did you go back to your room to relax whenever you had a chance?'

Tom was quiet for a moment, and then repeated.

'I didn't have the time.'

Lynda was in one of her persistent moods.

'But did you long to go back there when you were stuck in a meeting?'

'No,' he admitted reluctantly.

Lynda sat back in her chair, triumphant.

'There you are then. And you're a bloke, who should like all that wood and other manly stuff. You need to give the Tylers a room where his wife - what's her name?'

'Helen.'

'Where Helen feels she's somewhere special, but where she also feels she can make herself at home.'

'My, my!' laughed Patrick. 'This new member of the team sure has plenty of opinions!'

'Doesn't she just,' Tom agreed, half-amused.

Lynda, who had seen an opportunity, became very animated. 'Which room are you putting them in this time?'

'I've no idea.' Tom shook his head despondently. 'I'm afraid Tyler is going to tell me they all want re-furbishing.'

'Well, let's make a start, so he can see you have plans,' urged Lynda. 'Let's re-furbish one of the bedrooms in a way that will impress his wife. He does listen to his wife, doesn't he?'

'Not that I'm aware of.'

'Do they seem happily married?'

Tom hesitated. 'I think so.'

'Well, then, she'll be a big influence.'

Patrick gave one of this long slow grins, 'Lynda could be right, you know, Tom.'

Lynda looked at Tom Meredith with the eagerness of a child.

'Will you let me have a go, will you let me decorate a room for them? I'm pretty good at decorating. And we could get new curtains and a luxurious bedspread. That sort of thing can make all the difference.'

'That will all cost money, and to be quite frank, Lynda, I haven't got any to spare at the moment.'

'I'll pay for it,' she offered impulsively.

He was embarrassed now. 'Don't be ridiculous!'

'Sounds like a good offer to me, boss,' drawled Patrick.

Tom glared at him. 'No.'

Lynda knew she was risking making Tom angry with her, but instinctively she knew this was important. 'Please, Tom. I want to do this.' She paused, and then added quietly, 'I need to do this.'

He was startled at the pleading he saw in her eyes. He shook his head, got up and took a large bunch of keys from a hook in the corner cupboard. He went towards the door, but then turned to look at this woman who was glowing with longing and excitement.

'All right. You can have two hundred pounds. It's not a lot, but see what you can do with it.'

'Can I choose any room I want?'

He sighed, but said, 'Yes, I suppose so. And now I'm going to lock up.'

He marched quickly out of the room, closing the door behind him a little more forcibly than usual, so only Patrick saw Lynda dancing round the kitchen.

The room Lynda chose was one of the bedrooms at the front of the hotel, with a view across the garden to the silver reflections from the river. When she looked round the room carefully, she could see why Tom was worried about the hotel looking badly in need of re-furbishing and re-decorating.

The wall-paper was very old, with a pallid gold pattern of ornate lozenges which sought to imitate coats of arms. And above the bay window, which had obviously been letting in the rain, was a large patch which was now brown and grey.

The heavy damask curtains had faded in the sunlight which filled the room for most of the afternoon, and the carpet had a collection of stains which were never going to leave it. The room had a good en-suite bathroom with a bath and shower but it was looking a little grubby and dull.

Lynda spent a morning assessing and measuring the room, and taking down the curtains. She knew that Patrick was going into Guildford to pick up some guests in the afternoon, so she arranged to have a lift with him, and loaded the curtains into the boot. He quizzed her as they drove along.

'So, little Miss Whirlwind what are you up to with that room of yours?'

'I'm taking the curtains to be dyed and I'm going to re-decorate it with a plainer paper that I can paint over in the shade of pale gold I want. I'm going to make the room brighter but softer, and more welcoming.'

'Sounds good. If you need any help, you can ask me.'

'Thank you. Actually there's a couple of things that I need doing fairly soon.'

He groaned. 'I knew I shouldn't have made that offer.'

'The first thing is the roof above the bay window, it's leaking so I can't start re-decorating till it gets fixed.'

'That makes sense. I'll sort it, or get a man who can.'

'And I need that dressing table taking out, and a little sofa and a couple of tables I found in the attic bringing down.'

'Hey, just a minute, that sounds like heavy lifting.'

'You can get that young lad who does the garden to help you, he's always looking for extra work.'

He gave her a slightly sceptical look. 'You've got it all worked out, haven't you? I hope you've got the costs worked out as well.'

'I've a fair idea, and I'm going to see what negotiating I can do with shops in Guildford.'

'I may be able to help you there. I've met a girl called Amy, who's just set up her own little shop, and she seems pretty switched on about suppliers. I'll take you there and introduce you. She's very smart.'

'And is she pretty?'

'Of course.'

'I'd better warn her about you, then.'

'No. The deal is you tell her what a great guy I am, give her a list of all my good points.'

'That'll be a short one.'

When they arrived in the town, Patrick helped Lynda carry the curtains round to a dry-cleaners which would dye them for her. Then he led her up the steep, cobbled main street and along the little side-street where Amy Ford had opened her gift shop. The shop front consisted of a white-painted Georgian window, and a door decorated with a large white wicker heart shape with yellow ribbons woven through it. There was an old fashioned doorbell which sang out merrily as Lynda and Patrick entered the shop.

Amy Ford was a slim young woman in her early twenties, with short dark curly hair and hazel eyes which didn't miss a thing. She was dressed in tight jeans and a white sweater with a scattering of different shades of yellow which made it look as if it had collected flashes of sunlight.

Lynda could see why Patrick was keen on her, and wasn't surprised when, after he'd introduced her, he took the opportunity to arrange to go out with Amy. Then he had to hurry away to pick up the hotel guests.

Lynda and Amy exchanged a knowing look as he closed the door, looking very pleased with himself.

'He's gone away happy,' Lynda commented.

Amy smiled. 'Yes. He fancies himself a bit, but I can cope with that.'

Lynda's early impression of Amy was that she seemed the kind of girl who could cope with most things.

'I hope you don't mind him bringing me here to ask your advice.'

'Not at all. Have a good look round the shop while I make us a cup of coffee.'

Lynda was impressed with the way the shop had been set out with shelves and little alcoves with mirrors displaying the more costly items. She loved the range of goods on display, from children's wooden toys to baskets lined with frills of pretty fabrics.

'You've got something for everybody here,' she commented as she settled down on one of the two dainty white wrought iron chairs by a small round table positioned next to the counter.

Amy, placing two tall glass cups of milky coffee on the table, immediately asked, 'Have I got anything for you?' She laughed as she saw Lynda was taken aback.

'Sorry. I'm always looking for a sale. But I'm a bit too direct sometimes.'

Lynda grinned. 'That's what people say about me. I think we're going to get on. And don't worry, I won't leave until I've bought something.'

She found several pretty baskets and trays and, for the bathroom which she was painting and re-designing, she ordered a small white-painted cupboard with a set of dainty shelves and also a flower edged adjustable mirror to stand on the bathroom window-sill. She paid for her purchases and arranged with Amy that she would ask Patrick to drive into town and collect everything, when she was ready to add these finishing touches to the bedroom and bathroom.

She and Amy Ford took an immediate liking to each other, and they chatted for over an hour, quickly trusting each other with short versions of their life-stories. Lynda admired Amy for resisting her parents' attempts to persuade her to get the kind of 'steady job' they had done all their lives. To stop them worrying, she had made sure she'd passed her A-levels, and had done some accountancy and secretarial training but, when a great-aunt had left her a small bequest, there was no stopping her setting up her own business.

'I told them,' she recounted to Lynda. 'This is the 1980s. There are loads of women who are determined to have a career, and earn big money. Why should men have it all? I kept reading about women having a bright idea and setting up their own company, and I thought, that's what I want.'

'Oh, I envy you,' Lynda said. 'It would be absolutely fantastic to have your own business, be your own boss. I had that at the café to a certain extent, I could run it as I liked, and I made a success out of it. But to have your own business, that would be a dream. I really fancy that, wearing smart suits and driving a flash car. I'd have to learn to drive first, of course,' she laughed.

'You could do it. You'll find something that's right for you. And what you're doing now is good training, finding the right suppliers and negotiating the right price.'

Lynda waved the book she'd been filling with notes while talking to Amy. 'I'll have you to thank if I manage to do that. You've given me loads of useful contacts here. I just hope I can bring it all in on budget.'

'Just remember they need to sell stuff, and don't let them bully you. Only offer them what you can afford. And flutter your eyelashes a bit with the fellas, it always helps!'

Lynda felt exhilarated all the way home on the bus, but when she sat in her room that evening and went through her list of prices, she lost that heady excitement and had to do some serious calculations.

It was obvious that two hundred pounds wasn't going to cover what she needed, not with a new carpet to buy. She had to have the new carpet, otherwise the room would never look anything other than shabby. Tom Meredith had been very strongly against the idea of her using her own money to help pay for the re-vamp of the room, but she couldn't see any alternative.

She would do it. This was going to be her creation, and a big achievement if she could get it right. She decided she'd avoid letting Tom know everything she was doing, and would just not tell him that she was spending her own money.

He came into the bedroom the next morning and smiled when he saw her half way up a pair of steps, her hair scrunched up on the top of her head, and sweating as she scraped away the wallpaper. She was wearing an ancient pair of cotton trousers and an old shirt she had persuaded Patrick to give her.

'Not afraid of getting your hands dirty, are you?' he commented, thinking to himself that Suzanne would never have undertaken work like this.

Startled, she turned round and waved the scraper at him.

'You're not supposed to be in here.'

'Sorry! Were you serious this morning when you said you don't want me to see the room till it's finished?'

'Yes. I thought you'd promised!'

She could hear that she sounded a little panic-stricken, but she knew that if he saw what she was doing he would realise it was costing a lot more than the money he had allocated.

'Please. I want this to be my project, to do it my way. And I don't want you anywhere near it till I've finished.'

He raised his arms in a gesture of compliance. 'O.K. I'll keep away till you're ready to show it to me.'

'Promise?'

'Promise. But can I just ask you one thing? What have you done with the dressing table that was in the window?'

'Patrick and Charlie took it out to the stables, we didn't know where else to put it.'

'Don't you think Helen Tyler will want a dressing table?'

'Not one that takes up all that lovely space in the bay window. And anyway, what woman wants sunshine showing up all the lines on her face first thing in the morning?'

'I never thought of that. It's just always been the traditional place for a dressing table. Where will she put on her make-up and stuff?'

'In the bathroom. The en-suite is a big room, with a lovely window, and Patrick is going to put a new light in there. Don't worry, it will be fine.'

'I'm not worried. I trust you, Lynda Collins. And I look forward to seeing the transformation.' He blew her a kiss as he closed the door.

She started scraping at the paper again, but then paused and touched her cheek, and felt it glowing. She knew it was ridiculous, but she couldn't deny that she felt a thrill whenever Tom Meredith said her name. And he had blown her a kiss.

CHAPTER TWENTY SIX

Lynda put the final touches to the bedroom on the Tuesday morning before the Tylers were due to arrive on the Wednesday for their Easter holiday. She was excited, but also nervous, especially as Tom had had a phone call very late the previous evening to say that his wife and mother-in-law were arriving that morning. She knew that they would pass judgement on her creation, and she suspected that it wouldn't be very favourable.

Tom had cursed when he got the phone call, he didn't want Nicki and Suzanne there when he needed to concentrate on persuading Nathan Tyler about the hotel's potential. First thing that morning he asked Bridget, who had been on the staff for a while and was well-acquainted with the requirements of these two demanding women, to take some supplies over to The Gatehouse and make sure all the rooms were ready to receive their occasional occupants.

Mark, of course, was delighted when he was told the news at breakfast that morning. 'Fantastic! Will they be staying for a while?'

'Yes, apparently, they're going to spend most of your Easter holiday with you, though I gather they have people to see in London as well.' He looked at Patrick. 'A late change of plan, apparently.'

Patrick raised his eyebrows, 'I wonder what caused that.'

'Who knows?' Tom said resignedly.

Lynda could see that their arrival was an unwanted distraction for Tom, and wanted to help. 'Had I better go and give The Gatehouse a bit of a clean?' she asked.

'No, I've already asked Bridget to do that. And you have more important things to do, like showing us this room you've transformed for the Tylers.'

Lynda was pleased to see the sun come out as they went upstairs, she knew it would enhance the effect she had tried to create of a room always filled with warmth and sunlight. She had painted the walls the palest of gold, and on them she had arranged a few delicate prints of different species of pink and cream roses and a gold framed mirror.

Earlier that morning she had placed a bowl of pink and cream roses on the small, oval rosewood table which she had rescued from the attic. She had set the table in the centre of the bay window, together with a small sofa she'd also rescued from the attic. There was a gold satin trim along the scalloped edges of the cream blinds she'd hung in the windows. They were partly drawn up and the heavy gold damask curtains draped at each side of the window gleamed in the sunlight.

'Wow,' breathed Patrick as they walked into the room. He picked Lynda up and swung her round. 'You did it, girl. You sure did it! What do you think, boss?'

Tom looked amazed. 'It's a miracle. You've really transformed this room.' He kissed her on the cheek. 'Thank you.'

Mark shouted, 'Fantastic!' and then, remembering how important this was, asked, 'Do you think Mrs Tyler will like it?'

'What's not to like?' Patrick reassured him.

They watched Tom walking round the room and the en-suite, taking in the details. He came back to the centre of the room, and stood for a moment, his eyes fixed on the new, deep pink carpet. He looked up at Lynda and she was disappointed to see that anxiety bordering on anger had replaced the look of pleasure on his face.

'You didn't achieve this with the two hundred pounds I gave you. The curtains alone must have cost a fortune.'

'They're the old ones, I had them dyed. And that sofa isn't new, I found it in the attic and re-covered it, and made the cushions.'

Tom looked bemused. 'You've re-covered it? And made cushions? I didn't know you had so many skills.'

'There's a lot you don't know about me. My Grandma had the same settee for years, she could never afford a new one. A friend of hers showed her how to re-upholster it, and I used to help her.'

Patrick was worried that Lynda wasn't getting the reaction from Tom that she needed, and tried to push him towards a more enthusiastic response.

'This is a seriously talented lady you've got here, Tom.'

'Yes,' he retorted, 'but also a headstrong one.'

Lynda was disappointed enough to be angry now, but tried not to sound it.

'What do you mean, headstrong?'

'I made it clear I didn't want you to spend your own money on this. But you've bought a carpet, and there's a fridge over there that wasn't here before. None of our rooms have fridges.'

Lynda decided it was time for some straight-talking.

'But they should have, if you want this to be a really classy hotel. Guests like cold drinks, and fresh milk for their cups of tea, not that other nasty-tasting rubbish.'

Tom was looking exasperated now. 'That's beside the point. You've spent a lot of money. And I'll have to pay you back.'

'No rush.' She realised that she had embarrassed this proud man, and needed to give him a way out. She smiled and looked up at him beseechingly, 'I was hoping to stay for a while.'

'Were you, indeed?' Nicki Heston commented acidly as she stepped deliberately between her son-in-law and the woman standing too close to him. She looked Lynda up and down, and was obviously not impressed with her cheap black trousers and pale blue denim shirt. 'And who are you?'

Tom turned and saw his wife following her Mother. 'This is Lynda Collins. She works here. I'm sorry I didn't hear you arrive.'

Suzanne was still upset that Tom didn't care enough to come to the airport. 'We came in a taxi, as you hadn't offered to come and collect us.'

Tom had resolved not to let these two women place demands upon him like they used to. His tone was polite but indifferent.

234

'I'm sorry, I didn't think you would need a chauffeur. I thought you said you were travelling back with a friend, and I assumed he would have a car.'

There was a quick, guarded look between Nicki and her daughter before Nicki responded coolly, 'You made a wrong assumption, as you do so often, Tom.'

Patrick followed Tom's lead in discouraging Nicki Henson's habitual demand for her needs to be given priority. 'We had an important event to attend. The grand opening of this wonderfully transformed room.'

Nicki saw that his approval was directed at Lynda, and guessed that she was involved.

She looked slowly round the room. 'And who is responsible for this?'

Tom smiled at Lynda. 'Lynda has done it, all of it.'

Nicki smoothed her bejewelled hand across her immaculately styled ash-blonde hair before looking pityingly at Lynda.

'Well, I'm sorry, my dear, but it looks like a tart's boudoir.'

She laughed and Suzanne joined in. Tom was furious, and forgetting that his son was still in the room, hit back angrily at his wife.

'What are you laughing at, Suzanne? This room is fabulous. And what gives you the right to criticise what we do here? You never took any interest in this hotel, and you certainly would never have rolled your sleeves up and done the sort of work Lynda has done.'

Nicki Heston sighed and shook her head.

'Of course she wouldn't. You hire people for this kind of work, people who know what they're doing. Not amateurs! That was always the trouble with you,

Tom, you never understood how we do things in our family. You never had the class.'

'Mother. Don't,' protested Suzanne, not wanting to hear her Mother's reproaches again.'

Nicki was tired, and still annoyed at her plans being changed by Simon Lennox having been summoned home by his wife.

'I warned you, Suzanne not to marry this gold-digging opportunist, but you listened to your father instead of me. And that's how we have ended up having to deal with this wretched divorce. Now, let us get out of this appalling room and go back to the civilisation of our own accommodation.'

As she swept out of the room they heard a quiet voice, saying, 'Mummy.'

Suzanne turned and flung her arms round her son. 'Hello, darling! I didn't see you were here. Nicki!' she called after her Mother, who returned, a little discomfited that she, too, had not been aware of the presence of her grandson.

Nicki kissed Mark lightly on both cheeks. 'How lovely to see you, precious boy. Come and have lunch with us at The Gatehouse, we've brought a lovely hamper of food from France. And then we'll plan the lovely time we're going to have with you this holiday.'

Tom insisted that it should be Lynda who showed the Tylers to their room when they arrived on Wednesday afternoon. In spite of all his reassurances, she couldn't forget Nicki Henson's verdict, and she was terrified what the Americans' reaction would be.

Nathan Tyler was a big man in his early fifties, who preferred a leather jacket to a suit, and always looked as if he was ready to go out and chop down a few trees. His wife was petite and pretty, smart, and astute. Her husband, carelessly thrusting his large leather bag into Patrick's hands, declined to follow Lynda to their room, but went straight to the bar demanding a beer and a hot beef sandwich to make up for the airline catering he abhorred.

Patrick went to take the rest of their luggage from the Mercedes, and left Lynda to travel up first in the lift with Helen Tyler. She smiled up at the young woman who seemed so nervous. 'You're new here, aren't you?'

'Yes, I used to work at a hotel in Cornwall, but Tom, Mr Meredith, asked me to come and help out here.'

'And do you like it?'

'I love the place, I think Loveday Manor is wonderful.'

She opened the door and, wishing the sun was shining, watched Helen Tyler carefully as she entered. The curly-haired, doll-like creature stood in the centre of the room, looking all round it. She walked over to the window, running her hand across the back of the little sofa, and then turned to Lynda, smiling like a child in a sweet shop.

'My, my, isn't this just lovely!'

Lynda put her hands to her mouth and gasped with relief.

'Oh. Do you really like it?'

'I sure do. It reminds me of my Mother's room in our house in Monterey, the little town in Virginia, where I grew up. That view is so beautiful, and this little sofa is the perfect place to sit and enjoy it, and read. That's what I like to do on holiday, find time for some quiet reading.'

'There's a small bookshelf in the corner with books and magazines. I didn't know what you'd like, so I chose a few different authors and magazines.'

'You got the room ready?'

'Yes. I re-decorated it and chose everything in it. I hoped you'd like it.'

'I do. And I love the details, all the pretty things.' She walked over to the table set out for tea and coffee-making. 'Where did you get these cute little trays and baskets?'

'A friend of mine has a gift shop in Guildford, I bought them from her.'

Helen opened a small, gold and white tin. 'Home-made biscuits, and in a tin, not those irritating cellophane packs. You're a woman after my own heart, Lynda. It is Lynda, isn't it?'

'Yes, Lynda Collins. Well, I'll leave you to get settled in. Would you like me to set out a cream tea for you in the conservatory?'

'That would be lovely. I'll be down in about half an hour.'

Her husband joined her later, followed by Tom, who was looking a little anxious as his friend hadn't mentioned the subject of handing over the cheque for the rest of the money he'd offered to lend him.

'Shall I order some more tea?' Helen asked as she poured herself another cup.

'No, thanks. I'm going for a walk, I need some fresh air. Is the room O.K. this time?'

'It's perfect. I'll really enjoy being here. You'll be pleased, too, there's a nice thick cotton robe in the bathroom for you.'

Nathan turned to Tom.

'Glad you took my complaint on board. You can't call this a luxury hotel unless you provide that kind of thing.'

Tom, who had forgotten all about this demand, nodded, and said to Helen, 'I'm glad you approve of the changes. I'm planning to re-furbish all the rooms, depending on how the finances go.'

Helen looked at her husband, 'You'll have to have a talk with Tom about that, won't you, honey?'

'I guess so,' was the cautious reply. 'I can see you need to spend money on the place. It's a pity you also have to pay off your wife and your 'pain in the butt' mother-in-law.'

Helen rebuked him gently, 'Nathan we must be polite.'

'Why?'

His wife was well-practised in changing the subject when her husband was heading towards being belligerent. She turned to Tom. 'Will Lynda be involved in giving the rooms a make-over?'

'Oh, yes,' Tom replied, fairly sure that Lynda would agree.

'Lynda Collins is a new member of staff, a very good addition, by the look of it,' Helen explained to her husband.

Tom, delighted, seized the chance to talk about Lynda. 'She used to work at Springfield , the hotel you went to stay at in Cornwall.'

'Where your Mother was,' Helen remembered, and took hold of his hand. 'I was so sorry to hear she'd passed on.'

Nathan Tyler moved towards the door. 'Yeah. Not good, losing your parents.'

His wife watched his face darken, and knew which

memories were causing that. 'You go off and enjoy your walk. I'll take a little stroll in the garden and then relax in our lovely room for a while.'

Tom needed to leave, too. 'And I'll get back to the kitchen, if you don't mind, Helen?'

'You go ahead, I'm looking forward to one of your lovely meals. You're a great chef.'

'Thank you, but I'm lucky I have Patrick and Lynda to help me, too.'

'Lynda cooks as well, does she?'

'Yes.'

'A multi-talented lady.'

He smiled proudly.

'And she followed you here from The Springfield Hotel?' Helen confirmed, with a speculative look that reminded him of his Mother.

'Yes.'

That evening, discreetly observing the guests making their way into the dining room, Patrick signalled to Lynda to come and stand with him. He pointed to a table not far from the entrance, which Suzanne and Nicki had selected, and from where they were graciously greeting some of the guests.

'Just watch those two. You'd never know there was a divorce going on here. Nicki thinks she still owns the place and Suzanne is still acting like she's the hostess. Mind you, it was all she was good at.'

Lynda watched Suzanne thoughtfully, 'Do you think she really wants to lose all this? And Tom?' she added in an anxious whisper.'

'She no longer has a choice.'

Lynda moved towards the kitchen, 'We'd better get back.'

Patrick grabbed her elbow, 'No, wait, just watch this a minute.'

He was pointing to the Tylers who were entering the room. They saw Nicki spot them coming and immediately engage Suzanne in intense conversation to avoid looking at them.

Nathan Tyler marched past and chose a table as far from them as possible, but it was a moment or two before his wife joined him. Helen Tyler had seen the two women ignoring their arrival, but she walked deliberately over to their table, smiled and had a little chat to them before going to join her husband.

'Look and learn, Miss Lynda,' drawled Patrick. 'There's a real lady, who knows how to behave. Helen Tyler's great-grandparents used to own a plantation in Georgia, and they left a legacy of good manners, as well as a heap of dirty money.'

'Dirty money?'

'Wealth created by black slaves. Not Lady Helen's fault, though, and she tries to make up for it when she can, even though that husband of hers don't see things quite the same way.'

'What do you mean?'

'Nathan Tyler was brought up to believe the colour of a man's skin makes a difference.'

Lynda took one last look at the Tylers before turning to go back into the kitchen. 'He doesn't seem to like Nicki Heston, though. That's a big point in his favour.'

Patrick laughed. 'Tyler may have plenty of money, but in Nicki Heston's unassailable opinion, he's on a par with you - got no class!'

CHAPTER TWENTY SEVEN

Mark Meredith, who didn't like the formality of eating in the dining room, always had breakfast and his evening meal in the kitchen. For a couple of days that was the only time Lynda saw him, and he didn't seem to have much to say to her.

On Easter Saturday, however, he became more animated when she reminded him about the Easter Egg Hunt they'd planned, and early the next morning the two of them set off round the garden with the little nests of mini-eggs they'd prepared the previous weekend.

Nicki, who always liked to have a coffee in the conservatory before breakfast, saw them hiding the last few nests, and called out to her grandson.

'Mark, what are you doing?'

He ran towards her and told her excitedly, 'We've organised an Easter Egg hunt for the guests after breakfast.'

'What do you mean?'

'Amy told Lynda about it, she sells the little baskets and things for it in her shop. She started doing it after she went to her German pen-friend's house at Easter. We've got nests hidden all round the garden, and we're going to announce it during breakfast.'

'You're going to ask the guests to go hunting for eggs in the garden? You can't do that!'

'Why not? Dad said it was all right to give it a go.'

'Your father is a fool. You cannot ask guests to crawl around in the garden. It's been raining, for heaven's sake! You are not to do this, Mark.'

Her grandson stood his ground in a way Nicki had never seen before. 'Dad says I can. And Lynda thinks the guests will enjoy it.'

'Lynda Collins has no idea!'

'It'll be fun,' he cried as he went back to join Lynda who was watching anxiously from the edge of the slightly soggy grass.'

Nicki Heston was wrong. The guests, although some of them hesitated at first, wandered round the garden and into the shrubbery, joking and laughing, and shouting triumphantly as they held up the nest they had found. Nicki and Suzanne watched them for a while, smiling politely at the idiotic behaviour. A little earlier than they needed to, they waved goodbye to Mark, and set off to join some friends who had invited them for lunch at their elegant country house.

Tom and Patrick and the rest of the staff had come out to watch the egg-hunt, and Tom made sure his son and Lynda were standing next to him as the smiling guests came into the conservatory to have another cup of coffee, and eat their mini-eggs. They shared them out like children, and many of them told Tom how much they'd enjoyed the fun — and the eggs.

Charles and Mavis Hunter, an elderly couple who had stayed at Loveday on many occasions and over many years, were misty-eyed as they came over to speak to Tom.

'Thank you, very, very much for a lovely Easter morning. It was magical, being able to behave like children again. It's something everyone should do more often!'

Tom stepped aside, saying. 'It's my son you have to thank. And Lynda.'

He put his arms round the shoulders of both of them and pulled them close. Helen Tyler, sitting in a comfortable armchair, with a nest on her knee, sipped her coffee and thought how good the three of them looked together.

Helen Tyler had decided she liked Lynda Collins very much, and she took every opportunity to sit and have a chat to her. She often invited Lynda to join her for afternoon tea in the conservatory when she was free. Nathan Tyler disappeared most days to attend meetings in London, and when the spring season opened at Epsom he went to the races.

Lynda was surprised that his wife didn't accompany him. 'Do you not like going to the races?'

'I don't mind, but it's not my favourite pastime. I hate seeing the disappointment on people's faces when they lose.'

Lynda refrained from telling her that she'd love to go to a race meeting. Since coming to Loveday and listening to the guests, she was beginning to realise how limited her experience of life was.

'I prefer to go to the theatre,' Helen continued. 'I occasionally go to a matinée, but I have to admit I'm a little nervous of going into London on my own. Do you go to the theatre?'

Again, Lynda wasn't going to reveal that it was something else she hadn't experienced, apart from a couple of pantomimes when she was a child. 'No, but I'd love to one day.'

'Do you like musicals?' Helen enquired.

'I love them, me and my Grandma used to watch film musicals on television on Sunday afternoons.'

'There are two on in London I'd like to see. 'Les Miserables', which is fairly new but has had great reviews, and 'Me and My Girl' which is a revival, but sounds a lot of fun. Would you like to come and see them with me?'

'How much are the tickets?'

'Don't you worry about that, Nathan will treat you – he'll be so grateful if you'll go with me so that I don't have to drag him along.'

'Oh, I don't know if I can.'

'Please. I need someone to go with, Lynda. And I enjoy your company, as you'll have noticed. I hope you don't mind my taking up so much of your time. I don't want to be a nuisance.'

Lynda beamed at this charming little woman who seemed to want to be her friend. 'Helen, I love your company. I love talking to you, and I'd love to go to the theatre with you.'

Helen clapped her hands together. 'That's wonderful.'

'I'll have to see if I can have some extra time off those afternoons.'

'I don't think that will be a problem. Tom knows you work hard and deserve a break. He thinks very highly of you. And so does his son.'

'Mark's a lovely lad.'

'Yes. I wish I had a grandson like him. My boy, Peter, got married but it didn't last long, so I'm still waiting for him to meet somebody and have children.'

'You'd be a fabulous Grandma.'

'Thank you. I can't wait to be called Granny. It's appalling that Mark has to call his grandmother by her Christian name. Sorry, I've not right to comment about the family, but I'm quite fond of Tom. He's such a sweetie, isn't he?'

'Yes,' Lynda agreed, and her blush spurred Helen Tyler on to give free rein to the curiosity which her husband teased her about.

'He was lucky to find you at Springfield. Where did you work before then?'

'In a café, in Milfield where I come from. It's a town in the North of England.'

'But you left to live in Cornwall?'

'Yes.' Lynda had become used to needing to answer questions about her past, the guests often enquired when they noticed her different accent.

'Do you have family back in Milfield?'

Helen saw Lynda flinch a little at the question. 'Oh, I'm sorry, I've no right to be so nosey. It's just that I'd like to get to know you better. As a friend. We are friends, aren't we?'

'Yes. I'd be proud to call you my friend. And the answer to your question is that I have a daughter, and a grandson in Milfield.'

'Oh, lucky you, to have a grandson!' Then Helen paused and took hold of Lynda's left hand. 'But no husband?'

Lynda looked away, and Helen came to a conclusion. 'Oh, I'm sorry, are you a widow?'

246

'No.'

'Oh, divorced, then?'

'Yes.' Lynda hadn't intended to lie to Helen Tyler, but it seemed the right answer to give. And anyway, she realised, that was how she felt. Divorced. A free woman.

The next day she and Helen were walking in the garden, when Helen began a conversation which was to change Lynda's life. It began with a simple question.

'You really like working in the hotel, don't you, Lynda?'

'Yes, it's hard but very satisfying when you see people enjoying themselves, and feeling at home.'

'And you're going to have the chance to re-furbish the other rooms.'

'I hope so.'

'I told Tom he shouldn't give the job to anyone else. You know the value of getting details right, and you know when not to save money.'

Lynda laughed, 'Try telling that to Tom, he starts to look worried when I start talking about luxury items. I think I can keep the costs down, though. When I bought the stuff for your room, several people were willing to reduce the price when I talked about further orders.'

'Good for you. You'll make a great success of it all, I'm sure. Has Tom talked about a pay rise? Or making you an assistant manager?'

Lynda laughed. 'No.'

'He should. You're the right person to help him make this place a real success. Loveday Manor could be a real gold mine. It has great potential. Has Tom thought of really promoting the place as a venue for wedding receptions?'

'I don't think so.'

'No, well, he's a man, he won't be interested in weddings.' She giggled, 'Particularly when he's in the middle of a divorce. Sorry, I shouldn't laugh, divorce isn't funny. Weddings are something you should look into, though, Lynda. There are plenty of people in London and in this area who have money. Loveday Manor is so beautiful, it could become a very special venue. And if there's one thing people are willing to spend money, it's a wedding.'

Lynda's eyes were widening with excitement. 'Yes, I suppose you're right, Helen.'

'I know I'm right. That's what my business is, weddings and all the merchandise that goes with them.'

'You have your own business?'

'Sure. I have to do something when Nathan's off on his money-making expeditions. I set up a small shop and it grew from there.'

Lynda saw there was a lot more to this little lady than she had realised. As they talked, she saw a different Helen walking beside her, a woman charged up with an energy which came from the ability to be creative and successful.

Helen was pleased that Lynda was interested.

'I started off selling wedding outfits, but there were lots of people doing that, so I looked, like you, for the details which could make people feel special. I deal in all kinds of decorations and extras like little gifts for the guests.'

'I've never heard of people giving presents to the guests.'

'No, I don't think you do it over here — yet. I got the idea in Paris when I looked in shop windows and saw beautiful displays centred round sugared almonds.'

'Sugared almonds?'

'Yes, pink and white sugared almonds in exquisite little packages, they sell them as gifts for occasions like christenings and weddings. And I thought it would be lovely to have something like that by each guest's place-setting. I started with candy, but then realised it could be any small item which suited that particular wedding, things like toy cars, if the groom is into racing cars. People love fun things like that.'

'Doesn't it cost a lot, though?'

'No, it needn't be very expensive — and like you said, you can negotiate a good price if you're doing large quantities or a regular order. If you wrap something beautifully, it doesn't have to cost a fortune for people to feel they've been given something special.'

'What a brilliant idea.'

'It's a great little business. You could develop something similar with your friend Amy. She has a talent for finding unusual gifts. But get Loveday Manor established as a wedding venue first, then set up Loveday Manor Merchandise.'

'You're making me dizzy with all this.'

'It's just something to think about. You're at the age when a woman stops and decides what she wants to do with her life. Am I right?'

They'd reached the bank of the river and Lynda stared at the smoothly flowing water for a moment, remembering how she had changed her life in the last twelve months.

Helen went and sat on a small wooden bench and waited until Lynda was ready to talk to her.

After a while, Lynda came and sat beside her. She spoke slowly. 'When I was a teenager, Helen, I used to dream of a glamorous, exciting life, beautiful clothes and holidays in exotic places.'

'Like in the movies.'

'Yes. That's where I got it all from I suppose.'

'And did you want to be a film star?'

'No, I knew people from Milfield didn't become film stars. I wanted to be a secretary to some big executive, and fly round the world with him.'

'And did you train as a secretary when you left school?'

'No, my Dad had other ideas, he made me leave school early and got me a job in a cake shop.'

'What a shame. So you didn't get your dream.'

'No.'

'And what's your dream now?'

'To earn enough money to give me the freedom to choose what I do with my life.'

'There's only one way to do that, honey, and that's to have your own business.'

'You need a lot of money to be able to do that.'

'Perhaps we could lend you some.'

Lynda was horrified that Helen might think she was looking for favours. 'No! I wouldn't ask you for money. And anyway your husband is already helping Tom out.'

'And you're helping Tom. You'll be good for Loveday Manor, and you can build on what you do here. Why don't you start your business by charging a fee for the work you do re-designing the rooms? Don't just do it as part of your job. You have to value yourself, if you want others to value you, that's what I've found.'

'I don't think I could ask Tom to pay me separately for working on the bedrooms.'

'Tell you what, I'll suggest it, and then I'll let him think it was his idea. Go for it, Lynda! You don't want to be just an employee, do you? A woman like you needs to be her own boss.'

Lynda grinned. 'That's true. I never have been good at being told what to do. Now shall we go back, and I'll make you one of those cream teas you like so much.'

Helen sprang to her feet. 'You spoil me, Lynda. I'm very glad to say!'

Lynda surprised her friend by giving her a hug. 'You're an amazing lady, Helen Tyler. You make me feel I can do anything.'

'You deserve a chance to have your dream. And I'd love to see you transform this hotel your way, and make a huge success of it. I reckon that would really annoy Nicki Henson – and that would give me enormous pleasure!'

CHAPTER TWENTY EIGHT

Carolyn Sheldon loved going to work, she felt as if she'd been set free. She naturally felt guilty at leaving her child, but didn't worry about little Michael too much because she knew her Nana would take good care of him. Sheila didn't let her granddaughter know that she found it exhausting looking after her grandson, she just went to bed earlier. She was so delighted to see Carolyn taking this step towards the career she wanted her to have, and every morning she felt proud to see her dressed in her smart business suit.

She had had a lovely time taking Carolyn shopping for clothes and shoes to wear to the office, and Carolyn had been so grateful, especially as Sheila had insisted she needed several outfits, and that they had to be of the highest quality. As Ellen Heywood had said, it was important for her to look the part. She, too, was enjoying seeing her protégée start a career and had presented Carolyn with a black leather briefcase. She was gratified to hear from Andrew Howell that they were very impressed with the young lady she had recommended.

Carolyn had been terrified at first, walking into the offices of Howell and Jameson's Accountancy Firm, but everyone had been very welcoming and friendly. She'd found that she enjoyed the work she was given and, to her surprise, found it easy. She'd passed her A level maths, and managed to gain a good grade, but working with figures in this environment was a different experience, and she excelled. Her ability was soon noticed, and she had only been working there a few months when she was invited to take part in a training course.

This 'in-house training' was an idea introduced by Nick Allenby, a senior chartered accountant at the firm. He had been recently recruited by Andrew Howell's son, who had been impressed with Nick's knowledge of the latest accounting systems, and jargon. He was a very bright, good-looking, well-spoken young man in his mid-twenties whom rival male colleagues might have resented, had he not been so affable and charming. He came originally from Oxford, a fact which often led people to understand that he was an Oxford graduate.

There were four members of staff, two male and two female, whom he had selected to participate in the training sessions he held in his office on Thursday evenings, beginning at four o'clock so that no-one would have to go home later than six o'clock. He was so considerate about not keeping them away from their families longer than necessary, that he insisted on giving all four of his 'trainees' a lift home on Thursday nights in his 'top of the range' Audi saloon. The route he took meant that Carolyn was always the last of the group to be taken home.

Steve managed to get home early on most Thursday nights and, if for some reason he was late, Sheila or John would bathe Michael and get him ready for bed. Steve loved to spend every minute he could with his son, and it made him able to cope with all the frustrations at work, where there was a depressing atmosphere generated by Randerson acting like an arrogant nineteenth century mill-owner.

This Thursday Steve had delayed putting Michael to bed as long as possible, hoping that Carolyn would get home early enough to kiss her little boy goodnight. By twenty-past seven Michael was falling asleep, so Steve had to quickly give him his bottle of milk, and a final cuddle before lowering him gently into his cot.

He went downstairs and gratefully accepted the glass of beer which John had poured for him. John had already had his share of the pork casserole which Sheila had prepared for them, but Steve, although ravenous by now, had made it a rule to wait and have dinner with his wife.

It was a quarter to eight before she walked in.

'I'm sorry I'm so late,' she apologised before going upstairs to change out of her slate-grey suit and still crisp white shirt. They ate as soon as she came back down, and Steve was so hungry that he didn't speak to her until he had cleared his plate.

'What's the matter?' Carolyn asked. 'You've not said a word to me since I came in.'

'Haven't I? Sorry, love, I was starving.'

'You shouldn't have waited for me. You should have eaten with my Dad. Is he watching T.V.?'

'Yeah.'

'I don't like him sitting in there on his own.'

John had set up an old second-hand television in the front room, initially to enable him and Steve to watch sport in peace, leaving Carolyn to watch the programmes she preferred. Sheila had paid for them to have central heating installed before the baby arrived, and so, although, not quite as cosy as the living room it was always comfortable enough to spend the evening there.

Lynda had managed to convince John a while ago that it was important to let the couple have time alone together, but now, of course, he didn't have his wife to keep him company and it felt lonely to be sitting in there alone.

When Carolyn had first started work her Dad had stayed in the living room with them, enjoying seeing Carolyn so lively and full of news about all she was learning, and the people she was working with. Recently, though he had sensed a tension in Steve when he saw his wife come home in her smart clothes, still exhilarated by her successful day. Consequently, John had started moving off into the front room again, and tried not to hear them arguing.

Steve knew he was making a mistake, but couldn't stop himself from complaining.

'You've missed putting Michael to bed three times this week.'

'Counting, are you?'

'Yes. It's important for him to have that time with you.'

She bridled at the criticism, 'I know it is, but it's not often I'm late.'

'A lot more often than it used to be.'

'I can't refuse if they ask me to work an extra few minutes.'

'Or an extra hour! They don't pay you for it either. Have they not got a trade union?'

'No. It's not that sort of environment. And I get other benefits, like this training from Nick.'

'Nick?'

'Nick Allenby, I told you about him. But you didn't take it in, obviously. You're not really interested in what I do at work, are you?'

'Of course I am. I just don't like you coming home late.'

Carolyn stood up and began clearing the table. 'Well, I have no choice,' she protested, knowing she was lying. She had made the choice a few weeks ago now.

Nick Allenby flirted humorously with all the girls, and the older women, in the office and they had a lot of fun, teasing him in return. He'd flirted with Carolyn just like he did with all the others, and she loved it just as they did. She at first thought she was imagining that he looked at her more intently, or held her hand just that bit longer during these flirtatious skirmishes, but one Thursday before driving her home he had invited her to have a drink with him.

That first invitation had been so casual, so undemanding, that she'd felt she would have offended him if she'd refused. He'd taken her to Ashton House, the most expensive hotel and restaurant in Milfield, and a place not likely to be frequented by any of her colleagues.

She had felt awkward at first, and very guilty at being there with Nick, but couldn't resist the pleasure of the way he talked to her, and looked at her. It was not as if they were having an affair, she told herself, they were just two work colleagues enjoying each other's company. The fact that they always sat in a corner where they wouldn't be noticed by other guests was, she reasoned, just Nick being protectively discreet.

Tonight, however, had been different. When they got back in the car after their visit to Ashton House, he had kissed her. Only once, and afterwards he had just smiled, and they hadn't spoken again except to say goodnight. She thought of that kiss now as she went into the kitchen to wash up and make a cup of coffee.

Sheila Stanworth had decided to really splash out for her seventieth birthday in May, so she booked a weekend in London for herself, her daughter, Sylvia, and Carolyn. The three women were very excited as they set off on the train on the Friday, travelling first class. John wondered sometimes where his Mother found the money for such extravagant treats, but was glad that he would be spared having to put on his best suit for a formal dinner at some stuffy expensive hotel. He was happy, too, that the trip would be an exciting twentieth birthday present for Carolyn, whose birthday was on 9th May, the day after his Mother's.

Steve was disappointed that his wife wouldn't be home to share her birthday with him and he knew that Michael, who was a two year old toddler now, would get upset at his Mother's absence. The one compensation was that he and his son had been invited, along with John, to spend the Saturday at Old Manor Farm.

CHAPTER TWENTY NINE

Sylvia Stanworth's marriage to Graham Laycock, whose parents owned Old Manor Farm had been seen as a great social triumph by her Mother. The disadvantage of this union was that The County Bank had, for purposes of promotion, required Graham to move his family to Knutsford. Sheila enjoyed staying with them at their large new home, but had noticed that the invitations to visit them had become more and more infrequent.

Even more rare were the invitations to visit Graham's parents at the farm, which was now also the home of his brother, Sam, and his family. John and Steve were delighted to be there that Saturday afternoon, especially John, who loved the easy-going ways of the Laycock family and their legendary hospitality.

He had many happy memories of the times he and Lynda had spent in their home. After lunch he sat in the large dining kitchen with Graham's Dad, Harry Laycock, enjoying those memories, and several pints of beer, while his wife, Enid, devoted the afternoon to entertaining little Michael.

The Laycocks had liked Lynda, and Harry, who couldn't resist listening in to any gossip that was circulating in the bar at The Red Lion, knew all about her disappearance, but hadn't had a chance to talk to John properly. He wasn't going to miss the opportunity now and, in spite of his wife's warning looks, dived straight into the subject.

'It's a shame Lynda couldn't be here today, we miss her.'

'Not half as much as I do,' John admitted. He was glad to have a sympathetic audience who would listen to him talking about his wife. The subject had developed into a kind of taboo at Beechwood Avenue, especially when Sheila was there.

Harry topped up John's glass from the jug of beer on the table.

'It's a mystery, isn't it, her going off like that?'

'She left a note saying she just needed a break, and was going away for a few days.'

Harry shook his head in disbelief. 'Yes, but that's over a year ago now, isn't it? And you don't know where she is?'

'No.'

Enid didn't usually join in Harry's enquiries but she, too, was fond of Lynda. 'Have you not heard from her at all?'

'Not for a while. She hasn't even sent any birthday cards.'

Enid was shocked. 'Oh, I can't believe that!'

'No, neither can I,' John said.

Enid Laycock commented thoughtfully, 'That doesn't sound like Lynda to me, she loved sending people cards.'

260

'Aye,' Harry laughed. 'She used to send me ones to make me blush.'

His wife laughed, 'She did well if she could find one that would make you blush! Oh, I do hope you hear from her soon.'

'So do I,' muttered John. 'I wanted to go to the police, but everyone tells me that, because she left a note, and she's phoned, she's not really a missing person.'

Harry Laycock needing to lift his friend's spirits, clinked his glass against John's. 'Enjoy your freedom while you can, lad, your wife will be back soon enough!'

John tried to respond and become good company, but couldn't forget his disappointment and anxiety that they weren't receiving birthday or Christmas cards from Lynda. It would be a long time before he found out why that was.

Ever since she had, by chance, been at Beechwood Avenue to take delivery of the birthday card Lynda had sent for John. Ever since then Sheila Stanworth had made sure that she always arrived early to look after Michael. Thus she ensured that she was always at Beechwood Avenue before the postal delivery, and had managed to intercept Lynda's cards, and the Christmas present.

When he had seen that John had settled down to have a chat to his parents, Graham Laycock had invited Steve to join him for a walk. Graham was a gentle, reserved and intelligent man who knew a great deal about the ways of the world, but most of the time kept that valuable knowledge to himself. He was not looking forward to the conversation he had decided to have with Steve Sheldon, as he was not a man who liked to interfere in people's personal lives.

Steve was surprised, but pleased that Graham had sought his company. He listened to him with interest as they set off through the farmyard, and Graham proudly pointed out the improvements his brother had made to the farm. Steve had only met Graham a few times, but liked him a lot. He was also curious about this seemingly quiet man, especially as Lynda had told him the tale of how Graham Laycock had prevented Sheila Stanworth from refusing to attend her son's wedding.

He was amazed at Graham's generosity as he talked about his elder brother, and was prompted to be unusually forthright.

'Did you never wish it was you who got to take over the farm?'

Graham was a little taken aback by his companion being so direct, but realised Steve was genuinely concerned about how he felt.

'No. It's hard physical work, which I'm not suited to, and it's not easy to make a farm successful as a business. I hear you'd like to own your own business some day.'

Steve shrugged. 'Yes, but at the moment I have to concentrate on earning enough to keep my family, and hopefully save up a deposit for our own home.'

'Sylvia said that Carolyn is doing well at her job, that must be a help.'

'Yeah, but I'd rather she was at home looking after Michael.'

Graham sighed sympathetically.

'Unfortunately, society seems to be moving on

from the traditional pattern of family life. Sylvia has always been contented to be 'just a housewife' but many women aren't.'

'Carolyn certainly isn't, I don't think she'll ever give up work, she enjoys it too much. She never looks so happy as when she's putting on her smart suit, and picking up her briefcase. She can't wait to get out of the car when I give her a lift to the office, hardly remembers to give me a kiss some mornings.'

He fell silent then, feeling he'd revealed too much of how he felt, but there was something about Graham Laycock that made you feel you could confide in him, and trust him to be discreet.

They walked on for a while, enjoying the view of the fields coloured by the freshness of new growth, and breathing in the scents of the hedgerows. Eventually they reached an old stone trough painstakingly hollowed out by some farm-hand many years ago to collect rainwater for the cattle, and Graham paused.

'Would you mind if we sat here for a moment? It's my favourite view from the farm.'

Steve happily joined him. 'I wish I had chance to do this more often.'

'And me,' Graham agreed. 'It calms your soul.'

He took off his glasses, and spent a few minutes polishing them, even though they didn't need it. It was his way of collecting his thoughts before he had something important, and in this case, unpleasant, to discuss.

He began to speak in the circumspect manner which was so typical of him.

'It's good that Carolyn is enjoying her work,

Steven, and she's obviously one of those young women who seem to need the extra status that successful employment brings.

'Yeah, I suppose so. Like I said, she loves being at work.'

Graham took a breath, 'Which is fine, as long as it's for the right reasons.'

'What do you mean?'

Graham cleared his throat a little nervously.

'Sylvia and I have had long discussions as to whether I should have this conversation with you, but Sylvia is very worried that Carolyn may do something very foolish. You know me well enough, I think, to realise that I am not a man who normally indulges in any kind of gossip.'

Steve laughed out loud at the idea of this fastidiously correct and proper man being accused of being a gossip, but then saw the anxiety in the eyes behind those well polished lenses.

'Tell me.'

'I have been informed, discreetly, that Carolyn is being paid a lot of attention by a senior male colleague at Howell and Jameson's. It could all be construed as light-hearted dalliance, indeed the young man in question has a reputation for being skilled in charming his female colleagues.'

'Who is he?'

'A Mr Nick Allenby.'

'He's the guy who's been giving her this training on Thursday nights. He gives her a lift home.'

Graham nodded slowly. 'And therein lies the problem. They have been seen enjoying each other's company at Ashton House.'

'Just the two of them?'

'Yes.'

'So that's why she's been getting home late. I'll kill her!'

'I understand, Steven, why you are angry, but I hope you will give this some thought before you confront your wife with what could, after all, be just tittle-tattle.'

'You don't think it is, though.'

'No, the person who gave me the information is a loyal friend of mine. He hesitated for a long time, but when we had the opportunity to talk privately last week, he felt he had to express his concern.'

Steve sat with his head bowed and his fists clenched tightly in front of him. When he looked up at Graham his expression was one of misery as well as anger.

'I love her.'

'I know you do. And I'm sure she loves you. This is just one of those situations that can arise in an office when this type of man joins the staff. Young women like Carolyn are bound to respond to such flattering behaviour, particularly from a senior manager. But it needs to be stopped before any harm is done.'

'Too bloody right, it's got to stop. Wait till I see her!'

'And what will you say when you see her?'

Steve shook his head, 'I don't know.'

'Please take my advice and be very careful how you speak to Carolyn about this matter. I've told you about this unwise behaviour for only one reason, to prevent it from causing any real problem. This is the work of a very selfish and irresponsible young man. It is not a reason to abandon a marriage, especially when you have a child.'

'What do I do, Graham?'

'Talk to Carolyn.'

When Sheila and Carolyn arrived back late on Sunday afternoon from their weekend in London, they couldn't wait to tell John and Steve about their adventures. They sat side by side on the sofa, Sheila with shopping bags at her feet and Carolyn holding Michael on her knee, showing him the toy London bus she'd brought back for him.

'Oh, it's a different world down there, isn't it Carolyn?' gushed Sheila. 'Everyone seems to have money.'

'That must be nice,' muttered Steve, who was standing by the fireplace watching his wife and imagining her in another man's arms.

'There's so much to do,' Carolyn said, 'we didn't manage to see half the sights we'd planned to.'

'You managed to find the shops, though,' John commented dryly, indicating the Harrods bags they'd both brought back with them.

Carolyn grinned at him. 'Of course! We went all down Oxford Street, and then we went to Harrods – but we only bought a little tray each there, as a souvenir, just to get the bag really.'

'And we didn't forget you,' boasted Sheila, taking out two silk ties. 'They're from John Lewis.'

'Oh. Tell him thanks very much.' John held up the two ties. 'Which one do you want, Steve?'

'I'm not bothered, I don't wear ties,' was Steve's surly response.

Sheila's reprimand was sharp and swift. 'Well,

that's nice! Where are your manners, you could at least say thank you!'

Carolyn stared at her husband. 'Steve! What's wrong with you?'

'Nothing.'

Sheila looked with disdain at her son-in-law. 'He's just jealous it wasn't him giving you a birthday treat, so he's trying to spoil it. But don't you let him.'

'I won't,' Carolyn said angrily. 'I've had a lovely birthday. I thought you and Dad would be having a nice time, too, up at Manor Farm.'

'We did,' John reassured her. 'The Laycocks really looked after us and I had a good old natter with Harry and Enid. And Graham took Steve off for a walk.'

'Oh, that was good of him,' commented Sheila, who had never been able to stop herself feeling slightly deferential towards Sylvia's ultra-respectable husband.

Steve was ready for an argument. 'Why do you say that? Do you think I'm not the sort of bloke Graham Laycock would want to bother with, or something?'

Carolyn tried to play peace-maker. 'She didn't mean that. It's just that you don't know Graham very well.'

'Yes,' Sheila barged unknowingly into dangerous territory. 'I was just wondering what you'd find to talk about.'

Steve looked down at her sneering face, and all the resentment and anger which had been tearing him apart not only since that conversation with Graham, but for weeks as he'd watched his wife lose interest in him, couldn't be held back any longer.

'Oh, you'll be surprised,' he said, 'I know I was.

Shocked even. But then a husband is entitled to be shocked, when he hears his wife's being carrying on with another fella!'

John sat bolt upright. 'What? Who's been telling you rubbish like that?'

Steve had an aura of deadly calm about him now. 'That's what me and Graham found to talk about, Sheila. Or rather, he talked about it. He didn't want to tell me, but Sylvia was worried that Carolyn might be about to do something very foolish, like having sex with this other man.' He stared at his wife with eyes full of hatred. 'Mind you, for all I know, she already has.'

'No,' Carolyn whispered. 'No, I haven't, Steve. I swear, I haven't.'

White-faced, Sheila turned to her adored granddaughter. 'You mean it's true? You've been having an affair?'

'No!' Carolyn cried out. 'It, it was just a bit of silly flirtation. Nick flirts with everybody in the office.'

Steve leaned towards her. 'Oh, and does he take everybody to Ashton House as well?'

She looked up at him and tried, unwisely, to defend herself. 'Nothing's happened. He's just kissed me —once – that's all.'

Steve glared at her. 'And you think that's all right, do you? Letting another bloke take you out, and kiss you. Well, I'll tell you something, little Miss Stupid! It's not all right. And shall I tell you why? Because you're a married woman. You're my wife!'

There was a silence. Sheila had been horrified by this revelation, but now she instinctively sought to defend her beloved grandchild.

'But she never should have been! That's the

268

problem here. It's not Carolyn's fault. She married the wrong man, just like her father married the wrong woman. Perhaps it's as well this has happened. You can go your separate ways now and make a fresh start.'

'Mother, shut up! You keep out of this!'

John's shout startled them all, and Michael, who'd been staring round at these stern-faced adults, began to cry. Carolyn held him closer, and tried to comfort him.

John Stanworth's voice was shaking.

'I don't know what's gone on here, but you've got to sort it out.'

He looked at his daughter and the young man he'd begun to love like a son.

'You've got to talk about this. Believe me, I know that's what you've got to do. And then when you've talked about it, you've got to forgive her, Steve. Otherwise you'll regret it, and be as lonely and miserable as I am.'

CHAPTER THIRTY

One afternoon in late November Lynda walked into Tom Meredith's office and found him and Patrick drinking whisky. 'A bit early, isn't it?' she queried cheekily. Patrick gave her one of his slow, lopsided grins before turning to Tom.

'Like I was saying, Tom, this new member of staff will have to go. She's no idea how to behave with senior management. And we've just been given another perfect example of what I can only describe as her impudence.'

Lynda gave him a playful shove and declared, 'I'm just trying to protect the business from irresponsible men who spend too much time ogling young girls, and drinking away all the profits.'

'Hey!' Tom protested, 'I don't ogle young girls.'

'No, but he does.'

Tom raised his glass and grinned at Patrick. 'She might be right there. But what she doesn't know is that this drinking is entirely justified by our cause for celebration.'

'What are you celebrating?'

'This,' Tom replied waving a very official-looking letter in the air.

'His declaration of freedom,' explained Patrick as he helped himself to another splash of whisky.

Tom was smiling at Lynda, 'My decree nisi.'

'Oh, congratulations. Is that what you say when somebody's got a divorce?'

Tom gave an exaggerated sigh of relief. 'It is in my case. Especially when it means I've managed to hang on to Loveday Manor.'

Patrick wagged a finger at his friend, 'Not quite all of it. And not quite with no strings attached. You should have listened to me, and read the small print.'

Tom's smile was rueful now. 'I know, but I needed to be free of her, of them both. And I had other things on my mind.'

Both Lynda and Patrick knew that he meant his Mother's illness, and Patrick gave him a sympathetic pat on the shoulder.

'But you kept hold of your dream, and do you know something? I think there's a slim chance you might achieve it and make this place a big success.'

'It's looking more likely, thanks to you two.'

Patrick was prepared to hand on the credit.

'Thanks to Lynda, you mean. And you haven't even offered her a drink yet.'

She smiled but shook her head. 'No, thanks. I'll be asleep for the rest of the afternoon if I have a drink now.'

'You'll be having a drink tomorrow, though, won't you, on your birthday?' Tom suggested.

Lynda was astonished. 'How did you know it's my birthday?'

'Mark told me.'

'Oh, yes, I remember him asking me, but it was a while ago.'

'Well, he's remembered and he's bought you a present. I feel very guilty that I haven't bought you anything.'

Patrick looked at the two of them, and decided now was the time. 'How about you take her out to dinner, instead? I'll cover for you.'

Tom gave him a grateful look, and then smiled at Lynda. 'Would you come out to dinner with me tomorrow night?'

Lynda found she was a little breathless as she replied, 'Yes. That would be lovely. Thank you.'

She blushed as she saw Patrick wink at her. 'I'd better go now, work to do,' she stammered and fled out of the room before they could see her bright pink cheeks.

'At long last, Tom Meredith!' Patrick said teasingly, 'What is it with you and Lynda, that it's taking so long for you to get together?'

'There was a little matter of my being in the middle of a divorce, remember?'

'Yeah, I suppose so. But don't waste any more time now, my friend.'

Tom grinned at him. 'I won't!'

The staff didn't seem to notice that both Tom and Lynda were absent the following evening, and if they had Patrick would have told them not to gossip about it.

Tom chose a quiet little French restaurant just outside Dorking and had requested a table in one of the alcoves. They were greeted by the owner who showed them to their table and was obviously pleased to see Tom.

'Do you know him?' Lynda asked as she nervously looked round the restaurant.

'Yes, I've met him a few times at local business events.'

'He'll be wondering why you're not with your wife.'

'No, I've never been here with Suzanne. I'd never take her to a French restaurant because she'd just criticise, and compare it to the ones in France.'

'Well, you're safe bringing me here, I've never been to a French restaurant before so I've nothing to compare it to.'

'I'm sure you'll enjoy it. Is it all right if I choose the wine?'

'Of course it is.'

She picked up the menu and was relieved to see that it was in English as well as French, which was a good sign that the owner wanted everyone to feel at ease here. She had a look round and was pleased to see that the other women dining there were not wearing glitzy dresses, so she didn't feel out of place in the simple, soft woollen dress which she'd recently bought.

She had told herself that she'd bought it to wear at Christmas, as it was a rich shade of burgundy which would look quite festive, but the truth was that she had bought it in the hope that, one day soon, Tom Meredith would ask her to go out with him.

He was concentrating on the wine list, so she took the opportunity to enjoy looking at him as he sat back in his chair, so relaxed and so attractive in his well-cut sports jacket and open-necked shirt. He glanced up and caught her looking.

'I'm so glad you could come out with me tonight, Lynda. I've wanted to do this for a long time.'

'I understand why you couldn't ask me before. But I'm so happy to be here with you.'

He smiled and reached out for her hand. 'That's one of the things I love about you. You're so open, you don't play games, you just say how you feel.'

'Not always. It depends who I'm with, whether I trust them or not.'

He held on to her hand, and his blue eyes gazed at her intently.

'And do you trust me?'

'Yes.'

The waiter arrived, and they both ordered the same starter and main course, the Coquille St Jacques followed by blanquette d'agneau.

'We seem to share the same tastes in food,' Tom commented.

'No, I just ordered what you did, I thought you'd pick something good. I've never had any real French food like this before.'

She found herself thinking of Kath Kelly telling her about Jenny, being thrilled when Richard Heywood had taken her to a French restaurant on their first date.

'That looks like a sad thought,' Tom said.

'Sorry, just a memory of someone I knew in Milfield.'

'Do you think about Milfield a lot?'

'Not as much as I thought I would. I'm so happy here. It's as if there are two of me, one who lives in Milfield, and one who lives at Loveday Manor.'

'And which one would you rather be?'

'The one here.'

He poured more of the Vouvray he'd ordered, and then raised his glass to her.

'Here's to the one who I hope will stay here. Happy Birthday, Lynda Collins!'

It was so easy, chatting and appreciating the food, which they ate slowly, partly to enjoy it to the full and partly to make the evening last as long as possible. Lynda tried all the unfamiliar cheeses on the cheese board, and then they indulged in the delights of the dessert menu.

They were the only customers remaining in the restaurant when they ordered coffee, and they were shown into a small lounge area with comfortable armchairs, and a coffee table with a dish of dark chocolate mints in the centre. Tom sipped his coffee slowly and watched Lynda who had curled up in the chair next to his.

She saw him looking at her, and paused as she drank her coffee.

'I don't want to go home,' she said.

'To Loveday or to Milfield?'

'Neither.'

He was afraid to ask this question, but he knew the strength of his longing, and didn't want to make any mistakes.

'Will you ever go back to Milfield?'

She found this difficult to answer. 'I thought I'd decided I'd never go back, but sometimes I don't know.'

He leaned forward and took hold of her hand.

'I'm hoping you'll stay at Loveday with me. For ever.' He saw he had startled her, 'Sorry, am I going too fast for you?'

'Yes,' she gasped. 'Tom, we don't really know each other.'

'No, but we need to. You're right, we mustn't rush things. I want to be sure, Lynda.'

'So do I,' she whispered.

'Then we'll take it slowly.'

'Yes. Yes, please.'

He held her hand as they walked out into the night and through the garden where the trees were garlanded with tiny starry lights. He paused in the gateway and took her in his arms. He kissed her, and then pulled her closer and kissed her again until she was breathless. Then he forced himself to pull away. He looked at her and smiled.

'Slowly.'

When Rose Milner came to spend Christmas with them at Loveday Manor, she saw the change in their relationship and that Lynda had a new energy, a new confidence. She took Rose on a tour of the hotel, showing her all the changes she had made in the lounges and the hotel foyer, as well as the three other bedrooms she'd re-furbished.

'What do you think, Rose?' she asked excitedly.

'It's amazing how you've changed the feel of the place with all those little touches, the different pictures on the walls, and the brighter cushions in the lounge. And roses in the foyer.'

Lynda laughed. 'I thought you'd like those. A big improvement on those huge displays of lilies that made it look like a funeral parlour. Tom had never noticed that, but he could see what I meant. He'd just carried on letting the staff do the flowers the way Nicki had taught them.'

'But now he listens to you. He seems to be letting you have a free hand in making all these changes.'

'Yes, he thinks I'm a genius, a crazy one sometimes, but he just lets me get on with it in my own way and tells me it's all wonderful.' She paused. 'I've never had anyone encourage me, and believe in me like he does.'

Rose observed the way Lynda's eyes shone when she talked about Tom Meredith, and imagined her friend Janet nodding knowingly.

'He's told me he's lucky to have you, and so is Loveday. He says the bookings have gone up, though everybody wants one of what they call 'the new rooms', and you've had to open the whole hotel at Christmas because there was such a demand.'

'Yes, but to be honest we couldn't afford not to open fully at Christmas. Anyway, we like it, we want it to be similar to the way it was at Springfield – like a family Christmas, but with a very big extended family!'

Rose laughed with delight. 'Including me!'

CHAPTER THIRTY ONE

Mark had been disappointed that his Mother wasn't coming to spend any part of the Christmas holiday with him, and was beginning to realise fully that his parents now lived separate lives.

At the last minute, however, Suzanne arranged for him to fly over to Paris to see her at the beginning of the holiday, and during that time together she talked to him in a way she had never done before. She sat with her arm round him on one of the more comfortable sofas in Nicki's apartment in Neuilly, and talked to him, not as her child, but as her confidant.

'You know that a few weeks ago, your Father and I became finally divorced.'

'Yes.'

'I expect that has made you very sad.'

'Yes, though I've known it was happening for quite a while now.'

'It has made me miserable, so upset that I can't face seeing him. I don't know how long it will be before I'll feel able to visit Loveday. That's why I can't come and spend Christmas there with you. I hope you can understand, and not mind too much.'

He felt more confusion than understanding, but

saw that his Mother had tears in her eyes and, as always, couldn't bear to see her suffer.

'I understand, Mummy, though I'll miss you.'

She kissed him. 'Thank you, my darling. I'm truly sorry about Christmas, but we'll have a lovely time when you come and stay with me in Antibes at February half-term.'

Mark looked up at her, and felt he had to ask the question which had been in his mind for a long time. 'Leaving Daddy has made you so unhappy, Mummy. Did you really want to divorce him?'

A simple question, and such a look of innocence on her son's face, that it compelled Suzanne to answer it with complete honesty.

'No. No, I'm not sure I did.'

'Then why did you and Daddy get divorced?'

Suzanne could find no answer to this question, at least no explanation that she could present to a young boy who had a lot to learn about the world of men and women. She stood up and walked to the window, pulling back the gossamer thin curtain which held back the fading daylight.

'It's very complicated, Mark. Sometimes people do things they regret, but can't find a way back from their mistakes.'

'Do you still love Daddy?'

She turned to face him, with a bleak smile that made him run towards her and put his arms round her waist. She kissed the top of his head, and told him what she had never dared say to her Mother.

'Yes, I do. And I hope he might still love me. It all went wrong somehow. And that, I think, was mostly my fault.'

'Why don't you tell Daddy you're sorry, and make

him love you again?'

She stroked his hair and, with a slight air of defiance, looked across at the self-assured portrait of Nicki Heston which looked down with satisfaction from above the ornate fireplace.

'Perhaps I will one day.'

Amy Ford had so many parties to go to over Christmas that she'd run out of space to scribble all the details in her diary, but she had somehow found the time to make an unscheduled visit to Loveday Manor on the cold, frosty morning after Boxing Day. Patrick took her phone call and was at the door to welcome her.

'Come and have a coffee with me in the conservatory.'

'I'd love to, Patrick, but I haven't much time, I'm on my way to meet some friends. It's Tom and Lynda I came to see.'

He adopted his most mournful look. 'You really know how to make a guy feel wanted.'

She kissed him on the cheek, 'Poor boy. Now, where are they?'

'They've gone for a walk by the river to show Rose how they've renovated the old summer house.'

Amy grabbed his arm. 'Come on, then, let's go and find them.'

She was in such a hurry that they were both out of breath by the time they arrived at the summer house, a white clapboard clad building with a veranda overlooking the river.

'Hello! Happy Christmas if it's not too late!' Amy shouted as she sprang up the steps to give Lynda a hug. 'I've got some terrific news. Well, not terrific for the people who had a big fire at their hotel, obviously, but it's great news for you!'

Lynda laughed and gave her friend a little shake. 'Slow down, what are you on about?' She turned to Rose. 'This is the friend I told you about, Rose. Amy Ford.'

'Oh, yes, the one who owns the gift shop. Pleased to meet you, Amy.'

'Hi, Rose. Hi, Tom. I can't stay long but I had to come and tell you about a great opportunity.'

'We'd better all sit down,' suggested Patrick, indicating the wooden benches on the veranda. 'When Amy gets that look in her eye, you know she's got some grand plan cooked up, and will want you to hear all the details.'

Amy laughed as they all obediently found themselves a place on a bench.

'No details yet. But it is a grand plan.' She turned to Tom and Lynda. 'You know you said you were thinking about developing Loveday as a big wedding venue? Well, how do you fancy doing your first wedding in May?'

Tom blinked. 'In five months time - I thought people booked weddings about a year in advance.'

Amy nodded. 'Yes, my friend, Hannah, arranged it all ages ago, but the hotel she booked has had a huge fire, and she now has no venue for the reception. I suggested Loveday, and mentioned that you have this coach-house and wonderful stables, and she begged me to ask you. She's mad about horses, you see.'

'Whoah,' Patrick quipped. 'Slow down. I don't suppose you happened to mention that this coach-house and stables are in need of massive renovation?'

Amy pulled a face at him. 'I did tell her that,

actually, or rather that they need some work, but she said she didn't mind – she's desperate not to postpone the wedding and she thinks she has no chance of finding a venue at this short notice. Let her and her fiancé at least come to take a look and decide for themselves whether it's suitable or not.'

Lynda's mind was racing, but her voice was calm and determined. 'Give us a week to smarten the place up, and then bring them to have a look.'

Tom shook his head. 'Wait a minute, Lynda. We haven't got the money to transform the barn into a wedding venue.'

'I have,' Lynda said. 'The way I'm going to do it won't cost that much. Amy and I have had some brilliant ideas about what we can do with it, and worked out the costs, and it's affordable.'

Tom wasn't convinced. 'Not for me.'

Lynda stood up and faced him.

'Please, Tom. Let me do this. I have the money. Remember once I told you about my 'mad money'? Well, this is what I want to spend it on. It's a chance for me to start my own business, like Helen Tyler said. Please let's do this, together.'

She stood there, wrapped in a huge, fluffy white scarf, her nose and cheeks pink with the cold, her blonde curls stuffed into a matching woolly hat, and the eyes of a child full of dreams.

He sighed and looked at Amy. 'How many guests are your friends planning to invite?'

'Less than a hundred, I promise,' squealed Amy as she grabbed hold of Lynda and pulled her around dancing a jig.

When he'd sold his beloved Springfield Hotel, Robbie Skelton had passed on to Tom all the things from the hotel that were full of sentimental value to him and to Janet's family. He'd also given him his huge supply of silver and white balloons and Lynda used loads of them, together with some enormous lengths of white net which she borrowed from Amy's friend in the props department at the theatre in Guildford.

By the time Amy brought the future bride and groom to see Loveday Manor and the proposed venue for the reception, Lynda and Tom had transformed the coach-house enough to show them they could achieve the impression of a fairy-tale ballroom.

Hannah Newcombe and Ben Hampton were a bright young couple who had established careers in London, but who both came from local families. They hadn't been to Loveday Manor before and thought it beautiful, and they loved the whole idea of their wedding being set around the courtyard and stables. They were also very relieved to have found a new venue, and immediately booked all the hotel rooms still available for the weekend of their wedding. Tom gave them the menus he had prepared for them to choose from, and they promised to return in a couple of weeks, together with their parents, and finalise the arrangements.

After they had left, Lynda, Tom, Rose, Amy and Patrick sat in Tom's office and opened a bottle of champagne.

Tom proposed the toast, 'To Lynda Collins and Amy Ford, business women of the year!'

'And the poor fellas who are crazy enough to get

involved and say they'll help them!' added Patrick. 'You and me, Tom, we're going to be walking round like old men by the time we've done all the work these two have got lined up for us.'

Amy snuggled up against him. 'We'll be ever so grateful though,' she teased.

Tom smiled at Lynda. 'It's going to be a hectic few months, and we've a helluva lot to learn, but it will be fantastic.'

Rose was going back to Cornwall the next day, and Lynda made sure they had an hour on their own, sitting in the small bedroom which Lynda and Tom had designated as Rose's room at Loveday. Lynda had bought some rose-patterned material and made new curtains, and cushion covers for the small armchair which Rose was sitting in now.

'You look really at home in this room.'

Rose smiled at her. 'I feel at home, especially as you've taken the trouble to fill it with roses.'

Lynda had had a chat with Tom, as they'd both noticed how much more frail Rose had seemed when she'd arrived to spend Christmas with them. They'd decided to try to persuade her to stay longer, but so far she had not said she would.

'Are you sure you want to leave us?' Lynda asked again. 'We'll miss you so much, if you go. Tom and I would be very happy if you'd stay here until the worst of the winter is over.'

Rose thought how much she'd grown to love Lynda, and it was tempting to remain with her at Loveday Manor, but Rose knew she needed to be in her little cottage now.

'It's very kind of you both, but I'm ready to go

284

home. I'd like to come back and help with this wedding, though. I love weddings.'

'Oh, that would be great, come back as soon as you like.'

'The wedding is a big project for you to take on, Lynda, but I think you'll manage it.' Rose wondered if she should say this, but felt she had to protect Lynda. 'I'm a little worried that you're putting all your money into it. You'll have no escape fund.'

'I don't need one,' Lynda said with absolute certainty.

She went to stand by the window and look out at the garden and the stable courtyard.

'I feel as if I've been given a second chance, Rose. I've found what I've been looking for all these years. Working in the hotel and organising weddings is what I want to do. I'll be making new friends, looking after people, giving them a bit of Hollywood and enjoying being part of their dreams. Loveday offers me a new life, where I can be a success, and belong.'

Rose thought how happy she seemed, and how full of hope. She didn't want to spoil Lynda's dream, but experience had taught Rose Milner to be cautious.

'That's wonderful, but don't forget about yourself,' she warned. 'You need to earn a living, and you've always felt more secure with that 'mad money' to give you some independence. From what you've told me, at the moment you're working for love, not money.'

She saw Lynda bow her head and blush, but when she looked up again, there was a radiance about her which wouldn't have been out of place at a wedding.

'That's right, I'm doing it for love.'

'Love of Tom Meredith.'

'Yes.'

The second week in January was always a quiet time at the hotel, when all the New Year Festivities were over and people were getting back into routine at work. Tom often scheduled repairs or decorating the rooms during this period, and he took Lynda to a room on the top floor to discuss how it should be re-furbished.

It was one of only two rooms on that floor of the hotel, both of them faced the garden but had only small windows as they had once formed part of an attic. Lynda walked round the room, so busy assessing it as a designer that she didn't notice Tom locking the door. She went to look out of the two attic windows and then turned to him.

'Are you sure you want to give this room priority for re-furbishing? It's not suitable for some of our guests, with all those stairs to climb, and it really needs larger windows putting in, which would cost a lot.'

He came to stand behind her. 'Wonderful view though, isn't it?'

'Yes, it's gorgeous.'

'It would make a superb penthouse apartment, don't you think?'

'Yeah, but we'd have to spend a fortune to do that, and charge a much higher rate for it.'

He put his arms round her waist and held her tight, breathing in the scent of her hair.

'I wasn't thinking of it for guests. I was thinking it would be a lovely home for us.'

She wriggled out of his arms and backed away from him.

'What do you mean?'

286

'I want this to be our apartment as soon as we can manage to convert it. I want to be with you, Lynda Collins, and I want us to have this as our home, where we can come and be alone, and make love.'

As she listened to his words, spoken so softly, and with such longing, she lost the strength to move, and so he walked over to her and took her in his arms again.

'You said, slowly,' she whispered, 'you said we'd take it slowly.'

He gave her one of those tilting smiles, and said, 'Ah, but now I know you love me.'

Lynda felt bound to challenge that assertion. 'Oh, do you?'

'Yes, because you said so.'

'When?'

'To Rose, yesterday. You were chatting in her room and you'd left the door open. I was bringing you a tray of afternoon tea, and I heard you say it.'

'Overheard, you mean. You were listening at the door.'

'Only by accident, and I disappeared down those stairs pretty quick, I can tell you!'

She laughed. 'And you sent Bridget up with the tray instead.'

'Well, I didn't want to let a good pot of tea go to waste.'

They laughed together for a moment, and then he kissed her again.

'You do love me, don't you?'

'Yes. Yes, Tom Meredith, I love you.'

He gazed at her beautiful face.

'And I love you, Lynda Collins. And I want to be

with you, live with you here, and be truly happy for the first time in my life. That's how it will be for the two of us. We'll be happier than we ever thought possible.'

He was right. They made love that afternoon in the room that would become their own private hideaway, and it was love-making with a tenderness Lynda had never experienced. And later, as he lay sleeping in her arms, she caressed him and knew that she had to be with Tom Meredith, for ever.

CHAPTER THIRTY TWO

Nobody was pleased about Carolyn being pregnant. Carolyn had prayed that she wasn't going to have another baby so soon, and had kept the possibility to herself for a couple of months. It wasn't until she had been to the doctor's again in June, and had been informed that the baby was due in January, that she found the courage to tell Steve.

The only place they had any real privacy was in their bedroom, so she waited until they were getting ready for bed. He was still wearily undoing the buttons of his shirt when she stood in front of him wearing her prettiest nightie, and stroked her hand down his chest. He froze. They had avoided touching each other ever since the row over Nick Allenby.

'Steve, I've got something to tell you.'

He was immediately wary. 'What?'

'I'm pregnant.'

He stared at her, and tried to stop the thoughts that oozed their way into his mind. He turned away and took off his shirt.

'Steve, aren't you going to say anything? I'm expecting a baby in January. Aren't you pleased?'

'No.'

'Oh, don't say that! I know it's earlier than we'd planned, and we'll need another bedroom sooner than we thought, but it will be nice for Michael to have a little brother or sister so close in age. They say it's better to have them close together.'

He heard the words come out of his mouth, but they didn't seem to be from him, happy-go-lucky Steve Sheldon, they were from an angry, cynical, disillusioned man.

'And it's better for them both to have the same father.'

This was what she had been afraid of, this suspicion. But she wasn't going to let there be any doubt, and shouted indignantly, 'What do you mean? The same father! Are you saying it's not your child?'

'I don't know!'

'Well, I do! This is your baby, Steven Sheldon, and don't you dare say otherwise!'

The anger and jealousy which were clamped round his heart made him carry on, in that sceptical and bullying voice that didn't belong to him. 'But is it mine? Can you be sure?'

'Of course I'm sure!'

'There's no 'of course' about it. You had an affair, remember?'

'It wasn't an affair! I told you. I didn't sleep with him. Please, Steve, you've got to believe me.'

She tried to put her arms round him but he shrugged her away.

'Steve, don't be like this. I told you the truth, it was nothing, just a bit of stupidity. I love you.' She placed her hands over the little life that she already loved. 'And this is your baby.'

'You're bound to say that. But how do I know

whether it is or not?'

'It's due in January. We made love in April, a lot. Don't you remember?'

She had to look away for a moment. Unwillingly she'd recalled that it was the sexual excitement she'd felt at Nick Allenby's flirting that had driven her passion for her husband.

Steve hadn't forgotten that love-making, but all he could picture at this moment was the woman he loved giving herself to another man.

'April, when you were seen messing about with him!'

Carolyn cried herself to sleep that night, and Steve hardly slept at all. He was exhausted when he went to work the next morning, but he had no-one working with him, so it wasn't noticed that he made less progress with the job than he would normally have done. And the work he was doing now gave him pleasure.

It hadn't taken Tony Randerson long to realise that Steve Sheldon had talent or, more importantly, that he was worth money to the company. Randerson, always one to spot a trend, had started to expand beyond the production of kitchen units and to develop a kitchen and bedroom design department. Steve had volunteered to become part of that as it offered him the chance to produce higher quality work.

Soon clients had begun to pass the word around, and those who required a cheaper version of the 'top of the range' kitchens featured in the colour supplements of their Sunday newspapers, asked for him by name. They were willing to pay extra to have

Steve assigned to design and fit their kitchens, and Randerson made sure they did.

Steve had been pleased when Randerson had promoted him and was now giving him a monthly salary rather than weekly wages which varied with the amount of overtime available. Carolyn had been really impressed, or at least she'd made a big fuss about it. Since the row in May she'd been careful to show her appreciation of anything he did, but he knew why she'd started doing that, and it irritated him. The news of his promotion received a less enthusiastic response from his workmate.

'You're a mug,' Gary had told him. 'Randerson's making a fortune out of you, and paying you a fraction of what he's charging the clients for you.'

Steve was sorry he'd told Gary what his salary was, but Gary had a way of asking that made it hard for him to refuse. It was fortunate that Gary and his gossip-magnet wife, Jackie, didn't have any connections with employees at Howell and Jameson's, so didn't hear any of the rumours about Nick Allenby. Steve was praying that what Graham's discreet friend had found out would never be heard of outside the family.

Sheila didn't bother hiding her disapproval when, one sunny Saturday in early July, Carolyn found the courage to go to Stanhope Road to tell her about the baby. John, knowing how much his daughter was dreading this task, had offered to look after his grandson for a couple of hours so that she could give the conversation with Sheila her full attention. She found her grandmother in the large garden at the back of the house, sitting in one of her new reclining chairs and enjoying the scent of the roses her husband had lovingly tended for so many years. She was pleased to see her granddaughter, but when the reason for the visit was revealed it was greeted as a tragedy.

'Oh, no! Not another baby! This will put an end to your career before it's even started.'

That had been Carolyn's first reaction to this pregnancy, but she didn't want to admit it. 'No, Nana, it will just delay it for a while. I'll go back to work as soon as I can, and pick up where I left off.'

'That's assuming they'll have you back.'

Her words frightened Carolyn. 'Why wouldn't they?'

'You can't be sure no-one else found out about your reckless behaviour with that man. And now on top of that, you'll have to tell them you're pregnant. And you know how people can put two and two together and make five.'

'Oh, don't say that!'

'Well, they'll know you didn't want another one so soon. You'd only just started your career with them. Oh, Carolyn, how could you do this to me? Another unwanted pregnancy! I don't know how I'm going to tell Ellen Heywood.'

Carolyn now had another anxiety. 'Has Ellen heard the gossip about me and Nick Allenby?'

'I don't know. Let's hope not. But Ellen is going to be as disappointed in you as I am. I so wanted you to have a wonderful future, and so did Ellen. That was why she got you the job. It was a chance to put the shame of having to get married behind you and start again. You were doing so well. And now you've thrown it all away.'

Carolyn brushed away a tear, 'I'm sorry, Nana. I know it's too soon, but we did want a little brother or sister for Michael before he went to school.'

'Oh, did you? Or are you just making the best of another mistake?'

Carolyn resigned herself to a difficult afternoon with her Nana, and went into the kitchen to make some tea, and hope that it wouldn't be too long before her Dad came to pick her up. She tried talking about the garden, but that brought back memories of her Grandad and how he had deserted his wife. She tried talking about the forthcoming wedding of Sarah Ferguson and Prince Andrew, but Sheila didn't approve of the prince's choice of bride, and that led to the subject of the Duchess of Windsor who'd recently died, and Sheila's judgement of what a disgrace that affair was to the Royal Family. By the time John arrived, Carolyn was exhausted with trying to find something positive to talk about to her Nana.

John had hardly sat down with his cup of tea when Sheila confronted him with the question, 'What do you think about this baby, then?'

'What do you mean?'

'Well, it's too soon isn't it? They should have waited.'

'You can't always decide when these things should happen.'

'You can these days. They should have waited till they could afford a home of their own. They'll need a third bedroom now.'

Carolyn was silent, this was a big concern for her and Steve, especially with house prices going up. It was something John had been worrying about, too, and he had a solution.

He spoke with some trepidation, but the subject had to be broached. 'I've been thinking about that, Mother. This house is much larger than you need, and you can't manage a garden as big as this now. If you sold this place and bought a nice little bungalow, you could release some equity and help Carolyn and Steve towards getting a house.'

Sheila's response was sharp and shrill. 'No I could not! There is no question of my doing that.'

Carolyn and John were astonished at the panic this suggestion seemed to have caused Sheila, but she was able to quickly calm herself, because she had thought of another, far better answer to the problem.

'And anyway,' she said, 'Beechwood Avenue is Carolyn's home. It would make more sense if you moved out and let her have the house she's lived in all her life.'

'Where would I live?'

'You could move back here with me.'

John sucked in a big gulp of air and could not speak. This was not an alternative he had thought of, or ever wanted to think about. His Mother was disappointed that her son obviously didn't like the idea, but it was what she had dreamed of, having her son home with her again, and she was willing to give him time to realise that it would be the right outcome for the situation.

Pleased to have launched her idea, she decided now she could be pleasant company again, and that this baby's arrival might prove advantageous after all.

She smiled at Carolyn for the first time that afternoon. 'Anyway, it looks like I'll have to start knitting again. What will you need this time, Carolyn?

Something pink, I hope. I shall be very disappointed if it's not a girl.'

John watched his daughter work hard at trying to put her marriage back together. He comforted his little girl when she cried, and she told him how she'd had to endure the whispers and disapproving looks from her female colleagues when they'd found out she was pregnant. It had been noticed that the flirtatious behaviour between her and Nick Allenby had ceased and, when he announced he was leaving, many of them wondered, as Sheila had predicted, if his sudden departure had anything to do with Carolyn's pregnancy.

Steve often came home late, finding work which brought in the much needed extra money but also, John suspected, to avoid his wife's company. John also noticed that Steve had started inviting him to go to the pub more frequently since the row in May over Carolyn's silly flirtation. He tried turning down the offer, but then Steve went on his own, so John decided it was better to go with him.

This was their time for the conversations they couldn't have at home, and they were grateful that there was always a quiet corner available in The Britannia Inn. Steve usually spent some of the time talking about work. John hated even hearing Randerson's name, but he knew Steve valued his opinion about what went on at Bentham's, so he listened carefully to the latest instalment.

'Gary says his wife works for somebody I did a kitchen for, and she's going to see if she can find out how much Randerson charged them.'

296

'Can't do any harm to know.'

'I'm just glad to have more money coming in.'

'Still making progress towards that deposit?'

'Yeah, we're saving as much as we can. And we've been looking, but prices keep going up.'

'You'll need the extra bedroom with the new baby.' John paused and observed Steve carefully as he asked the question. 'Things are getting better between you and Carolyn, aren't they?'

'I suppose so.'

'You've got to get over it, Steve. And that guy's left now.'

'Yeah.' Steve couldn't keep the bitter satisfaction out of his voice. 'Helluva shock to Carolyn when he announced he'd got a job in America, and was leaving at the end of the month. She hadn't seen that one coming. Good timing as well, wasn't it, before people started noticing her bump?' He drank the rest of his beer and banged his empty glass down on the table. 'Time for another.'

'No. Carolyn will be wondering where we are. What do you mean, good timing? What's that fella leaving got to do with Carolyn expecting?'

'You tell me!'

'No! You stop this, now, Steve! She told you, she didn't sleep with him. I believe her, and so should you. Our Carolyn doesn't tell lies. This is your baby, and I never want to hear you say any different!'

Steve had never seen John so angry. He didn't want to upset this man who treated him like a son, so he nodded and said, 'O.K. We'll go if you don't want another pint.'

They walked home in silence for a while, but John couldn't bear to see Steve so unhappy.

'Carolyn does love you, you know. I found her upstairs crying when you were working late last week. She's terrified you'll leave her. You can't have her feeling like that, Steve. Everybody deserves a second chance.'

Steve continued to walk along without speaking, so John tried again. 'What are you going to do about all this, Steve? Walk out on your wife and your little boy, the only family you've got?'

'No.'

'Then you've got to stop tormenting yourself, and you've got to make your marriage work.'

John felt saddened as he looked at the young man who had once been known for his mischievous grin, and for always finding humour in any situation. His son-in-law had more the look of a careworn old man now as he said, 'I know. But it's not easy, John.'

'I know.'

John Stanworth had been weighed down with some unwelcome thinking these last few weeks, and his body felt as if it were bowed under the sorrow of the decision he'd had to make. Nevertheless he forced himself to utter the words which would condemn him to a life he didn't want.

'It'd be easier if you had your own house. Has Carolyn told you what my Mother said about that?'

'Yeah. What a bloody awful idea, you moving back in with her!'

'That's what I thought at first. I was really hoping that she'd sell up and give you a share, but she won't hear of it.'

'We can't expect her to. It's something we have to sort out for ourselves, buying a house.'

'But you can't. You'll never manage it before the baby is born, however hard you work. And you work damned hard, Steve. I really admire you for that.'

'Thanks. But don't worry about us, John. We'll manage, if you don't mind putting up with another baby yelling and stinking the place out with dirty nappies!'

'I won't have to put up with that, because I've decided my Mother is right. It makes sense for me to move in with her, she has me round there half the time anyway, doing jobs for her.'

'No, John. I can't let you do that.'

'You can't stop me, lad. I've thought it all through. We'll agree a price you can afford and get the house sold to you and Carolyn, and that's it, problem solved.'

'No, John,' Steve said, but his father-in-law could see the light had come back in his eyes.

'Stop arguing, and let's get home and tell Carolyn the good news.'

They'd reached Beechwood Avenue by now, and both of them stopped and stared at the house they lived in. Steve looked at John who nodded and held out his hand. Blinking back tears, Steve took that strong, work-chastened hand in both of his.

'Thank you, John.'

CHAPTER THIRTY THREE

Christmas 1986 was a low-key affair, more a period of waiting than a festive season. Steve's twenty-fourth birthday on January 6th also passed almost unnoticed. A few days later Sheila was with Carolyn, watching the snow begin to fall, when her granddaughter began having contractions. Both Steve and John came home early from work, and Carolyn phoned the hospital, who told her she should come in straight away.

She became tearful. 'I wanted to put Michael to bed first.'

'He'll be all right, he's got his Grandad to put him to bed.'

'I wish his Grandma was here as well,' sighed John.'

'Well, she isn't,' Sheila said sharply, 'Nor is she ever likely to be.'

Steve, too, had been thinking of Lynda. 'It's crazy that she doesn't even know she's about to have another grandchild. I can't believe she didn't leave an address where we could contact her, or at least some clue as to where to look for her.'

Like an irritating fly, guilt flitted briefly across

Sheila's face, before she hissed, 'Will you shut up talking about Lynda. Can't you see it's upsetting Carolyn? Now let's get to the hospital.'

In the delivery room Steve, waiting anxiously for the midwife to come back, found that Lynda was still on his mind.

'It's all wrong that your Mother's not here. It was such a lovely moment, you and her, and Michael.'

Carolyn finished breathing her way through another painful contraction and then turned angrily to her husband. 'Did you not listen to what my Nana said? I don't want to hear about my Mother! She's not here when I need her. She never has been. My Nana's the one sitting out there in that draughty corridor, worrying about me. She's always been the one who's looked after me.'

'Yeah, and that was always the trouble, her being there.'

'I can't believe we're having this conversation. I'm about to have a baby and all you can talk about is my flaming Mother.' She gasped with pain again, 'Well, as far as I'm concerned my Mother is dead!'

The midwife heard Carolyn's anger as she came back in, and nodded knowingly to her assistant, in mutual recognition that their patient had reached the transition stage. Steve stared at his wife, and wondered for a moment not only if he loved this bitter, unforgiving woman, but if he really knew her.

A little while later Gemma Sheldon entered her parents' lives and added to the tension between them. Her Mother held her close and told her she was beautiful. The midwife smiled, but then turned away and found herself a task in a far corner of the room, as she heard Carolyn speak to her husband in a tone which did not suit the occasion.

'Well? Aren't you going to hold her?'

Steve reluctantly took the baby in his arms, and searched the tiny wrinkled face for some feature which would instantly reassure him, but found none. His body tensed, and the baby stirred fretfully. He looked at his wife who stared at him, waiting for the loving words he couldn't bring himself to say. He looked at the child again, and said, 'Gemma. That's what you want to call her, isn't it?'

'Yes, Gemma Sheldon,' Carolyn said firmly, and then added in a whisper, 'She is yours, Steve, I swear she's your daughter.'

He handed the baby back to her. 'I'll go and let your Nana come in. She'll be desperate to see you both.'

Steve didn't go home, he went for a walk round the streets of Milfield, and didn't stop until he came to Bennett Street. He stood outside number twenty-one, the large, stone terraced house which had been the home of Kathleen and Bernard Kelly, the couple who had looked after him when he was a teenager who had needed a home and a Mum and Dad.

The new owners had painted the windows and the door a dark blue instead of the emerald green which Kath and Bernie had chosen because of their home in Ireland – and the Frankie Vaughan hit 'Green Door' which had 'an old piano playing hot' behind it. The curtains of the houses on the street were closed for the night, so no-one saw the young man standing outside the Kellys' house for a long time, and staring up at the front window. Steve thought about Kath and Bernie, who had been his family before he had married Carolyn and started a family of his own. He knew for certain that they would have said exactly what John had said to him.

When he went back to the hospital at visiting time that evening, he found Carolyn feeding the baby with tears streaming down her cheeks. He passed her some tissues, and then sat quietly at the side of the bed until she finished feeding and moved little Gemma to a sitting position. The baby burped and seemed to smile.

Steve leaned forward to take hold of her tiny fingers, and looked up at his wife. 'She's beautiful like her Mother, but she's got my cheeky grin.'

Ellen Heywood declined the invitation to the home-made buffet lunch which was held at Beechwood Avenue to celebrate Carolyn's twenty-first birthday, but she did invite Carolyn to afternoon tea at Kirkwood House a few days before that homely celebration. She presented her protégée with an Edwardian pendant and the assurance that she would always be a welcome visitor to Kirkwood House, whenever she could arrange to have the children looked after for the afternoon. Carolyn came home happy that Ellen was still fond of her and interested in her future.

Dan Heywood was happy to accept the invitation to Beechwood Avenue, but he wasn't very pleased when he saw that his Mother had given Carolyn a piece of jewellery that, in his opinion, should have stayed in the family. It was not a valuable pendant but it had belonged to his beloved Scottish grandmother.

And nothing similar had ever been given to Ellen's daughter-in-law, Jenny, or, as yet, to Alex or Katie, her granddaughters. It was yet another example of Ellen's actions causing her son distress, but Dan decided to try to forget about her for a few hours and enjoy chatting to John and his family.

'How are things, John? I haven't seen you for a while.'

John, with baby Gemma in one arm, bent down and fixed his grandson's toy train together for the third time. 'No. I've been busy with these two,' he smiled. 'And doing as much overtime as I can get.'

Dan, glancing towards the door to make sure Sheila wasn't about to enter the front room, lowered his voice as he enquired, 'How's it working out, living at your Mother's?'

John shrugged resignedly. 'Well, you know how it is, being in the same boat. I could strangle her sometimes, but on the whole I'm coping. And the food's good.'

Dan laughed, 'You've one up on me there, I still have to do the cooking most days.' He paused before asking the question that was important to him. 'Has Lynda been in touch, with it being Carolyn's 21st?'

John shook his head. 'No.'

'Is Carolyn upset?'

'She seems more angry than upset, but I think she was secretly hoping her Mum would come back for her birthday. I know I was. I felt sure she would have at least sent a card, but there's been nothing.'

'That's not like Lynda.'

'No. I'm worried to death that something's happened to her.'

'You'd have heard from the police if it had.'

304

'I suppose so. It's not right, is it, Dan? She's got a granddaughter here that she knows nothing about.'

Dan shook his head and smiled at the baby. 'Never mind, Gemma, your Grandma will come back and see you one day.'

Steve came over to join in the conversation. 'According to her Mother, Gemma hasn't got a Grandma. She won't let us talk about Lynda, will she, John?'

'No. It's terrible. She says she'll never speak to her Mother again, especially after today.'

Steve looked at Dan. 'It's pretty bad, isn't it, not turning up for your daughter's twenty-first?'

'Yeah,' Dan agreed. He sought something positive to say. 'It's nice having a party at home.'

Steve readily picked up the change of subject. 'Yes, we decided that with these two lively little beggars it'd be chaos trying to go to a hotel. I'm taking Carolyn out for a meal tonight, though. I've booked us in for the dinner-dance at The Peacock, Carolyn's always wanted to go.'

'And he's hoping he can remember how to dance,' laughed John, watching the door open and Sheila enter with the birthday cake. 'Oh, grab hold of Michael, here come the candles.'

Sheila placed the cake on the small table in the centre of the room, and was closely followed by Sylvia and Jean Haworth carrying trays full of glasses, and Graham brandishing a bottle of champagne. The other guests, Carolyn's school-friend, Tricia and her fiancé Philip Lawson shuffled into a corner to make room for Carolyn to stand by the table. Graham poured the champagne and Steve stepped forward.

'I'd like to propose a toast to Carolyn, my beautiful wife and fantastic mother of my children. At twenty-one her life and her dreams are only just beginning, and I look forward to sharing them with her.' He raised his glass, 'Happy Birthday, Carolyn.'

Everyone drank the toast and sang 'Happy Birthday to You', and made sure that they didn't mention the one person who should have been there and wasn't.

Steve did remember how to dance and, as they sat in The Peacock Hotel, enjoying the meal and each other's company, he and Carolyn laughed as they remembered Bernie and Kath teaching him the slow waltz.

'They were a lovely couple. I was always at their house when I was a kid, getting away from my Dad. I'll always be grateful to them, especially Bernie, for getting me my apprenticeship, and for arranging for me to meet you at that New Year's Eve party, of course!'

'You think he planned it, for us to get together?'

'Yeah, he loved to do a bit of match-making, did Bernie. And he and Kath always wanted to see me happily married and settled down.'

'And are you – happily married?' Carolyn asked, still a little unsure of how Steve felt.

'Yeah. Are you?'

'Yes.'

'Even though I messed up your life, getting you pregnant?'

Carolyn remembered the passion which had overwhelmed her that first time with him. 'You know what they say, it takes two. I've no regrets, Steve. I've got you, and a home and two gorgeous children. What more could I wish for?'

'A helluva lot!' He reached across and took hold of her hand. 'I'll make sure you get all the things you've dreamed of Carolyn, I promise.'

When they arrived home later that night John was delighted to see them so happy together, and quickly ushered out his Mother and Jean Haworth, who had stayed on after the party to help clear up and to enjoy John's company for a few hours. Sheila had observed her eagerness to help and the way she looked at John, and was forming the opinion that Jean Haworth might prove to be a useful member of the family. Sheila was finding it harder to ignore the signals her body was giving her that she needed to think, very unwillingly, that there might soon be a time when she would not be there to take care of her family.

John drove his Mother home first and Jean noticed his grim expression as he came out of her house and got into the car.

'What's the matter?'

He sighed as he switched on the ignition. 'It's like being a kid again.' He raised the pitch of his voice into a attempt to convey his Mother's whine. 'Have you got your key? Drive carefully, there'll be drunks driving home from the pubs.'

'She just worries about you.'

'Yeah, I know, but I'm forty-four years old, Jean, and here I am living back home with my Mother.'

'It was very generous of you, letting Carolyn and Steve have the house,' Jean commented, not really having approved of his giving them such a bargain.

He drove slowly, glad of the opportunity to talk to

someone who was sympathetic. 'They needed it, but I must admit it's got me down, moving back into Stanhope Road. It's like I'm standing in for my Dad, and I feel like an old man.'

'You don't seem like that to me.' She looked at his dark, handsome profile, and the yearning she had always had for this man gave her the impetus to declare her feelings. 'You're still young, and as good-looking as you've always been in my book.'

He was both startled and pleased to hear this, and rewarded her with a confidence.

'I'm lonely, Jean. I suppose I'm missing Lynda. I was hoping, I was convinced she'd come back for Carolyn's twenty-first.'

'Yes. She should have done. It's beginning to look like she's forgotten about you.'

John didn't say anything else, but felt that perhaps Jean was right. The angry thoughts he'd had about Lynda's desertion of him gathered in his head again as he drove to Jean's cosy little home.

When she invited him in for a drink, he accepted and, after a large whisky, was also ready to accept everything else she was blushingly, yet so explicitly, eager to offer. In front of the fire in her cosy living room he satisfied his need of her, a need driven by a masculine frustration and a desire for revenge. But Jean's love-making was the release of a passion she had nurtured since he had danced with her at the Carlton ballroom, when she was sixteen years old, and crazy about him.

When John arrived home he was annoyed to find that his Mother had waited up for him. She didn't question his lateness, but knew her son well enough to guess its cause. The following morning, she initiated a pointed conversation about Jean Haworth.

'She seems very fond of you. She's had a crush on you for a long time, hasn't she?'

'A crush! Don't talk daft, Mother!'

'Well, a crush is probably not the right word at her age, but she's obviously very keen on you. And you could do worse.'

'What do you mean?'

'You could marry Jean, sell her cottage and buy a nice little bungalow together. You'd need to get a divorce first, of course, but there's nothing to stop you doing that.'

Like his father, so many times in the past, John didn't say anything, but walked out of the kitchen door and found some work to do in the garden.

CHAPTER THIRTY FOUR

Rose Milner had been looking forward to returning to Loveday Manor and helping Lynda organise the wedding, but one cold, windy afternoon in February she settled down for a little nap on her rose-chintz covered sofa and fell asleep for the last time.

It was almost exactly a year since Janet Meredith had died, and Tom and Mark grieved for her again as they and Lynda travelled down to Cornwall for the funeral. They stayed at The Springfield Hotel and tried not to notice the changes that had been made, they wanted to remember it just as it had been when Robbie had owned it. He, too, could not bear to return, but phoned them from his new home in France and sent a huge box of roses to decorate the little church.

There were also snowdrops and early daffodils from almost every family in St Benedict, and after the funeral all the flowers were taken away, as Rose had requested, and given to local hospitals and nursing homes. Only Lynda and Tom's oval wreath of her favourite pink and white roses were placed on the grave next to that of Janet Meredith and her husband.

Tom and Lynda stood there after everyone else

had gone. Mark had been invited to spend the rest of the afternoon with friends in the village. He would meet them back at the hotel that evening, where in accordance with Rose's instructions, there would be a party to celebrate her life. Mark was glad to leave the graveside and walk back through the village, letting the sound of the sea blur the edge of his thoughts about losing loved ones.

The wind had brought a salty chill as it chased the mourners out of the graveyard, and Tom kept his arm round Lynda's shoulders and pulled her close.

'Two friends back together, eh?'

Lynda wiped away more tears and whispered, 'Two wonderful women. I wish I'd had more time with both of them.'

'You'll never forget them, so you'll still have their company.'

She laid her head on his chest and looked up at him. 'That's a good way to think about it.'

Hesitantly Tom asked, 'Shall we go back to Rose's place and make a cup of tea? Or is it too soon to go to her cottage?'

Lynda took a deep breath, 'No, it would have been just what she and Janet would have done.' She reached into her pocket and drew out the key she had gripped so hard during the service that it had dug into her hand. 'I can't believe Rose left me her cottage.'

Almost as soon as they had arrived at The Springfield Hotel, Lynda had received a phone call from Ernest Latimer, Rose's solicitor, asking if he could call and see her on his way home from the office that evening. When this thin, bespectacled gentleman arrived, having insisted that he would meet them in the small quiet room to one side of the foyer, he had shyly handed Lynda an envelope.

'This is most irregular, most disconcerting,' he had murmured sotto voce, 'but Rose, Mrs Milner, left me strict instructions that I was to come and inform you, straight away, that she had left you her cottage, and to give you this envelope which, I believe, contains a letter and a key. If you would be good enough to call at my office the morning after the funeral, say ten-thirty, I shall be able to read you her will.'

Lynda's eyes filled with tears again as she walked up to the door of Rose's cottage with the key in her hand. She stepped inside and looked round at the cosy furniture and Rose's ornaments, trinkets and treasures. For a moment she found she couldn't move, then Tom led her gently over to the armchair by the fire.

'I'll put the kettle on.'

They stayed in the cottage for over an hour, remembering the happy times with Rose, but avoiding looking at the little sofa where Rose's friend, Biddy, had found her, she had assured Lynda, looking content and peaceful.

'Will you keep the cottage, or haven't you decided yet?' Tom asked.

'I'll sell it. Rose expected me to, she said so in the letter she sent with the key. She knew that I'd be living at Loveday, and probably wouldn't have time to come to Cornwall often enough to justify having a home here.'

'It would be somewhere to escape to,' he suggested with a wry smile.

'Escape from you, do you mean? I don't think I'll

want to do that. And if you don't mind leaving for Loveday a bit later than planned, I'd like you to come with me to the solicitor's for the reading of Rose's will. I'll be too emotional to take in what Mr Latimer is saying.'

'Yes, of course. I wish I could stay and help you sort out the cottage and everything, but you know what it's like. And Mark has to get back for school.'

'Don't worry about me, I'll be fine here. And I think Mark might be glad to have you to himself for a bit. Has he said anything about us being together? He seemed a bit surprised that we were sharing a room at Springfield.'

'Yes, I'll have to have a chat with him.'

Tom was not going to tell her that he'd already had one emotional conversation with his son, who was not finding it easy to understand how parents might move on from being divorced. He smiled at Lynda.

'Don't worry. He thinks the world of you.'

Rose Milner had enjoyed life, but she had also known what it was like to be short of money and had learned to be a prudent business woman. The consequence of this for Lynda was, as she and Tom discovered during the meeting in Ernest Latimer's office, that she inherited not just Rose's cottage, but also a large sum of money. Lynda felt dazed as she left the solicitor's office, and she and Tom went for a walk along the beach, to enjoy the unexpected sunshine, and to give her chance to recover from the shock of such astonishing news.

'Rose explained in the letter she sent me with the key, that I was more than a friend, I was her connection with Ted, who had made her so happy. So I have Ted Stanworth to thank for this as well. But, Tom, so much money, and the cottage.'

'You'll have to think very carefully about what you want to do with it,' Tom said solemnly.

'Oh, I already know what I'm going to do with a big chunk of it. I'm going to give it to you so you can pay off the bank loan, and make Loveday Manor the four-star hotel you've always dreamed of.'

'No.' The single word was uttered so forcefully that it made her stop and look at him.

'Why not? I love you. And we're a couple, aren't we?'

'Yes. But I can't let you give me money like that.'

'Of course you can! We love each other, don't we? And we both want Loveday to be a success, we love the place. It's what I want to do with my life, Tom. I told Rose that.'

'And I bet she warned you not to give it to me.'

Lynda, becoming exhilarated with the power she now had to shape her future, laughed out loud. 'Yes, she did. But she understood when I told her how I felt.'

He spoke sternly again. 'She was right, though, Lynda. You mustn't give me the money. It's yours. Rose left it to you, not to me. She generously left me and Mark part of her hard-earned cash, in memory of my Mother, and that's all we should have. I won't let you give it to me. I've already borrowed what you call your 'mad money'. And I shouldn't have done that, really. You can't make that kind of financial commitment to me and Loveday Manor, you can't predict what the future will be.'

She felt as if she'd opened her loving arms to him

314

and he'd turned away. 'What are you saying, that we're not going to be together?'

'No, I'm not saying that. But you need to think about all this. I know from experience how things can go wrong, and I don't want you to go through the kind of financial minefield that I've just struggled through. Do you understand?'

'Yeah, of course I do,' she lied. She didn't want him to see her disappointment, and the anger that made make her want to beat him with her fists. She looked at her watch. 'You'd better go, you told Mark to be ready to leave by twelve. He'll be waiting for you.'

He checked his watch too. 'Yes, I hadn't realised the time.'

She looked at him steadily, almost coldly, 'I'll see you in a few days time. When I've sorted out everything down here.'

'Aren't you coming to see us off?'

'No. I'll stay here. I need a walk. Like you said, I need to think. Tell Mark I'll see him back at Loveday.'

'O.K.' He stepped towards her but was only allowed to kiss her on the cheek.

'Safe journey,' she said softly, refusing to look into his bewildered eyes.

He walked away slowly, raising his hand to blow her a kiss. She waved, and then walked towards the waves feathering their way on to the sand. Before he reached the road he waved to her again, but she didn't turn round to see him.

Lynda felt it was one of the worst things she'd ever had to do, going through everything that made up the history of Rose's life, and having to decide what to do

315

with each item before she could eventually leave the house empty and ready to be put up for sale. By the time she returned to Loveday Manor she had no tears left, but had done a lot of thinking – and had read a book on hotel management which she'd borrowed from the new owner of Springfield.

She arranged a formal meeting with Tom Meredith, and was very pleased at how surprised he was at the new persona she presented, Lynda Collins, potential business woman of the year. She laid out her plans in front of him, and then calmly sat by his desk and waited for him to read them. When she spoke it was with scarcely a trace of her Northern accent – she'd been practising this speech standing in front of the full-length mirror in Rose's bedroom.

'As you can see, I've thought about what you said, and I hope you will accept this as a sensible approach. I intend eventually to set up a company but, in the meantime, all the weddings I organise will be financed by me, and Loveday Manor will take a share of the profit and receive income for any in-house catering involved.'

He nodded, trying not to look amused at the formal way she was speaking to him. 'Sounds good to me. And in return I think Loveday Manor should give your company a share of the extra hotel bookings we receive as a result of the accommodation requested by the wedding guests.'

'Yes, I'd expect that.' She paused, wondering how long she could keep up this act, and leaned forward to lay down the conditions she knew he might object to. 'However, for the hotel to reach the standard I will require for the wedding guests, a certain amount of

316

investment of capital will be needed. I propose to make that investment in return for a small share in the hotel.'

She waited anxiously for him to respond. He teased her by taking a while to re-read the documents Amy had typed out for her. He then stood up and held out his hand.

'We'll have to work out some of the details, but as far as I'm concerned, it's a deal.'

They shook hands, then he swiftly moved round the desk to stand beside her.

'And now, please may I have a kiss?'

CHAPTER THIRTY FIVE

The next few weeks were incredibly hard work but the most exciting time Lynda had ever had in her life. She had a wonderful time running round checking the work being done on the coach-house and stables, ordering curtains and carpets for the bedrooms and for the dining room, which she thought, as well as being a bit faded, looked far too cold and formal to be the right setting for two families and their guests to socialise and get to know each other. She also arranged for a section of the floor to be made suitable for dancing.

She spent hours designing and making the blue, white and silver drapes, decorations and flower arrangements for the coach-house. She decided to make the table decorations herself and, with some help from Amy, the small gifts which Helen Tyler had suggested.

Lynda was especially pleased when a sample of the chairs arrived, complete with their white damask coverings and blue satin bows – another idea she had picked up from listening to Helen. The delivery van blocked the driveway for a while, and Suzanne, who was arriving to stay at Loveday for most of Mark's Easter holiday, sounded the horn of her hired car impatiently as she waited to drive up to the hotel.

'What are you having delivered to the stables?' she asked Tom.

'Not me, Lynda, it'll be something for the wedding.'

'What wedding?'

'The one Lynda is organising at the beginning of May.'

'By Lynda, do you mean the woman who was working on the re-furbishing of the bedrooms?'

'Yes, Lynda Collins. She's done a lot of work on quite a few of the bedrooms, and the dining room, she's working her socks off to get them ready for the wedding.'

'Why on earth have you given her the responsibility for all that? I do hope it wasn't because of her blonde hair and other rather obvious physical attributes.'

'Don't be silly, Suzanne.'

'She doesn't seem to me to have the background or experience for that kind of work, and her idea of style leaves a lot to be desired. How long did you say she'd been working for you?'

'Not long.'

'So she wasn't a factor in your hastening our divorce?'

'It was your Mother who was setting the timetable there, if you remember.'

Suzanne didn't want to acknowledge that, and so returned to her original subject. 'I thought you had no money left after the divorce. Where have you found the finance for all these changes?'

'I don't think my financial arrangements need concern you any more now that we're divorced,' Tom replied coolly. 'Mark's just got home from school, he'll be in the kitchen with Patrick I expect. Do you want to go and look for him?'

'No, you go and tell him I'll be in the conservatory having a coffee, will you?'

'Certainly, Madam,' Tom replied sarcastically, and marched off, trying to suppress his irritation at being treated as a servant – a habit Suzanne had copied from her Mother.

Lynda tried to avoid Tom's ex-wife during her visit, which wasn't difficult most of the time as she was, like the rest of the hotel staff, kept very busy as the hotel was fully booked over Easter. Occasionally she found herself serving her at dinner, as Suzanne saw no reason to cook in the kitchen at The Gatehouse when she could dine for free at the hotel.

Mark now joined Suzanne every evening for dinner, and Lynda saw that he seemed to feel a little awkward talking to her in front of his Mother. She was also aware that Suzanne watched her closely, and she once overheard part of a conversation which indicated that Suzanne questioned Mark about her.

On Easter Sunday, he was even hesitant about helping with the Easter Egg Hunt which Lynda had organised again, and which he knew his Mother disapproved of, but in the end he couldn't resist the madcap fun of it.

When most of the guests had left after Easter, Suzanne Meredith, she had decided to keep her married name, for the sake of her son, demanded to be taken on a tour of the changes which had taken place. Tom declined to accompany her, but could not refuse Mark's request to be allowed to act as his Mother's guide. Tom did, however, instruct his son not to include the rooms on the top floor which were being converted into an apartment.

Mark didn't like the way his Mother made sarcastic comments about the changes Lynda had made, but found himself joining in her laughter as she mocked Lynda's taste.

'I'm really surprised that your Father has allowed her to take over the re-decorating, and buying new curtains and carpets.'

'I suppose he hasn't got the time to do it himself,' the boy explained.

'I assume she has to discuss it with him?'

'Oh, yes. And they argue about it sometimes.'

'Do they?'

'Yes, like when Lynda wanted to make one of the bedrooms a sunflower room. She got the idea when they sold that sunflower painting for £24 million.'

'The van Gogh, you mean? What an awful idea! He didn't let her do it, did he?'

'Yes, he did. But she had to tone the colours down a bit. Lynda says my Dad's making her learn to compromise.'

Is he? Do they spend a lot of time together talking about the hotel?'

'Oh, yes. Lynda's always coming up with ideas. Dad says she's a crazy little whirlwind.'

'He seems to like her, though.'

'Yes, he does.'

'And you like her, too, don't you?'

'Oh, yeah!' Mark said, but, realising he had perhaps sounded too enthusiastic, he added, 'But not as much as you, Mummy.'

Suzanne saw her son's anxiety, and smiled. 'I should hope not!'

The following morning, when Tom had taken his son fishing, Suzanne used her old key to go into her ex-husband's bedroom, and was furious at finding Lynda's clothes and toiletries there. She was looking through the dressing table drawers when Lynda, having spilled green paint down the front of her shirt while giving the stable doors a final coat, came back into the room to change. She was startled to find Suzanne there, but instinctively confronted her.

'What are you doing in here?'

'This is my husband's bedroom, our bedroom. Why should I not be here?'

'Because it's not your room any more. He's your ex-husband, in case you hadn't noticed. And those are my bloody things you're poking your nose into!'

'My goodness, you do have a temper. Tom won't like that, or perhaps you've managed to keep it from him so far? And it makes your accent become even more noticeable. Northern, isn't it? And you have a family in the North, I believe. But obviously not one you can go back to, as you seem to have decided to stay here and try to steal mine.'

'What a load of rubbish.'

'Rubbish? Well, if we're talking about rubbish, let's discuss your taste in decoration and furnishing. You're ruining this hotel, destroying everything my Mother and I have created.' She walked across to draw back one of the curtains, 'at least he hasn't let you spoil our bedroom.'

322

Lynda wondered why she didn't tell Suzanne that the only reason she and Tom had decided not to change this room was that they would be moving into the new apartment, which would soon become their home. She saw her reflection in the mirror, dishevelled hair flecked with the green paint which also adorned her grubby shirt, and then looked at the confident, elegant, and expensively dressed woman standing by the window. Suzanne smirked as she saw Lynda making the comparison.

'You see it, don't you? You're not what he needs to make a success of Loveday Manor. You haven't got the class and culture that I and my family provided for him. He needs a lot more than a cheap, gold-digging tart in his bed.'

Lynda felt herself losing the strength her anger had given her as she tried to withstand the unwavering contempt in her rival's eyes. For that was what Suzanne Meredith was, she realised, a rival who kept Tom's name and was the Mother of his son. She guessed that this woman regretted losing her home and her husband, and perhaps was still in love with him.

Lynda felt vulnerable as she realised she wasn't sure of Tom Meredith's love, and wondered if she ever would be sure that someone could love her. She knew why she hadn't stood up to Suzanne more strongly, why she hadn't told her that she and Tom planned to live together in the apartment upstairs.

She saw Suzanne's eyes begin to gleam with triumph and intent, and knew she had to fight back. It was difficult to square her shoulders, tilt her chin and look confident wearing paint-spattered jeans with holes in them, and a shirt that was becoming glued to her skin as the paint dried, but she did her best.

'I think you'd better leave,' she said, wishing she sounded less like an actress in a B-Movie.

Suzanne just laughed at her, and as she walked out, she turned and said, 'You do realise don't you, you stupid little tart, that I can have him back any time I choose.'

Lynda had organised what she called 'a singing supper' for the Friday night before Ben Hampton and Hannah Newcombe's wedding. The bride and groom's parents, bridesmaids and ushers were all staying at Loveday Manor, together with various other relatives and some of the couple's closest friends. Hannah and Ben were a little anxious about how all these people would mix, as many of them didn't know each other. Even the parents of the bride and groom hadn't met very often. As everyone filed into the dining room there was a sense of restraint, especially among the Newcombe family, who weren't as used to such grand surroundings as Ben's wealthier parents.

Wearing her glamorous new 'wedding hostess' dress, Lynda stood nervously at the door of the dining room, where the atmosphere was just what Ben and Hannah had feared. Wishing Tom could be by her side instead of cooking and supervising in the kitchen, Lynda took a deep breath and signalled to the pianist, Josh Taylor, a friend of Patrick's, to join her as she walked across to the grand piano. She took her mind back to those Saturday nights long ago, when she had entertained the customers in the piano room of The Black Bull, and summoned the reckless teenage confidence she used to have then.

As soon as she began to sing the 1920s jazz standard 'Making Whoopee' all the muttering, awkward clearing of throats and scraping of chairs ceased as the guests relaxed and smiled at Gus Khan's tongue-in cheek lyrics. When the guests' enthusiastic applause had died away a little, Lynda looked round the room and smiled.

'Good evening, ladies and gentlemen – I apologise for getting the month wrong, I do know it's May not June. And I also know that we're going to have a great time this weekend at Ben and Hannah's wedding. The fun starts this evening with a lovely supper and wonderful music provided by Mr Josh Taylor here, who will play for you while you're enjoying your meal and afterwards for us all to have a sing-song. This may be a new experience for some of you, to have to sing for your supper, but I think you'll enjoy it. Now, gentlemen, can I ask you to take off your jackets and ties and, ladies, please kick off those high heeled shoes that feel too tight. Go on, I mean it!'

There was a shuffling and murmuring of embarrassment. Then Ben Hampton's father, Roger, stood up and with a flourish took of his jacket and tie. Dave Newcombe, who had been sitting opposite him, getting hotter and more tongue-tied by the minute, also stood up, grinned at Roger and followed his example. There was a lot of noise and laughter as the guests obeyed Lynda's orders, and relaxed into the enjoyment of an evening they would talk about for years to come.

The next morning they all greeted each other like

the old friends many of them were to become, and after breakfast strolled around the garden until it was time to get ready to drive to the village church where the wedding was to take place. When Tom, standing by the main entrance, had watched the last of the cars and taxis disappear down the driveway he saw that Mark was sitting on a bench among the trees, watching the final preparations for the reception. He went and sat beside him.

'Hello. Haven't seen you for a while.'

'You've been too busy.'

Tom had heard that resentful tone before, and knew Mark had some justification for feeling neglected.

'Yeah, I'm sorry. But it's a big thing, this wedding, it could do Loveday a lot of good.'

'I know. People are always willing to spend money on weddings.'

Tom forced himself not to smile at Mark's desire to sound like a business-minded grown-up. 'So I've heard. It's the women who spend the money, though, that's what Lynda says.'

He saw Mark's expression become even more sullen, and decided to test out his son's feelings. 'Good thing we've got her to show us what they want, isn't it?'

'I suppose so.'

Tom had been expecting trouble from Mark ever since Suzanne had left. He'd watched her questioning him, and had been aware that she had encouraged him to share her criticisms of Lynda. He was wondering what to say next when Mark asked a question which surprised him.

'Did you and Mum have a big white wedding like

this one?'

'Yes, we did.'

'So you really loved each other, didn't you?'

Tom hesitated, but remembered how he had felt about Suzanne Heston on that day. 'Yes, we did.'

'Mum still loves you. She wants you back.'

'I don't think so.'

'She does, she told me.'

'Well, it's too late for that.'

'Why? Because of Lynda?'

Tom was worried about what, or who, was behind that question, but had always been as honest as possible with his son.

'Yes, partly.'

Mark turned to his father accusingly. 'Did you get divorced because of Lynda?'

'No,' Tom answered firmly, knowing who that idea had come from. 'Your Mum and I were getting divorced before I knew Lynda.' He put his arm round his son's shoulders. 'Listen, Mark. I know it has really upset you that your Mother and I have split up. But it's my fault and your Mother's. I don't want you to blame Lynda. She'd be very upset if she thought you did. She thinks the world of you, you know that, don't you?'

He could see Mark struggling with choices and divided loyalties that no child of his age should have to be troubled with.

Mark sat there, very quiet and still for a moment, and then blurted out, 'Yes. But she's not my Mum!'

'No,' Tom said softly. 'I know she's not, and never could be.'

He didn't like the brief flash of what looked like hope in his son's eyes.

'You're not going to marry her, then, Dad?'

Tom didn't know how to answer that question, but ended up shaking his head.

At one o'clock the bridesmaids, ushers and all the guests stood in the sunshine by the entrance to the stable courtyard and watched the newly married couple arrive in a flower-trimmed pony and trap which had belonged to Hannah's great-grandmother. Sparkling white wine was served in the courtyard, where the stable doors had been decorated with balloons and satin ribbon, and Lynda and Amy beamed at each other as they stood by the door to the coach-house and heard the sighs of pleasure as the guests entered the silver, blue and white magical palace which they had created for the reception.

The wedding went on until late. It grew dark but the guests were still dancing in the courtyard or sitting at tables enjoying a few more glasses of wine. The Loveday Manor hotel staff, having served a copious buffet supper which was just as delicious as the lunch the guests had enjoyed so much, were sitting at a table in a corner of the courtyard enjoying their own supper, and the glow of success. Patrick reached over and chinked his glass of wine against Lynda's.

'Well, you did it, girl, gave them the wedding of the year. Congratulations!'

All the staff raised their glasses and joined in the toast, and Lynda, with Tom sitting beside her, smiled happily and her eyes sparkled as she looked round at all these people who had become her friends.

'Thank you, and thank you all for your hard work and for making this happen. Extra thanks to Amy and

Patrick, and to Tom, of course. I think after today Loveday Manor will become number one choice for wedding receptions, and it deserves to be, because it's a very special place, full of wonderful people. And I love it so much.'

The following morning, enjoying the stillness after the wedding, she went for a walk by the river with Tom. She was still feeling the thrill of what she had achieved.

'It was marvellous, wasn't it?'

'It was wonderful,' Tom smiled at her eagerness to be reassured yet again.

'I was teasing Patrick, telling him it'll be his wedding I organise next.'

'Who to?'

'Amy, of course! Have you not noticed what's going on between those two?'

'Yes, but I don't think Patrick's sister will let him marry anyone who's not from a Jamaican family.'

'She'll want him to be happy. And Amy would make him happy, she's just what he needs.' She reached up and kissed him on the cheek. 'Like you're just what I need.'

He paused, he didn't want to spoil the day, but he needed to warn her about Mark's anxieties. 'We've got some family opposition to contend with, too.'

'Mark?'

'Yes, Suzanne has been 'confiding' in him. He thinks you are stopping me going back to her.'

Lynda was outraged. 'What?'

'I know. He's upset and confused. All children want their Mum and Dad to get back together again.' He paused.

'I've had to tell him we're not getting married.'

'Oh.'

'I'm sorry.'

Her pride kicked in strong and hard.

'Well, of course we're not. Like I told you on our first date, I'm not keen on the idea of getting married again. And anyway, as far as I know I've still got a husband.'

He put his arms round her. 'Lynda, don't get upset.'

She tried to pull away from him but he held her tight until he felt her resistance melt away. He kissed her, and they clung together.

'I love you,' he whispered.

'And I love you.' She smiled at him, and tilted her chin. 'And we're going to make Loveday Manor the best hotel in the world, and everyone will want to come and celebrate their wedding here, because it's a magical place filled with love.'

He laughed as he shared her dream. 'Yes, and the ninth of May 1987 will go down in history.'

She cried out in pain and horror.

'Lynda, what's the matter?'

'The 9th of May 1987! Oh, God! It was Carolyn's twenty-first birthday yesterday. And I forgot! I should have been there, but I didn't even send her a present, or a card. Oh, she'll never forgive me now. What kind of a Mother am I?' She leaned against him, sobbing. 'Oh, dear God, she'll never forgive me.'

CHAPTER THIRTY SIX

Carolyn, sitting in the August sunshine in Sheila's garden, read the page again, and tried to memorise the wording of the regulation about bankruptcy. She was finding her study of law and accountancy fascinating but difficult to remember, especially as she was also supervising Michael and Gemma playing in the sandpit.

Sheila, pruning some of the shrubs at the side of the fence, paused to wipe some damp leaves off her secateurs and heard her sigh.

'Are you finding it hard?'

'Yes, but I'm enjoying it. It's really good to have something to think about besides sorting out the washing and 'what shall we have for tea?' And I'll be qualified by the time Gemma goes to school.'

'You won't need me then.'

Carolyn smiled at her. 'I'll always need you, Nana, you know I will.'

Sheila's eyes were bleak. 'I thought about your Grandad would always need me, but he didn't in the end.'

'What's wrong? Why are you thinking about Grandad? You know it only makes you unhappy.'

'It would have been our wedding anniversary today.'

'Oh, I'm sorry, I didn't realise.'

Sheila returned to hacking savagely at the strong branches of a large fuschia bush full of deep pink flowers.

'This damned fuschia is getting out of hand. Ted loved the way it flowers every summer. Always reliable, he used to say.' She cut off a tall, wayward shoot, and muttered, 'Like him, till he met that woman!'

She reached up and tugged angrily at a thick branch which sprang away from her. She jumped up after it, lost her balance and fell to the ground, clutching her chest. Carolyn dashed across to help her.

'Nana, are you all right?'

Sheila stared up at her and Carolyn saw that she was struggling to breathe. 'I'll call an ambulance.'

'No!' Sheila clutched her hand. 'Stay with me.' She screwed up her eyes in pain.

'Nana!'

Carolyn knelt down and instinctively cradled her grandmother's head in her arms. Sheila opened her eyes and gave a little smile. This searing pain had tormented her many times before, but somehow she knew that this was the last time she would have to suffer.

'Do well, Carolyn,' she said, struggling to breathe. 'Make me proud of you. And, and ask John to forgive me.'

'Oh, what for?' Carolyn asked tenderly. 'There's nothing to forgive, Nana, you've always . . '

She stopped as she saw Sheila trying to shake her

head. With her last breath she whispered one word.
'Lynda.'

The sun had refused to put in an appearance, and as they stood by the grave in Holy Trinity churchyard, the group of mourners tensed their bodies against the unseasonably cool breeze.

They were invited to follow John and the Sheldon family back to Stanhope Road, and quite a few of them went there, if only as a sign of respect. They were glad of the cups of tea, and sandwiches and cakes made by Sylvia and Carolyn, and Sylvia's mother-in-law, Enid Laycock.

Sylvia and John stood awkwardly in the centre of their Mother's front room, brother and sister who were now orphans. They listened and responded as best they could to the carefully chosen words of Sheila's friends from church, and of neighbours who had known her since she and her husband had moved into Stanhope Road.

Graham looked across at his wife to check that she was coping with sharing reminiscences of her childhood and her parents. There were tears in her eyes but she gave a little smile to reassure him she was all right.

He went off to volunteer for the task of ferrying more trays of tea-cups from the kitchen where two ladies from the church had taken charge of the kettle and the teapots.

The vicar had dutifully agreed to join the relatively small group of mourners returning to the home of the deceased, but had the firm intention of staying only long enough for a ham sandwich and one cup of tea. He sipped this as he endeavoured to engage his church's patron, Ellen Heywood, in conversation.

'Very nice to have the gathering at Sheila's home. But quite a lot of work, doing the catering in the circumstances.'

Ellen didn't seem to be listening to him, so he looked round the room for another subject.

'Alice Smith usually turns out to help at these occasions, I believe, but she doesn't seem to be here.'

Ellen decided it was time this relatively new vicar, who had not yet earned her approval, received a little education about his parishioners.

'Mrs Stanworth had stipulated that Alice Smith was to be informed that her services would not be required here.'

Her sharp tone made the vicar hastily replaced his cup in its saucer. He steadied it as it rattled. 'Indeed?' And then he foolishly added the question, 'Why was that?'

As if speaking to a naive young schoolboy, Ellen explained, 'The last time Alice Smith was in this room was when she behaved inappropriately at the funeral of Mrs Stanworth's husband.'

'Oh, I see,' the vicar said, not seeing anything but the door through which he would very soon make a grateful exit.

When he had gone Ellen spoke briefly to a few of the other people she knew, and then sought out Carolyn, who was standing in a corner of the bay window, clutching her handkerchief.

'Try not to get too upset, my dear. You've spent many happy hours in this house, Carolyn, and those memories are what you must hold on to now.'

'Yes.'

'She was so very proud of you.'

'Yes.'

'I shall miss her visits and our afternoon teas together. I hope that you will continue to come to Kirkwood House and have tea, and remember how your grandmother loved to sit in my conservatory.'

'You were always very kind to her, Ellen, and she told me she felt honoured to be your friend.'

Ellen Heywood was gratified to hear that, but her mission was to comfort Sheila Stanworth's granddaughter, and strengthen her influence over her.

Ellen Heywood was a someone who avoided physical contact with other people, but she now placed her arm around Carolyn Sheldon's slim young shoulders, and tilted her head, so that she could look into her eyes. She spoke softly, confidingly, to the beautiful young woman whom Sheila Stanworth had presented to her as a child.

'I know I can never take your grandmother's place, Carolyn, but I hope you will feel you can call on me whenever you need someone to talk to. Will you promise me that you will not hesitate to do so?'

'I promise. And thank you, Ellen.'

'I shall leave now. I find funerals even harder since I lost my beloved Richard.'

'Of course.'

Ellen turned as she reached the door.

'Promise that you will come and see me soon. You are very precious to me, my child.'

Dan Heywood, who had been observing his Mother's expressions as she talked to her protégée, heard this last piece of the conversation, and wondered how Carolyn's Mother would have felt if she had been there to witness her daughter being 'adopted' by her enemy. Dan had been learning not to think about Lynda, but couldn't avoid it today. He walked over and shook her husband by the hand.

'Sorry about your Mother, John.'

John was glad to look into the honest eyes of the man who was the only friend who really understood what his relationship with his Mother had been like.

As teenagers they'd spent many hours in various hideaways, experimenting with any brands of alcohol and cigarettes they could get their hands on, and sharing their resentments and frustrations. Many of these had been focused on the ways their Mothers had tried, often with too much success, to control their lives.

John held on tight to his hand, and muttered gruffly, 'Thanks for coming.'

Dan nodded, and knew that John would need to talk to him, but some other time, and not in his Mother's house.

'I'll have to be going now, but I'll give you a call and we'll meet up for a pint and a quiet talk in The Red Lion – when you're ready.'

John understood and there was gratitude in his smile. 'Yeah. That'll be good. See you, mate.'

He watched Dan leave, and then turned to find Jean Haworth holding out a mug of tea and a plate of sandwiches. Jean had been glad to see she was not needed to make cups of tea and coffee, and was free to take on the position of co-hostess. She had been delighted when one of the people from church, who knew of her long connection with Lynda and John, had described her as almost one of the family.

'You haven't had anything to eat, John. Take these and find somewhere to sit down for a while. You've spoken to enough people now.'

He took the plate and the tea gratefully. 'Thanks, Jean. I think I'll go and sit in the garden. Sylvia's lads are out there, aren't they?'

'Yes. They're ready to go back to the farm, I think.'

'They will be. A funeral's no place for kids.'

'No. I'm glad Steve took Michael and Gemma back home after the service. Now you go and give yourself a break.'

She watched him edge his way past the few mourners who were staying on for a livelier chat with each other, now that the initial duty of condolences had been fulfilled. Jean could not suppress a little sigh of happiness; John Stanworth would need looking after now, and she would be very happy to have the chance to do that at last.

Steve took the afternoon off work, and looked after the children while Carolyn went to the solicitor's with her father and her aunty Sylvia to find out the contents of Sheila's will. Afterwards Carolyn decided that they should return to Stanhope Road rather than Beechwood Avenue, so that they could be in a quiet place to recover from the shock, and discuss it all between the three of them.

They sat at the table in the living room with mugs of tea and the documents in front of them. John trying to control the fury he felt inside, stared out at the garden.

When he spoke, there was a harshness in his voice. 'I've been working overtime and saving up, so that when she'd gone I could buy you out of your share of the house, Sylvia, and live here and look after my Dad's garden.'

Sylvia, who had never managed to forgive her father for leaving, corrected him.

'It hasn't been his garden for a long time. Mum used to spend hours out there. She loved the house as well, she's spent quite a bit of money keeping it nice.'

John tried to keep the bitterness out of his voice, but failed.

'She spent quite a bit of money on everything!'

Sylvia continued to defend her Mother. 'Only after Dad left her. She was devastated, and she needed to boost her morale, so she treated herself to new clothes and new furniture. You could understand that.'

'Yeah. But that was with the money her Uncle Freddie left her. I knew she'd probably spent all that, but I didn't know she'd done this equity release thing, taking money out of the flaming house as well!'

Sylvia glanced anxiously round the room.

'John, be quiet. My Mother will be turning in her grave hearing you shouting like this in her living room. I can understand you being upset, but my Mother had a right to spend the money, it was her house, after all.'

'It's all right for you, Sylvia, you've got a home. You don't need the money as much as I do. I've got to buy somewhere to live now, and thanks to her 'treating herself' I won't have much to do it with!'

Carolyn, with tears streaming down her cheeks, said quietly. 'You can move back in with us, Dad.'

His voice was gentler now. 'Thank you, love, but you know I can't really. You need the rooms for the

338

kids, and I need my own place.'

'I feel awful,' Carolyn confessed. 'She spent most of that money on me. She always got me everything I wanted, and she paid a lot towards the wedding, and all the stuff we needed for the kids.'

Sylvia, who had often been a little resentful of the favouritism Sheila had shown towards her granddaughter, decided not to say anything. She had learned from her husband that it was better to be charitable, or at least to keep some uncharitable thoughts to herself.

Carolyn was remembering so much that her Nana had done for her. 'She even took me to Paris when I'd passed my O-level exams. She obviously couldn't afford it really.'

John put his arm round his daughter. 'Don't beat yourself up, love, your Nana loved every minute of that. And her birthday trip to London with the three of you, didn't she, Sylvia?'

His sister was crying again now, 'Yes, she was so happy that weekend. Oh, I can't believe she's gone.'

John stood very still, and then walked off into the kitchen so that they wouldn't see his tears. His anger left him now as he stood in the room which was his Mother's domain, and where she would never again cook meals and bake cakes. He pictured the way she used to present them with a flourish and wait for the praise she craved. He bowed his head and wished he had been a better son.

When he and Carolyn returned to Beechwood Avenue and told Steve about Sheila's will, John hid his disappointment at what his inheritance might now amount to. Steve, he knew, would blame himself for Sheila having to find money for him and his family, but John didn't begrudge him that money. Steve worked hard, and had even found the courage to ask Randerson for a pay rise. John had been very proud when Randerson had had to agree, albeit with a bad grace, to reward the employee whose skills were so much in demand.

John tried to talk positively about looking for a nice little house for himself, with a bit of garden or an allotment nearby. When, later that night, he walked back into the empty house on Stanhope Road, he felt that he would be glad to move out of it, away from the bad memories, but he knew the future he had once imagined was no longer possible.

CHAPTER THIRTY SEVEN

While John was at work the next day, Sylvia and Carolyn came into the house and went upstairs to begin the task of sorting out Sheila's possessions. Jean Haworth had volunteered to come round to Beechwood Avenue and look after Michael, so they only had Gemma, who was happy to sit on the floor and play with her toys.

The house was eerily silent, and the two women didn't talk at unless they had to have a brief discussion about which clothes and ornaments should go to the charity shop. They each shed tears as they came across items which had special memories for them.

In the afternoon Sylvia decided to sort out some towels and bed-linen for a charity as well, and when she reached down into the bottom of Sheila's oak bedding box in she found a letter and postcard from Cornwall, and the birthday card Lynda had sent soon after she'd gone away.

Sylvia read them and sat down on the edge of the bed, trying to decide what to do. Carolyn, who had gone downstairs to give Gemma some food, came into the room as she was sitting there.

'I've made us a cup of tea, I thought we could . . . whatever is the matter, Sylvia?'

'I've found this postcard, and a letter from that woman to your Mother. Goodness knows how they got here.'

An image and the sound of paper being crumpled flashed into Carolyn's mind, as she remembered a moment in another bedroom, when she had seen her Nana shove something into her pocket, and give her a look which had told her not to ask questions.

Carolyn took a deep breath. 'What does it say?'

Sylvia held the letter as if it were badly soiled. 'It's just going on about how lovely it is in St Benedict, this place in Cornwall, and how she's desperate for your Mum to go and visit her there. And my Dad, if he wanted to.'

'Oh. When was this?'

Sylvia checked the rose-garlanded heading. February 1985. That was just before she left, wasn't it?'

'Yes.'

'There's a house address, and this postcard with a cross on it to mark where the Springfield Hotel is, where she works.'

Sylvia hesitated, but knew if Graham had been there he would have insisted on her telling Carolyn everything.

'There are also two birthday cards that your Mother sent to your Dad and you, not long after she left, judging by the postmark. There's an address on your Dad's card.'

Carolyn didn't want to think about her Mother. 'I've got to go back down and see to Gemma.'

'We have to talk about this, Carolyn. My Mother

had an address, but she didn't give it to John, did she?'

'No, or he'd have gone there to find her.'

'Do you think we should give him this?'

Carolyn had no doubt.

'No, I don't. It would only upset him, and it was over three years ago. She'll have moved on from there by now. Jean said she was going to London, and we haven't heard from her since then. She doesn't want us to go and find her.'

She walked to the door.

'What do you want me to do with these, then?' Sylvia asked her niece.

'Throw them away!'

'There a phone number as well as the address.'

'Well, I'm not going to call that number, I don't want any more phone calls with my so-called Mother! She's forgotten about us, Sylvia. She didn't even send me a present for my twenty-first birthday. We're out of her life. Throw it all away!'

'All right,' Sylvia agreed. 'Let's go and have that cup of tea.'

She was about to follow Carolyn downstairs, but then stopped and put the cards and letter in her bag. Like her Mother before her, she wasn't sure she had the right to throw them away.

When she got back to Old Manor Farm, she found she didn't want the responsibility of such a secret and so that night she told her husband about it.

'There's an address and a telephone number. Do you think we should give it to John? Carolyn didn't want to, she told me to throw it away.'

Graham sighed as he sat up in bed and cleaned his

glasses, his usual habit when he had some tricky thinking to do. He read the letter again, and checked the date.

'As Carolyn said, it's three years ago and Lynda may have left by now, but we should at least try the number. And it would be better if we did it, rather than have John get upset for nothing.'

He saw the expression on his wife's face. 'Do you want me to do it?'

'Yes, please.'

The following morning, with Sylvia sitting anxiously beside him, Graham Laycock phoned the number of Rose's cottage but found it was no longer connected. A man with a reputation for perseverance, he then obtained the number of The Springfield Hotel.

He was informed that they had not heard of anyone called Lynda Stanworth or Collins, but one of the staff knew that Rose Milner had died over a year ago, and that her cottage had been sold. Sylvia hoped that they could now forget about the possibility that Lynda had gone to stay with the woman who had torn the Stanworth family apart. Graham, however, was adamant that John had a right to know about the letter.

The whole family sat, a little crowded, in the living room at Beechwood Avenue and listened to Graham speaking in the calm and authoritative voice which his late mother-in-law had admired. When Sylvia saw the anguish on her brother's face she thought that, for once, her husband had been wrong.

'You're sure there's nobody there who will know where Lynda has gone?' John asked, sitting at the dining table and turning the postcard over and over in

344

his hand.

'It doesn't seem likely.'

'I ought to go there and find out for sure.'

Carolyn wished the letter had never been found.

'Why? You have to face it, Dad, she's left us, she's forgotten about us, and I want to forget about her. And you should do the same.'

John looked at his daughter, and bowed his head. 'Sometimes I wish I could.'

Steve wanted to encourage John to go to Cornwall and look for his wife, but was afraid of how Carolyn would react. And, having realised more than the rest of them how unhappy she'd been, he also wondered if Lynda wanted to be found. He guessed that there was only a slim chance of finding her, and was glad to hear Graham confirm this opinion.

It was John who voiced the question no-one else wanted to ask.

'What worries me is that my Mother had this letter and the birthday cards, and didn't tell us about them. Lynda left Rose's letter and the postcard for me to find them, I'm sure she did. And as for my birthday card – why didn't I get that? My Mother must have picked it up and hidden it. She had no right to keep all these things from me.'

Carolyn had her Nana's defence ready.

'She did it for the best, Dad. My Mother caused too much trouble between us. You don't know she left that letter for us to find it. And she's only ever sent those two cards, why has she never sent us any more cards, or letters or anything?'

Steve felt compelled to speak now. 'We don't know that she didn't.'

Carolyn spun round and stared at him. 'What do you mean?'

'Think about it, Carolyn, your Nana always insisted on being here early in the morning. She was the one who was here when the post came.'

Carolyn was glaring at him now. 'What are you implying? That my Nan would hide the post from us? What a terrible thing to say!'

There was a long silence, then John said. 'He could be right, Carolyn. I wouldn't put it past her to take any letters or birthday cards if she saw they were from Lynda. She didn't want Lynda back, I know that.'

'No,' Carolyn cried, 'and neither do I! And neither should you. And I won't have you saying things like that about my Nan. You have no right, Dad!'

'And she had no right to come between me and my wife, but she did. She wanted all her own way, all the time, my Mother! Wanted to rule our lives, and she ruined mine. She drove Lynda away. May God forgive her, because I won't!'

CHAPTER THIRTY EIGHT

Tom Meredith was right, by the spring of 1989 Loveday Manor had become one of the area's top venues for wedding receptions. The hotel was fully booked almost all the year round, partly due to the weddings but also because the guests who had attended them often returned for short holidays, or remembered the venue when booking company events. Easter was even busier than usual and another wedding reception was booked for the weekend after. All the staff were looking forward to the following week which would be relatively quiet.

'We ought to take a couple of days off that week,' Tom suggested to Lynda as they sat on the sofa in their apartment one evening.

'I can't, I've arranged to go to that wedding event in Brighton with Amy.'

'Can't she go without you?' he asked, slightly irritated.

'No, we've booked a stand, I can't leave her to run it on her own.'

'We need a break, Lynda, we hardly see each other these days.'

'Well, it's like you warned me, the hotel business

takes over your life.'

'We can leave Patrick to run the hotel, it's your wedding merchandise business that's stopping us from taking time off now.'

'It's important to me, and it's vital to get a hold on the market before everyone else starts to copy what we're doing.'

'Spoken like a true business woman,' he commented wryly.

'Well, that's what I am.'

'Yeah.'

She sensed his disapproval, and was annoyed. 'I want to be a success, Tom, to feel I've really achieved something. There's nothing wrong with that, is there? You have the hotel, that's your achievement.'

'And yours.'

'Only a small part.'

He sighed and got up. 'I could argue about that, but I'm not going to. We do enough arguing at the moment. I promised Mark a game of chess, so I'll see you later.'

'O.K.' she said quietly and noticed that he didn't give her a kiss before he left. She knew he was right, that they weren't finding enough time for each other, but she didn't know what she could do about it. She curled up, cuddled a cushion and soon fell asleep.

A few days later she was sitting in the kitchen with Patrick, working on a new set of menus, when Tom walked in, his face pale and his voice a little shaky.

'Nicki has been killed in a sailing accident. Suzanne is devastated and is begging me to go and help her. I'll get the first flight I can to Nice. Will you be able to manage here?'

'Of course,' came Patrick's instant reply.

'What happened?' Lynda asked.

'A speed boat race to St Jean Cap Ferrat, and there was a collision. It was pretty messy, apparently. Suzanne was hysterical on the phone.'

'What will you tell Mark?'

'As little as possible. He'll want to come with me, but I can't let him. Not till things are sorted out. There'll have to be an inquest and we'll have to arrange the funeral. I'll come and get him then.'

'He'll be fine with us,' Lynda reassured him. 'You'd better go and pack.'

'Yeah.'

Tom left for Nice the following morning, and it was almost two weeks before they saw him again. Then he only stayed one night, and slept the deep sleep of exhaustion before taking Mark with him to Nice to say farewell to his grandmother, and comfort his Mother.

Lynda and Patrick worked well together, and the staff all gave extra help when they could, so that everything ran smoothly while Tom was away. He phoned a couple of days later to let them know when they would be back, but it was only a brief call, and Lynda found she was desperate to talk to him. All the time he was away she had missed him so much, and she'd kept dreaming of being in his arms again.

Patrick drove to the airport to collect them on the Friday afternoon and Lynda wished she could go with him, but she was organising a wedding on the Saturday, so she had to stay to welcome the families and guests, and supervise the final preparations.

She was waiting outside the hotel, desperate to see

her love again, when the Mercedes drew up by the entrance. She ran towards it and then stopped as Tom got out of the car and walked round to open the rear door. Suzanne, dressed in black, stepped out gracefully and very slowly.

'Suzanne!' Lynda gasped, and caught Patrick's look. They had both assumed that Suzanne would have to stay and sort out her Mother's property, and that it would be only Tom and Mark returning to Loveday.

Lynda realised she was standing there open-mouthed, and took a deep breath. 'I was so sorry to hear about your Mother.'

Suzanne looked at her blankly, and then reached out for Tom's arm as she walked unsteadily into the hotel, followed closely by her son.

Patrick retrieved the suitcases from the boot, and entered the foyer in time to hear Lynda apologising and saying that she would go and prepare The Gatehouse herself.

Tom said quietly. 'Suzanne doesn't want to go to The Gatehouse, she'd find it too lonely. She's going to stay in the hotel. We'll find a room for her, won't we?'

'Of course.' Lynda's brain switched into overdrive as she worked out how she could make one of the best rooms available for her. 'Would Room 10 be O.K?'

'That's a single room, isn't it?' Suzanne sounded weary, and her voice was without strength but still had an echo of petulance.

'I'm so sorry,' Lynda apologised. 'There's a wedding here tomorrow and all the double rooms have been booked for that.'

Suzanne, clinging to her ex-husband's arm spoke in a whisper to Tom, but it was loud enough for Lynda to hear it.

'Oh, I was hoping we might stay in our old room.'

Patrick had also heard the pleading request, and picked up the cases again, saying firmly, 'Room 10.'

Lynda stood and watched them get into the lift, Tom had his arm round Mark's shoulders. Neither he nor his father looked at her.

She was so busy with the wedding the rest of the day she only caught glimpses of the three of them in a corner of the dining room or walking in the garden. And always they were close together, a family. She went to bed alone, it wasn't until after midnight that Tom came in. He sat down on the edge of the bed and stroked her hair.

'Are you all right? You seemed a bit upset when I turned up with Suzanne,' he said.

'It was stupid of me. I should have realised you'd bring her back with you.'

'She said she had nowhere else to go. And Mark wanted her to come.'

'Of course.'

'It's hard for him, losing Nicki so soon after his other Grandma. And Rose, too. I imagine his world doesn't seem very secure any more, especially with the divorce as well. He needs his Mother at the moment.'

'And you.'

'Yes, and me,' he said, and his shoulders and head bowed down with tiredness. She reached up and kissed him, pulling him close.

'Come to bed, my love.'

She held him tenderly as he slept, and the next

morning watched him trying to help with all the work that the wedding entailed, but having to go off and comfort Suzanne who kept appearing on the edge of the festive crowd of guests and calling for him.

Lynda could see that she felt lost and very lonely and, remembering how she had felt when her Grandma had died, she tried to not to mind that Tom never had time to be with her. But when Suzanne had been there over a month, Lynda was beginning to think she would never leave, and could see that she was getting stronger and more demanding. She understood that Tom felt great pity for his ex-wife, and he had explained to Lynda that he still felt responsible for her, especially now she had lost both her parents.

Suzanne was with Tom so much that the guests who knew her thought that she and her husband were together again, and she encouraged that impression. Then, one morning, Lynda was taking her turn at cleaning the bedrooms on the floor where Suzanne's room was, when she heard her talking to Tom. The door of her room had been left ajar, and Lynda knew she shouldn't listen, but couldn't resist.

Suzanne spoke in a clear and dramatic tone. 'We were good together, Tom, you and I. Please! I need to be here, to be with you. I need you so much. And Mark needs me. He would be so happy if we were a proper family again.'

Lynda couldn't hear what Tom's response was, but knew it concerned her when Suzanne said dismissively, 'But she's married, isn't she?' Then she spoke so caressingly that Lynda could imagine her arms entwined round Tom's neck.

'We should never have got divorced. Please let's try again. It will be different now, Tom, I promise. You still care for me, I know that you do.'

Lynda listened hard, and in vain, for Tom's denial.

She couldn't bear to hear any more of this, and decided to hurry away but had to step behind the door as she saw Tom coming out of Suzanne's room. There was a silence. Lynda looked round the door and saw them standing in the corridor, kissing, with their bodies locked together in an embrace so intimate that it made her recoil away and shut herself in the room, leaning against the door, and trying not to believe what she had seen.

She watched them at every opportunity from then on, and was relieved that she never saw Tom alone with her again. In fact it started to look, Lynda hoped, as if he was avoiding her. Suzanne spent more time in her room, and Patrick commented to Lynda that the staff on room-service duty were being asked frequently to deliver bottles of wine to her room.

Mark noticed that there was a half empty bottle of white wine on the table when he went up to say goodnight to his Mother. She usually came up to his room to kiss him goodnight, and he had become a little anxious when she hadn't arrived that evening, and so he had come up to her room to look for her.

She stood up, a little unsteadily, and kissed him enthusiastically on both cheeks.

'I'm sorry, my darling boy. Were you worried about me, mon petit chat?'

She sat down again on the chair by the little table,

and sipped her wine mournfully.

'I'm so glad I have you. I have no-one else now, you know.'

'You have Dad.'

She shook her head. 'Not any more. He says he's fallen in love with that woman, that little bitch.'

He was shocked to hear his Mother talk like this, and was about to protest, but then she began to cry.

'You won't leave me, will you Mark? You won't desert me. I have no-one else. Simon has grown tired of me, I'll never see him again.'

Mark remembered that name. 'Simon? The guy who said he didn't want me around?'

His Mother didn't realise what he was saying, she was concentrating on her need of another glass of wine.

'He's gone back to his wife, for good, he says.' She put down the bottle and gave a little laugh. 'He was scared to death when he heard she might have found out about me, so he went scampering back to her.'

She paused, and drank more wine. 'It had nothing to do with her money, of course,' she said with heavy sarcasm. She shook her head and stared at him with eyes full of self-pity. 'Oh, Mark, I've wasted so many years on that man.'

'Was he the reason you left Daddy?'

'Yes. I was a fool. And now your Daddy says he won't have me back. He says he's found someone who loves him more than I ever did. How could he say that?'

She leaned forward eagerly. 'You can make him change his mind, can't you? Will you talk to him, tell him you need to have your Mummy and Daddy back together again.'

354

He stood up, and said solemnly, 'It's too late for that.'

She looked up at her fourteen year old son who was no longer her little boy. He kissed her.

'Goodnight, Mummy.'

Suzanne found it impossible to tolerate seeing her ex-husband and Lynda working together and being happy, and a few days later accepted an invitation to visit her friends in Sardinia. Lynda could not hide her relief at seeing her leave, but she was upset to see how sadly Mark waved goodbye to his Mother.

'We'll have to plan a treat for him, to cheer him up,' she suggested to Tom.

He gave her a hug. 'I already have. I thought we could take him to Epsom when we go with the Tylers.'

Lynda had been looking forward to having the American couple staying with them again, and to showing them all the improvements and developments at Loveday. Almost as soon as they arrived, Helen insisted on going to look at the stables and coach-house and clapped her hands with delight at the transformation.

'It's absolutely wonderful, isn't it, Nathan?' she exclaimed.

'Looks fine, but is it making money?'

'He's such a romantic!' his wife commented with the dry humour Lynda loved.

'It's making a lot of money,' Tom claimed proudly, placing his arm round Lynda's shoulders, 'and it's mostly down to this little lady.'

'Who's not wearing a ring yet, I see,' Helen Tyler

observed cheekily. 'Why not, Tom?'

Lynda blushed, and took Helen's arm to lead her away.

'It's complicated. Let me show you the shop and café I've set up in what was the saddle room. We still sell goods in Amy's shop but she's short of space so we decided to use this as another outlet. When people come to look round, even if they don't book a wedding reception, they usually buy some of our accessories. It's closed at the moment, but I can show you round and make you a coffee.'

Nathan waved them away. 'You go ahead, Helen, Tom and I have an appointment with a cold beer or three.'

Helen walked slowly round the shop, picking up tiaras, posy bowls and all kinds of small gifts, and fingering the bridal fabrics and lace hanging on display where saddles and harnesses had once been stored.

'Its' a really good idea to have fabrics displayed here as well as accessories, it gives the bride a chance to envisage how everything she chooses for the wedding can all fit together. And she and her Mother can sit in this cute little café to have a rest, discuss all the possibilities, and decide what they want.'

'Yes, that's the idea.'

'Good thinking, girl!'

Lynda grinned. 'A bit devious, aren't I? And we have a couple of ladies who live locally and make the most superb wedding dresses and veils, and another in the farm up the road who runs a nice side-line in making stunning hats.'

'Wow, that's great. And you're enjoying it all,

aren't you?'

'I love every minute!'

'And you love him, too.'

Lynda wasn't going to pretend she didn't know who Helen was referring to. 'Yes.'

'And does he love you?'

Lynda looked away. 'Shall I make us some tea, or coffee?'

'Tea, please. I love your English afternoon tea. And I see you've made sure there are some of my favourite scones and cream on the counter.'

Helen settled herself happily at one of the small tables, and flicked through the brochure advertising Loveday Manor wedding accessories.

When Lynda had served the tea and scones, Helen sat back in the comfortable little cane armchair and gave Lynda what her grandmother had called 'an old-fashioned look'.

'And now I'd like an answer to my question, Lynda. Does he love you?' she repeated.

Lynda couldn't avoid the gaze of those mischievous but perceptive eyes, but she paused for a long moment before she said, 'I think he does.'

'But you'd like to be certain.'

'Yes. He's so detached sometimes in the way he deals with me and the business, it's not like we're sharing it.'

'Don't worry about that. I quizzed Tom about your business relationship. He told me he's being very careful to look after your interests as well as his own. That's the kind of guy he is. Do you feel more sure about him now?'

'I would if it wasn't for Suzanne. When she came here after her Mother died, he let her take him over.'

'He was just being kind to her, I guess, after such a terrible loss.'

'Yes. But it went beyond being kind.' In her mind she saw Suzanne and Tom in each other's arms.

'She's not letting him go.'

'No. I don't think she ever will, and she'll always have the right to be here. The Gatehouse belongs to her, and she'll even have a share in the profit if ever Loveday is sold. Tom was too uptight about the divorce to read the small print properly.'

'Don't tell Nathan that, he's already wondering if he should leave his investment in the hotel.'

'Oh, no. He doesn't want his money back now, does he?'

'Nathan is a man who likes to think of himself as an adventurer in the world of finance, he's always looking for the next money-making scheme to impress his parents.'

'Aren't his parents dead,' Lynda asked bluntly.

'Yes, but it makes no difference, he still thinks he has to prove they were wrong not to make him their favourite. And talking of favourites, Tom mentioned that we're all going to Epsom, to watch The Derby. That will be fun.'

Lynda smiled at her, 'Yes, I'm really looking forward to it.'

Helen squeezed her friend's hand, 'Tell you what, let's go to your lady on the farm and buy ourselves a stunning hat.'

Lynda got up to clear away the cups and plates. 'That's a great idea, I've never owned a posh hat.'

'Well, now's your chance. And don't you worry about that fella of yours. I'm sure he loves you. He's probably just forgetting to say it enough. I can't remember the last time Nathan said he loved me.' She picked up the empty cake stand and, with a wicked look, said, 'But I think nowadays I almost prefer to hear those other 'three little words' from him.'

'What are those?'

'You were right!'

CHAPTER THIRTY NINE

On Derby Day it seemed as if a wave of excitement had rolled across from the chalk downs and swirled its way through the crowds of race-goers.

Lynda had gone shopping with Helen and had bought a white skirt and a white jacket embroidered with gold thread. The white hat Helen had urged her to buy was decorated with an exuberant gold silk flower which matched the colour of her hair which she'd allowed to fall in natural curls on to her shoulders. She looked at Helen in her deep pink dress and neat pink and cream hat, and linked arms with her.

'This is the first time I've been here and felt confident I look right. Thank you so much for helping me choose my outfit.'

'I don't know why you always feel so unsure of how you look, a gorgeous girl like you! You should forget everything Suzanne said, she was just jealous.'

'I know. But she was right, I've got no class, and no education compared to her.'

'Will you stop putting yourself down! You're beautiful and you've got a good and generous heart. That's what I call classy. And what's more, you appreciate whatever fortune presents you with.'

Lynda joked to cover her embarrassment. 'Wow, if I ever need a reference, I'll come to you.'

'You do that, and in the mean time the trick is to hold your head up real high – that way nobody will dare criticise you. Now where have those men gone?'

'They're over there checking out the odds for the race.'

She and Helen joined Tom, Mark and Nathan but found the two men weren't talking about horses, they were continuing a discussion they'd started the day before.

'It's a big investment, building an extension,' Nathan was saying.

Tom, sounding defensive, said, 'The bank manager seems O.K. about it.' He turned to Lynda, 'I've been telling Nathan about our plan to add more bedrooms and an extra dining room.'

'An extra dining-room?' queried Helen.

'For the hotel guests who aren't involved with the weddings,' Mark explained. 'Some people find it a bit noisy at meal times when there are wedding guests getting a bit too lively.'

Helen patted him on the back, 'My, you've got quite a young business man growing up here, Tom.'

'Yes, he's taking a real interest, aren't you, Mark? And he's absolutely right, we don't want the weddings to spoil the other guests' evenings, so the extra dining room does make sense.'

Nathan was still frowning. 'Extra rooms cost a lot of money, both to build and to maintain. It sounds risky. I was saying to Helen last night, you're a bit too much of a risk-taker for me sometimes, Tom.'

He was surprised to be strongly contradicted by Lynda.

'He isn't, he just sees that Loveday needs more accommodation. We can't afford to turn people away when they're queuing up to stay. You have to go with success and build on it, fast.'

Nathan shook his head, 'You also sound like a risk-taker to me, honey.'

Helen thought her husband was being unfair, and said, 'I don't know about that, Nathan, but she's a great little entrepreneur with her wedding business. Or should that be entrepreneuse? Do you speak French, Lynda?'

She shook her head, 'No, I passed O-level French but I can't speak it, I've never been to France to learn.'

'Would you like to?' asked Helen.

'Yes, I've always wanted to go to Paris.'

'Have you? I didn't know that,' Tom said.

Helen was in an impertinent mood. 'Well, it's about time you took her there, Tom!'

'Be sure to take plenty of money with you, if you do,' Nathan warned, 'it's a real expensive city.'

His wife gave him a nudge, 'Oh, be quiet, Nathan, you're no fun today!'

Tom decided it was time to be tactful and change the subject.

'Have you ladies decided which horse you're going to back to win The Derby?'

Helen winked at him to let him know she appreciated his diplomacy, and checked the list of runners again.

'I'm fancying Cacoethes.' She snuggled up to her husband. 'What do you think, honey?'

He gave her a teasing little smile. 'Not a bad choice, for a girl, but I'm sticking with the favourite, Nashwan, he's not going to be beaten today.'

Lynda was looking at the odds. 'You won't win much on the favourite.'

'No, but I'll win.'

'I'll take a risk, seeing as I'm a risk-taker. I fancy Terimon.'

Nathan Tyler laughed, 'At five hundred to one? You're crazy.'

'He won a race not so long ago,' Tom said thoughtfully, 'and his trainer is Clive Brittain. He's pretty shrewd, though I've heard that the owner didn't really want Terimon entered for the Derby, she doesn't want to be embarrassed.'

'She? Who is the owner?' asked Helen.

'Lady Beaverbrook.'

'The woman who married two millionaires?'

'That's the one,' Tom laughed, and Nathan joined in.

'My wife doesn't read the racing press for tips, she prefers to rely on the gossip magazines.'

'Well, it's interesting. We'd all like to follow her example and marry a millionaire, wouldn't we, Lynda?'

Lynda grinned at her. 'Yes, but in the meantime, I'm going to make my own fortune. I'm betting ten quid each way on Terimon, I like grey horses, and I like long odds.'

'Hope you can afford to lose your money,' Nathan cautioned.

Helen was intrigued. 'You know about each way bets? You continue to surprise me, Lynda.'

'My Grandma used to bet on the horses, she taught me all I know – which isn't a lot!'

Mark was still studying the list of runners. 'Michael Roberts is riding Terimon, he's a good jockey. I'd back him.'

Tom smiled at his son, 'Well in that case, so will I.' He put a £20 note in Lynda's hand and gave her a kiss. 'Make that £20 each way, my Lady Luck, we risk-takers should stick together.'

Helen Tyler pulled off her hat and waved it wildly when Cacoethes took the lead, but Nashwan won by five lengths. Michael Roberts held Terimon back and he was last but one when they turned for home, but thundered up to the finishing line to take second place.

Mark was jumping up and down with excitement. 'We've won! He came second, he did it! He got a place!'

Lynda stared at Tom, 'How much will we have won?'

He shrugged his shoulders. 'Oh, over two grand,' he said coolly, then lifted her up and swung her round. 'Two thousand pounds, my Lady Luck! Two thousand!'

Helen beamed, and then nodded at her husband, 'Lynda's not a bad risk taker, is she?'

He laughed. 'I guess not.'

Mark grabbed his Dad by the arm.

'Come on, let's go and collect our winnings. Come on, Lynda!'

'O.K!' she yelled, waving jazz hands in the air, and laughing as she ran with them.

They opened champagne when they got back to Loveday, and Helen Tyler suggested that they should spend some of their winnings on a holiday in Paris. Tom and Lynda looked at each other and decided that now was the time to take that holiday they both needed so much.

They managed to book flights and Helen contacted a friend who had a small apartment in the centre of Paris. A day later it was all arranged. Lynda couldn't believe it was all happening so quickly, and was absolutely thrilled at the idea of flying to Paris.

'I can't believe you've never flown before,' Mark said to her.

He had seen her sitting on a bench in the small rose garden she had planted in memory of Rose Milner, and had gone to sit beside her.

'I've never been abroad before. I've never had the money,' Lynda explained simply.

Mark pretended to study the cover of the Paris guide book Lynda had been reading, and then he said, 'I suppose I was a lucky little boy spending all those holidays in France with my Mum and Nicki.'

'Yes. And I'm sure you'll have more lovely times there with your Mother.'

He didn't respond, and she looked at him questioningly. 'Are you upset that your Dad and I are going to Paris without you?'

He replied in that serious, grown-up way of his which always made her smile.

'No. I'm not that keen on Paris, as a matter of fact. And it will be nice for you and Dad to have a holiday together, even though it is only four days.'

'I'm glad you're O.K. about it.'

'Yeah.' He nervously flicked through the guide

book for a moment and then said quietly, 'I am O.K. with the idea of you and Dad being a couple. I understand now.'

'Oh,' Lynda said, and tried not to notice his embarrassment.

'And I want to apologise for, for the way I've been with you.'

She hesitantly took hold of his hand. 'There's no need to apologise to me, Mark. I just want us to be friends.'

'So do I.' He stood up, took a deep breath and stared into the distance as he said, 'I know about my Mum and Simon.'

'Oh.'

'No wonder Dad wanted a divorce.' He was fighting back tears now. 'Why did she have to go and mess up our family?'

'People do crazy things sometimes. I know I do. And you need to forgive them. Your Mother loves you, Mark. Remember that. Whatever happens, she does love you.'

He sighed and seemed to relax a little. 'I know. And I love her. But I love you and Dad as well. That's all right, isn't it?'

Lynda was overjoyed, she'd never expected Tom's son to say that he loved her. She got up and grabbed him by the arms. 'All right? It's more than all right.' She hugged him tight. 'It's bloody marvellous!'

Tom, looking out of the lounge window where he was chatting to one of the guests, observed the scene in the rose garden, and that night, as they were getting ready for bed, he asked Lynda about it.

366

He sat on the edge of the bed and made a confession.

'I know it sounds bad, but I'm glad he found out about Suzanne. In fact, I think perhaps I should have told him a long time ago. It would have saved you having to be upset when he seemed to turn against you. God knows what she told him about you.'

'The same as she told me, I expect.'

'And what was that?'

Lynda stood there and didn't know whether to be angry or ashamed, but she felt she had to let Tom know how Suzanne had undermined her and made her suffer.

'She told me that I was a liability to you, that I had no taste, no class, and that I was just keeping you warm in bed, till you went back to her.'

'What? That'll never happen.'

'It doesn't seem so far-fetched to me! I saw you, Tom, outside her room, holding on to each other and kissing like you'd never stop!'

He stared up at her in disbelief, and then realised what she had seen. 'In the corridor, outside her room?'

'Yes, I was sorting out the bedrooms on that floor, and I saw you.'

He stood up and put his arms round her.

'What you saw was Suzanne clinging on to me, desperate, because I'd told her I was in love with you.'

'Are you? Are you really in love with me? I need to be sure, Tom. I need you to love me as much as I love you.'

The look in his eyes showed her she should have no doubt.

'I love you so much, Lynda Collins. And I know I'll always love you.' He smiled at her tenderly, and took her by the hand.

'Now come to bed and let me prove it.'

CHAPTER FORTY

Paris seemed to Lynda, like a beautiful, graceful woman, waiting to welcome them. She'd never expected the majesty, elegance and exhilaration of the city's wide straight avenues and spectacular buildings. On their first night she stood with Tom in the centre of The Avenue des Champs Elysées, gazing towards the floodlit splendour of the Arc de Triomphe at one end and the lights of the Place de la Concorde at the other, and knew she was in a magical city.

The apartment Helen's friend had lent them was on the third floor of a beautiful nineteenth century building which faced the river Seine and the cathedral of Nôtre Dame. There was a small balcony, and in the morning they opened the shutters and had their breakfast sitting by the tall, elegant casement window, and gazing at the view.

Every moment exploring the city was an adventure to Lynda and she seized on each new experience. On their first morning she had insisted on going out to buy a baguette and some buttery croissants from the little boulangerie-patisserie they'd found in a side-street close by. She was delighted when, after stumbling over the words at first, she gradually made her O-level French understood.

'I'm so glad we're not staying in a hotel,' she said to Tom on that first morning, 'it's much more fun to try to feel like a Parisian, living the way they live.'

Tom grinned. 'Yes, I'd have been taking notes all the time if we'd been in a hotel. Now, let's have a look at that list of yours, and decide where to go today.'

'The Eiffel Tower, and the Louvre. I have to see the Mona Lisa.'

'We'll have to queue for both of those. But who cares? I'm so glad to be here with you.'

They went to the Louvre first as it wasn't too far to walk from the apartment, then they took the Metro to Trocadero and were thrilled that they arrived in time to see the sunshine creating diamonds in the spectacular fountains at the Palais de Chaillot.

Lynda made Tom laugh when she went for a ride on one of the gaily coloured horses of the carousel close to the Eiffel Tower.

'It reminds me of being a kid on a trip to Blackpool,' she said. 'Oh, I wish I hadn't thought of that, I don't want to be reminded of living in Milfield, especially while we're here.'

He put his arm round her, 'You're bound to think of it sometimes. And you don't want to forget the happy memories. Now let's get in that queue for the tower, I've never actually gone up it, you know, and I can't wait to see the view.'

The weather was kind to them during their few days in the city and they walked whenever they could.

They wanted to see everything, not just the famous buildings and monuments, but also the small shops as well as the famous, fashionable and expensive ones.

Lynda was especially thrilled when they came across a local market with its beautifully presented fruit and vegetables, bunches of fresh herbs and huge variety of cheeses. They bought some fruit and cheese and had a picnic on the banks of the Seine, waving to the tourists enjoying a more sophisticated lunch aboard the Bateaux Mouches.

One afternoon they went to Montmartre to see the gleaming white Basilica of The Sacré Coeur, and sat for a while on the steps, gazing at the spectacular view over Paris. As they walked back up the hill, Lynda couldn't take her eyes off the white splendour of the building.

'It's the most amazing looking church I've ever seen, those white domes make it look as if it floated down from heaven.'

She paused at the top of the steps and looked up at him.

'Paris is such a special city. I'm so grateful that we could have this holiday, and I'm so glad I came here with you.'

He kissed her, and thought again how beautiful she was.

'It's wonderful to show you all of this. It's as if I'm seeing everything for the first time. Now, let's go round to the Place du Tertre, it's one of my favourite places.'

'Where the artists are? Fabulous!'

She took his arm as they walked into the square filled with artists, umbrellas and cafés.

Lynda refused to have her portrait sketched, but bought a small painting of Montmartre with the white domes of the Sacré Coeur in the background. Then they sat in a pavement café and watched the world go by, as they had so often during their wanderings round Paris.

After a while Lynda looked at her map and said, 'It's not far to the Moulin Rouge from here, is it? I'll have to make sure you don't get kidnapped on Pigalle and lose your innocence.'

He laughed. 'What innocence?'

On the last day Lynda didn't want to think about going home. Being alone together had brought her so close to Tom, it was as if they'd managed to go back and begin their relationship again. They realised that they hadn't really been allowed to enjoy their romance; time they had needed just for themselves had been taken from them by what was happening around them, and the need to work hard.

That morning Lynda went to the boulangerie as usual but didn't just buy croissants for breakfast, she bought extra treats as well. When she came back the sun was already shining on the little table by the window, and Tom had placed a small posy of red roses in the centre.

'Tarte aux abricots for me and tarte aux fraises for you,' Lynda announced, holding up the neat package with its pale pink ribbon. 'I thought we'd have something special for breakfast this morning.'

'Wonderful.'

She was delighted with the roses. 'Where did you get these?' she asked, her eyes shining.

'I went into that florist's round the corner while you were getting ready to go out last night.'

'They're lovely, thank you.'

She set the bread and pastries out on the little table, and as Tom poured the coffee he saw that she was close to tears. 'Do you not want to go home?' he asked gently.

'No. I don't want this to end, being here, just the two of us.'

'We'll come here again, and we'll take Helen up on her invitation to visit them in America. We'll go everywhere you want to go, do whatever you've dreamed of.'

'You don't have to do all that for me, Tom. I just want to be with you.'

'For ever?'

'Yes.'

'There's a small white box in the centre of those roses. Would you open it?'

She stared at the tiny white velvet casket and then gasped as she saw the beautiful antique gold ring, with a heart edged with small diamonds, and a small sapphire in its centre. He took the ring out of the box and, taking hold of her hand, drew her to stand in the sunshine.

'Here, looking down over Paris, this is where I want to give you this ring. Do you like it?'

'It's beautiful.'

'I thought of Cornwall. Gold for the sand, sapphire blue for the sea and your eyes, and a heart for my love. Will you marry me, Lynda Collins?'

'I can't,' she whispered, with tears in her eyes. 'I'm still married.'

'Perhaps. But you love me, don't you?'

'Oh, yes. I love you, Tom Meredith. More than I have ever loved anyone in my life.'

He placed the ring on her finger. 'Promise that you will be my love for ever, and that one day you will marry me.'

She looked into the loving eyes of the man who made her happy and complete, who always made her feel she was the most wonderful woman in the world.

'I promise.'

The Lynda Collins Trilogy
by
Liz Wainwright

Book One

~~~~

The Girl who wasn't Good Enough

Book Two

~~~~

Second Chances

Book Three

~~~~

A Long Way Back

www.lizscript.co.uk

Made in the USA
Charleston, SC
02 May 2013